Praise for
*Newton and Polly*

"Amazing Grace, indeed! *Newton and Polly* is one of the most powerful love stories I have ever read, wrenching the heart and waking the soul. If you read one book this year, this should be it."

　　—Julie Lessman, award-winning author of The Daughters of
　　　Boston, Winds of Change, and Heart of San Francisco series

"A powerfully moving account of one man's epic journey from doubt and despair into a world of radiant faith. *Newton and Polly* is impeccably researched and punctuated with glints of genuine humor . . . I loved it!"

　　—Elizabeth Camden, RITA® and Christy award-winning
　　　author

"A sweeping tale rife with adventure, love, and God's relentless pursuit of his own. With her signature depth and detail, Jody Hedlund plunges her readers into a fascinating and powerful story that has gone untold—until now. Set sail with *Newton and Polly* and become anchored in amazing grace."

　　—Jocelyn Green, award-winning author of the Heroines
　　　Behind the Lines Civil War series

"In this story of the lives of John Newton and Polly Catlett, author Jody Hedlund skillfully weaves together the history, romance, and Christian faith that inspired the world's best-loved hymn. Evocative and illuminating."

　　—Dorothy Love, author of *Mrs. Lee and Mrs. Gray: A Novel*

"Jody Hedlund's historical detail is immaculate, and her storytelling will bring you to tears. Newton's conversion was truly remarkable, sparking a legacy that has impacted millions of lives. *Newton and Polly* invites readers into that powerful experience."

—SIGMUND BROUWER, award-winning author of *Thief of Glory*

### Praise for the Christy and ECPA Novel of the Year
### *Luther and Katharina*

"Jody Hedlund's *Luther and Katharina* is an absorbing and deeply researched look into the life and ministry of a figure in church history I'd previously known only from a few dusty facts. Jody breathes life into those facts with this fascinating and intimate portrayal of Martin Luther's life. *Luther and Katharina* is a compelling tale of tested faith, tumultuous church history, and incredible courage against daunting odds—and one of the most unique love stories I've read in ages."

—LORI BENTON, author of *The Pursuit of Tamsen Littlejohn* and *The Wood's Edge*

"Complex and emotionally rich, *Luther and Katharina* gripped me from the very start and never let go. Not even when the final page was turned. The history, the love story, the depth of faith in this novel is masterfully woven by Jody Hedlund."

—TAMERA ALEXANDER, *USA Today* best-selling author of *To Win Her Favor* and *A Lasting Impression*

## Books by Jody Hedlund

*Luther and Katharina*

### The Hearts of Faith Series

*The Preacher's Bride*
*The Doctor's Lady*
*Rebellious Heart*

### The Michigan Brides Collection

*Unending Devotion*
*A Noble Groom*
*Captured by Love*

### The Beacons of Hope Series

*Out of the Storm: A Novella*
*Love Unexpected*
*Hearts Made Whole*
*Undaunted Hope*
*Forever Safe*

### Young Adult

*The Vow: Prequel to An Uncertain Choice, A Novella*
*An Uncertain Choice*
*A Daring Sacrifice*

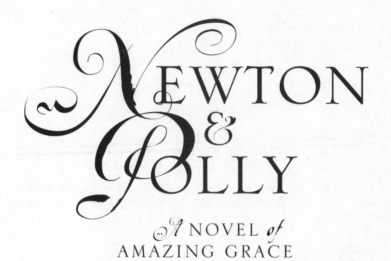

# Newton & Polly

## A NOVEL *of* AMAZING GRACE

# JODY HEDLUND

AUTHOR OF LUTHER AND KATHARINA

**WATERBROOK**

Newton and Polly

Trade Paperback ISBN 978-1-60142-764-9
eBook ISBN 978-1-60142-765-6

Copyright © 2016 by Jody Hedlund

Cover design by Kristopher K. Orr; cover photography by Loïc Bailliard (ship) and Kristopher K. Orr (woman)

Published in the United States by WaterBrook, an imprint of the Crown Publishing Group, a division of Penguin Random House LLC, New York.

WATERBROOK® and its deer colophon are registered trademarks of Penguin Random House LLC.

Library of Congress Cataloging-in-Publication Data
Names: Hedlund, Jody, author.
Title: Newton and Polly : a novel of Amazing Grace / Jody Hedlund. Description: First edition. | Colorado Springs, Colorado : WaterBrook, [2016]
Identifiers: LCCN 2016022221 (print) | LCCN 2016027477 (ebook) | ISBN 9781601427649 (softcover) | ISBN 9781601427656 (ebook) | ISBN 9781601427656 (electronic)
Subjects: LCSH: Newton, John, 1725-1807—Fiction. | Man-woman relationships—Fiction. | Hymns—Authorship—Fiction. | Hymn Writers—Fiction. | Clergy—Fiction. | BISAC: FICTION / Biographical. | FICTION / Romance / Historical. | FICTION / Christian / Historical. | GSAFD: Biographical fiction. | Historical fiction. | Christian fiction. | Love stories.
Classification: LCC PS3608.E333 N49 2016 (print) | LCC PS3608.E333 (ebook) | DDC 813/.6—dc23
LC record available at https://lccn.loc.gov/2016022221

Printed in the United States of America
2016

10  9  8  7  6  5  4

*To my mother:*
*Thank you for the seeds of faith*
*you planted in your children.*
*Thank you for remaining steadfast*
*during the turbulent storms.*
*Thank you for always praying, always loving,*
*and always forgiving during the darkest of days.*
*You exemplified the Father in running*
*to your prodigals with open arms.*
*I pray now I will do the same.*

# PART ONE

# ONE

DECEMBER 1742
CHATHAM, ENGLAND

*I* fear that our wassailing has become a nuisance." Polly Catlett slowed her steps, her toes aching in the stiff leather of her boots, the damp chill of December finally taking its toll.

"Nonsense." Susanna Smith linked her arm into Polly's and dragged her toward the front door of the tenant farmhouse that stood across the road from the Blue Anchor Inn. "You've such a pretty voice. You could never be a nuisance."

One of Susanna's friends, an older Quaker widow who held the beribbonned wassail bowl, knocked on the farmhouse door, while the others in the wassailing group formed a semicircle for the singing. A mangy mutt had announced their presence with deep-throated barking that echoed in the crisp cloudlessness of the coming night.

The fading golden brocade that streaked the sky overhead was all that remained of the daylight but enough to show the frozen rosy splotches on each of their noses and cheeks. Enough for Polly to glimpse tension on the face of the older Quaker widow.

"This is the last house," Polly whispered to Susanna, flexing her aching fingers inside her wool mittens. "Then we shall return home."

"Of course," Susanna conceded as the door opened and bright light poured out upon them, illuminating a spark in Susanna's eyes, a spark Polly knew all too well. A spark that meant something was afoot.

The Quaker widow stepped away from the door and took her place among other Dissenters in the group who were attired in plain and unadorned garments as was their custom. Earlier, after Susanna had convinced Polly to join her for the wassailing, Polly wasn't entirely surprised to discover that their company was made up of Susanna's Dissenter friends. Susanna made no pretense about her strong political views and never passed up an opportunity to gather with like-minded friends whenever she came to visit.

Although Polly would have preferred to wassail with friends from her own social circle, she hadn't been able to begrudge Susanna the favor. Nor had she been able to resist an opportunity to sing, even if the group was strange and sober.

Susanna's poke through her heavy cloak was Polly's sign to begin her song. As the open doorway filled with several women, Polly took her place at the fringe of the group and hummed several notes before starting, "A jolly wassail bowl, a wassail of good ale . . ."

The others allowed her to sing the first stanza by herself, and her voice lifted clear and pure with the melody of the traditional song. A hush fell over the women who were now stepping out of the farmhouse. As her song rose, even the dog stopped its barking.

At the Blue Anchor Inn across the road, she could feel the attention of several patrons upon her, men who were either coming to or going from the alehouse. Out of the corner of her eye, she could see that one stocky man had leaned his shoulder against the weathered clapboards and was staring at her from beneath the triangular brim of his cocked hat.

Susanna glanced toward the barn at the rear of the farmhouse and squeezed Polly's arm. "Sing another verse." Susanna's request was met with a murmur of assent from the hefty woman facing them, likely the farmer's wife with her milkmaids and scullery girls behind her.

Polly didn't need much prodding to continue. Her song filled the air, drawing the plump, almost square-shaped farmer away from the barn toward them. With a limping gait, he lagged behind several boys, likely his sons. Polly was warmed with a small measure of satisfaction that her singing could please others so readily.

Later when she was alone, she would offer prayers of contrition for her vanity, but for now, she was helpless but to release the melody. She sang several more stanzas by herself as the crowd expanded the same way it had at their previous stops. Finally, Susanna and her friends joined in, finishing the song. Together they sang the chorus two more times before offering the wassail bowl to the farmer and then to his wife.

The drink was no longer bubbling hot as it had been at their first visit. Nevertheless, everyone sipped from the bowl and praised the sweet spiciness of fine ale and roasted crab apple blended with cinnamon, nutmeg, cloves, and ginger. In exchange for the songs and drink, the farmwife had her maids pass out an apple to each of the wassailers.

The chatter of the singers mingled with those of the farmer and his family, but the laughter this time was different, louder, more forced. Or maybe Polly was merely unnerved by the young man who continued to lean nonchalantly against the Blue Anchor and stare at her. The other patrons had listened for a verse or two before hustling on their way. But this one hadn't budged, not even when they'd finished singing. The shadows of the early evening prevented her from seeing his features clearly, but from the glimpse or two she'd caught, he was certainly dashing enough to make her squirm.

Polly focused her attention on Susanna, who was speaking to the farmer's wife. "'Tis true. We are ahead of the festivities for our wassailing as we've not yet celebrated Twelfth Night. But we were in a joyous mood this day and thought to spread our cheer."

The farmer's wife boxed one of the boys in his ear for drinking too long from the wassail bowl. "We won't complain that you've come. Especially since your sister has such a pretty voice."

"I'm not—" Polly started to explain that Susanna was her aunt, her mother's youngest sister, but Susanna cut her off.

"I concur," Susanna said with a smile and toss of her dark ringlets from beneath her wide-brimmed straw hat. "She does have a pretty voice."

Susanna was vivacious even in the fading daylight. Next to Susanna's ravishing beauty and charm, Polly often felt like a pale golden embroidery thread set against a dark lush tapestry. Although she'd inherited her mother's fairness, there were times when Polly secretly lamented that her mother hadn't given her more of the French ancestral heritage, which had apparently been bequeathed upon Susanna to the fullest.

"If I were making the laws," Susanna continued, "I'd deem the entire month of December—and not just twelve days—be devoted to celebrating Christmas. But unfortunately, I'm not part of the monarchy." Susanna peered around the farmyard and beyond to the stretch of road that led away from Chatham into the open countryside.

If Polly didn't know better, she'd almost believe Susanna was looking for someone. Her Quaker friends, too, were glancing around more than usual. With the coming of night, perhaps they were merely nervous about the need to return to their homes. Nothing good ever happened after darkness, particularly near the River Medway where dangerous smugglers had become all too common in recent months.

"Shall we be on our way?" Polly leaned into Susanna as far as the fan hoops on her petticoat would allow. "I vow, it's time to go before we're left to wander in total darkness."

Susanna lifted one inky brow at her widowed friend, who in turn gave a slight shake of her head as though to tell her "Not yet."

The unspoken communication between the Quaker widow and Susanna only made Polly more wary. Something more than wassailing was happening tonight. Of that she was growing certain. Were Susanna and her friends arranging one of their protests tonight? During her last visit, Susanna had secretly participated in passing out pamphlets expressing disapproval of the slave trade and stressing the need for reforms. Polly hadn't known of the clandestine activities until she found a stack of pamphlets in Susanna's bag. When she confronted Susanna, her aunt swore her to silence.

"Perhaps one more song from my dear sister Mary?" Susanna asked, raising her voice along with Polly's mittened hand. Susanna's slanted glance told Polly not to question her pretense over being sisters or the use of her given name, Mary, rather than her nickname.

Susanna's squeeze told her to just sing. At the ensuing enthusiasm from the farmer and his household, Polly had no choice but to indulge them in spite of her unease.

Once the last notes of melody drifted away, she was relieved when the members of their wassailing group tightened their cloaks and with brief good-byes started down the lane toward Rochester where many of the Quakers lived.

"Needn't we go the other way?" Polly asked, increasing her stride to keep up with Susanna's lengthy one. She caught the edge of her flat straw hat to keep it from blowing off her head. Underneath she wore a bonnet-like cap edged in lace, which although stylish did little to keep her ears warm.

"We shall accompany our friends a short distance before turning around," Susanna said tersely, with a sharp look over her shoulder toward the farmhouse. They were already on the outskirts of Chatham on the highroad that would eventually wind its way through Rochester and north to London. The road ran close to the bank of the River Medway, and the dampness from the river and the nearby North Sea made the December air especially biting.

As they walked Polly's breath came in cloudy bursts that disappeared into the lengthening twilight shadows. No one spoke, and in the complete silence, their footsteps against the hard-packed, frozen dirt sounded choppy and hurried.

If she didn't know better, she'd suspect they were running away from someone. "Why are we so somber—" Polly started, but Susanna cut her off with a harsh *shush*.

When they came to a fork in the road, Susanna peered over her shoulder again, her pretty features taut with anxiety. Woods hedged them in, preventing them from seeing the farmhouse and the inn.

But sudden shouts from the area whence they'd come drew alarm upon every face in their small group.

"Hide!" the Quaker widow hissed as she picked up her heavy skirts and broke into the hedgerow between the road and the river.

Susanna grabbed Polly's arm and dragged her the opposite direction down the road that led to the nearby hamlet of Luton. "Quickly." Susanna pulled Polly along at a near run. Polly didn't resist as a sense of dread rapidly spread through her limbs, chasing away the frigidness that had gripped her.

Susanna had apparently gotten herself into trouble again. The question was, what kind and how much?

Polly raced after Susanna until her lungs felt seared with the effort. It wasn't long before the heavy clomp of horse hooves pounded the road behind them. Without slowing her pace, Susanna veered into the woods, and Polly had no choice but to follow. They stumbled over windfall and low branches, their crackling and crashing suggesting an advancing army rather than two delicate young ladies.

"Halt." Susanna held out an arm, steadying Polly.

"Susanna, why are we running? What have you done?"

"Not now. For mercy's sake, be silent and hide."

Susanna crouched behind an ash tree, but the hoops at her hips made concealment impossible behind the trunk. Polly slunk to a fuller hedge that was still covered with a smattering of dried leaves. Her hoops were cumbersome too, but she bent low nonetheless. Thankfully the falling darkness would veil them more than the woodland did.

The rapid thudding of her heart and her labored breaths momentarily drowned out the approaching horse. As the rider came

nigh and slowed the horse's gait, Polly held herself motionless, praying the newcomer would pass by.

When the rider reined his horse on the road in front of them, she
sucked in a breath at the same time as Susanna. For a long moment, he sat silently atop the beast and surveyed the woodland on
either side. When he seemed to turn and look directly at Polly, she
stiffened. She didn't know if he could see her through the thick
growth and darkness, but when he hopped down from his saddle,
her body tensed. He began to move to the edge of the woods. She
ducked her head and glanced at Susanna for some indication of
what to do. Should they attempt to run, perhaps deeper into the
woods?

Susanna merely put a finger to her lips and gave her head an
imperceptible shake.

He stopped at the side of the road and tipped up the pointed
brim of his hat revealing his face. Polly sucked in another breath. His
features weren't clear in the deepening shadows, but she could see
enough of his strong jaw and broad shoulders to recognize him. It
was the young man who'd leaned against the Blue Anchor Inn and
watched her sing.

At the thundering of more horse hooves, the man pivoted away
and bounded to the other side of the road. His easy swagger and hair
tied back in a queue identified him as a sailor. He fumbled at the
clasp of his trousers, and within seconds Polly thought she heard a
distinct splatter of rain against dry leaves. Only it wasn't rain . . .

Was the man relieving himself?

Polly had to cup her hand over her mouth to catch her surprise.
With the approach of darkness, the moon had made its appearance and illuminated him, but thankfully his horse sidled into the

middle of the road, shielding her from the display. Nevertheless, she was mortified.

To make matters worse, the man began to whistle a ribald folk song. Seemingly without a care in the world, he whistled the merry tune, even as two men on horseback came upon him and reined abruptly, causing his horse to shy sideways and nicker.

The sailor glanced over his shoulder at the newcomers. His whistle tapered off as did the other sound. "If you're thinking of robbing me," he said in a slurred voice, "you're in for a sore disappointment. I gambled away my last halfpence at the inn."

"I don't care the devil about robbing you." Polly recognized the square face of the farmer at the home where they'd just been wassailing.

The sailor gave an unsteady laugh. "Good that, since all I have to give you is the shirt off my back."

The farmer and his companion didn't laugh. Instead, they surveyed the woods. "We're looking for a group of women that came a-wassailing by the farm."

Again the sailor laughed and lurched toward his horse, grappling for the reins but missing and nearly falling to the ground. "If you find them, let me know; I'll join you in the fun."

Polly's muscles turned rigid at his implication.

"Then you haven't seen any women?" the farmer demanded, examining the road that led to Luton.

Polly wasn't sure if the sailor had seen them, but she readied herself to bolt should he divulge their location.

"Women? I sure wish I had seen some," the sailor said finally, maintaining a grip on the reins of his horse. "But alas, if my game of hijinks is any indication, then this looks to be my unlucky night."

Polly didn't know much about alehouse games, but she'd heard enough criticism of the dice and drinking game to know it was one of the bawdiest.

The farmer spoke to his companion in low tones before addressing the sailor again. "If you see the women, you'll earn yourself another cup of ale at the Blue Anchor if you report back to me."

"Aye. I like that bargain," the sailor said. "Make it two cups and a bed for the night, and if I find them, I'll bring them to you myself."

Polly could only pray that he was too drunk to be any threat. From the farmer's snort, she surmised he was rapidly concluding for himself that the sailor wouldn't be of much help. Within moments, the night air echoed with the clomp of retreating horses.

The sailor made a show of stretching his arms high in the air with an obnoxious yawn before scratching his belly. Then for several long moments, he adjusted the length of his stirrup.

Except for the soft neigh of the horse, silence hung in the air. Polly's legs had begun to cramp from staying in one position for so long. Slowly she straightened and arched her back to work out a kink, but in the process her foot shifted against a twig, causing it to snap.

Polly froze and turned her attention back to the sailor. But thankfully, he didn't appear to have heard and was now fiddling with the leather strap and buckle of the bridle. She glanced at Susanna, who remained motionless. Polly cocked her head toward the deep woods behind them, hoping Susanna would follow her lead in sneaking away.

Before she could move, however, the sailor spoke in a surprisingly clear voice that hinted at humor. "I think it's safe for you to come out now. I give you my word I won't hurt you." The sailor finally turned around and once again looked through the shrubs. Although darkness had now almost completely fallen, his eyes found Polly first and then Susanna.

Susanna remained motionless, apparently still not intending to show herself until the stranger passed by. Polly hesitated, but then took a step away from her hiding spot.

"I saw everything that happened back at the farmhouse," the sailor continued. "And it was a clever plan. Freeing those slaves during the singing."

"Freeing slaves?" Polly's ire rose as swiftly as a breeze on the North Sea. She spun on Susanna. "Are you mad?" Such an exploit was not only a theft and illegal but could—already had—put them in grave danger.

"We were just wassailing," Susanna chided. "This drunken fool is speaking utter nonsense."

At that the young man laughed. "I suppose a farmhouse so close to the River Medway is in just the right location to hide smuggled goods. I have no doubt some local gang unloads their goods on the dock behind the Blue Anchor and pays that farmer a hefty amount to store their overflow in his barn, including a couple of young slave boys smuggled into Kent. The singing was a nice diversion to draw everyone away from the barn. I doubt anyone else saw the Quaker man leading those boys in chains to his waiting shallop."

There was nothing slurred in the man's speech now. Obviously, he'd put on a drunken show for the farmer. And everything he said made perfect sense. If only Polly had acted upon her unease earlier and left before singing the last couple of songs.

Even as she rebuked herself, she conceded that Susanna was

stubborn. Though her aunt was only three years older than her own fifteen years, once determined to do something, Susanna was difficult to sway. Usually her activities were relegated to temperance meetings or peaceful demonstrations. Even the delivery of the anti-slavery pamphlets had been relatively harmless. But this time Susanna had gone too far. Those slaves had been someone's property, and abetting in their escape was equivalent to stealing. English laws were strict concerning stealing of private property. If they were caught and implicated in thievery, they could be hung for their crime.

Although the large majority of slaves were shipped to British plantations in the West Indies, according to Susanna there were still plenty of the rich in England who kept slaves too. She'd disparaged some of her London friends for keeping slave boys, especially the darkest skinned, like little pets in order to have a decorative contrast to their own fashionable white skin.

While Polly certainly didn't condone such practices, she hadn't figured it was her place to work at eradicating an institution that had been in progress for her entire lifetime and beyond.

"We were wassailing," Susanna said more firmly, finally moving from her hiding spot. "And now, if you please, we need to be on our way home."

The young man only laughed again and stood back as Susanna stepped onto the road. Susanna's parents had made no secret that they'd hoped in Chatham, Susanna would mature and stay out of the trouble she often stirred up in London. If only they could see their daughter tonight.

Polly followed Susanna until she was free of the woods and out in the open. The sky overhead was bright with the first stars, and the moon gave off enough light that she could see the sailor's features more clearly.

His face was deeply tanned as was befitting a man who spent weeks at a time under the sun on the open sea. The slight bend in his nose spoke of a past brawl. But rather than marring his strongly lined features, it only added a rugged appeal.

At the same moment she perused him, she realized that he too was studying her face. She expected he'd turn his stare to Susanna and scrutinize her equally, but his attention stayed riveted to her. She wasn't accustomed to men taking a second glance, especially when she was with the vivacious Susanna, who drew the interest of men the way the queen drew a crowd.

"Where are you ladies headed?" He directed his question to Polly. "I wouldn't be able to live with myself if I allowed you to continue your journey without making sure you arrive safely to your destination."

"We shall be just fine without an escort." Susanna grabbed Polly's arm and moved forward in jerking steps.

The sailor fell into step next to them, deftly handling his horse's reins and leading the creature with a gentle tug. "Would you deprive me of peace of mind?" His cocked smile showed even white teeth.

"We've only a short distance to go," Susanna responded.

"Short?" Polly started.

"It may seem long since you're cold. But our home in Luton isn't overly far." Susanna's tone warned Polly not to contradict her again.

Apparently Susanna wasn't planning to trust this man. And perhaps she was right. After all, he'd agreed to turn them over to the farmer for two cups of ale and a bed for the night. What if even now he was plotting how he might lure them back to the farmhouse?

Polly glanced sideways at the young sailor. His smile faltered as though he sensed their mistrust. "I hope you know I'm neither drunk nor planning to inform the farmer of your whereabouts."

"You have nothing about which to inform the farmer," Susanna insisted. "Unless, of course, wassailing has become a crime. Now let us be on our way without further hindrance. I wish you good evening."

The sailor shrugged. "Aye, then. Have it your way." He came to a halt as did his horse, allowing them to move ahead of him.

Polly's footsteps slowed. The man seemed to be kinder than Susanna was allowing, but Susanna clung to Polly's arm, forcing her to keep the brisk pace. As they rounded a bend in the road, Polly couldn't resist taking one final look at the sailor over her shoulder.

He'd angled his head and was watching them with an amused smile. When the curve in the road rapidly took him from her sights, she hurried to keep up with Susanna.

"Let's run," Susanna whispered once they were alone. As Polly lifted the thick layers of her skirt and petticoats and began to race forward, one thought almost stopped her.

The sailor had intercepted their discovery when he'd distracted their pursuers with his theatrical performance. He'd quite possibly saved their lives.

And she'd neglected to thank him.

# TWO

$\mathcal{T}$he crumpled paper in John Newton's inner coat pocket shouted for his attention. He'd ignored it there for the past several days. But its voice had grown steadily louder over the last hour until he could no longer hear much else.

He blew a hot breath against his leather gloves trying to loosen his frozen fingers, and then he nudged his father's steed away from the shadows along the River Medway where he'd found a secluded spot to watch the comings and goings of the farm and Blue Anchor Inn.

His limbs ached with cold, and his toes were numb. His belly rumbled for want of a meal. And his temples throbbed with the intensity of his scrutiny.

"All for naught," he grumbled under his breath, urging his horse onto the road. His disappointment was keen. He hadn't wanted to lose track of the two young women, particularly the one with the face and voice of an angel. He only thought to let the women travel ahead of him a bit before following at a safe distance. With the coming of night and all the danger that came out to play, he'd decided two pretty young ladies needed an escort whether they wanted one or not.

But when he finally rounded the bend in the road to creep along after them, they had disappeared. At first he thought mayhap they'd walked far ahead of him. So he'd ridden all the way to Luton. After wandering the streets there, he'd realized that either they'd already gone inside or they had deceived him into thinking that's where they lived.

Deciding it was the latter, he'd scoured the road on the way back to Chatham. Without a lantern to guide his search, the darkness had prevented him from tracking broken branches, footprints, crushed foliage, anything that might have shown him where the young women had veered off the road. All the while he searched, a strange fear had seized him, the fear that perhaps the smugglers had caught up to the women and captured them after all.

His only recourse had been to return to the farm and Blue Anchor and see if the women were being held there. He'd waited in the shadows and hadn't noticed anything unusual. When finally several men, including the farmer, returned empty-handed, Newton allowed himself to relax in his saddle. He was fairly certain all the members of the wassailing group had escaped to safety.

Even so, he was disappointed. He couldn't deny that he'd wanted to see the golden angel again. There was something about her singing that made his chest ache in a way it hadn't in a long time. Aye, her singing could make the coarsest seafarer cry.

"All for naught," he said again, spitting into the gravelly mixture of dirt and pebbles that filled the ruts in the road. He turned his horse toward London and home, home for Christmas before he set sail for Jamaica, where he would be trained as a manager of a sugar plantation. The dark shadows that splayed across the road warned him of the danger he'd face from highway robbers and press gangs if he attempted his journey now.

His father had expected him to ride directly home from Maidstone after visiting an elderly uncle. And he could have easily been home by dusk. But he'd lost track of time at the gaming table that afternoon. Then he had to stop to listen to the wassailers. When he finally readied his horse, the farmer had burst out of his barn yelling about his missing slaves. Of course, the Quaker and his shallop had slipped into the river mist as if they'd never existed, leaving the wassailers to take the blame. Another clever move of deception. If any of the women were stopped, there would be nothing to link them to the missing slave boys except speculation. Nevertheless, Newton didn't have any choice but to warn the women that their ploy had been discovered. One thing led to another, and now here he was, hours past when he was due home.

He may as well stay in Chatham for the night and leave at first light. Whether he went home tonight or left in the morning, either way he'd earn his father's censure for being late.

He touched a hand to his breast and felt the paper crinkle beneath his fingers, and the voice of the letter spoke to him again. "Dear John, We received news that you are now home after your many years away. It would give me great pleasure to see you again. Your mother was not only my closest cousin, but she was my dearest friend. Please visit us so that we might make your acquaintance and so that I might have peace in light of the vow I made to your mother to check on you from time to time."

Newton tugged the reins of his horse, and the beast shifted away from London and tossed its head toward Chatham. He hadn't planned on visiting his mother's cousin. But these relatives might be the solution he needed for the night. At the very least he'd have a warm meal and bed. The visit would also provide an excuse to give his father for why he was late.

He nudged his horse forward toward High Street but then hesitated. Chatham with its strategic location on the River Medway had been commissioned by Queen Elizabeth I to host the Royal Navy Dockyard nearly two hundred years ago. Now the shipbuilding yard employed hundreds of men and launched many of England's finest vessels. Not only that, but the winding river provided a safe place for both merchant and navy vessels to anchor away from the harsh conditions of the North Sea. The defense fortifications of Upnor Castle and the batteries at Cockham Wood Fort in Gillingham also made Chatham a protective place for ships to moor away from French warships.

None of the merchant vessels he'd served on had ever anchored there, but like most seafaring men, he was familiar enough with Chatham to know the town wasn't necessarily a safe place for a man like him. One wrong step and he could end up impressed on a navy ship, forced into the king's service.

If he was completely honest with himself, he knew that wasn't the real reason he hadn't planned to accept this cousin's invitation to call. The truth was, he had no desire to visit the place that had taken his mother from him. Ten years ago his mother had come to Chatham for help and healing, but she'd been returned to London in a wooden box.

His stomach gnawed at itself, reminding him that he hadn't had anything to eat since he'd left his uncle's home in Maidstone at midday.

"Ahoy the ship." He dug his heels into his horse and urged it onward. He may as well pay the call. He had no better options. The directions at the bottom of the letter indicated the house wasn't too far off the highroad, at the edge of Chatham on one of the chalk ridges.

As he ascended out of the river valley, the breeze grew stronger, bringing with it the familiar scent of salt and sea. Many believed that breathing deeply of the sea air could cure consumption. It was one of the reasons his mother had given him for leaving London.

If only it had worked . . .

After a short distance, he paused in front of a double-gabled brick home. It was set off the road behind a tall wrought-iron fence with decorative points that resembled the tips of pikes. The arched windows hadn't been shuttered for the night, and the amber glow of oil light spilled out of several of them, illuminating the front door with a semicircular fanlight that, like everything about the house, attested to the growing affluence of the middling class.

Several other homes stood in close vicinity, detached unlike the narrow terraced house he'd lived in for much of his life in Wapping on the north bank of the River Thames. Instead, these houses of modest size likely belonged to professionals who oversaw and profited from the Royal Dockyard.

The slate roof and the classical-style parapet were just as his mother's cousin had described. So he dismounted and rattled the front gate, which swung open easily. He tied his horse just inside and bounded up the short walkway. Without another moment's hesitation, lest he change his mind in the face of ghosts from his past, he rapped on the door.

He was fully prepared for a servant to answer, knowing a household of this size would have at least two, if not more. So when the door cracked open mere inches and the angel-faced young woman from earlier peeked out at him, he took a rapid step back before catching himself. "Smite my timbers," he said. "It's you."

Her eyes widened and flashed with fear before she backed away and began to close the door.

Thankfully he was quicker than she and wedged his foot into the crack, preventing her from locking him out. She pushed against the door, but the wide brass buckle on his black leather shoe prohibited her efforts.

"Go away." She spoke in a low urgent voice. "We weren't doing any of the things you said." She cast a worried glance to the hallway behind her.

"I only want to ask you a few more questions," he said, unable to resist the urge to tease her.

"No."

"One more?"

"No. None." Her whisper was rushed, and she again shoved the door against his foot.

"Then you must at least sing another song for me."

She eyed him warily, and her pressure against the door lessened. If he'd wanted, he could have easily flung the door wide and forced his way inside. If there was one positive thing that had come from his years at sea, it was his strength. He hadn't struggled to hold the tiller or man the pump or lift half hogsheads without gaining plenty of muscles.

"Please," he said in a gentle whisper. In the dim lighting of the hallway, her features were obscured. But there was no hiding her beauty, the delicate curve of her chin that led to high arched cheekbones that only served to make her wide eyes more pronounced. "To be honest, I didn't come to ask you any questions. I came to hear you sing again."

She shook her head, swishing long golden ringlets. "Of course I can't sing for you—"

"Why not?" He knew his tone was coaxing, the tone he used to ply maidens for stolen kisses. "One song. That's all I want. Then I'll leave you alone forever."

Her fair eyebrows came together in a crease at the bridge of her elegant nose as though she was considering his request.

"I fear that I may never again hear a voice like yours on this side of heaven. Surely you wouldn't torture me with waiting until I reach the celestial gates, not when I can have the pleasure right now."

She hesitated again and this time her lips twitched with a smile she was holding back. "If I sing one song," she said, "then you'll not speak another word about what you may or may not have seen tonight?"

He leaned against the doorframe. "My lips will be locked." He pressed his lips together and pretended to turn a key.

This time she couldn't contain her smile. "You are quite persuasive, sir."

He gave a mock bow, sweeping his hat from his head. "If you must know, I'm also easily persuaded."

"Polly, darling," came a woman's voice from down the hallway. "With whom are you speaking?"

The young woman gasped then tried to shut the door on him again. "Go," she hissed, turning her back and covering the crack in the door with the full length of her body as though to hide his presence.

"It's nothing, Mother," said the young woman. "There's no need to trouble yourself."

"Did you answer the door?" There was sudden alarm in the

mother's voice. "You know how dangerous that can be at this time of the evening." Footsteps came closer and before he could straighten and present himself at his best, the door was yanked wide revealing a lovely woman. From the maturity in her expression as well as the lines next to her eyes and in her forehead, he could see that she was about the age his own mother would have been if she'd lived. She had the same fair Saxon complexion as her daughter, although paler.

"Mrs. Catlett." He inclined his head, presenting her with what he hoped was his most dashing grin.

The older woman had already pushed her daughter behind her and now stood facing him, her shoulders stiff, her posture regal in a striking green bodice and matching overskirt. The daughter wore garments of a similar style, although slightly plainer but no less comely. Since he'd spent the majority of time at sea in recent years, he was admittedly far from knowledgeable about women's fashions. But even a simpleton could see that they were well attired, quite the contrary to his own humble garb.

Of course, he'd cleaned himself up, put aside his work clothes, and donned his going-ashore rig before he left his ship. Nevertheless, his striped yellow waistcoat was faded, and his blue wool coat was patched at the elbows and several of the cloth-covered buttons were frayed. As Mrs. Catlett took in his apparel, he was tempted to adjust his neckerchief as though that would make him more presentable.

"Do I know you?" Mrs. Catlett asked. Behind her, the angel was shaking her head, her eyes pleading with him not to reveal their earlier encounter. Now in the light of a simple pendant oil lamp, he could see that the young woman's eyes were blue, the same shade as the sky he often saw on a clear day on the Mediterranean.

For a moment he was tempted to set himself adrift in that blue. But in the presence of her mother, he had the sudden urge to make a good first impression. "Madam, I am your most obedient servant. I'm heartily glad to see you, Cousin."

As he spoke the word, his pulse gave a strange lurch at the realization that if Mrs. Catlett was his cousin, then her lovely daughter was also his cousin, though thrice removed.

The matron's eyes widened, and she fluttered one hand with its ruffled sleeve above her heart. "John?"

With a flourish, he removed the crumpled letter from his pocket, unfolded it, and held it out. "Aye, madam." He bowed. "It is I, John Newton, and none other."

She took in her own letterhead and handwriting before lifting a gentle but curious gaze to his face. She studied him a moment before responding. "You have a little of your mother in your eyes. But you strongly resemble your father in your carriage."

"So I've been told." He tried to keep his tone congenial although he wasn't keen on the comparison with his father. He might share the same brawny build and swarthy complexion, but that was as far as the similarities went.

"Please come in." She stepped aside and waved at the front hallway where more of her children had gathered and were now watching him with curiosity.

Mrs. Catlett took his coat and hat and hung them on a corner coat tree. Then she proceeded to make introductions of her six children, starting with a boy of about seven ranging to a young girl named Eliza, who appeared to be about thirteen. Then Mrs. Catlett turned to the angel. "And this is my oldest daughter, Polly."

Polly stepped forward hesitantly, the same petition still afloat in her eyes. As tempting as it was to tease her further, he gave a slight bow and what he hoped was a sincere smile. "It's a pleasure to meet you, Miss Catlett."

He knew he'd done the right thing when she rewarded him with a dazzling smile, one that contained not only her relief but also her appreciation. The smile transformed her delicate features from pretty into stunning.

"You must call me Polly." She glanced at her mother for approval of the informality.

"Of course," Mrs. Catlett responded, nodding her head in approval of Polly's kind welcome. "We are family after all."

Amid the flurry of the children, he was ushered into the drawing room and given a wing chair at the center of the semicircle of settees and chairs. The room was modestly decorated and colorfully painted with an Oriental patterned carpet at the center. The long tapestries in the windows and the several small paintings on the walls gave the room an elegance that matched the lady of the house.

He sensed a kindness in Mrs. Catlett's manner that reminded him of his mother and brought a pang to his chest. The last time he'd seen his mother was when she'd poked her head out the carriage window and waved a weak good-bye as she left for Chatham, where she hoped to recover from her lingering illness. She'd arranged for him to stay with a neighbor, Dr. Jennings, the minister of their church. Only a few weeks later, Dr. Jennings pulled him aside after a service and informed him that his mother was dead.

With the loss of the one person who'd loved him more than life itself, he'd been lost. His body was so numb that he wasn't able to cry. All he was able to do was go through the motions of living, like a carved toy figure. He didn't realize that he'd been waiting for his father to return from his sea voyage, until the broad-shouldered captain stalked into Dr. Jenning's house months later to retrieve him. When Newton glimpsed the strong, bronzed features, he wanted his father to wrap his arms around him, hold him, let him cry, and share his sorrows over the woman they'd both adored. He wanted his father to tell him that everything would be all right, that he'd stay home and take care of him, that he'd love him the way his mother had.

But his father didn't hug him, didn't cry with him, didn't speak a word about the death. Instead, he drowned himself in rum for two weeks. It was the first time he'd ever seen his father drunk. On the third week his father dragged himself out of his stupor, dressed in his best, and went away. When he returned, he brought home a new wife.

All the many years hitherto, Newton had tried not to think about his mother, had done his best to push the haunted longings for her out of his mind. But here in this inviting and bright home, the wistful memories of her came rushing back to the front of his mind.

"When your mother last brought you for a visit, you were but a lad of five," Mrs. Catlett said from her spot on the settee next to Polly. "Polly was just a waif of three and Eliza a newborn."

"I wondered why you looked so familiar, Polly," Newton said, feigning seriousness. "Now I know it's because we've met before."

Polly's brows rose as though she wasn't sure whether to be alarmed or amused by the double meaning of his statement. "Your powers of recognition are remarkable."

He couldn't contain a grin. "Aye." He wanted to tell her that he'd never forget a face like hers but restrained himself in Mrs. Catlett's presence. He vowed he'd find a way to tell her later.

Before he had the chance to tease Polly further, Mrs. Catlett asked him to tell how he'd occupied himself in recent years. He skipped over the years at a boarding school in Stratford, Essex, where his father sent him. Those years were a blur of pain and heartache, missing his mother and secretly hoping his father would get rid of his new wife and call him home so they could make a life together, just the two of them.

But his father had called for him only after the schoolmaster complained about his wild behavior and impudence. He knew his father had sent him to school because it was what his mother had wanted. Her own father had been intelligent, a maker of mathematical instruments. She was well educated, and he remembered fondly the hours she spent teaching him at home, having him memorize long passages from the Westminster Catechism, Scripture, hymns, and poems. His mother had always told him he had a bright mind, that he was made to do great things.

Apparently his father didn't share his mother's optimism. Even though at ten Newton was at the top of his Latin class, his father deemed his time in school over and decided to take him to sea.

Newton had spent the past seven years on one voyage or another, most in the Mediterranean area. As he shared about his travels, the Catletts listened to him, spellbound. He'd become proficient over the years at embellishing his tales and making a seafaring life sound more exciting and adventurous than it really was. In truth, most days were dull and monotonous with very little to do.

"By Jupiter," came a voice from the parlor door, interrupting his sharing of his time in Venice. Staring at him with flashing dark eyes was the other young woman from the escapade earlier in the evening. Now in the light of the glowing sconces with mirrors behind them to reflect their brightness, he could see that she was young and lovely too, very much like Polly.

"Susanna, my dear," Mrs. Catlett chided softly. "Mind your tongue, please."

"What is this stranger doing here?" Susanna asked, taking in his comfortable position at the center of the family.

"He's no stranger." Mrs. Catlett offered Newton an apologetic smile. "He's our cousin Elizabeth Newton's son, John."

Susanna scrutinized him with narrowed eyes before the lines of tension in her face eased. As she moved forward, Newton rose. She crossed to the fireplace, which was graced on either side by Greek columns that upheld a mantel with flowers carved across the front. Susanna stretched out her hands to the cast-iron basket grate that contained smoldering coals, and Newton could see that her hands were red and chapped, likely from overexposure to the cold.

"John," Mrs. Catlett continued with introductions, "this is Susanna Smith, my youngest sister. She's from London and visiting us for the month."

"More accurately, Mother and Father have banished me."

"You make it sound like you're in a dungeon here. We're not so bad as that, are we?" Mrs. Catlett rose from the settee and held out a hand.

Susanna reached for her sister's hand and squeezed it. The age difference between the two was such that Mrs. Catlett could have been Susanna's mother. If their parents were getting older, it would be easy to see why they were having a difficult time with a child as spirited as Susanna seemed to be.

"You certainly enjoyed tonight's wassailing, did you not?" Polly cut in, rising from her chair.

"Of course I enjoyed it." Susanna glared first at him and then at Polly, who gave an impish smile in return. "I always love the opportunity to sing."

"Then perhaps you can give us the pleasure of singing right now," Newton suggested. "One of the songs you sang earlier?"

Amid the clamoring from the younger children, Susanna laughingly agreed. "But only if Polly sings with me."

Polly protested, but he could see from her slight smile that she wouldn't need much convincing.

"How can you say no?" Newton asked. "If you do, then I'll be obliged to sing in your stead. And then I'm afraid Mrs. Catlett will boot me from her home without delay."

To the tune of laughter, Newton sank into his chair strangely stirred. When was the last time he'd participated in wholesome company and listened to laughter that wasn't bawdy or harsh? His thoughts returned once more to his mother. She hadn't laughed much. She'd been a devout and serious woman.

But whenever his father returned from one of his voyages, he'd walk through the door of their cramped home, pick her up, and kiss her on the mouth long and hard. And when he would set her back down, her cheeks had always been flushed and her laughter breathless.

After several songs—not quite enough to satisfy Newton—Mr. Catlett arrived home. As Mrs. Catlett served her husband a meal and offered a plate to Newton as well, he learned that the quiet but kindly man was a customs officer and often worked past dark, depending upon the coming and going of merchant vessels in Chatham.

When Mr. Catlett finished his meal, he, too, was interested to hear all that John had been doing over the years. Finally, when the hour was growing late, Mrs. Catlett ushered her children toward the stairway that led to the second floor.

"You can bed down with the boys," Mrs. Catlett instructed, nodding toward her oldest son, Jack, a gangly lad Newton guessed to be about twelve years.

"Think you can abide my snoring?" he asked the boy.

Jack had his father's thin build. He'd likely had a fair complexion when he was younger, but the maturing into an adult was darkening his hair to a plain brown. Jack mumbled a shy response before bounding up the stairway.

Newton set to follow him, but Mrs. Catlett's touch on his elbow halted him. "I'm glad you came, John." Her expression was tender and motherly. For a moment he even got the feeling that she would hug him if he let her.

"I'm glad I came also." He was surprised at his own sincerity.

"I'm only sorry that it had to take so long," she said wistfully, the regret in her eyes palpable. "I wrote your father several times over the years . . . I hoped he might consider letting you come stay with us from time to time."

Of course his father had never mentioned anything to him about the possibility. "You were kind to inquire, but I'm sure you must remember that my father isn't easily swayed."

She nodded, her face pale in the dim lighting of the hallway. "Only your mother had the power to influence him."

Newton murmured his agreement.

"Whatever the case may be," she continued, "I'm glad you're old enough to make up your own mind on the matter and have come."

Was he old enough to make up his own mind now? For so long he'd been doing what his father told him to do that he hadn't stopped to question what he wanted. He supposed at seventeen he

was a man in his own right and could set the course of his life as
he saw fit.

"I want you to know that you'll always have a place in our home.
You're welcome here anytime."

His throat constricted. He couldn't remember the last time anyone had treated him with such warmth. "Thank you, Mrs. Catlett,"
he managed.

"Your mother would have done the same had our situations been
reversed."

He nodded and knew it was true.

After Mrs. Catlett left him, he ascended the steps two at a time.
As he reached the top stair, he caught sight of Polly scurrying away
from the railing.

"You weren't eavesdropping, were you, Cousin?" he whispered.

She stopped in the center of the hallway and spun to face him,
shaking her head adamantly. "I was only going down to say good
night to Father."

Three of the four bedroom doors were already closed, and the
only light in the hallway was the faint glow that came from below.
He couldn't see her features clearly in the darkness, but there was no
mistaking her chagrin.

"I don't mind you listening in on my conversations," he said
lightly. He forced himself not to budge from the top step and to
maintain appropriate boundaries. "It just means that you like me
and want to learn more about me."

She gave a snort. "I see that not only are you easily persuaded,
but you're also easily puffed up."

He smiled at her quip. "You've only known me a short while, and
you already have me all figured out."

"Is that all there is to you?" she parried. "Surely I haven't so easily unlocked all of your secrets."

His resolution to keep a proper distance from her evaporated. He started toward her, careful to keep his tread light and his voice a whisper so that he wouldn't draw attention from the other family members already in their beds. "Mayhap if I stay, you'll be able to discover for yourself if I have any more secrets."

"Perhaps." She took several steps backward until she bumped into the wall.

"I must warn you that I'm not always well behaved."

"I have noticed that already."

He grinned. "Mayhap you will make it your mission to reform me?"

"I do my best to accept people for who they are, not who I wish them to be." She smiled shyly in return, revealing her youth and innocence in that one smile. Yet there was a mature confidence in her words and an unconditional acceptance that wrapped around his heart and soothed him. He was accustomed to disappointing people. But this young woman, without knowing anything about him, had already put her faith in him. And that was a rare gift, to have someone believe the best about you.

"I must bid you good night." Although he wished he could stay and talk with her longer, remaining in a dark hallway in close proximity to Polly would only earn him censure from her parents. He took a step back, releasing her from the intensity of their encounter. She slid to the closest door and opened it a crack. He expected her to leave him without another word. But she paused with one hand on the doorknob and cast a glance over her shoulder.

"I didn't have the chance to thank you yet."

"Thank me for what?"

"For providing a distraction to the men who were trying to find Susanna and me."

"I was quite the distraction, wasn't I?"

She laughed lightly. "You put on a good show."

"I can give a grand performance when I need to."

She was silent for several heartbeats before speaking more seriously. "You saved us. And I won't forget it." She slipped through the doorway and closed the door behind her, leaving him in the dark staring at the spot where she'd disappeared.

He'd have to remain for at least another day. Even if he stayed for two, he'd still have time to ride to Liverpool and board his ship for Jamaica and his job there on the sugar plantation. His father's friend and new employer, Joseph Manesty, would be expecting him the day before the *African* was set to sail, but so long as he arrived before the ship weighed anchor, what difference would it make exactly when he showed up? Although Manesty was a successful Liverpool merchant with profitable investments in the New World, he was also a close family friend and a kind man—at least he seemed kind on the couple of occasions John had met him. Surely Manesty wouldn't mind a short postponement in his arrival.

His father, on the other hand, wouldn't be so easily appeased if he discovered Newton's delay. That just meant Newton wouldn't be able to go home before he left for Liverpool. He'd have to avoid his father altogether.

Newton turned to the boys' room. Images of Polly's golden hair, sweet smile, and bright blue eyes swam in his vision. Aye, the delay would be worth any consequence that came his way.

ou used me last night," Polly whispered to Susanna when the young woman walked into the house.

Susanna thrust two heavy baskets laden with the strong scent of mackerel and oysters into Polly's hands. The young serving maid who had accompanied Susanna to market carried two other baskets. Susanna waited to speak until the girl closed the door and disappeared down the stairway. "I had no choice." She yanked off her scarf, and tendrils of her dark hair sprang up with static. "I needed your beautiful singing voice to mesmerize everyone."

Polly glanced to the door of the morning room where the rest of her siblings were still working on their school lessons with Mother and their visitor, John Newton, who'd offered to help Mother. Like the others, Polly had been surprised to discover that John was quite learned. His Latin was advanced, as were his mathematical skills.

She hadn't been able to keep from peeking at him as he worked with Jack. Not only did he help Jack, but he also found witty ways to help the younger children learn their lessons, so that George and Sara practically worshiped him by the end of his time teaching them.

When he finally looked up and winked at Polly, she'd been mortified to have been caught staring and had needed to escape from the room. Susanna's homecoming had provided her with a ready excuse. Besides, she'd wanted to confront Susanna about involving her in last evening's escapade. Even now her chest constricted at the possibility that someone might connect her and Susanna to the missing slaves.

She'd hoped to speak to Susanna last night. But after she left John in the hallway and entered her room, Susanna was already buried deep under the covers. And this morning when Polly arose, she spent the first hour of her morning kneeling beside her bed in prayer, particularly petitioning for forgiveness for her role in the crime. By the time Polly finished her prayers and grooming, Susanna had already left for town.

"You should have told me your true intentions," Polly insisted.

Susanna tossed her scarf onto the coat tree, and when it fell to the floor, she didn't bother to pick it up but rather began to unbutton her coat. "You're no good at keeping secrets," Susanna explained. "If I'd breathed a word to you about any of the plans, your expression alone would have given us away."

"I'll thank you next time you decide to put my life in jeopardy to consult me first."

Susanna stopped in her unbuttoning to place a hand on Polly's cheek. Her fingers were frigid and stiff against Polly's overly warm face, which Polly told herself came from the sunshine warming the morning room and not from John's presence.

"You've the purest heart of anyone I know." Susanna smiled at her in a way that made Polly feel like she was a mere child. "The main reason I didn't say anything was because if anyone had detained us, you would have been completely innocent of any wrongdoing and could have gone free."

"But I became guilty by association."

Susanna dropped her hand and resumed fumbling with her coat.

"Did you stop to consider the implications of your involvement?" Polly lowered her voice. "This was too radical, too risky—"

"Saving another human being from the bondages of slavery and suffering isn't too radical," Susanna retorted in a harsh whisper.

Many of the slaves brought to England and America came from Africa. Her father had indicated that it was a profitable business for many merchants. They traded goods and trinkets along the coast of Africa in return for a cargo of slaves, which they then sold. Most people in England accepted the practice of slavery, and some even claimed that slavery helped Christianize the pagan Africans. But of late, the Dissenting Quaker group was speaking out. And was apparently now taking action.

Polly shook her head. "Your Quaker friends are influencing you too much, Susanna."

"Yes, they are influencing me. They're opening my mind to the ills of slavery." Susanna's eyes flashed with familiar passion.

"There may be ills that need addressing." Polly had already heard Susanna's litany of complaints against slavery over the past few days since she'd arrived: the poor working conditions, the ill-treatment, and more. "But that doesn't mean you must resort to illegal activities, does it?"

"Those young children were ripped away from their families, Polly. From mothers and fathers who loved them. How do you think those parents feel not knowing where their children are or what is to become of them? And can you imagine the fear those boys are experiencing in a new land away from their families and all they've ever known?"

Susanna's passionate speech silenced Polly. She couldn't imagine such a situation. It was indeed cruel.

"The Quakers hope to at least give the boys their freedom among the free blacks in London." Susanna's voice had grown louder, and she lowered it as she spoke again. "Sometimes drastic measures are needed to bring about true and lasting change."

From the edge to Susanna's voice, Polly knew she had no hope of winning the verbal spar. She'd spent enough time with her aunt over the years to realize Susanna wouldn't be dissuaded, at least until she discovered a new and more important cause upon which to focus her time and attention.

"I may not be able to sway your opinion in this matter," Polly finally said, "but I hope I can convince you not to involve me again. Especially when the consequences could be severe."

Susanna met her gaze levelly. "You're right. I'm sorry for involving you."

"We were very fortunate that Mr. Newton came along when he did."

"Did I hear my name?" John stepped through the door of the morning room. In the brightness of day, his features were stronger and more rugged than they'd appeared last evening. That her attention shifted so easily to his countenance made her squirm.

"I don't mind being the center of conversation between two pretty young ladies," he said, striding to them with the rolling gait of a man accustomed to the sway of a ship. While he wore the same clothes from the previous day, he'd obviously taken time that morning to comb his long hair back into a neat queue. His hair was light woodland brown, with sun-bleached streaks that gave him a fair appeal.

"Were you on another rescue mission this morning, Miss Smith?"

John asked in a secretive whisper, and although he addressed Susanna, his dancing eyes met Polly's. She was struck again today at the beautiful green, the color of lush marsh grass that grew along the river in the summer.

"I have no idea what you're referring to." Susanna spun away from him, draping her coat over another on the crowded coatrack.

John chuckled. "And I believe you as much today as I did last night." He reached for the baskets that Polly still held. When his fingers brushed against hers, the soft graze startled her. She released her grip on the baskets so quickly that John almost dropped them.

His brows quirked with an unspoken query. As the heat stole unbidden into her cheeks, his eyes lit as though he guessed her reaction to him.

She'd had attention from young men in the past year. It was no secret that her best friend's brother, Billy Baldock, was sweet on her. Billy was nearly John's age, almost a grown man. Even so, in all of the parties and gatherings they'd had so far that fall and winter, she'd never reacted as strangely to Billy as she was to John. Of course, she'd known Billy all her life, and most of the time she thought of him the same way she did her brothers.

But John was different from any young man she'd met before. He was unconventional, even somewhat uncouth, and somehow larger than life. She bent to retrieve Susanna's scarf from the floor and busied herself with hanging it up, all the while attempting to ignore his attention.

"There you are, Susanna," Mrs. Catlett's voice came from behind them. "I was beginning to think you'd gotten lost."

*Lost?* Polly wanted to laugh at the absurdity of her mother's assumption, especially since Susanna had been the one to guide them home last night through a narrow forest path that not even Polly had known about.

"I'm just fine," Susanna said, smiling innocently at Mother. "It's such a beautiful morning that I couldn't help lingering."

The cheerful sunlight streaming through the fanlight above the door called to Polly. "Since it's such a fine day, perhaps I can surprise Father with a warm lunch?"

The walk downtown to the customs offices took less than half an hour, and Polly enjoyed the opportunity to deliver a meal to her father. Although he was usually busy, he never failed to take the time to sit down with her for a few minutes.

"That's a kind offer, Polly," Mother said, peeking in one of the baskets that John held. "You and Jack may take soup and bread."

Polly started to nod, but John interrupted. "It would be my pleasure to accompany Polly. Then you won't need to tear Jack away from his studies."

"Thank you, John." Mother smiled at him and squeezed his arm. The skin on her hands had become paler in recent years so that the veins protruded more prominently. "Your help this morning has been a blessing. And I'm sure Jack would appreciate not having to escort Polly."

Mother and Father had decided to give Jack the opportunity to go away to school since he had the inclination to become a lawyer. As they could only afford to send one child at a time, Polly tried not to be envious that Jack would get to go to school instead of her. She'd reached an age where many of her peers had begun to leave for boarding schools in London. Girls' schools didn't offer the same academic curriculum as those for boys, but Mrs. Overing's Boarding School where Susanna had attended was more progressive and taught literature, poetry, and even some foreign language in addition to the customary sewing, embroidery, painting, and music. Polly longed for the day when she'd have the chance to go and improve her composing.

She suspected her father could find a way to earn more if he wanted to, like many of her friends' fathers who worked as customs officers. They had no qualms about accepting bonuses from ship captains or local smugglers for turning a blind eye to the smuggling of goods. They considered the extra payment one of the benefits of the business. However, Father called it bribing and had made a private decision not to accept the frequent bonuses even if that decision meant his family had to go without some of the luxuries that others could afford—like schooling for her.

Whatever the case, she still loved her father and tried to respect his choices, even if at times she felt left behind.

As she started on her way down the sloping road that led toward the center of town and the dockyard, she lifted her face to the sunshine and let the warmth settle over her. Next to her, John carried a small basket that contained a crock of soup and toasted bread lathered with a thick layer of fresh butter that Susanna had brought back from the market.

"Do you like country living?" he asked amiably as he scanned the bare rounded summits beyond which lay Sheerness and the North Sea. They couldn't see the vast sea from Chatham, but the taste and feel of it was in the air. A herd of sheep grazed nearby on the downs, which had turned a pale yellowish green, and the stands of beech, yew, and juniper were leafless and brown.

"A quiet and peaceful life suits me just fine." She tried not to feel self-conscious walking along next to him, but she was too aware of the crunch of gravel underneath his feet and the carefree swing of his arm.

"You don't ever crave more than this?" There wasn't contempt in his voice. Only curiosity.

"Someday I hope to go to school in London, especially so that I may be able to become more proficient with my music."

"You never long for excitement or adventure?"

"Excitement and adventure are for Susanna. Not me. But I have the feeling that's what you desire."

He laughed, and she was beginning to realize that laughter came easily to him. She liked the carefree tone of it as if he had not a worry in the world, and she liked the way his eyes sparkled brightly in his sun-browned face.

"Aye, adventure and I have a longstanding relationship," he said. "Sometimes too close."

She'd relished learning about him last night when he entertained them with tales of his adventures at sea. And now in the quietness of midday, with only the two of them on the path toward town, she couldn't deny that she wished to hear more of his adventures.

"Once," he began, "when I was home from a voyage, I arranged with a friend to visit a man-of-war anchored off Purfleet in the Thames near Long Reach. On my way I stopped to quench my thirst—only cider, mind you."

"I'm sure," she replied dryly, having no doubt he'd had drink much stronger than cider.

He smiled and continued. "I reached the quayside just a few minutes late. But the longboat had already headed off to the man-of-war. I shouted at my friend to persuade the crew to come back for me. But they were already full and refused to oblige us."

His smile faded and his sights grew distant. "Not more than a couple minutes later, as I watched and grumbled from the shore, the longboat hit jetsam and capsized. Most of the passengers, including my friend, drowned before my very eyes."

Polly halted her steps. "How awful."

He stopped next to her and was silent for a long moment. He swallowed hard before forcing a smile. "Aye, that. Another time, I was riding my father's horse, returning home from visiting friends in Essex. It was a stormy evening, and a crack of thunder spooked the horse so that it threw me."

Polly held her breath.

"A hedgerow cushioned my fall and kept me from breaking my back. But when I brushed myself off and got to my feet, I noticed that mere inches from where I'd fallen was the sharp pike of a fence pole. I'd come a hairsbreadth from impaling myself on that spike."

"Providence was watching over you both times."

He shrugged. "Mayhap. Or mayhap I was lucky."

"You certainly don't discount God's sovereignty, do you?"

"Who's to say what is God's sovereignty and what's mere chance?"

She started walking again, attempting to think of an answer to his sacrilegious question. He fell into an easy step next to her. They walked along quietly for a few moments, the puffs of their breath crystallizing in the cold air.

Finally, she spoke the words she felt she must, even if they were nothing profound. "It sounds to me like God has intervened in your life in each of the occasions, miraculously saving you from death. Perhaps he deemed that your time on earth isn't finished, that he has more in store for you yet in this life."

She waited for him to scoff at her. But he responded slowly, thoughtfully. "To be honest, I'm at a point in my life where I'm searching for spiritual wisdom. Lately I've been immersing myself in the Earl of Shaftesbury's second volume of *Characteristicks*. And I'm attempting to understand better how man fits with God's laws."

He quoted passages from the book that he'd memorized, and he shared some of Shaftesbury's philosophies. She didn't want to admit that his thoughts and rationalizations were far above her ability to understand. She didn't want him to think her young and naive, even though she was a simple woman of faith and had no desire to question God or his ways.

"You sound so learned," she said as they turned down High Street and neared the proximity of the river front. The busyness of the town pushed in around them.

"You mean for a sailor?" His voice was light and teasing.

"I meant it as a compliment."

"Good that. Then I'll take it as such."

The narrow street was crowded with sailors, merchants, and naval officers loitering about the inns and seamy taverns that populated the town. In addition to the ships' chandlers, sailmakers, and other shops that catered to the nautical community, the street was also lined with the usual cooper, blacksmith, tailor, glover, milliner, grocer, and more.

"You are an interesting contradiction," she said as a woman and her two small children passing by jostled her, causing her to bump against John.

He took hold of her elbow and steadied her. "I hope a good contradiction?"

The calls of deck hands and dockworkers mingled with the faint sounds of hammers and saws from the nearby dockyard. Even so, she was strangely attuned to the pressure of his fingers on her arm.

"I have the feeling there is much more to you than meets the eye," she said.

"Aye," he replied with a smile. "I can admit that I'm a bit of a complicated mess."

"There you go again." She nudged him playfully. "You're twisting a genuine compliment."

He nudged her back. "Mayhap I'm not accustomed to praise and don't know what to do with it."

"Then perhaps while you're visiting, I shall have to teach you to accept compliments more graciously."

"I'll look forward to the lesson." His voice dipped and his gaze alighted on the light wisps of her hair that the breeze was swirling around her head. "What shall I teach you in return?"

Something in his tone and the flicker of his eyes made her stomach flutter. "I'm sure I have a great deal to learn from someone much older and wiser, like yourself." She attempted to infuse her voice with humor, but his usual mirth was gone and something much more serious and intense darkened his eyes.

The look was unlike any she'd ever received, and it did something to her that was difficult to define, except that she was aware more than ever that she was almost a woman and that he was very much a man. Thankfully, they were at the front of the Customs House, and she could feign avid interest in the goings-on behind the wrought-iron gate.

The Customs House was a large three-storied building near the waterfront, where the river was filled with a fleet of cutters. The small boats were used to transport officials out to anchored vessels so that the officers could inspect them and ensure the safe discharge of the goods and the payment of duties.

"Polly Catlett?" came a familiar voice from one of the cutters that had just docked. A young man at one of the sets of oars raised a hand in greeting. Behind him at the deepest part of the River Medway, at least a dozen large ships were anchored, along with several smaller clipper ships. The traffic as usual was busy, especially since the relatively calm waters of the river further inland were a safer place for the vessels than the more temperamental sea along the coast.

"Good day to you, Billy." She smiled in greeting at her childhood friend. He stood then and climbed gracefully over the bow and onto the dock. He was attired in loose ankle-length pantaloons and a dark blue coat with a row of polished brass buttons. He wore a knit cap for warmth, but his cheeks were slapped red from the sea breeze. Strands of his hair curled at his neck, and the bright sunlight turned the color almost a blue-black.

As he bounded down the planks and leaped onto the rocky knoll, he surveyed John, from his cocked hat down to the buckles on his shoes. At the sight of John's grip on her elbow, Billy's eyes frosted into a cold winter blue without a trace of warmth.

When he reached them, he folded his arms across his chest and nodded at John. "Who's this?"

"My cousin, John Newton," Polly replied, feeling as though she ought to tug away from John and put some distance between them, but not knowing how to do so without embarrassing herself or John. "He came last night and will be visiting for—"

She stopped then, realizing she didn't know how long John

planned to stay. She looked up at him hoping he'd fill in the missing information.

"I'll be visiting the Catletts for a while." He gave a curt nod back at Billy.

For a while? She hadn't suspected he intended to stay long. But apparently she'd been mistaken. "John," she said, "this is my friend Billy Baldock. His father works here at the Customs House too, as a Searcher like my father. Billy is in training with the hope of someday receiving a customs position."

"I'm heartily glad to see you," John said.

"Likewise." Billy's response was formal and stiff and anything but glad.

An awkward silence fell between the two, who seemed to be appraising each other.

"I came to bring Father lunch," she said, hoping to distract the men.

Billy cocked his head toward the river. "Last I saw, Mr. Catlett was on the *Bounty*." She started to ask why her father had gone out when he was in charge of other officers who did the actual searching for smuggled goods, but Billy answered first. "He's training someone new."

Polly couldn't keep her shoulders from drooping in disappointment.

"I beg of you not to worry," Billy said. "I'll deliver the lunch when he returns. He'll be sorry to have missed seeing you." He grabbed the handle of the basket John was carrying. For a few long seconds, Billy didn't move away from John. Instead Billy's dark brows furrowed, and he drew himself up to his full height, which was almost the same as John's.

"So what brings you here, Mr. Newton?" Billy asked.

John released his grip on the basket. "As you can see, I'm escorting Polly—"

"No. Why are you here in Chatham?"

"My dear cousin Elizabeth invited me, and since I was passing through the area, I decided to stop." John paused and smiled down at Polly briefly before returning his attention to Billy. "I'm glad I did."

"How curious that you have nowhere else you need to be."

John didn't answer and a tension Polly didn't understand swirled between the men.

"Billy," she said, "would you be so kind as to give Father my love?"

"Anything for you, Polly." He gave her one of his charming smiles and stepped away from John.

With a cheerful farewell, she led John away from the Customs House and back the way they'd come. As they retraced their steps through Chatham, John's lively conversation surrounded her. She'd never had a friend, boy or girl, as open and talkative as John, and she found herself enjoying conversing with him. Something about him put her at ease so that she felt as though she could share openly.

As they neared her home, their footsteps slowed. She realized she was dawdling, but she wanted to stretch their uninterrupted time. Once back in the house, her siblings would clamor for John's attention again, and with his winsome grin, he would oblige them in whatever they wished as he had since he'd arrived.

John ambled slowly next to her and was suddenly quiet.

She glanced sideways at him. Although she knew she ought to view him in a brotherly manner, she found herself admiring his profile, the strength of his jaw and chin, and the taut lines of his cheek. There was an edge of danger that warned her John was like no one she'd ever known before. That should have scared her. But for a reason she couldn't explain, she was fascinated by him.

"So Billy's a suitor?" His tone was nonchalant, but his jaw flexed.

"No. Not a suitor." She laughed at the awkwardness of speaking of such personal matters. "Billy's just a friend."

"*'Anything for you, Polly,'* doesn't sound like something *'just a friend'* would say."

"Billy's a very sweet boy—man."

"Boy."

"He's probably the same age as you," she said. "So if he's a boy, what does that make you?"

He grinned. "Much more of a man than that monkey."

Polly stumbled to a halt and put a finger to her lips. "Shh. He's not a monkey."

"Oh that's right, he's a donkey—"

"John!" She glanced at the windows of the elaborate house that sat a short distance away. It was similar in style to the Catlett home but was more palatial looking with a terrace made of four columns surrounding the doorway, resembling a small ancient temple. "This is Billy's home. I don't want any of the Baldocks or their servants to hear us."

John peered with new interest at the home standing before them.

"I've grown up with the Baldocks. Billy's sister Felicity is one of my dearest friends."

"Is Felicity one of Susanna's accomplices in crime too?"

"Oh no." Polly shook her head even as she admired the thick

tapestries that hung in the windows, apparently new since the last time she'd called upon the Baldocks. "Felicity is much too proper these days for any capers."

"Then she sounds rather dull."

"I'm actually the boring one."

"I haven't had a dull moment since I met you," he said earnestly.

Warmth seeped into her cheeks, and she prayed John would attribute any red there to the cold and not to her embarrassment.

"If you stay long enough, Mr. Newton, you shall see my true self."

"Well, Miss Catlett," he said with all seriousness. "Then you've dared me to find out the truth. I don't suppose you played any games as a child in these woods?" He tilted his head toward the hedgerow that bordered the woodland.

"Of course I did."

"Mayhap you still have some of that liveliness within you."

She started to deny him, but when he yanked her hat from her head, she was rendered speechless.

A slow grin spread across his countenance. He dangled the hat out in front of her, the lacy ribbons beckoning her like fingers. "Come and get it."

She shrugged. "I don't need it."

He fluttered it closer so that one of the ribbons brushed her nose.

She feigned disinterest for another moment before swiping at it.

But he jerked the hat out of her reach leaving her fingers grasping only air. "I don't think you can get it back. You're not quick enough." He held it out to her again.

She pretended to start walking away but then spun and lunged for it.

With a laugh, he jumped back. "I told you that you wouldn't be able to get it from me." This time he plopped the hat on his head. The hat was too small, and the ribbons and lace surrounding his head made him look like a court jester. She couldn't contain her laughter.

His eyes shone. He taunted her again by leaning in. Soon she found herself chasing him through the woods, until finally they both stumbled to a stop, breathless and laughing.

"You put up a good chase, Miss Catlett," he said from his bent position, where he attempted to catch his breath.

"Are you always so wild, Mr. Newton?"

"Almost always."

She put a hand against the nearest tree trunk to rest but leaned in at an awkward angle and almost fell. John caught her, and she found herself laughing again, this time at her own clumsiness.

His laughter mingled with hers, echoing in the crisp air. She bumped her chin against his arm, and at the same moment she felt the pressure of his fingers upon her waist. At the warm contact her mirth faded, and his expression turned serious. His face was mere inches from hers, close enough that she could feel a burst of his breath near her cheek.

She didn't dare move, not to back away as she knew she ought. She stood taut and silent, listening to their mingled breathing and the rapid *thump* of her heartbeat.

He didn't move either. "It appears that you're not so dull as you might think," he finally whispered.

She couldn't form a coherent response.

The pressure of his hands left her waist, and he took a step away from her. She allowed herself a small breath before it caught again, this time as he gently replaced her hat on top of her head. He tilted it just slightly, the way she'd had it before. Then he dropped back another step, his gaze never once wavering from her face.

The chattering rebuke of a red squirrel in an overhead branch startled them. "I should get you home."

"Yes." She reached for the ribbons grazing her chin and began to tie them. "Yes, that's a good idea."

She followed him back to the road, and for a few minutes they strolled in silence side by side. Was he attempting to understand what was happening between them too? She'd never experienced such strange emotions. She'd never been close enough to a man to feel his breath. She'd never had any man look at her with such intensity.

Even now as she walked, her heartbeat tapped an unsteady rhythm at the nearness of his presence.

Perhaps she was more aware of him as a man because he'd rescued her and Susanna last night. Or perhaps she felt closer to him because he'd been so real and open with her about his spiritual struggles during their trip to and from town. Whatever the case, she couldn't deny that something was happening between them, and it filled her with both anticipation and fear. When her home finally came into view, they slowed their steps again.

"John?" She had to say something but wasn't sure exactly what.

"Aye?"

She twisted her mitten. "I see that we have the start of a genuine friendship—"

"Good that. I'd hoped for friendship too."

She stumbled slightly, caught off guard by his admission. "You did?"

"Aye. I'd like friendship very much."

From his slight emphasis on the word *friendship*, she had the feeling his definition of the word was different from hers. Against her better judgment, she let the delight of it settle deep inside.

John halted and uttered an expletive under his breath.

Polly cringed at his coarse language. "John—" She began to softly chastise him, but he cut her off by grabbing her arm and thrusting her behind him.

"What are you doing?" she asked.

"You need to hide." His voice contained an urgency that sent a shiver up her backbone. When he propelled her toward a nearby hedge, she didn't resist. "Stay here and don't show yourself until I come for you."

"What's going on?" She started to follow him.

"The farmer from last night is on your doorstep." His words stopped her. A peek through the barren branches showed a horse on the road in front of her home. "Promise you'll stay hidden?"

A chill moved to her heart, a chill that was deeper than the one that had numbed her toes and fingers.

"Promise?" His question was terse, and his expression more severe than she'd seen it.

She nodded, suddenly mute. He didn't have to spell out the seriousness of the situation for her to understand that if the farmer implicated her or Susanna, they could very well never get to experience another Christmas.

As John walked toward the house, she crouched low, praying the farmer wouldn't spot her. She strained to hear what he was saying.

"Everyone I asked said your daughter and sister were among the wassailers last night." The farmer's voice boomed with anger.

Polly swallowed the sudden lump of fear that rose in her throat.

"That's true." Mother's reply was faint. "They were wassailing. But I'm sure you're mistaken that they were involved in any plot to steal from you. They're just young girls—"

"Then let me question them for myself and determine their innocence."

"That's not possible—"

"What's the problem?" John interrupted her mother.

A moment of silence was followed by the farmer uttering an oath. "You were the drunk last night on the road to Luton." It was less of a statement and more of an accusation.

"Aye." John's answer was a bit too impudent and made Polly shiver again.

"Are you connected to this family?"

"Mrs. Catlett is my cousin."

"Then you're involved in the theft too." The farmer's voice rose.

"You're mistaken."

"It's no mistake that you were on the road near my farm at the same time I was robbed."

"I have no knowledge of any robbery. Neither do the girls. If a robbery happened while they were wassailing, it was by pure chance."

The lies flowed off John's tongue as smooth as lantern oil. Polly just hoped he wouldn't get burned in the process of defending them. She closed her eyes and began to silently chant the Lord's Prayer. Maybe if she prayed hard enough, God would hear her and save not only her and Susanna but now John as well.

For a moment the cold winter air seemed to freeze with silence.

But then the farmer released a string of frustrated oaths. John uttered several back, while telling the farmer to be on his way.

"I'll be watching you and those girls," the farmer finally said.

Polly chanced a glance around the hedge to see that the farmer was mounting his horse. She sat back on her heels, relief giving way to shaking.

Finally, the fading stamp of hooves against gravel told Polly the farmer had taken his leave. John ushered her rapidly inside. And when the front door closed behind her, she exhaled a long breath. At the sight of her mother's face creased with anxiety, the tightness returned to Polly's chest.

"I don't think we have anything further to worry about," John assured Mother, after he'd briefly relayed the previous evening's events.

"You don't think he'll go to the constable?" Mother asked.

John shook his head. "He can't. Then he has to admit to his own crime, that he was a part of smuggling the slaves rather than paying the required duties."

Mother didn't look convinced.

"Even if he had proof that the girls were involved—which he doesn't—he has no legal recourse for accusing them of anything."

Polly prayed John was right but couldn't keep from agreeing with Mother. She had the feeling this was only the beginning of trouble.

ou need more bookshelves," Newton said to Mrs. Catlett as she returned several volumes to a small shelf overflowing with more books than he'd ever seen in one place. In fact, books filled every corner and spare nook of the breakfast room. "I'd be happy to build you a larger shelving unit."

Mrs. Catlett paused with her hand on the spine she was attempting to wedge into too narrow a spot. Her elegant brow rose. "Why, John, I didn't know you were a carpenter."

"I'm not." He assessed the wall space and quickly calculated the footage of lumber he'd need. "But I've helped the ship carpenter enough that I've learned a few basics."

"Is that so?"

"Aye. I could do something simple. Nothing fancy, mind you. But it would be better than the floor."

Mrs. Catlett glanced to the various piles stacked around the room. "I cannot deny that in recent years I've longed for more shelves."

"Then I insist that you allow me to do it. I shall draw out a proposal this very day and present it to Mr. Catlett when he arrives home."

She smiled and the beauty of her features reminded him of Polly. "You have the same sweet spirit as your mother."

Newton wasn't so sure about that, but he returned her smile anyway. He pushed back from the table where he'd spent the morning next to Jack, tutoring him on his Latin verb conjugations. He slapped the boy on his back, then stood and stretched.

In addition to the tutoring, he'd also used the opportunity to thumb through several books. He tried not to appear overly eager at the thought of getting a chance to read some of them. He'd been mocked enough by fellow sailors for his thirst for learning, and he'd learned to hide his enthusiasm.

Even though years had passed since he'd been in school, he'd always found opportunities to continue educating himself. He hadn't admitted to his father how much he craved knowledge and how he regretted not working harder when he was in school. But he wondered if his father sensed it, because on each voyage his father happened to have a new book in his captain's cabin—once a volume of geography, another time mathematics, and yet another Latin. As far as Newton could tell, his father didn't read any of the books himself, but he also never said anything when Newton spirited the books away to read in secret.

Of course, his father wasn't always so calm. Newton didn't want to think about how angry he must have been yesterday when the day had passed with nary a word from him. The thought of his father's frustration had nagged Newton all morning and had urged him to be on his way if he hoped to make his ship in time. The job his father had arranged for him in Jamaica as a manager on one of the Manesty sugar plantations was too good an opportunity to pass up. First he'd learn how to oversee the slaves and process the sugarcane.

Eventually he'd have the prospect for advancement and perhaps one day could become a planter himself. A life in Jamaica would give him the chance to accumulate a large fortune, maybe not as much as Joseph Manesty's, but certainly much better than he'd ever make as a seaman.

But now that he'd just offered to build Mrs. Catlett a bookshelf, how could he leave? Mayhap he could stay another day or two and at least start the bookshelf. It wouldn't hurt to stay for some of the upcoming Christmas festivities, would it?

"I remember the last time your mother brought you to visit us," Mrs. Catlett said, as she walked around the morning room and picked up more books and discarded papers. "She was involved in a Dissenting church at the time."

Newton nodded. It had been years since he'd stepped foot inside the Old Gravel Lane Chapel he'd attended with Mother. But he hadn't forgotten those days of sitting in the chapel next to her and listening to their pastor, Dr. Jennings, preach directly from Scripture for at least an hour every Sunday morning. As a young boy, he'd paid rapt attention to the detailed exposition. Even if he hadn't understood everything, he remembered being moved by the sermons.

"I never did comprehend why she wanted to break away from the Church of England," Mrs. Catlett said, "although she sure did try hard to explain her position."

Newton pictured his mother's devout face above his, her eyes closed, her fingers gentle in his hair as she prayed for him and kissed him good night. He hadn't understood at the time what it meant to be a Dissenter, to break away from the king's church and join an independent meetinghouse. He knew now that the repercussions were swift and strong against Dissenters. Although the days of fearing

being hauled off to prison were over, the religious tolerance for anyone outside the Church of England was still low, with fewer job opportunities, lower pay, and disdain. In fact, no Catholics or
nonconformists were allowed to hold any crown offices, including
customs positions.

"She was so intent upon teaching you God's ways." Mrs. Catlett's
thin fingers lingered on the frayed binding of a Bible that rested on a
mahogany end table, and her eyes held a faraway look in them. "I
always admired her determination to put your spiritual training
above all other educational endeavors."

"Aye, I think I can still quote whole sections of the Gospels." He
tried to infuse humor into his tone, but guilt chafed him as it did
whenever he wondered what his mother would think if she could see
his skeletal faith now and the type of life he'd been leading, giving
in to the desires of his flesh whenever it suited him.

"Did you know she wanted to send you to University of St. An-
drews in Scotland to be educated when you were old enough?"

The question surprised him. "Then she was determined to make
a Dissenting minister of me?"

It was too late for him to even consider a life in ministry. Not
only was he not educated enough, but too many doubts had crept
upon him in recent years, too many things about the faith he questioned now that he was more enlightened and thinking for himself.

"As much as my husband and I are staunchly devoted to the true
Church," she said, "your mother's sincerity of faith and devotion to
God were an inspiration that I have sorely missed over the years."

Regret lingered in her tone, a regret that in his opinion was entirely unworthy. From what he'd been able to tell from the two days
he'd stayed with the Catletts, they were almost as pious as his mother

had been, especially Polly. That morning, when she'd come downstairs with dark circles under her eyes, Susanna had explained as though it were an everyday occurrence that Polly had stayed up late and arisen early to pray.

Not only was Polly pious, but she was also completely guileless and innocent of the wiles of men. He had realized that when they stood together in the woodland yesterday. He'd never in his life wanted to kiss a woman as badly as he did at that moment. And he was accustomed to doing whatever pleased him. But the innocence in her eyes stopped him. He knew that in kissing her he would be using her, and in using her, he would hurt her.

"Thank you again for coming to my defense yesterday, John." Mrs. Catlett crossed to him, her petticoats swishing in the quietness of the room. Except for Jack, the children had gone outside for a "breath of fresh air." And every now and then, he heard their distant laughter. She stopped in front of him, close enough that he could catch the scent of her rose water. She reached for his cheek and pressed a hand there. "You put your own life in jeopardy to protect the girls, and I can't thank you enough."

The tenderness took him off guard. "It was nothing."

Last evening, when Mr. Catlett had learned about the doings, he'd been grave. He'd listened to Susanna's impassioned speech about the evils of slavery. But like Newton, Mr. Catlett understood that the English economy depended upon slavery. Britain's ships dominated the slave trade, delivering thousands of chained captives each year to Dutch, Spanish, and Portuguese colonies in addition to its own. Without the wealth made from the slave trade and the many English plantations in the West Indies that relied upon slaves, England would be weak and easily fall prey to her enemies, namely the French.

Whatever the case, Newton had echoed Mr. Catlett's request that Susanna refrain from any further involvement with the abolitionist lawbreakers.

Before Mrs. Catlett could speak any further about the issue, a servant announced their noon meal was ready. Newton offered to call the children inside. Of course he couldn't pass up the opportunity to wrestle with young George or tickle Sara as she bounded up to him, clearly delighted to see him. If only Polly were equally delighted.

Once the rest of the children had gone inside, he found Polly standing beside a giant spruce in the side yard.

Bundled in her heavy wool coat, mittens, and flat-crowned straw hat, she looked as she had that first night he'd watched her sing at the farmer's house. The vibrant blue of her coat served to contrast her porcelain skin and blond hair, and the bleak gray of the leafless trees and shrubs highlighted the bloom in her cheeks.

She was staring into the tree and pleading with someone to come down. The distress in her voice moved him. Heedless of the cold, he crossed the yard and stood next to her, peering into the thick spruce. Scanning the dark shadows of the branches, he couldn't spot the source of her concern.

He hadn't had the opportunity to talk to her alone since their walk to the Customs House yesterday, when she'd delivered her line about being friends.

He felt slightly guilty that he hadn't taken her declaration too seriously because the truth was, he felt anything but platonic where Polly was concerned. She'd captivated him not only with her singing but with her wit, her smile, and her sweetness. She listened — really listened — to him yesterday when he spoke of matters on his heart.

He hadn't scared her away with his doubts and insecurities. Instead, she seemed to accept him, faults and all.

He hadn't needed much time to realize she was not only the most beautiful girl he'd ever met but also the most amazing.

Even now as her big blue eyes met his, he was rendered utterly helpless by the silent plea there. And when her long lashes fell and then lifted, his heart did the same, dropping in his chest with a *whoosh* before pattering back to life again.

He didn't know exactly how to describe what he was feeling about this young woman. It was quite possible he was falling in love with her, if that could happen after so brief an encounter. Whatever it was, he knew he'd never be satisfied with mere friendship.

Suddenly all he could think about was winning her, making her feel the same way about him that he did about her. He couldn't imagine leaving her. If he departed today as he knew he should, he wouldn't see her for at least five years, for the duration of his contract with Manesty. Five whole years. And he'd be halfway around the world from her in Jamaica. He wouldn't have even a passing glimpse of her. No visits. No chance to hear her sing. No opportunities to win her heart.

The most he could hope for would be letters, but the correspondence with the colonies and West Indies was untrustworthy and infrequent. There was the very real prospect that if he walked away from her today, he'd lose her before he even had the chance to start winning her. The thought lodged in his chest and held fast just like a harpoon sinking deep into the layers of a whale.

The chill of the winter day rippled the thin linen of his shirt sleeves. "Who's in the tree?"

"Pete," she said, returning her distressed gaze to the spruce. "And he won't come down."

"Pete?" Newton mentally ticked off the rest of the Catlett children. Who was Pete? "Would you like me to climb up and get Pete?"

At his offer, her shoulders eased and she nodded. "Oh, would you?"

He didn't need any further urging. He ducked through the spindly branches and pushed them aside with ease. The sap was sticky on his bare hands, and the long spines prickly. He glanced up through the branches and could make out a slight form sitting on a high branch, a form with pointed ears and a long tail. He hoisted himself up to the first branch, testing the weight to see whether it would hold him.

"Be careful," Polly said, watching him through the evergreen boughs.

When he was out to sea, he spent hours in the rigging in both sunshine and storm. He'd had to drop the topsails in plenty of squalls, with the lightning flashing in his eyes, the wind whipping his body, and the rain slickening every step. He certainly wouldn't have any trouble climbing a mere tree.

"I may not be good at much," he said, "but have no fear. I'm quite the expert at climbing. The past seven years in the rigging haven't all been for naught."

"Even so, watch your step . . ."

"It sounds like you really care about me."

"Of course I care." Her voice echoed with a thread of embarrassment. "I'd care about anyone climbing a tree on my behalf."

"Admit it, Polly." He couldn't resist teasing her. "You like me."

"Yes, I do—I mean, no, I don't. At least not in the way you're insinuating."

He laughed and climbed higher. "That's right. You don't *like* me. You *love* me."

"As a brother."

"I'm no brother. I assure you of that." He cast a glance down to see her eyes widen at his comment. He grinned at her speechlessness and hefted himself to the next branch. He could see that Pete was just a kitten, perhaps several months old. The fluffy gray creature peered down at him with big eyes and then meowed a long, loud howl.

"Is he all right?" Polly called up.

Newton reached a hand for the furry bundle. But the kitten meowed again and scooted backward on the branch toward the trunk, moving out of Newton's reach.

He shifted on the branch and debated whether to tuck the kitten in his shirt or make the descent one-handed. Before he could make up his mind, the branch beneath him cracked. Without thinking he latched onto the branch that held the kitten. Thankfully his reflexes were honed, and he was able to make the connection before he fell.

"Are you safe?" Polly asked, squinting her pretty eyes in an attempt to discover what was happening.

"Aye." He hoped she couldn't see him hanging there like an idiot. "I'm perfectly safe."

A loud crack told him he was in trouble. Springing into action, he lunged for Pete and snatched up the kitten just as the branch he was hanging on to broke.

The kitten decided at that moment to turn into a demonic waif. It scrambled and howled and hissed, all the while attempting to break free from him. The commotion and the pain of the creature's claws digging through his shirt into his chest distracted him from getting a firm grip on another branch so that he found himself slipping downward, branches bumping and scraping him until at last he hit the ground with such impact that it forced him to his backside.

At once Polly was kneeling at his side. "Are you hurt?"

"Of course not." He'd only slipped. That's all.

The kitten gave another screech of panic and released his claws again, this time into Newton's arm. He winced at the sharp pain tearing into his skin and couldn't maintain his grip on the cat any longer, nor did he want to.

He let go of the tiny demon. With fur sticking out in all directions, Pete shot away from him and scampered across the yard, disappearing around the house with nary a backward glance, as though Newton were the source of all his torment instead of his rescuer. "You forgot to say thank you," Newton called after the creature while nursing his arm.

"He's too frightened to remember his manners," Polly said. "I'll make sure he apologizes properly later."

He tried to push himself up but had to admit his backside ached a tad too much to move.

"You're bleeding." She pointed at his arm.

He shrugged. "It's just a little scratch. That's all."

"And your chest." She gaped at the blood seeping through the linen that wasn't covered by his waistcoat. "Perhaps you were scraped during your fall."

"I didn't fall."

"Forgive me, O ye climbing expert," she said dryly. "Perhaps you were scraped during your rapid descent."

"Nay, 'tis only the cat's handiwork." He glanced inside his shirt at his chest to assess the damage. Deep red scratches crisscrossed his skin, only surface deep, but stinging nonetheless.

"I'm sorry," she offered. "I should have warned you that Pete is easily frightened."

"'Tis not your fault. I should have known when I saw so ferocious a creature that I was in for a terrible battle."

His attempt to ease her guilt was rewarded with a smile. "He was a fierce enemy, wasn't he?"

"The fiercest."

"Consider them your battle wounds. And I shall knight you for your heroic rescue."

"Sir John Newton." He pretended to mull over the title. "I like the sound of it."

Her smile widened. "You're now a noble hero."

"Will you write a song about me so that my brave deeds will be lauded through all generations?"

Her eyes took on a merry twinkle. "I shall do my best to come up with something worthy of you."

"Something epic, mayhap very similar to *Beowulf*?"

She laughed and the sound melted his heart into a puddle of tallow.

The nearby yap of a dog startled him at the same moment it did her. She quickly scrambled away from him and up to her feet.

"How do you do, Miss Donovan?" Polly said, smoothing her hands over her skirt as though she didn't know what to do with them.

A tall woman stood in the yard on the opposite side of the wrought-iron fence. With raven black hair and equally dark eyebrows, the woman at first appeared to be scowling at them, but her darting eyes spoke more of nervousness than rebuke. She held a curly-haired white dog in her arms, and her gloved fingers were rapidly stroking the dog's fur.

"This is my cousin, Mr. John Newton," Polly spoke again, motioning at him. "And Mr. Newton, this is one of our neighbors, Miss Donovan."

He scrambled to his feet, trying not to wince at the pain in his tailbone or the throbbing in his chest and arm. "Good day to you, Miss Donovan." He bowed with a flourish.

"I was just examining Mr. Newton's condition," Polly said quickly. "He fell from the tree and he's bleeding and we were discussing the nature of his injuries . . ." Her voice trailed off, and her cheeks flushed a deeper pink.

Still Miss Donovan didn't say anything. Her fingers only moved faster in the dog's hair. Red seemed to steal into her thin cheeks as well, and she merely nodded before finally turning away from them and gliding toward the house that stood a short distance from the Catletts'.

When she disappeared inside, Polly pressed her fingers first against one flushed cheek and then the other. All the while she glanced everywhere but at him—at the spruce tree, at the large front windows, at the dirt road that led to a small stable behind the house.

"You have such friendly neighbors," he offered, wanting to put her at ease.

She shifted her attention to the imposing brick house Miss Donovan had entered. A large tapestry in one of the side windows fluttered back into place hiding whoever had been peering out at them. "Miss Donovan moved here only last year and lives with her younger brother and his family."

"Then she's a spinster?"

"Unfortunately." Polly rubbed her mittened hands together. "And unfortunately, Mr. Donovan, her brother, isn't very kind to her. He treats her as though she's an imposition to his family."

"Perhaps he doesn't have the means to take care of her?" Judging from the home, he suspected Mr. Donovan was likely of the middling sort, the same as the Catletts, and had more than enough to live comfortably.

Polly shook her head. "No one wants to take care of a spinster sister, even if they have the means."

"Means or no, a man ought to do his duty by his family." His father's wife, Thomasina, had given birth to three children over the years—two boys and a girl. Newton had never considered them his siblings, and he'd been away on voyages too often to get to know them. And yet, if anything ever happened to his father or Thomasina, he'd find a way to help his stepbrothers and stepsister.

"We should get you inside," Polly said. "And have Mother dress your wounds."

He didn't need anyone to take care of a few little scratches. Besides, in spite of his banter with Polly, he wasn't looking forward to admitting to everyone else that he'd been wounded by a kitten. That wasn't exactly something a man boasted about. Nevertheless, if it gained him Polly's further doting . . . "I'm sure your mother will be much too busy to worry about me. Mayhap you could take care of me."

She started back to the door with rapid steps, but not before he caught a glimpse of the pretty pink coloring her cheeks again.

He chuckled and then jogged after her.

"Polly?" The call from down the lane stopped them both. A

horse cantered toward them carrying a man in a customs uniform—the same young man they'd met yesterday down at the river front.

"Good day, Billy." Polly's greeting was as warm as her smile, and she veered toward the front gate.

John had an overwhelming and completely irrational urge to grab her arm and steer her into the house so that she couldn't talk to Billy Baldock. It had been clear from the very first moment Billy had rushed to see Polly that the man was infatuated with her. Although she claimed they were only friends, he could see that Polly liked Billy too. Mayhap she didn't like him as a suitor. But with Billy's ardor, he'd win her soon enough.

A strange urgency prodded John to follow closely on Polly's heel. As she stepped out of the gate to the side of the road, he joined her.

Billy reined his horse next to Polly and beamed down at her, ignoring John altogether. "You look lovely today." He flashed a grin that revealed perfectly white and straight teeth. In his finely tailored coat, with his dark hair and blue eyes, the man was too handsome. He looked like a real knight on his steed.

"I was in the area delivering a message for Father," Billy said. "And Felicity asked me to bring you this invitation." He leaned down and handed Polly a crisply folded note.

"That was kind of you." Polly smiled her thanks. It was the sort of guileless smile that said she always saw the best in people, that she genuinely cared about those around her, and that Billy was no different from him in that regard.

In fact, she'd known Billy a lot longer than she had known him, and who was he to think he could waltz into Chatham and in two days' time make her fall in love with him? Because that's what he wanted to do, wasn't it? Because that's exactly what had happened to him, hadn't it?

Billy hadn't taken his attention off Polly's face. "Felicity is hosting a party next week, and she wanted to make sure you and Susanna will be there."

Polly finished reading the invitation but hesitated. Newton hoped she'd say no. He didn't want her to go. He wanted to keep her all to himself, although that was unrealistic considering there would likely be many parties and activities during the twelve days of Christmas.

"I'd like to attend." Polly started folding the note. "However . . ."

Newton couldn't stop himself from lifting a hand and grazing her elbow. He wasn't sure why he did it, except that perhaps it was his way of laying claim to Polly, of telling Billy that she was his now and that Billy would do well to stay clear of her.

Billy didn't miss the message. His mouth thinned, and everything in the taut flexing muscles of his face shouted at Newton to back away and take his hands off Polly.

Newton was tempted to slide his arm around Polly's waist and draw her into the crook of his body. But she'd bolt away from him like a frightened doe if he made such a bold move. Instead he circled his fingers about her elbow more possessively. He didn't look away from Billy's stare but returned it with a half grin, hoping to irritate the man.

Polly glanced between them and, seeing the growing tension upon Billy's face, spoke quickly. "I'd like to attend Felicity's party, but only if Cousin John can come along too. That way the two of you will have the opportunity to become better acquainted."

Newton almost snorted. He'd rather drink the foul bilge water that sat beneath the floorboards of a hull than become friends with Billy.

"I'm sure Felicity would like to meet John as well," Polly added.

"It's only a small party," Billy replied.

"Please, Billy?" Her plea, her big eyes, her beauty—combined, they were simply too hard to resist for even the strongest man. "I wouldn't feel right abandoning my cousin during the festivities."

For the briefest moment, guilt churned in Newton's gut like a rancid meal. His father's voice at the back of his mind demanded that he leave today for Liverpool. He had a decent job waiting for him in Jamaica, a job his father had negotiated on his behalf. The rational part of him urged him to go, to do the responsible thing, to follow through on his commitment.

But then just as rapidly, he tossed the guilt overboard and let it sink far, far out of sight. There was no way he could leave now, not in light of the party next week. He couldn't allow Polly to go without him. Not with Billy Baldock following her around like a besotted puppy dog.

Besides, he promised Mrs. Catlett he would build her a new shelving unit. He'd offered his help, and he couldn't withdraw it now.

Nay, he couldn't go. Not yet. He'd at least stay through next week. The job in Jamaica could wait. He would devise an excuse to give his father and Joseph Manesty for why he was late. And at some point he'd find another ship leaving for the West Indies.

Billy finally nodded at Polly reluctantly. "I'm sure Felicity would much rather have you come to the party with your cousin in tow than be absent altogether." Billy cast Newton a quick sharp glance that told him the truth: that Felicity didn't care a farthing who came to the party, that Billy would rather see Newton dead than anywhere near Polly, but that he'd do anything to make Polly happy.

"Thank you, Billy." Her face radiated her pleasure. "You're a dear."

At her words of endearment, the young man's features softened.

Newton stiffened. The matter was settled. He was staying. And he was going to the party.

## FIVE

*P*olly tried not to gape in envy as a footman led her into the Baldocks' drawing room. Every time she visited the Baldocks, she imagined that she was stepping into one of the rooms of the king's palace at Hampton Court. Maybe it was the oval moulding of the decorated plaster ceiling that gave the room its elegance. Or perhaps the intricate cornice and frieze that contrasted with the deep burgundy color of the walls that made her feel as though she were stepping into the royal household. With the Christmas evergreen and holly draped about the room as accents, it was more beautiful than usual.

Whatever the reason, she always lifted her shoulders just a tad higher when she entered the room. Its enormous gilt-framed pictures and polished dark mahogany tables and chairs gleamed under the glow of the oil lamps. Even the carpet, with its design of birds and foliage, was thick and plush, making her feel like a wealthy gentlewoman, although she most certainly was not.

"I dare say, it's about time for your arrival," Felicity said, rising from the settee where she had perched as she visited with several other guests.

Polly smiled at her childhood friend, but Felicity was staring directly at John, who had entered the room behind her. Earlier as they prepared for the party, Susanna had insisted on outfitting John in one of Father's suits. Although John was about the same height as Father, he was decidedly broader and more muscular, and therefore the waistcoat stretched at the seams. Susanna wasn't able to button any of the wrist buttons of the coat, leaving more of the shirt ruffles on display. He refused to wear one of Father's wigs but gave in to Susanna's prodding to allow her to tie a cravat at the high collar of the waistcoat.

"So this is the handsome cousin I've heard so much about." Felicity approached them, all the while studying John with open curiosity as one might a foreigner. Though Polly had questioned Susanna's efforts at dressing John up, she was glad now that Susanna had enough foresight to save John the embarrassment of feeling ill at ease and out of place at the Baldocks'.

Polly made all the proper introductions. Fortunately, John wasn't easily embarrassed, and he responded with warm charm to Felicity, who tossed her thick auburn curls over her shoulders and gave John full view of the womanly curves that her bodice and overskirt emphasized to perfection. Polly had to suppress a momentary pang of jealousy at the newest mantua Felicity was wearing. The open robe was buckled at her waist with a girdle and revealed a flowered petticoat in a lovely violet that contrasted with the gold skirt.

Polly swallowed the familiar envy she experienced whenever she was with Felicity and other friends whose fathers could afford to buy new garments. She pushed aside the thought that her father could be doing the same and reminded herself that he was a man of principle and integrity and she loved him for it.

"You're jealous," John whispered as he took a place on the settee next to her.

Polly buried her fingers in the layers of her silky skirt and rebuked herself for her discontentment. How had he noticed? And had anyone else noticed her vanity? She glanced around the room. Susanna had accompanied them to the Baldock home, but she'd already disappeared. Billy was nowhere in sight either, and he was usually one of the first to greet her.

"Envy is indeed one of my faults," she whispered.

He grinned and puffed out his chest. "You don't have to be jealous."

"I'll try not to be the rest of the evening." She would have to refrain from looking at what all the other young ladies were wearing, and she'd have to stop admiring the decor of the drawing room and comparing it to theirs. After all, while their home might not be quite as lavish, it wasn't as though they were beggars living in a poorhouse.

"Miss Baldock is a lovely woman." John leaned closer so that she caught his scent, one that was a mixture of sea and wind.

"Yes, she's a dear friend." Felicity had taken up a conversation with several other young ladies near the fireplace. Her voice, her laughter, her expression were vivacious and irresistible. She was already making plans to leave for boarding school in the spring, and Polly was trying not to envy her for that either.

"Aye, you don't have anything to worry about," John continued. "As lovely as she is, I could tell right away that she's not the type for me."

Polly shifted so that she gave John her full attention. Did he think she was jealous of Felicity's wiles and ability to attract his attention away from her? Did he believe she was worried that he'd like Felicity better than her?

His grin told her that was exactly what he thought.

"I'm not concerned in the least that you'll become smitten with Felicity or she with you."

"Good that. Apparently you know you already have my heart to the fullest."

She laughed. She couldn't help herself.

"I'm glad I easily amuse you."

"You do know how to make me laugh." She was more delighted than amused, but she didn't want to encourage his insinuations of affection, since he was already lavish enough with them.

The past week of his visit had been one of the merriest weeks of her life. Even though he spent the bulk of his time with a hammer and nails in the breakfast room constructing a wall of shelves, they'd still spent hours together. He helped her with chores, began to teach her Latin, listened to her practice the pianoforte, and read to her and her siblings with such animation that they clamored for his stories every evening. Best of all, he spent Christmas Day with her. They went to church and then returned for a goose dinner and the lighting of the yule log. He teased and bantered with her about their relationship from time to time, but overall, he interacted with her in the same friendly manner that he did with her brothers and sisters. She felt safe with him. And that made his teasing about liking him even more delightful when it happened.

"Aye, then. I'm good for something." A glint of hurt passed through his eyes. It was there one second and gone the next. If she hadn't been paying attention, she might have missed it altogether.

Her humor faded. She loved his jesting, the easy way he could make people smile, his ability to laugh at himself and not take life so seriously. But there had been times, like now, when she sensed deeper pains.

She shifted on the settee so that she was facing him. "I haven't known you long. But it hasn't taken much for me to realize that you're a good man."

"I am rather good at rescuing kittens stuck in trees, aren't I?"

"I'm serious. You're one of the kindest men I've met. And one of the most helpful." He was always jumping in and assisting others with no thought to himself.

"Then you clearly haven't met many men."

"John." Her tone rebuked him, but she couldn't keep from smiling.

"Polly." He smiled back, and it was the kind of genuine smile that made her really like him, much more than she should.

At that moment Susanna bustled into the room, her dark eyes flashing and her face tight with an urgency that told Polly her aunt was conspiring once again. As Susanna crossed the room, Polly braced herself. What was Susanna planning this time? Another abolitionist rescue perhaps?

When Susanna reached her, she bent over the scalloped edge of the settee and whispered, "I must temporarily excuse myself from the party."

"Why?" Polly demanded, wanting Susanna to know that she wouldn't be so gullible this time. Susanna may have fooled her once, but she wouldn't again.

"I need to return home at once." Susanna splayed her fingers over her gown. "I've spilled mead on my bodice. I must change and have the servants treat the spot before it stains."

The crimson blotch of honey wine on the silvery satin glared at Polly. "Of course."

Susanna nodded and began to leave. "I won't be long. I promise."

"You can't walk home unattended," Polly protested, glancing out the windows to the darkness of the winter evening.

"Of course I can. It's only a short distance—"

"I'll accompany Susanna," John offered.

"I don't want to trouble you or make you miss any of the party—"

John cut Susanna off with a narrowed look. "It won't trouble me."

For a moment the two seemed to be having a private, unspoken battle. Then finally Susanna sighed. "Very well. I shall accept your offer." And with that she turned and stalked across the room.

Polly wanted to chastise Susanna for her lack of manners and ungratefulness. But John rose from the settee with an unruffled grin.

"Don't miss me too much while I'm gone," he said in a tone that made her insides flip, and before she could find a witty response, he spun away and strode across the room, the suit coat stretching to display his strong shoulders and the power of his upper arms. He moved with confidence and toughness, a man who could easily defend himself and overcome an opponent in a fight.

Only when he reached the door did he wink at her over his shoulder, the kind of wink that said he knew she'd been watching him.

"I vow," she whispered and covered her cheeks with her hands, "if I'm not more careful, John Newton will be my undoing."

For a while she did her best to mingle with Felicity and her other

friends. When Billy finally joined them a short time later, he provided a distraction as well. Soon enough Felicity started the game
Find the Ring, and they all sat in a circle and held on to a piece of
string long enough to go around the inner circumference. As they
passed a ring on the string from one hand to the next, a player stood
in the center and tried to discover whose hand contained the ring.

They completed several other games before Susanna and John
finally returned, their cheeks red from the cold and their eyes sparkling. From his spot next to her, Billy studied them intently. "Where
have you two been?" The lilt to his voice implied the two had been
away having a romantic tryst.

Polly was surprised when neither denied his insinuation. Susanna squeezed John's arm and whispered in his ear. In return
John gave a half grin to the crowd that seemed to confirm Billy's
assumption.

Polly wanted to believe he was only playacting in a role of Susanna's making, but a tiny part of her was unsettled at the thought
that they'd been together.

During the game of Blind Man, Polly plastered herself to the
wall near the door. Felicity had insisted on extinguishing the
lamps, closing the grate on the fireplace, and locking the shutters
so that they had to play in the dark. Only a tiny sliver of moonlight
came in through the crack in the shutters. It wasn't enough light to
see where anyone was; however, titters and hushed laughter gave
away locations.

"There you are."

She jumped at the sound of John's voice so close. Close enough
that she could feel the warmth of his breath in the hollow part of
her ear.

"You've been avoiding me since I returned." The words came out soft and feathery against her skin.

She shook her head. "I'm sure you're mistaken."

His shoulder leaned into hers. "Susanna and I only kissed, that's all."

"You did?" Her question came out louder than she'd intended.

John laughed lightly. "No. Of course not."

She relaxed against the wall. But he tugged her forward in the dark, sliding along until they were wedged into a corner. For a long moment they were both silent, listening for anyone else who might be nearby.

Then John's voice was near her ear again. "I told you that you were jealous." At the cockiness of his tone, she gave him a playful push. He feigned falling away from her and grabbed her hand as though needing it to keep his balance.

As his fingers closed around hers, she sucked in a sharp breath at the contact. He resumed his position next to her in their hiding spot, this time their intertwined hands resting between them.

At his nearness she was rendered immobile.

"I like that you're jealous," he whispered.

"I'm not—"

"I can admit that I'm jealous whenever I see you with Billy." His confession stopped her denial.

Was he teasing her again? She didn't think so. His voice was much too serious. "You needn't be jealous."

"Aye, but I am." He pressed his face into her hair and took a deep breath. "You're beautiful. And Billy knows you're a treasure just as much as I do."

*Beautiful? A treasure?* Was she dreaming his words? Her pulse doubled its speed, and her legs liquefied like melting snow. Without the solidness of the wall bracing her, she would have collapsed.

"And just so you know"—his words brushed the hair near her ear—"I would never consider kissing Susanna."

"That's good to know." Her whisper felt incoherent.

"There's only one woman I'm considering kissing."

She shivered, whether from his implication or his proximity, she knew naught. All she knew was that she needed this sweet torment to end before she swooned. She needed to pull away from him and return to their safe camaraderie.

At that moment the door of the drawing room swung open with a crashing bang, and light from the hallway pierced the room. Polly jumped away from John. For an instant he held fast to her hand, but at her jerk he released her.

Felicity and the other guests complained loudly, and within moments the lanterns had been relit. There were several other couples standing rather close together, guilt coloring their faces. At the sight of them, Polly tried to put even more distance between herself and John, but the settee in front of them prevented her escape.

"We have a traitor in our midst," boomed a hard voice.

Filling the door was a burly man whose body was nearly as wide as the opening. At the sight of the wooden peg leg that started at one of his knees, Polly recognized Billy's uncle, Charlie Baldock, the leader of the biggest smuggling gang in the Kent countryside. Polly had seen him from time to time over the years during her visits at the Baldocks' home, and she'd always done her best to stay away from him. She was embarrassed to admit that his booming voice and strange leg had always frightened her.

Even now that she was older, something about him intimidated her. And the gossip surrounding him made him even scarier. Her father hadn't meant for her to overhear his latest tale about the dock-yard worker who'd been accused of stealing two gunnysacks of con-traband tea. The smugglers had found him, stripped him, and then whipped him until he confessed to the whereabouts of tea. The bat-tered body had been discovered later in a ditch. Dead. Of course, no one was willing to step forward and indict Charlie and his gang for the crime.

With an ominous *thump, thump* against the wooden floor, Charlie took several steps forward until he was inside the room and standing on the carpet. "Someone here was listening to something they shouldn't have been."

"Now, Charlie," Mr. Baldock's calmer voice came from the hall-way. He was a thinner man than his brother, more darkly handsome, like Billy. "I told you that you can't make that assumption. Anyone in the area could have learned of the whereabouts of the tea."

"No!" Charlie retorted. "It was one of these young people. I'm sure of it."

A hard knot coiled in Polly's chest. She didn't dare look at Susanna for fear of bringing her unwanted attention, but something told her that Susanna was involved in this new situation. Hadn't she learned from the last escapade that she was flirting too closely with danger? Although the farmer hadn't come back again, Polly wasn't able to walk the roads of Chatham without fear that he was lurking, waiting to capture her and make her pay for what she'd done.

Charlie Baldock was attired in a tight suit and a simple bob-style wig. He carried a hat under one arm and walked with a cane in the other. As he hobbled further into the room, his furrowed gaze jumped from one guest to the next until it finally came to rest on her.

He lifted his cane and pointed it at her. "You're one of George Catlett's children, aren't you?"

Polly was tempted to shrink back. But she reminded herself that she wasn't at fault for anything. "Yes, I'm Polly Catlett—"

Billy stepped forward and squared off with his uncle. "Don't accuse her of giving away the location of the tea. She would never do that."

"She listened to our meeting and then ran home and told her daddy," Charlie said in a tone that abided no further arguing.

The coil in Polly's chest cinched tighter.

"Polly is the sweetest girl I know." Billy spoke again, his voice wavering just slightly, showing her the courage it cost him to stand up to his uncle. "She would never involve herself in matters that don't concern her."

Billy's glance cast her a silent plea to agree with him.

She nodded, grateful for his defense. "I've been here at the party all evening." Again she had to refrain from looking at Susanna, who hadn't budged from her spot in one of the wing chairs near the fireplace.

"If not her," Charlie said in a growl, "then who?"

Billy turned then and looked directly at John. "Why don't you ask Newton here. Apparently he disappeared for a while after he first arrived. Maybe he heard the news and went straight to Mr. Catlett."

"Of course Mr. Newton wouldn't do such a thing," Polly spoke before thinking. Once the words were out, she prayed they were true, that Susanna hadn't unwittingly involved John.

John held himself tall and stiff. His chin rose a notch, and his eyes sparked with defiance. If anyone in the room looked the part of a troublemaker, John did. Even though he wore her father's suit, there was still something slightly wild spirited about him that no amount of grooming could hide.

She waited for him to deny Billy's accusation, to make some excuse about how he had only gone out with Susanna to have a few minutes alone with her—at least that's what she desperately hoped he'd say. But he remained silent.

With a low growl, Charlie started toward their corner, his peg leg tapping ominously on the carpet like the prelude to an explosion.

She was surprised when John took hold of her arm and propelled her away from him and toward Billy. Billy readily maneuvered her out of harm's way.

"Who are you?" Charlie demanded as he bore down upon John. "And why are you interfering with my business?"

"You have no proof that I interfered," John said in an equally hard voice.

"All I know is that nobody knew the location of my tea until this party started tonight. It was safe and sound, and now it's been confiscated by Mr. Catlett and one of his officers in training."

"Maybe you have a traitor in your ranks."

"My men are loyal." Charlie's voice dropped dangerously. "I pay them to be loyal."

John shrugged. "Maybe you aren't paying them enough."

"Or maybe you're a fool to think you can tamper with my affairs." Before anyone could stop him, Charlie swung his cane upward so that it caught John between his legs. The hit was swift and severe, doubling John over with a grunt. Charlie didn't wait for John to catch his breath but instead lifted his cane again, this time higher, striking John across his bent back. The crack of the cane reverberated through the silent room.

Polly cried out in protest at the same time that Billy's father in the doorway called out for Charlie to stop, even as the big man whacked John again, this time across his shoulder. Susanna too was out of her chair and would have rushed to John, except the Polly caught her arm and held her back.

"Stop!" Susanna yelled, her features contorted with both anger and fear. "It isn't his fault!"

John lifted his gaze and caught Polly's. Though it was brief, it was long enough to see the pain in his eyes. And something more, a silent appeal to keep Susanna quiet. To let him take the blame.

Although she didn't want him to be hurt, her grip on Susanna tightened. "Hush, Susanna."

But Susanna shook off Polly's hold. "It's my fault."

Charlie's cane stopped midway down toward John's back.

"Don't listen to her," John said. "She had nothing to do with it."

"I am entirely to blame," Susanna insisted. "If anyone deserves a caning, let it be me."

Charlie stared from John to Susanna and then back. He gave a low growl of frustration. Then with a swift jerk, he brought the cane down upon John's back again. The blow sent John to his knees.

Susanna cried out, and Polly struggled to restrain her. Polly doubted that Charlie would go so far as to cane Susanna. In fact, Polly doubted Charlie believed Susanna; likely he attributed her confession to a desire to protect the man she cared about. Even so, Polly's grip on her aunt tightened.

"Charlie," Mr. Baldock said, approaching his brother from behind. "You can't beat up the boy. You'll get me in trouble, and then what will you do without me here to help you?"

Mr. Baldock glanced around the room, particularly at the

young women cowering against one another and the other men who were fidgeting uncomfortably as if they'd rather be anywhere else in Chatham at that moment than in the same room as the notorious Charlie Baldock.

"Someone is lying to me," Charlie shouted. "And I aim to find out the truth. One way or another."

John sneered. "If you want to find the biggest liar and thief in this room, then take a look at yourself—"

Charlie whacked John again.

John gritted his teeth, clearly holding back a groan of agony.

"Charlie, Charlie." Mr. Baldock's tone grew more placating, and he hesitantly placed his arm across Charlie's shoulder as though to comfort him. "These are all just young people. Don't be too hard on them. We don't really know who's to blame."

Charlie glared at John, and Polly prayed John wouldn't say anything more. She realized now he was trying to protect Susanna, and she was grateful to him for that. But he was only getting himself into more trouble.

"You better watch your back, boy," Charlie ground out before finally allowing Mr. Baldock to usher him from the room. No one spoke as his stilted steps faded down the hallway. "His blabbing will cost me!" Charlie roared. "That tea was valued upwards of five hundred pounds."

Mr. Baldock's response was calm. "I've been told we can expect a shipment of Flanders lace this week."

When finally another door closed with a loud reverberation, Billy turned to Polly and exhaled a shaky breath. "Are you all right?"

She nodded but was watching John attempt to straighten his back, his face contorting. The others in the room were murmuring among themselves and moving toward the door, clearly anxious to leave the party before Charlie came charging into the room again.

"I'll walk you and Susanna home," Billy offered apologetically.

With tears pooling in her eyes, Susanna captured a half sob in her hand and stumbled toward John.

"I'm sorry about my uncle." Billy said. "I shouldn't have said anything about Newton. It's just that I didn't want Charlie hurting you."

Polly nodded, feeling suddenly numb. Both Billy and John had only sought to protect her and Susanna. But she couldn't ignore the truth. Susanna had overheard Cutthroat Charlie talking about the smuggled tea. Polly had no doubt Susanna had spilled the mead upon her gown to conjure an excuse to leave the party without arousing suspicion. And then she'd run home to tell Father. In the process she'd dragged John into the danger.

"Will you forgive me, Polly?" Billy reached out as though he wanted to touch her face but then let his hand drop to his side.

"Of course I will." She offered him as much of a smile as she could. It wasn't generous, but it seemed to be enough for Billy, who exhaled a breath with obvious relief.

Susanna helped John into his coat. With Billy on one side and Polly on the other, they managed to lead him up the hill to the Catletts' home. When Billy was gone and they were in the kitchen in the lowest level of the Catlett house, Polly's father helped settle John into one of the chairs at the servants' table. Susanna collapsed into another and laid her head down on the table, her body shaking with soft sobs.

Thankfully the servants were already retired to their dormer rooms, and the kitchen was empty of prying eyes. Her father helped

John take off his shirt, and her mother began making a poultice. Polly figured they had forgotten about her, or they would have demanded that she leave rather than be exposed to John's half-naked state. As it was, they were too busy asking questions and tending to him to pay attention to her standing against the wall.

"It's my fault," Susanna said, wiping her cheeks dry with her sleeve. "I'm the one who overheard. If anyone should suffer, it should be me."

John shook his head and grimaced at the pain even the tiniest motion caused him. "Nay. Let the suspicion fall upon me. Better me than either you or Polly."

"I hope you finally learned a lesson tonight, Susanna," Mother said, stirring flour and comfrey together. "Your rash actions have consequences. That's what Mother and Father have been trying to tell you all along."

Susanna glanced at the swollen red welts on John's back that gleamed in the candlelight and then shuddered. "I only wanted to do the right thing."

"And it was the right thing," Father assured her as he laid a cool cloth across another of the ugly welts. "But you didn't tell me that Charlie Baldock was there, or I wouldn't have allowed you to return for the evening."

"Susanna is too young to be involved in such things," Mother protested.

Father didn't disagree, but neither did he chide Susanna. He must have concluded that her own misery at John's condition was chastisement enough.

Apparently Mother wasn't convinced of the same and stopped mixing the poultice to give Susanna her sharpest glare. "Young ladies your age should be concerned about having suitors and training for marriage. Not worrying about freeing slaves or disempowering smuggling operations. Think about the trouble you could have brought upon Polly if Mr. Baldock had decided to go after her instead of John."

The rattle of the lid on the copper kettle commanded Mother's attention, and she turned to remove the boiling water from the hob on the coal grate. She poured a small amount into the mortar, and the liquid turned the dry mixture into a grayish paste.

While they didn't know if the farmer from the wassailing incident was linked to Charlie, the fact was, Susanna had no business interfering then or now. And perhaps Father had no business interfering either.

Her father was still attired in his heavy wool coat that he'd apparently thrown on when he left on his raid to confiscate the tea that Charlie had smuggled in from the coast or from one of the ships anchored in the River Medway.

"Will Charlie come after you, Father?" Polly asked. She'd known her father faced danger as a result of his stand against smuggling, but she had never before realized exactly the extent of the threats.

Father refused to meet her gaze but focused instead on dipping the cloth into a basin of cold water before applying it to another of John's welts. John's head hung low, and his forehead rested against the table. Polly suspected it was his way of hiding the pain that each touch brought. "We will always encounter danger when we stand up for what's right," Father said, "particularly when we try to expose the ills of our society. But I've learned I must fear God more than man. If he calls me to challenge evil, then I can no more resist his call than I can be content with complacency."

Mother clunked the pestle against the mortar. "God may be calling you to challenge evil, dear husband. But he doesn't need Susanna or Polly to join in."

Her father's brow was deeply grooved above his kind eyes. He laid a gentle hand on John's head as if John were one of his own sons. "I'm doing my job, and there isn't much Charlie Baldock can do to stop me. But my concern is that he may attempt to hurt John again and make an example of him. He certainly doesn't want anyone to think they can double-cross him and get away with it."

Susanna groaned and buried her face in her hands.

"Don't worry about me," John said without lifting his head. "I won't let that lunatic touch me again." The plank table seemed to capture his words and make them small.

Polly prayed he spoke the truth but dreaded that his declaration was as hollow as his voice.

Polly's knees ached from her position on the floor next to the bed, and her toes were numb from the cold. She stifled a yawn and offered one more final plea for forgiveness. Forgiveness for all her sins that day—her envy of Felicity's gown and the Baldocks' prosperity, the strange longings for John she'd experienced when they stood in the dark together during the game, and her anger at Susanna for getting in trouble again.

She started to rise, the warmth of the blankets and the softness of the feather mattress summoning her. Susanna was curled up in the bed, likely having already forgotten the evening's incident.

Polly clutched the edge of the coverlet and wished she could so easily put to rest all the turmoil in her chest. But even after her prayers and recitations of the Psalter, she couldn't shed her guilt and the feeling that somehow God was displeased with her. Should she pray longer? Perhaps if she fasted on the morrow, God would smile down on her.

A chill swept under her nightgown and wrapped around her legs. With a shudder, she climbed next to Susanna and pulled the heavy blankets up to her chin. Even then her body shook in protest at having been exposed for too long in the unheated room.

She melded against Susanna's warmth.

"By Jupiter," Susanna said sleepily, shifting her legs quickly away from Polly. "Your toes are freezing."

"Oh good, you're awake," Polly said.

"Of course I am now," Susanna replied. "How could anyone sleep next to an ice sculpture?"

"I don't know how you can sleep after what happened tonight." John's back was a patchwork of red welts and purple bruises. After Mother's nursing, Father had to assist him up the stairs to his bedroll in the boys' room.

"Sometimes we must make sacrifices for what is right," Susanna said, although her voice lacked the usual fervor.

"Were you freeing slaves again?" Polly wanted to understand why Susanna had put her and John in danger again tonight.

"No, not tonight."

"Then why? Why was it so important to reveal the smuggling?"

Susanna released a noisy yawn. "It's wrong, that's why."

"Surely if so many God-fearing people accept the smuggling as a normal part of the economy, then the issue can't be so entirely evil." Polly understood her father's stand against it, but there were times, like now, when she questioned whether he was too legalistic or old-fashioned in his views.

"And that's exactly how I feel about slavery," Susanna replied, her voice losing its sleepy edge. "Just because so many God-fearing people accept slavery as a normal part of the economy doesn't mean that it's right."

Polly stared through the dark at the faint glow of moonlight slanting in through the cracks in the shutters and tried to make sense of Susanna's logic. She knew Susanna had twisted her words and backed her into a corner, leaving her no room to argue. At times like this, she felt like a simpleton compared to Susanna, who'd had the privilege of going to school, of learning more about the world, and of associating with important and educated people in London.

"I'm not saying I agree with everyone about the smuggling," Polly said, trying to formulate a coherent response. "But I can't help but wonder if it's as bad as we think."

"Smuggling is stealing," Susanna said firmly. "Just because the whole world changes its opinion about something doesn't mean God changes his."

"Billy says that they are just stealing back from Parliament what Parliament has stolen from us with the high taxes."

"Greed can lead us to justify many wrongdoings."

She didn't know why she bothered to argue with Susanna. She never won the word sparring. Not that she really wanted to. For the most part she accepted Susanna's arguments about smuggling, knowing her father would say the same.

It was just that sometimes she wished faith was simpler and easier, that it wasn't so difficult to please God. Polly rubbed her arms to bring warmth to her body. Even under the covers she was still so cold.

"Come here." Susanna's arms wrapped around her, drawing her into a warm hug. "Let's go to sleep. We can't solve all the world's problems at once."

Polly closed her eyes and snuggled against Susanna, drawing from both her heat and her strength.

SIX

*L*aughing and jesting, Newton stumbled through the front door of the Catlett home with the rest of the revelers. The January cold raced inside with them and clung to their hats and coats. The playacting and singing in the Chatham streets was still ongoing and likely would continue long into the night around the bonfire at the village green. But the wintery breeze of that Twelfth Night had driven their party back inside for "Lamb's Wool," a sweet cider that had beckoned them even before they stepped inside.

Many of Mr. Catlett's relatives had visited during the Twelve Days of Christmas for one party or another. And tonight on the culmination of the festivities, the house was full of visitors. Mrs. Catlett had served a feast earlier in the day, and they'd already had the traditional Three Kings Cake. One of Polly's cousins had found the bean hidden in his piece of cake and had been crowned king of the day.

Ahead in the circle of young ladies, Polly's laughter tinkled, sweet, innocent, and delighted. He couldn't keep his attention from drifting to her as she slipped out of her coat and scarf, her cheeks rosy and her eyes bright as always. He wanted to push through the others and stand next to her, talk to her, and monopolize her attention.

But he'd already done so plenty of times that day. Truthfully, that's all he had done over the past week since Christmas. He spent the majority of his waking hours with her, if not directly, at least in the same room. He liked it when she joined her siblings in watching him work on the bookshelves. The project had taken much longer than he had anticipated, but once started he couldn't very well leave it half-finished. Could he?

And after he finally added the last touches, Polly worked with him over several days to organize all the books by subject and author. Of course, he wasn't able to resist stopping and reading passages aloud. As usual she was a willing listener and a fast learner.

"You can't keep your eyes off her, can you?" teased one of Polly's cousins, shoving him from behind good-naturedly.

Newton grinned and held himself back as she entered the drawing room, where there would be more singing and games for hours yet to come. He would make sure to request a solo from her, and his heart gave an extra *thump* at the anticipation of hearing it.

"Why don't you just kiss her and get her out of your blood," the cousin suggested.

"No worries there, my good man." Newton shrugged out of his coat and draped it over several others on the coat tree. "I will kiss her someday. No doubt about that. But a kiss won't get her out of my blood. That's for certain."

Several of the men laughed a little too loudly at his comment, but then abruptly fell silent. When John pivoted, he saw why. Mr. Catlett stood at the base of the stairway and was looking directly at him. Although his expression gave nothing away, Newton had no doubt the man had heard his boasting.

Mr. Catlett nodded curtly at the others to dismiss them, and they hurried to follow the young ladies into the drawing room, leaving Newton alone to squirm under Mr. Catlett's censure. Although Mr. Catlett was tall and slender of build with nothing remarkable about him, there was a strength about him that defied his appearance.

When Mr. Catlett started toward him, Newton straightened his shoulders and sucked in a breath, preparing himself for the punch to his gut that he deserved.

Aye. He shouldn't have talked about Polly like that to anyone. He deserved to be hit.

Mr. Catlett didn't stop until he was close enough that Newton caught the spicy whiff of Lamb's Wool on his breath. His thin face was placid, but there was a sharpness in the man's normally kind eyes that wasn't unexpected given the circumstances.

Newton braced himself. Should he apologize first? Was that what Mr. Catlett was waiting for?

"I've been meaning to talk to you today, John."

"Sir?"

"Miss Smith—Susanna—is going home to London on the morrow."

"Aye." Neither Polly nor Susanna had made mention of the plans, but he wasn't entirely surprised by the news. Since the night of the party at the Baldocks' home, Susanna had apologized to him on numerous occasions. He hadn't faced any further threats from Charlie Baldock, but she had limited her secretive activities. As a result she'd grown increasingly bored. He had the feeling that only the steady stream of visitors and the parties over the past week had kept her from getting herself into some new trouble.

"Mrs. Catlett and I would be grateful to you if you would accompany Miss Smith," Mr. Catlett said. "Make sure she arrives home safely, that she's delivered into the care of her parents without any delays or detours."

All of Newton's thoughts rolled to a stop as he grasped the true meaning of Mr. Catlett's request. The man was asking him to leave. Albeit he was doing so subtly. But he was most definitely telling him that it was time to raise the anchor and set sail.

"Besides"—Mr. Catlett shifted, and the movement put Newton on the defensive again, mentally readying himself for a blow, but Mr. Catlett merely clasped his hands together almost as though he was uncertain what to do with them—"we have already imposed on your time long enough. You have been gracious to indulge Mrs. Catlett with your presence. She has missed your mother, and so it has meant a great deal to have you here. She valued your help in tutoring the children, especially Jack. And we are indebted to you for the fine craftsmanship of your bookshelf. But we realize that you must have other obligations that you need to attend to."

Although his words were a statement, his eyes held questions—questions Newton couldn't answer, questions that had been roiling around in him like vessels in a storm-tossed sea. What was he planning to do next with his life? Where would he go from here? How could he better himself?

During the past couple of weeks with the Catletts, he had done his best not to think about the future. He hadn't wanted to ruin the merriment with thoughts of what awaited him when his time at the Catletts' home came to an end. But no matter how much he tried to focus on the present, there was always a shimmer of dread on the horizon, a dread that had to do with his father's reaction when he discovered his son had missed the ship to his new job in Jamaica.

Part of him considered not returning home and facing his

father's wrath. Mayhap he'd be better off going directly to Joseph Manesty, making an excuse for his tardiness, and then catching another ship to the West Indies. The problem was, he didn't know if Manesty would still offer him the job. Perhaps the merchant had already found someone else to be a supervisor in his stead.

In truth, mayhap Newton had to finally admit to himself, and at some point to his father, that he didn't really want to go to Jamaica. It had been his father's idea, not his. Deep down Newton realized he hadn't wanted to leave England even before he met Polly. Now he wanted to leave even less. In fact, the prospect of saying good-bye to return to London was daunting enough, much less going halfway around the world.

The laughter and music from the pianoforte drifted from the open door of the drawing room. Mr. Catlett hadn't moved, and the questions in his eyes hadn't dissipated. "What are your plans, John?"

Newton had the feeling that the man's desire to know went deeper than just a casual curiosity. Obviously after Newton's flippant remark about kissing Polly, the man would want to know his intentions toward his daughter. Newton supposed his infatuation with her hadn't gone unnoticed by either Mr. or Mrs. Catlett. It was only natural that Mr. Catlett would question his future plans before allowing him to pursue Polly any further.

What could he say without making himself look like a fool? In all his time among the Catletts, he never once mentioned his opportunity in Jamaica. He simply told them he was between shipping assignments. He certainly couldn't admit now to Mr. Catlett that he'd thrown away a perfectly good chance to make a great deal of money because he didn't want to leave Polly for so long.

And he couldn't admit he had no other job awaiting him, not even as a sailor.

After their last voyage, his father had finally retired from the sea. He'd been granted a position as an agent with the Royal African Company and so wouldn't be captain of any more ships. Newton wasn't so sure he wanted to be a sailor anyway. Maybe he could retire from the sea like his father and find some other kind of work.

"I'm not certain of my plans yet, sir," Newton said slowly, knowing that his answer was important, especially if he wanted any chance at winning Polly. "I have a couple of prospects but need to pursue them a little further." The half truth came easily. He *did* have prospects even if they weren't good ones.

Mr. Catlett studied him for another long moment before clamping him on the shoulder in a friendly squeeze, careful to avoid the tender spot that yet remained from where he'd been caned. "Why don't you take some time to figure out where you're headed?"

It wasn't exactly a dismissal, but Mr. Catlett's message was clear. He wasn't welcome to consider courting Polly unless he laid out a course for his life and a means to provide for her. As much as he dreaded facing his father again, he'd have to make the trip to London and pray that after his father's anger subsided, he would use his connections to find him a different job, preferably one close to Polly.

"Good that," Newton said. "You can count on me, sir. I'll deliver Miss Smith to her home and then attend to my business."

The angular lines in Mr. Catlett's face softened. "You're a fine man, John. And I believe in you."

The praise took Newton by surprise. He wasn't accustomed to compliments. His father believed that truthful criticism was more helpful in the long run than flattery. Perhaps it was, but he couldn't deny that Mr. Catlett's words moved through him like a strong current, pulling him deeper into the family whether Mr. Catlett intended it or not.

"Thank you, sir," Newton said, his voice cracking unexpectedly. Here he had found a home unlike any he'd ever experienced, even when his mother was alive. Now that he'd experienced such family life, such acceptance, such stability, he didn't want to leave.

But if he ever hoped to have a chance at winning Polly, he had to go out and prove himself first. Mr. Catlett would clearly have it no other way. And even if he wasn't ready to leave, Newton knew Mr. Catlett was right. It was time to go.

The next morning the hired carriage came early. The driver loaded most of Susanna's bags and trunks as Susanna raced around the house with Mrs. Catlett, packing small items that she had missed.

Newton waited silently inside the front door. His horse was saddled and ready. He'd said good-bye to Mr. Catlett that morning before he left for work, and he'd already said good-bye to the children who stood in the hallway quietly watching Mrs. Catlett and Susanna. Polly waited a few feet distant, but she could have been a league away for all the communication they'd had.

Her face was pale, having lost all the glow of the previous evening. The dark circles under her eyes were especially visible today, the sign that she had lost sleep to her praying. What did she have to pray about today? He wished he could ask her to pray for him, even though he wasn't sure anymore if God really cared about answering petitions regarding his welfare.

Why not ask her? Before he could talk himself out of it, he reached for her coat on the rack. "Come out with me for a minute," he said draping, the garment over her shoulders. "I have something I want to show you."

Polly shrugged into her coat.

"May I see it too?" asked one of the younger girls.

Newton smiled at her but shook his head. "Nay, this is a secret for Polly."

"Will she be able to show it to me later?"

He winked at the girl. "If she wants to."

Polly followed him outside and around the side of the house. He glanced around at the barren landscape, the thin dusting of snow on the grass and tree branches, the icicles hanging from the eaves of the roof. The small cluster of hedges, several trees, and even the spruce that he'd climbed to rescue Pete offered no privacy. Newton wanted a more secluded spot where he could be alone with Polly to say good-bye.

The stable behind the house seemed to offer the only place they could be alone. And yet, taking her there would surely raise her swift objections.

"You have nothing to show me, do you?" she asked from behind him.

"Of course I do."

"Are you sure?" Her voice teased him. "Or are you just tired of standing around waiting for Susanna and in need of one last adventure before you leave?"

"What makes you think I'm seeking an adventure?" He started toward the stable and hoped she would follow. "What if I simply want to say good-bye to my favorite buddy, Pete?"

"Are you wanting a few more of his scratches that you can take with you?" Polly's footsteps squeaked in the frosty grass as she followed him. "I'm sure he'd be happy to oblige."

Newton laughed, thinking of the marks left on his chest from the little demon. "I have no doubt he would."

He opened the stable door and peered around the dark interior. The earthiness of damp hay and a lingering scent of horseflesh greeted them.

"Here kitty, kitty." Newton put on a show of looking for Pete although he had no desire to come face to face with the creature ever again.

Polly stood in the light of the open door and watched him, her smile only growing bigger. "Would you like some help finding him?"

"You wouldn't deprive me of this last good-bye to dear Pete, would you?" Suddenly he wished he had something to give her, something of his possessions that she could keep, something that would remind her of his affection while he was gone. But of course, he hadn't brought anything with him. His journey, after all, had started as a short trip to his uncle's home in Maidstone to deliver a missive for his father. The uncle was really his father's uncle, a wealthy older man who didn't have any children. Newton suspected that his father had sent him in order to remind his uncle that Newton was a prime candidate to inherit his estate once he passed away.

Whatever the case, the visit had been meant to be brief. Now he was left with nothing to give Polly, nothing but his heart.

She moved away from the door and peered into one of the empty horse stalls. "Perhaps Pete is hiding in protest of your leaving."

Newton stepped behind her. A sliver of sunlight wedged through a crack in the roof and touched her head, highlighting her hair and turning it golden like a halo. She was an angel. He'd thought so the moment he first saw her and heard her sing. And it was still true now more than ever.

As though sensing his presence behind her, she didn't move.

He lifted a hand and hesitated only a moment before giving in to the pleasure of touching her hair. He grazed a long curl, letting it slide between his fingers.

She didn't move, didn't pull away, didn't stop him.

The silk against his fingers was exquisite and only made him crave more of the texture. He brushed the full length of his fingers against the soft strands. Then he combed deeper, sweeping the hair away from her neck and exposing her bare skin there.

Still she remained motionless except for the rapid rise and fall of her chest.

He combed the strands back again, this time letting his fingers graze her neck.

At the slight contact, she sucked in a breath.

The long column beckoned to him, and when she tilted her head slightly, as though to give him permission to touch her there again, it was his turn to draw in a quick breath. He wanted to bend in and kiss her beautiful skin, wanted to breathe deeply of her. But he gritted his teeth against the temptation and instead pulled her back against his chest and slid his arms around her middle.

Her body molded itself against him, as pliable as an apple blossom. He had an overwhelming urge to twist her around so that she was facing him, but if he did, he knew he'd be utterly helpless to resist his desire for her, that he'd kiss her long and hard, something he had no right to do.

His limbs shook faintly at his need for her, but he satisfied himself with pressing his face into the back of her head and letting his lips linger in her hair. He dragged in a gulping breath, trying to gain control and trying to still his trembling lest she realize how much she affected him.

"John?" The waver in her voice, the uncertainty mingled with desire, sent a shot of heat through him like a swallow of strong whiskey. "I thought you wanted to show me something."

*Aye, I want to show you my undying affection.* The words were on the tip of his tongue and yet he swallowed them to refrain from saying so. Instead he released her, gently turned her, and then dropped to one knee before her. He had no choice. If he didn't put some distance between them, he'd cave in to temptation.

Her eyes widened at the sight of him kneeling before her. He forced a grin and then reached for her hand. "I wanted to show you this," he said. And then without breaking his gaze from hers, he lifted her fingers to his lips and placed a kiss on the back of her hand. It wasn't a brief kiss as he'd intended. Instead he pressed harder, and her eyes grew wider by the second, the slant of sunlight now turning the blue of her eyes into deep oceans where he could drown if he let himself.

Gone was the playful teasing about their relationship that had kept the boundary of friendship in place during his visit. He supposed she'd already guessed by now that he considered her more than just a friend. But before he left, he would make sure she had no doubt.

"And I wanted to show you this." He turned her hand over so that her palm faced up. And then he pressed a kiss there too, another lingering one in the warm center of her hand. He was loathe to let go, but with a will he didn't know he possessed, he ended the kiss.

"I wanted a moment to say good-bye to you." He didn't release her hand. He couldn't yet.

"I wish you didn't have to go." Her words were hardly more than a whisper, but they shouted through him and filled him with hope.

"Then you won't object if I visit again sometime?"

"I would never object." Her admission brought a rosy hue to her cheeks.

"I would never stay away, even if you objected."

She smiled. Then she reached into the slit in her skirt and fumbled for her pocket. "Since we're saying good-bye," she said pulling out a delicate, white lacy handkerchief, "I wanted you to have something by which to remember me." She handed him the piece of linen with her initials embroidered in the middle with white silken thread.

He fingered the raised monogram and almost brought the handkerchief to his nose to breathe in her scent. Did this mean she was finally accepting that they had more than a friendship? He hoped so.

He could feel her eyes upon him waiting for his reaction. He pressed it against his heart with a dramatic flair. "Now I will never be able to forget you. As long as I live."

"Be sure you don't," she jested, her eyes dancing.

He rose to his feet then, brushing hay from his baggy trousers. He ought to keep the moment light now. He'd already been serious enough. But his emotions were too raw to pretend a lightness that he didn't feel. "You should know that even without your token, I could never forget you."

Her long lashes dropped, but not before he caught sight of the pleasure his words brought her.

"I will never forget you, Polly Catlett." His voice lowered to a hoarse whisper. "Ever."

"How long will you be gone?" Her voice was low now too.

Before he could answer, a knock sounded on the open barn door. "I hate to interrupt your little tryst," Susanna said wryly. "But I told your mother that I was sure you were in the kitchen sneaking John leftover tarts from last night."

Polly skittered past him and was out the door before he could protest. He stared after her, wishing he could draw her back so that it was just the two of them again.

Susanna's lips curved into a knowing smile. "I tried to give you as long as I could."

"It wasn't quite long enough."

"Would any length ever be enough?" Her smile teased him.

He ducked outside, aching too much to return the smile. It was finally time to go. "Nay. Not even a million years would suffice."

ewton stepped over the fish entrails half-frozen on the cobblestone and approached the familiar door of the narrow terraced structure that had been his home for as long as he could remember. The hand-hewn brick was rough and cracked and worn away in spots, the gray faded and dismal as it was on all the other homes squeezed next to each other in the crowded Wapping district.

Along the River Thames the streets teemed with sailors, ships chandlers, dockers, deck hands, sailmakers, and all the others who made their living from the ships that anchored at the Pool of London.

After seeing Susanna to her parents' home, he'd stabled his father's horse, stopped by several of his favorite pubs, and wasted as much time as he could. But he couldn't put off the inevitable forever. He had to face his father sometime.

He rested a hand on the doorknob. Faint light came from the dusty glass of the only window on the first floor. He'd spent many hours sitting on a stool in front of that window, his mother next to him teaching him everything she knew.

Now his father's wife, Thomasina, reclined in his mother's chair, cooked over her fireplace, slept in her bed. Thomasina bustled about and chattered away and always tried too hard to take his mother's place. He wanted to tell her she never would and to just stop trying, but he wasn't cruel.

His father would be home too. Newton's discreet inquiries had confirmed that his father wasn't off somewhere for his new job outfitting ships or organizing supplies for a voyage.

The captain was likely supping even as Newton lingered outside the door, the damp nip of river air urging him inward. His heartbeat thudded faster at the thought of his father's anger, frustration, and disappointment. This wasn't the first time he had failed his father's expectations. He'd done so often enough already. In fact, it seemed to be the one thing at which he consistently succeeded.

He drew in a fortifying breath, his nose having to adjust again to the stench of London streets after so many weeks away, the sourness of waste that mingled with the ever-present smoke that came from burning coal.

It was now or never. He pushed open the door and stepped inside to warmth, soft lamplight, and low voices. Next to the hearth, his father sat in a tall-backed chair with a young girl on his lap and two boys at his feet. Thomasina was sitting in a chair across from him.

Immediately the talking ceased and all eyes fixed on Newton. The children had their mother's Italian complexion, dark brown eyes and olive skin. He didn't know their ages—except that they were all born in the past ten years since his mother had died.

"John." Thomasina was the first to rise. She donned a tentative smile, took a step toward him, then stopped. "We weren't expecting you."

His father's dark eyebrows arched high, and he stared at John for several moments without speaking.

"I'm sorry to impose," Newton said to Thomasina.

"You're not imposing." The petite but broad-boned woman crossed the room. She wasn't as pretty or graceful as his own mother had been. But he couldn't deny that she was sweet.

When she stopped in front of him, she raised then lowered her hands several times as though to hug him before finally crossing her arms beneath her portly bosom. "We're always glad to see you, John."

His father's brows fell, and thundering clouds cascaded across his features. "Why are you here?"

"So I guess I'm not welcome then?"

"You're supposed to be in Jamaica!" The captain rose from his chair holding the little girl gently, but his tone must have frightened her, for her eyes grew wider than a half crown.

All the words Newton had rehearsed, all the excuses he'd carefully planned during the six-hour ride back to London deserted him. He could think of nothing to say that would exonerate him. So he jutted his chin and braced himself for his father's anger in whatever form it took.

As though sensing the coming storm, Thomasina bustled back across the room and reached for the little girl, who all too willingly went into her arms. "Come, sweet one. It's time for beddy-bye." Then she touched the heads of the boys. "You both come too. I know you're excited to see John again, but you'll have plenty of opportunity to be with him on the morrow."

The two boys stood. Their gazes hadn't wavered from Newton since the moment he stepped into the house. With their short-cropped brown hair, wide faces, and stocky builds, they could have been twins except for the difference of several inches in height. They didn't look particularly excited to see him, and considering that he'd rarely seen them over the years, he didn't expect much of a welcome from them. But they did as their mother bade and followed her to the steps that led to the bedroom above and the dormer room at the highest level of the house.

Newton watched them until they disappeared. With only the patter of footsteps and the squeak of floorboards overhead, Newton chanced a glance at his father.

The tall, broad-shouldered man had lifted a hand to his hair and jammed his fingers into the loose brown strands. In the flickering light that emanated from the coal fire, Newton caught a glimpse of sadness in his father's sea-weathered face, the slight droop of his eyes and mouth, before frustration hardened them again.

"What happened?" His father's voice was clipped and demanding. He faced Newton head on, and even though he was still across the room, Newton tensed. "Was the ship delayed? Did Manesty change his mind?"

Should he lie to his father? It would save them from another argument. And devil be hanged, he'd already had enough of those to last a lifetime. But if he lied, he wouldn't be able to get his father's help in locating a different job.

At his hesitation, his father's scowl turned darker. "Don't tell me you were late and missed the ship. I should have known when you didn't make it home that you'd been irresponsible again."

"The first thing you always think is that I've been irresponsible." Newton didn't like the way he seemed to turn back into a six-year-old every time he talked with his father. Why couldn't he argue with the captain without his voice turning petulant?

"Because you have been. Just like you were with the job I lined up for you with the Spanish merchant in Alicante."

"He was cruel."

"It was a position that offered good prospects for your future."

A good prospect in Spain? Newton almost laughed. Campos was a brute. The living conditions were less than desirable. And he missed England. As a result, his father shouldn't have been surprised that he hadn't exactly been on his best behavior. After only three months of working for Campos, he walked out and found a ship home. His reception by his father then was vaguely reminiscent of the one now.

"Now you've lost another valuable job because of your inability to make it to the ship on time."

"I didn't miss the ship. I decided not to go."

"And you don't consider that irresponsible?"

"No, I don't. I made the decision that was best for me."

His father muttered something under his breath before turning his eyes upward. His jaw muscles flexed as though he were holding back a slew of expletives. Newton had heard his father swear only once, during a squall when he'd ordered Newton below deck. When Newton had disobeyed and nearly been swept overboard, his father had shoved him down the hatch and told him with a few choice words not to come out again.

"After I went to all the work to line up the position, after I put my reputation on the line for you, after I assured Manesty that you would work hard for him, you decide not to go?" His father's voice rose with each word.

"I didn't want to go to Jamaica."

"What you *want* to do and *need* to do are often two very

different things. And now you just threw away the best opportunity you'll likely ever have."

"It's my life."

"It's your life?" His father was already moving across the room toward him, his stride choppy, his shoulders stiff. "You're only seventeen, and you think you know everything about life?"

Newton clenched his fists. "I know more than you give me credit for."

His father barreled into him and shoved him so that Newton's back slammed into the door. "You don't know anything yet." The captain jerked Newton's shirt into a fist under his chin and pushed his hand against his windpipe, cutting off air. At the same time, his father rammed his other arm into Newton's stomach making him gasp for breath. But with the choking hold at his neck, Newton couldn't get the slightest air into his lungs.

He had seen his father make plenty of wayward sailors submit to his authority with such a move. His father had done it once or twice on him too. Maybe he deserved the discipline in the past, but he didn't now. He hadn't done anything wrong by turning down the job opportunity in Jamaica. He simply made a choice that was different from what his father wanted. What right did his father have to crucify him for that?

With a strong upward thrust, Newton knocked his father's hand loose from his neck, sidestepped, and slipped away from the captain's grasp. But before Newton could get far enough away, his father's fist barreled into the small of his back with such force that it sent him crashing into the table. A jug tipped and rolled to the floor where it crashed and broke into shards, splashing ale over the hearth.

Newton scrambled to right himself and avoid another blow. But now his father stood unmoving, his attention focused on the broken jug, his chest rising and falling with the exertion of their fight.

Newton used the opportunity to put the entire table between himself and his father. Even if he'd known the discipline was coming, a familiar helpless rage simmered deep in his gut.

"I shouldn't have come home," he said hoarsely. "And I shouldn't have expected you to understand."

His father stared at the shards of pottery a moment longer before uncurling his fists. The tight muscles in his jaw slackened, giving way to a weariness that made his jowls sag. The sign of weakness didn't last long before the captain wiped it away with another scowl. "I understand you much better than you think."

"That's right. You have me all figured out because you listen so well and take the time to understand what I really need." Bitterness burned in Newton's throat.

"You may not like the decisions I make regarding your future," his father said. "But surely you can see that I'm only trying to help you better yourself, that I only want what's best for you."

"Or mayhap you're more concerned about keeping *your* standing. Mayhap the job was a way to make *you* look good."

His father shook his head and released a long-winded sigh. "You're impossible."

There was that disappointment again. And frustration. He'd never measure up to what his father wanted for him. Somehow he would always fall short.

"For the love of all that's holy, John," his father said in a wearisome tone, "then tell me. Why didn't you want the supervisor position in Jamaica?"

"I decided I didn't want to leave England for so long." He couldn't tell his father about Polly, could he? Would such a revelation help or hurt his cause?

His father's lip curled with disdain. "Likely, you were too busy at the pub to make it to the ship on time."

"Aye, go ahead and think the worst of me. Again."

"If it's not the truth, then tell me what is."

The footsteps on the floor above them had stopped. Newton had no doubt Thomasina and the children were listening to every word. Newton focused on the oval picture above the fireplace. It was a small Baroque painting of the conversion of Saint Paul that his father had bought in Venice, one of the few treasures that graced his home. His mother had always loved the painting because she said it reminded her that no one was ever too evil or too far beyond the reach of God's grace.

"Tell me why you didn't want the job." His father's tone told Newton he had little choice but to tell the truth, that his father would demand it of him sooner or later.

Newton lifted his chin and met his father's sharp gaze. "I met a girl." He braced himself for scoffing, for a laugh, for some snide remark.

His father didn't say anything for a long moment. Instead he seemed to look deep into Newton's soul before settling his attention on a pair of silver candelabras on the mantel that had once belonged to his mother. "Who is she?" his father asked softly.

"George and Elizabeth Catlett's daughter."

"So that's where you've been?"

Newton nodded.

His father's attention shifted to the creamy porcelain figure of a delicate woman next to the candlesticks. It was another gift he'd bought Mother during one of his voyages. "Then you're serious about her."

"Aye. I want to marry her." Once the words were out, Newton knew them to be the absolute truth. Polly was too young to consider a union now. But in a couple of years, when she was older, he would ask for her hand. In the meantime he had to start preparing, start showing himself worthy.

"Will the Catletts allow it?"

"I think so. If I'm able to provide for her, then I believe Mr. Catlett will give me his blessing."

"She'll be accustomed to a lifestyle that you may not be able to give her, at least right away."

"She's young. So I have a couple of years to work and save."

"What will you do now?"

*Now that I've thrown away another good opportunity?* His father didn't say the words, but John knew that's what he was thinking. "I don't know, but I couldn't leave her for five years."

His father didn't speak for a long minute. Finally, he sighed and his shoulders sagged. "I can get you a job on a merchant ship, the *Expedition,* heading to the Adriatic, as an able-bodied seaman."

The position and pay would be better than that of captain's boy or a common seaman, which was all he'd been on previous voyages. He'd be gone for months, which would still be too much time away from Polly. But it was better than five years.

"If you come back with good reports," his father continued, "then you'll have more opportunities for advancement for the next voyage."

Newton hesitated.

"The *Expedition* is leaving in two days," his father said bluntly.

"Two days?" That was too soon. Newton's whole body resisted. What if Polly forgot about him while he was gone? What if she fell in love with Billy Baldock? Or what if Susanna involved her in some new danger and he wasn't there to protect her? "You can't find me any office work with the Royal African Company so that I can stay here?"

His father shook his head. "It's a miracle I was given a job with them. They would never bring on a man as young and untried as you."

"And there's nothing anywhere else? No other work?"

"Except for the jobs you decided not to take."

Newton pressed his lips together to keep from releasing his frustration. He had never been apprenticed for any trade. He had never been educated for any profession. All he knew was the sea. And like his father, that was the surest course before him.

He'd be a fool to spurn the offer to earn his pay as an able-bodied seaman. He'd be a fool to throw away another chance his father was giving him.

He would simply have to console himself that the time would pass quickly and soon enough he'd be back with both money and experience in his pocket. And then he could visit the Catletts again, and when he did, he'd make his claim on Polly once and for all.

# PART TWO

---

## One Year Later

# EIGHT

*M*y father says I may have a chance at becoming a riding officer in a couple of years," Billy said, rubbing his gloved hands together for warmth. Though the gray January day was mild, after the walk home Polly felt the nip of cold also.

"That would be a fine position," Polly responded as they stepped through the front iron gate and onto the walkway, her sister Eliza trailing two steps behind them. Polly's attention shifted again to the neighbors. Mr. Donovan was on the front walkway, arguing loudly with his sister, who stood in the doorway in only her petticoats. Half of her dark hair was pulled up into a coiffure and the other half hung over part of her face as though she'd been interrupted in the middle of her grooming.

"The children are purposefully letting him out." Miss Donovan's voice had grown shrill.

"When the dog yaps at all hours of the day and night, what can you expect?" her brother snapped back.

"I expect that they'll leave him in my chamber where he isn't bothering anyone." Miss Donovan's expression was distraught, and her gaze darted around the front yard.

"I told you I didn't want the dog here," Mr. Donovan said, turning away from his sister and starting down the path to a waiting coach. "It's already burden enough to have you residing in my home without having to worry about an idiotic dog too."

Miss Donovan flinched as though her brother had slapped her in the face.

"I say good riddance," Mr. Donovan said.

"You must tell the children that they need to put on their coats and shoes and commence a thorough search for Prince."

He waved a dismissive hand in the air.

"I insist that the children make every effort to locate him," Miss Donovan called after him.

He spoke to the coach driver before stepping up and ducking inside.

"Prince can't be left to wander outside on his own!" Miss Donovan yelled, stepping out the door. The tangled hair falling across half of her face did nothing to hide the angry flush. "He won't survive the cold, and he'll go hungry."

Mr. Donovan responded by slamming the coach door shut. As the driver urged the team forward, Miss Donovan took several more steps outside. She opened her mouth as though to call her brother back, but as the coach rolled away, her shoulders slumped and she clamped her lips together.

She glanced around the yard anxiously before her gaze landed upon Polly. Billy had stopped with his hand on the doorknob and was watching the coach wobble down the rutted road with narrowed eyes. Eliza was staring with an open mouth at Miss Donovan. Apparently neither Billy nor Eliza had been able to ignore the neighbors' spat any more than Polly had.

Polly felt she ought to say something to her neighbor. Should she apologize for eavesdropping? Should she tell the woman she was sorry Mr. Donovan was so calloused?

Raw, undisguised pain flashed into the woman's eyes. Miss Donovan lifted shaking fingers and pressed her knuckles to her mouth. She turned back to the door but wasn't quick enough to hide the swell of tears that came to her eyes.

Once the door closed and hid Miss Donovan from their prying eyes, Billy whistled softly under his breath. "That man is an imbecile."

Polly wanted to agree, but propriety demanded that she say only good things aloud and keep her unkind thoughts to herself. She peered around the barren yard, but saw no sign of the curly haired white dog that Miss Donovan often carried about like a baby. "Shall we do a quick search for the dog about our premises?"

Eliza started to nod, but Billy's reply cut her short. "I wish I could, but I don't have the time right now. As it is, I'll need to run most of the way back to the Customs House if I'm to return to my position before anyone notices how long I've been gone."

"Of course." Polly smiled up at him. He'd gotten into the habit most days of accompanying her and Eliza home after they took Father a basket of lunch. Now that Jack was away at boarding school, Mother insisted that she take Eliza with her anytime she went out. At fourteen, Eliza was two years younger, but still pleasant company. Even so, Polly always enjoyed Billy's conversation and attention for the walk home.

Eliza opened the door and stepped inside. Polly followed but paused at the threshold. "Thank you for walking us home."

His dark eyes regarded her with apprehension. "I don't want you to go out searching for the lost dog on your own."

She laughed softly. "You know me all too well, Billy."

He didn't smile or laugh in return. "Promise you won't get involved in the matter?"

She knew without him saying anything that traveling around the countryside had grown increasingly dangerous over the past few months. New gangs of smugglers roamed up and down the Kent coast. French pirates were seizing English ships with increasing frequency, which meant that fewer goods were reaching England from America and the West Indies. The sugar, tobacco, lumber, and other imports that did make it past French pirates ended up costing much more. Thus the demand for cheaper smuggled goods had increased.

Her father was working longer hours to patrol the waters of River Medway. Even though the parliamentary Board of Customs had appointed more officials to help catch the smugglers, many were easily bribed to overlook illegal goods. Her father remained among the minority who couldn't be swayed. But as a result, of late he'd been harried and haggard. Only last week he'd been threatened at gunpoint by a smuggler.

Billy had been the one to confide in her about the incident, about how close her father had come to losing his life. Although Billy understood her father's position, he insisted that her father shouldn't be so strict in his stand against the smuggling, because the next time he might not get away so easily.

He didn't have to remind her of the incident only last month when the cordwainer and riding officer in West Sussex had been tortured to death simply because smugglers had assumed the two men were out to ruin their gang. The smugglers had tied the men to their horses and made them ride with their heads under the horses' bellies. Then after the harrowing ride, the gang had broken every joint in the men's bodies, cut off their noses, and finally hurled them into a well. Even if several members of that gang had been captured and hung for their crimes, the incident had only reminded everyone how dangerous smuggling gangs were.

Billy's dark blue eyes warned her even now.

"I can't promise I won't search for Miss Donovan's dog," she said, her heart still aching at Mr. Donovan's treatment of his sister. "But if I search, I shall convince Eliza to go with me."

Billy's frown told her he wasn't completely satisfied with her response, but she reassured him with another smile before he took his leave. When she closed the door behind her, she was surprised to find the younger children standing in the hallway watching her with wide eyes and silly grins.

"What?" she asked, feeling for her hat. "Do I have gull droppings decorating me again?"

Young George grinned wider and started to say something, but Sara, one of her younger sisters, shushed him and nodded to the drawing room. "You're urgently needed."

Polly didn't bother to undo her coat but started toward the open door. "Is Mother home already?"

Mother had left shortly before Polly to take food and other supplies to the almshouse. Although Polly often asked if she could go with her mother, Mrs. Catlett insisted that she was still too young to witness the depravity and conditions of the poorhouse where privacy was always in short supply.

Polly didn't wait for an answer from her siblings as she walked into the drawing room. She stopped abruptly at the sight of the empty room.

"Why am I so urgently needed—" she started. But the clicking shut of the door behind her startled her. She spun and found herself standing mere inches from the one man she'd given up hope of seeing again. "John?"

He was bigger than she remembered. His shoulders were broader, his chest and arms thicker and more muscular, his face sun-browned, making his green eyes brighter. Those eyes danced with a mingling of delight and desire that made her pulse patter with a strange tempo, one she hadn't experienced since the last time she'd seen him a year ago. His jaws and cheeks were covered with a light layer of scruff that lent him a ruggedness and maturity. His hair was longer and more sun-bleached but tied neatly back.

For several seconds he openly stared at her the same way she was staring at him, taking in every detail about her. He seemed to be the first to recover as he leaned against the door, crossed his arms over his chest, and gave her a half-cocked smile.

"Good day, Cousin." His grin crooked higher. "Are you excited to see me?"

She was suddenly too breathless to respond and utterly embarrassed by how happy she was. She'd had plenty of time over the past months to analyze all the new and strange feelings she had in regard to John. She still flushed when she thought about the good-bye he'd given her in the barn, when he'd held her from behind and buried his face in her hair, when his lips had pressed into her hand.

Even now, the thought made her stomach jump. No matter how many prayers she'd said and how much penance she'd done, the sounds and scents of that good-bye were burned into her mind and came back to taunt her mercilessly, especially late at night during sleepless hours when she would hug her arms across her chest and pretend it was him instead.

She told herself that even if she liked John last year, he wasn't the type of man she should consider for a more serious relationship. Although he was funny and easy to talk to and sweet, he was somewhat reckless and wild spirited, lacking the stability that a woman needed in the long term. Not only that, but he openly questioned his faith in God. How could she consider a man who didn't have the same values or beliefs as she?

She warned herself not to set her heart on a man like him. And she worked hard to convince herself that she didn't miss him, that she didn't care if he ever visited again.

But now standing before him, she knew that she had lied to herself over the past months. She'd cared. She'd been waiting for him. She'd hoped for this moment. The very fibers of her being had yearned for him.

"Is your delight at my presence rendering you speechless?" he asked with that same playful smile he'd leveled at her during his last visit.

She had to conduct herself like a proper lady. So she took a step back and offered him what she hoped was a composed smile. "I am delighted to see you, John. How long has it been since your last visit? A few months?"

She felt foolish once the words were out.

He gave a short laugh that told her he knew what she was doing. She started to turn away, embarrassed again and knowing she was still just as naive and inexperienced in these matters as she was the first time she'd met him.

His laughter died and he quickly reached for her arm so that she couldn't move away. "It's been three hundred and seventy-five days, four hours, and twenty-three minutes since I last saw you."

She didn't dare look into his eyes. But the words soothed her and brought a smile to her lips.

"I haven't been able to get you out of my mind," he continued in a low voice, "not even for a second."

Her smile widened.

The door creaked open then and little George poked his head into the room with a grin that stretched across his freckled face. "Did you like your surprise, Polly?"

"Yes, George," Polly replied. "I liked my surprise very much."

John reached for George and snaked his arm around the boy's neck. Then he proceeded to knuckle George's head. Laughing, George returned the affection by tackling John. Of course, John made a show of letting the young boy wrestle him into a tight hold. For several moments the room rang with laughter and chaos as John made a point of teasing each of the children before finally turning back to Polly.

"You're not planning to go out again today, are you?" John asked, reaching to help her out of her coat.

She clutched it closed. "Miss Donovan's little white dog has run away, and she's upset about it. I thought I'd search around outside in the yard for it."

"I'll help you," John said. She ought to insist that he stay inside where it was warm and comfortable, especially since he'd likely traveled all day to reach Chatham. But as he donned his coat, she couldn't find the words to protest.

Once the front door closed behind them, he sauntered with his rolling gait toward the towering spruce tree he'd climbed during his last visit. "Do you think the dog is up in the tree? Will I need to make another daring rescue?"

"Don't you mean another dangerous tumble?"

"I'll have you know that I've improved in my climbing skills since the last time I was here. After nearly a year at sea, I could climb the tallest tree in the dark. Backward. And upside down holding on only by my toes."

She laughed. "I should like to see that."

He started to shrug out of his coat. "Very well. If you insist."

"No!" She reached to stay him. "I don't relish the idea of you killing yourself on the first day of your return."

He pressed a hand against his heart and stumbled backward as though mortally wounded, even as he grinned. "My dearest girl, how little faith you have in me. Mayhap I have grown over the past year into a stronger and better man."

Her gaze dropped to his chest and then to his thick arms bulging against his coat sleeve. He curled his arm and flexed his bicep.

"I'm sure you have grown quite strong." Silently she berated herself for gawking and spun away. With burning cheeks, she started toward the back of the house. His laughter followed her, and he easily caught up and fell into stride next to her.

"I suppose we shall need to look for the dog in the stables," John said casually, but there was a teasing glimmer in his eyes that told her he remembered their good-bye every bit as much as she did. Once again her thoughts returned to the warm pressure of his lips at the center of her palm. Her skin tingled just thinking about it. But the idea of being alone with him and of giving in to her desires to be in his arms frightened her.

It was too soon. They'd only just seen each other again after months and months apart. All her reservations about him came rushing back. He was so much more worldly wise than she was, and that intimidated her more than she wanted him to know.

"Actually, I was thinking of searching the woodland behind the houses." She veered toward the back gate that would take her out to the hills. "I saw the Donovan children playing out in the woods earlier today. I suspect they left their gate open, and poor little Prince unwittingly made his way out."

"I'm sorry, Polly," he said, trailing after her. "I don't mean to be so forward. It's just that I'm so excited to be with you that I keep letting my mouth run ahead of me."

She passed the ash bin and privy and then unlatched the back gate.

He pushed it open for her. "I promise I won't say or do anything else to make you uncomfortable."

She wanted to tell him that the discomfort was her fault, that she'd clearly dreamed about him too much while he was gone and had allowed herself to care for him more deeply than she ought. But she couldn't admit all of that, so she strode ahead, forcing him to lengthen his stride to keep up.

"You offered me friendship on my last visit," he said. "Will you extend the offer to this visit too?"

At the anxiety in his tone, she stopped and faced him. His features were shadowed with an insecurity that made her realize that for all his teasing and bravado, he was still trying to understand the nature of their relationship too. Certainly there was nothing wrong with going back to the kind of relationship they had last time—the playful teasing that hinted at more but was safe.

Yes, that would work. She smiled to reassure him. "Of course we shall be friends. I should like nothing better."

Although his grin broke free, there was something more reserved in his manner as they walked along the edge of the woodland. While she loved the stomach flips and heart flops, she was also content simply to talk, to listen to him describe his year sailing the Mediterranean to the Adriatic Sea. As always, he had her laughing at his many experiences, the silly escapades as well as the dangerous. And she loved that he listened to her just as attentively as she told about Jack leaving for boarding school in London and Susanna's betrothal to Daniel Eversfield and the upcoming wedding. Susanna had met Daniel shortly after returning to London last year, and thankfully the budding romance had kept her too busy to involve herself in any more trouble.

"And what else have you done this year besides rescue lost animals?" he asked as they ambled back toward home. The overcast sky was thankfully quiet, without wind or rain. The edge of the woodland was silent and still, as if every creature had gone to sleep for the remainder of the winter.

"I'm afraid my life is not so exciting as yours," she said, stepping over a dead branch, her shoes squishing in the damp leaves that covered the ground. "I cannot yet go away to school as most of my friends have done. But Father has told me I might have the opportunity next year."

"You would do well in school." His sincerity warmed her. "And your singing and composing? How is that going? Have you written that epic song about me yet that will give me renown through all generations?"

She smiled. "Not yet. Mother keeps me very busy these days. She has begun to give me more responsibility so that I may learn how to manage a household."

"Are your parents making marriage arrangements already?" There was more than curiosity in his tone.

"Not at all," she replied. "I want to go to school before I marry, and they know that."

"Surely young men are vying for your hand."

"You're flattering me, John."

"What about that monkey-boy who was sweet on you? What was his name? Billy-bald-donkey-head?"

She pushed John in the arm playfully. "You're naughty."

He grinned in acquiescence. "Is he still trying to win your hand?"

"He never was trying to win my hand."

"I very clearly heard his voice when you walked in the door today."

"Billy has always been a good friend."

John stopped walking. She continued several more paces before halting and turning to face him. His expression was devoid of humor. In fact, the seriousness with which he regarded her made her pulse flutter. "He truly means nothing more to you than a friend?" His voice demanded honesty.

She thought of all the many ways Billy had helped her over the past year, his attentiveness, his willingness to go out of his way to walk her home, the efforts he made to include her in activities with the young people who weren't away at boarding schools.

"Please tell me you're not thinking seriously about Billy."

"I'm not." At least not too often. After all, she couldn't completely ignore Billy's continued devotion and attribute it only to friendship, especially when he hinted from time to time that he'd like more.

The worry in John's eyes didn't go away. But before he could say more, a flash of white in the woods caught their attention.

Polly peered more closely through the low branches and twigs. "There's Prince." The dog's curly-haired white body was unmistakable against the backdrop of grays and browns.

"Prince!" she called. "Come here, Prince!"

The dog lifted its head, sniffed the air with its scrunched snout, and then turned and trotted away.

Polly darted into the woodland after it. She pushed back barren branches and attempted to hasten in spite of her hooped petticoat getting caught in the brush. The canine, as if sensing the pursuit, scampered ahead, much faster on its legs than she was. John crashed through the brush next to her in pursuit as well. With his long legs and agility, he moved ahead until he almost had the dog in his grasp.

"Come here, you little devil!" John lunged toward the dog and grabbed it around the torso. But as John crashed to the ground, his hold on the dog loosened for just a second, and the creature jerked free. With a yip of victory, he bounded off again.

"Are you all right?" Polly stopped next to John.

He jumped up and brushed at the leaves clinging to his breeches. "Nothing's injured except my pride."

"You made a marvelous effort."

John scowled after the dog. "Never fear, my lady. I shall get the sneaky, slippery eel yet." He charged through the brush again, and Polly chased after them both. By the time they stopped, Polly could hardly catch her breath. They were at the bottom of a hill, and the woods had thinned during their descent.

"He disappeared over there," John said between gasps as he pointed to a rocky area.

Polly combed her hair out of her face. The tightly drawn and twisted knob at the upper back of her head had come loose, leaving her hair a tangle of waves.

"Come on." John reached for her hand, giving her little choice but to race after him. "We're not letting that weasel get away from us now. Not after we've come this far."

"Maybe we're scaring him," she managed to gasp out. "Perhaps if we tried a gentler approach?"

John laughed at her over his shoulder. "Too late for that. We've already frightened him into thinking we're two giants who'd like nothing better than to skin him alive."

Laughing, she stumbled after John. As he rounded a bend in the hill, he came to an abrupt halt. She bumped into his backside and would have loosened her hand from his and distanced herself from him if he hadn't tightened his hold. He pulled her forward, and she was startled to see a large stone shoved aside to reveal a tunnel.

"He went in there." John nodded to the gaping dark hole.

Her thoughts immediately turned to Billy's warning earlier. "I don't think we should go in."

"Of course we should."

John tried to tug her closer, but she resisted. "Let's go home. It's not safe here. This is probably a smuggler's cave." Her father had talked about the smugglers devising new and more creative places to store their goods, including underground tunnels and caverns. Some of the tunnels were left from Roman occupation centuries ago, aqueducts that had been enlarged. If the risk of being spotted by a smuggler wasn't danger enough, she didn't want to add on the prospect of being buried by a crumbling ancient cavern.

"The little devil couldn't have gone too far." John's voice contained a note of excitement.

She didn't budge. "The problems with smugglers have gotten worse over the past year since you've been gone, John. Gangs are roaming all over the coast."

When John released a breath of disappointment, remorse pooled in her chest. He clearly craved adventure. Danger didn't thwart him. Rather it seemed to feed his appetite for more, much like it did for Susanna. She started to explain herself further, but her words were cut off by a distant shout followed by a high-pitched bark.

"It's Prince," Polly said. "And it sounds like he's been hurt."

"Wait here." John released her hand. "I'm going in a little farther to see if I can grab him."

"I don't think you should," she started, but he'd already moved away from her. "Someone else is here. We should leave before we're spotted."

"I'll be fine," he said much too confidently. "Just stay out here and I'll be back shortly."

Before he could duck inside, the shouting grew louder and Prince shot from the tunnel yipping in terror. He knocked into John before scampering directly into Polly's skirts. She reached down and scooped up the dog, which was shaking as if he'd seen the ghost of a Roman legionnaire.

Her fingers made contact with his wet nose. She allowed him to sniff her fingers and then gently stroked the top of his head. He gave a soft whimper. "You're safe now," she crooned.

"Where's that mutt?" an angry voice called. "I'm gonna kill him for biting me."

John's eyes widened, and he began to back away from the mouth of the cave. "Go," he whispered to her. "Run now."

At the anxiety in his voice, she didn't stop to argue. Billy's earlier warning clanged in her head, urging her to retreat the way she'd come. She expected John's heavy footsteps to follow. But after a moment of running and hearing only the crunch of her own steps in the windfall, she stopped and turned.

To her horror, John was lying on the ground not far from the cave. A man the size of two oxen was on top of him, wrenching his arm behind his back. The man's face was as brown as wet leather and just as crinkled. He reminded her of some of the burly men she'd seen with Charlie Baldock from time to time.

She dragged in a shaky breath.

John muttered something but was cut short by a punch to the side of his head.

She cried out in protest.

"Run, Polly!" John called, lifting his head from the ground.

"I won't go anywhere without you," she insisted. Prince burrowed into the crook of her arm, still trembling. She glanced around for anything she could use to free John, a hard stick, a big rock, anything. At the edge of the forest there were a dozen things she might wield as weapons, but she couldn't make her body work to pick something up.

"Snooping around Charlie's cave, are you?" the man groused.

So Charlie Baldock had a hideout close to his brother's house? No wonder Billy had warned her not to stray too far from home. He'd likely known about the cave and wanted to prevent her from stumbling upon it.

The ox unsheathed a knife and pointed it at John's throat. "For that I'm gonna tie you and your lady friend up. And then I'm gonna make you watch as I roast your dog alive."

Even with the knife pricking his neck, John struggled against his captor's hold and uttered several colorful curses.

The man slapped the side of John's head again. "Watch your filthy mouth."

"Devil hang you!" John yelled as he spat a glob of blood to the dirt. He attempted to roll away, but the huge man jerked John's arm up sharply behind his back again. He cried out in agony, and when his eyes found hers, the desperation there unnerved her. And pleaded with her again to run.

Her pulse pounded erratically, and her stomach clenched with the need to be sick. For a moment she could only stare, unwilling to depart but knowing the best way to help him was to get her father. He'd know what to do to save John. As much as she loathed leaving him at the mercy of the brute, she'd only make matters worse if she attempted to help him on her own.

She tucked Prince under her arm. His body was still shaking and hers was now too. And then she ran.

## NINE

*P*olly buried her face in her hands. Her mother's gentle
fingers rubbing her back didn't bring any comfort. Neither the heat emanating from the morning-room fireplace nor the
heavy wool blanket draped over her shoulders could warm her.
Nothing could take away the cold grip that had wrapped around
every limb.

"Your father will know what to do," Mother assured her, although her voice didn't contain any confidence.

After finding her way out of the woods, Polly had gone down to
the Customs House only to discover that her father had ridden out
on a search with several junior officers. Thankfully, Billy noticed her
with the dog and escorted her straight home, even though she begged
him to return to the cave. He promised to go there and investigate
the matter. But they hadn't heard anything from him.

"I shouldn't have left John," Polly said into her hands. "He's
probably dead by now."

"I doubt they'll kill him," Mother responded weakly, likely remembering the murder of the cordwainer and riding officer in West
Sussex. If Mother only knew about the recent threat to Father's
life . . . But Polly wouldn't tell her. She reasoned that if Father hadn't

told Mother about the incident, it was because he hadn't wanted to frighten her any more than she already was.

"I wish Father didn't have to be a customs officer," Polly said. "At the very least, why does he have to be so strict in his stand against the smugglers? He's putting himself in great danger." Even though she was repeating Billy's admonition, the fear in her heart made the words hers now.

Mother sighed as though she'd wrestled through the issue herself many times. "Your father is an honest man who lives by his convictions. Just because so many others turn a blind eye to the evil going on around us doesn't mean we should too. Imagine if everyone sat back and looked the other way. Who would be left to fight for righteous living and justice?"

Polly lifted her face and wiped the tears from her cheeks. "But what if smuggling isn't so evil after all? Maybe the fault lies with Parliament trying to enlarge the king's treasury with burdensome taxes." She had heard Billy say as much plenty of times. Without the cost of the import duties, the smuggled tea, coffee, tobacco, spirits, and silks were more affordable. What was wrong with that?

"Do we fight dishonest gain with more dishonest gain?" Mother said gently. "Or should we rise above the corruption and fight with truth and integrity, no matter the personal cost?"

Before Polly could respond, a loud banging on the front door made her jump.

Her mother crossed rapidly to the window and peered outside, her hands fluttering above her heart. "I can't see who it is." Her mother didn't have to say the exact words for Polly to know she was afraid the smugglers had decided to come after Polly since she knew the location of their hideout.

The pounding on the door came again, this time more urgently.

Polly rose from her chair and tried to still the trembling in her legs. She would go hand herself over before anyone else in her family was hurt.

But Mother was already gliding across the room to the door. "Stay here, Polly darling. I'll send the visitor away."

"No, Mother. Let me answer it." Polly attempted to follow, but with a stern shake of her head, Mother commanded her obedience. Polly sagged against the wall, closed her eyes, and began praying the Lord's Prayer.

The *click* of Mother unlocking the front door was followed by its squeak open and then Mother's gasp. "John, thank heaven you're safe!"

John? Polly pushed away from the wall.

"Where's Polly?" He gasped out the words. "Is she here?"

"Yes, and she's fine."

Polly moved into the doorway, the sluggishness of moments ago disappearing. At the sight of John standing in the hallway framed by the gray sky and lifeless January landscape behind him, she drew in a shaky breath and blinked back sudden tears. He was alive.

His frantic gaze landed upon her, his eyes wild, his hair disheveled. His nose had stopped bleeding, but his shirt and cravat were splattered with bright red. "Are you all right?"

She rushed to him with the urge to throw her arms around him, but she stopped short. His chest heaved in and out from his recent exertion, his warm breath reassuring her that he was safe. A bruise was beginning to rise on his cheekbone. His nose was slightly puffy, and she wondered if the huge man had broken it. "Are you in much pain?"

"None now that I'm here with you."

She tried to smile but her lips were tremulous. "I'm glad Billy found you."

"Billy?"

"Yes, he brought me home and told me he would go back to the cave to help you . . ." The blankness in John's eyes told her he hadn't seen Billy.

He gave a half grin, one that didn't reach his eyes. "I freed myself."

"You did? How?"

"Polly, darling," her mother admonished with a nod toward all the other children watching with wide eyes from the drawing-room door. "Little ears are listening."

Once John was settled in a chair in the morning room, Polly pressed a hot cup of tea in his hand and her mother draped the wool blanket over his shoulders. Polly started to back away from him, but his fingers snaked around her wrist, and he glared up at her. The anger in his eyes took her by surprise.

"You shouldn't have turned back."

She bristled at his tone. "I was worried about you. Is that wrong?"

"Aye."

She jerked free of his grasp and fisted her hands on her hips. "What kind of friend do you take me for? I only regret that I didn't do more to help free you instead of running like a coward."

"Your hesitation only put you under suspicion. Now Charlie's gang knows you were there with me. And they'll be watching you closely."

Her ire escalated. "I only wanted to help you."

"As you can see, I didn't need your help."

"Well, pardon me for not wanting to leave you with a knife pointed at your throat."

"Polly." Mother's gentle reprimand ended Polly's tirade, but not her indignation.

Polly dropped into the chair next to John's, not sure if she was more irritated at herself for making matters worse by bringing herself under suspicion from the smugglers or at John for being right.

"Let John tell us how he freed himself," Mother suggested.

Polly crossed her arms and glared back at John.

He addressed Mother. "I don't think the man intended to kill me. Frighten me. Aye. Scuff me up a bit. Aye. But not kill."

Mother folded her fingers in her lap but not before Polly caught sight of the trembling.

"He dragged me into the cave and started to tie me up," John continued. "But when he went around my backside, I used the opportunity to kick over his torch and stomp it out." He lifted one of his shoes to reveal a blackened sole that was nearly burned away.

"Thankfully the torch had only a small flame and went out easily, leaving us in complete blackness. In the commotion I was able to slip out of the cave and back the way I'd come."

"Did he chase you?" Polly asked with a glance toward the doorway at the same time as her mother, knowing her mother was thinking the same thing, that at any moment Charlie's gang would be knocking down their door.

"I didn't hear anyone following me," John answered. "I hid for a while just to make sure. But that doesn't mean they won't come after me. Eventually."

Mother was silent, studying John as though deciding what to do next. Finally, she reached over and took one of his hands in hers. "As much as we are glad to see you again, John, I wonder if perhaps you should depart from Kent for a while—"

John started to shake his head.

"Just until this incident has the chance to defuse," Mother continued. "We wouldn't want to see anything worse happen to you as a result of being here in plain view of Charlie Baldock and his gang."

Polly wanted to deny her mother, to tell John to stay. How could she bear his leaving when he'd only just arrived? But at the same time, her mother was right. John would be in danger if he stayed.

Newton leaned back in the cushioned elbow chair. The green damask had probably been new and fine at one time but was now pale and frayed around the edges. He suspected that's why the chair was relegated to Mr. Catlett's closet-like study across from the dining room at the back of the house. It was no longer fine enough to have a place in the drawing room, the showplace of the house.

Mr. Catlett sat in a hard-backed oak chair with scrolling detail on the legs and arms. It too had likely been a fine, polished piece of furniture at one time, but now it was scuffed and faded. With each move Mr. Catlett made, the chair wobbled as though it might fall. But Mr. Catlett didn't seem to pay any attention to his surroundings. Newton had learned during his last visit that Mr. Catlett was more concerned about honesty than making good impressions.

They'd already spent the past hour discussing the looming threat of war with France. Many believed that the exiled heir to the English throne, Bonnie Prince Charlie of the Stuart line, would attempt an invasion in an effort to regain the throne from the Hanoverian King George, whom some believed to be a usurper.

"Rumors abound," Newton said, "that the Young Pretender, Charles, is even now in France assembling an army of French, Scottish, and disgruntled English, and that he's planning to invade England in the spring."

"The problem is that we've been expecting a French invasion for years," Mr. Catlett replied. "There has always been a lingering fear, ever since the Stuart king was deposed, that he would eventually attempt to regain the throne with the help of France."

"But never so much talk as now," John insisted. "In every port I visited on the voyage home, people were saying that this time the invasion will happen. In fact, British agents in Paris have gotten word of preparations of forces at Dunkirk along with information that the crossing is feasible."

Mr. Catlett's expression was grave. "That would account for the increase in active troops around the area and naval vessels sailing up and down the coast. The king is apparently preparing to defend London and Southeast England, including Kent."

Newton's recent voyage was rife with the stress of avoiding French pirate ships, which were more numerous than ever before. "Too many English merchant vessels have been needlessly seized by our archenemy," Newton said. "Now we've reached the point where most convoys need a naval escort if we hope to survive capture."

Mr. Catlett perched his elbows on the armrests and steepled his hands in front of his grimly set lips. "As much as I hate war, perhaps it's necessary to put an end to the French bullying. If we're finally able to stop the French from confiscating English goods, perhaps then we shall be able to control the smuggling and restore law and order to our coastal towns."

Newton had already relayed the day's confrontation to Mr. Catlett and had learned too late about the threat Mr. Catlett had recently received. He realized now he should have heeded Polly's warning not to go near the blasted cave. Even if he was lucky to have escaped alive, his recklessness had put not only him in danger but now Polly, perhaps even the entire Catlett family. And he loathed himself for that. He silently cursed himself as he'd done a hundred times that afternoon and evening.

Again, as before, Newton couldn't keep from bringing their conversation back to the incident. "I think Charlie Baldock's gang will be watching Polly closely."

"And watching you too?"

"Aye. He likely won't take his eyes from me."

The hollow, ominous ticking of the square pendulum clock on Mr. Catlett's desk seemed to agree with his prediction. Only one brass wall sconce was lit, lending little light to the dark-paneled room, which did nothing to quell Newton's fears. His scalp pricked at the thought that even now Charlie might have a man outside just waiting to break in and slit his throat.

"I think we can both agree," Mr. Catlett said, "our primary concern is keeping Polly safe."

"Aye, sir. I'd have it no other way."

"Then what do you propose that we do, John? Should I attempt to have Charlie arrested? Without his leadership, the gang might fall apart." The suggestion was empty. They both knew how difficult such an arrest would be. Mr. Catlett had been unable to prove that Charlie had been associated with the illegal tea that he'd confiscated during Newton's last visit. It was almost always impossible to prove a smuggler's connection with the goods, especially because anyone who spoke out against the gangs feared reprisal.

Newton shook his head. "If you go anywhere near that hidden tunnel with your officers and confiscate the smuggled goods, then Charlie will know we betrayed him. He'll take revenge upon both Polly and me at some point."

Mr. Catlett sighed wearily. "I don't like ignoring crime, especially one as large scale as this. But if I pursue it, I'll be putting Polly into grave danger."

Newton's body eased against the chair pads. He'd been concerned that a principled man like Mr. Catlett might put integrity and justice above the personal safety of his family. He was relieved to hear that Mr. Catlett wasn't planning to do anything that would bring Polly further risk.

"Something like this was bound to happen sooner or later," Mr. Catlett said, his shoulders sagging and his face pale. With new threads of gray in his hair, he looked to have aged ten years rather than one since John had last seen him.

"I think the safest course is for Polly and me to stay close to home until this all blows over."

"And what if it doesn't blow over?"

"It will. Once Charlie sees that we didn't give away his location, he'll realize we're not working against him, and he'll leave us alone." At least Newton hoped so.

"My wife was right to encourage you to leave," Mr. Catlett said. "Charlie didn't like you the last time you visited, and he'll like you even less now."

"I won't turn tail and run at the first sign of danger. In fact, consider that by staying, I might be of use in protecting your family if any gang member should come calling."

Mr. Catlett met his gaze directly, as Newton was learning was his custom. "I'm grateful for your willingness to protect them, John. Truly I am."

*But . . .*

The word hung unspoken in the air.

"I don't want Polly to get hurt."

"I don't either. Believe me, sir. That's the last thing I want."

Mr. Catlett glanced down. "I don't want Polly to get hurt by you, John."

Newton sat back. He wanted to pretend he didn't know what Mr. Catlett was referring to. But he did. He wasn't yet the man he needed to be for Polly. He'd spent much of his free time during his last voyage gambling and drinking gin and rum with his mates. Without his father there, he hadn't had the advantage of being able to sneak into the captain's cabin to borrow books to read. With little to occupy himself, he'd all too easily given in to the pursuits of the other sailors.

Now that he was back on land, the guilt for his indulgences had reared up to wrestle with his conscience, especially now that he was with Polly. What would she think of him if she knew what he'd done over the past year?

He had consoled himself during dinner and evening activities by telling himself that he would be a better man for her, that he wouldn't drink again, that he'd try to be more responsible, especially now that his father had lined up a new position as a ship's officer for his next voyage.

"She likes you," Mr. Catlett said. "And I can see why. You're a charming young man."

"I vow that I'll cherish her affection."

"She's still very young."

"I have all the time in the world to wait." He didn't consider sixteen all that young. But he'd wait an eternity for her if necessary.

Mr. Catlett sat quietly for several minutes, and again the ticking clock grew louder. Finally, he unfolded himself from his chair, unbending his long limbs slowly. "Since she's still young, I shall trust that you'll remember to regard her as a sister at all times."

A sister? He'd never be able to see Polly as a sister. A friend? Mayhap. But his feelings for her ran too deep to ever think of her as a sister. "Aye, aye, sir. You have no worries with me."

Mr. Catlett clamped him on the shoulder. "I like you, John. I pray that God will continue to guide you in the paths that he has planned for you."

John was tempted to respond that he wasn't so sure God was guiding him at all and that it was up to him to make sure he was his own wind in his sail. "Thank you, sir," he said instead, knowing he would only prove himself more unworthy if he revealed his spiritual struggles to Mr. Catlett.

Newton bade Mr. Catlett a polite good night and then excused himself.

The truth was, during his last voyage he'd had a lot of time to think about his faith. He couldn't be certain that God was involved in anyone's life. He'd almost begun to wonder if the concept of God was merely a buoy for weak-minded people to rely upon instead of truly working things out for themselves.

After all, he'd tried plenty of times in his past to live a righteous, God-fearing life. On one of the voyages with his father, he'd resolved to renounce the world, the flesh, and the devil. He had turned to asceticism with hours of prayer, Bible reading, meditation, and even fasting. But in the end, nothing had changed in his life through the experience. He hadn't felt any closer to God. He'd only become boring, morose, and unsociable.

In hindsight, he couldn't reason out any benefits in denying himself. Why work so hard to please a God who didn't seem to care? Why strive to be perfect, when perfection was unattainable? Why deny the desires of his flesh, when they were so prominent? Mayhap, religion offered some people a way to feel better about themselves with all their rules. Mayhap they found security and safety in their traditions. Mayhap the idea of a loving God comforted them.

But his experience with God had been much like his experience with his father. So far he'd only managed to be a disappointment and failure. And he didn't really care all that much anymore about trying to gratify a God who was so hard to please.

He plodded silently up the stairway, then stood on the landing for a moment and stared through the dark at Polly's door. He'd been harsh with her earlier and now wished he'd taken a tender approach. He needed to apologize and make sure everything was still all right between them.

The voice of reason warned him to go directly to the boys' room, that he shouldn't put her into a situation that might compromise her reputation. Or his. If he went into Polly's room, Mr. Catlett would shoot him on the spot if he learned of it. But a deep need to see her rose strong and swift. Before he could talk himself out of going to her, he crossed the hallway, turned the doorknob, and opened the door a crack.

In the darkness of the room lit only by starlight, it took him a moment to realize she wasn't in the bed but rather was kneeling beside it. Her head was bowed on her folded hands and her long hair was loose and flowing down her back.

He stepped farther into the room and closed the door behind him as quietly as he could. The *click,* however, was enough to gain her attention, to cause her head to snap up and for her to swivel. At the sight of him, she gasped and jumped to her feet. Her plain nightdress covered her from head to toes and even the length of her arms. Even so, Newton's mouth went dry as he took her in.

"John," she whispered. "What are you doing in here?"

For the briefest of moments, he imagined what it would be like on their wedding night. He would have every right to walk into her room, sweep her into his arms, and kiss her all night long. He would never have to leave her again. She would be his.

She didn't move except to hug her arms across her chest.

He didn't dare move either for fear that he might do something he'd regret, something that would likely scare her and most certainly get him thrown out of the Catlett home. And what's worse, they'd never let him back in the house.

"You shouldn't be in here," she said. But thankfully she didn't sound angry, only surprised.

He reached behind him, his fingers fumbling against the cold brass doorknob. "I wanted to apologize for getting angry with you earlier. I should have realized that you aren't the sort of woman to flee from danger."

At his admission, her stiff bearing seemed to relax slightly. "I didn't want to abandon you, John."

"I know. So will you forgive me for being cross with you?"

"Of course."

He gripped the doorknob to hold himself in place.

"Will you leave on the morrow as mother suggested?" she asked.

"You should know that I'm not the sort of man to flee from danger."

"I'm worried for your safety."

"Good that. I like knowing you're worried about me."

"Charlie Baldock is much too dangerous a man to offend."

"I'll be fine, Polly."

Her silence told him she didn't believe him.

"After being away from you for almost a year, you can't expect me to leave again so soon."

This time she gave an exasperated sigh.

"If you honestly don't want to be with me, I'll go." He was stretching the truth. He didn't know that he'd be able to leave her even if she demanded it. "Just say it. Say, 'I don't want to be with you, John.' Then I'll leave." He didn't care that he was baiting her to declare her affection for him. Even if it would never match his own, he wanted her to admit her feelings.

"John," she chastised softly.

"Do you want me to leave?"

She was silent again. Finally, she uttered one low word. "No."

He smiled. "Aye then." Before he took the implication of her admission to a new level and neglected to leave her bedroom, he forced himself to turn the doorknob. "Good night, Polly."

Her breathless good night followed him out of the room and almost made him lose his willpower to close the door behind him.

Polly squeezed Eliza's hand from her spot on the edge of the settee. Everyone watched John pace back and forth, eight steps to the window and eight steps to the pianoforte.

The moment the constable and two superior officers from the customs office had arrived, Mother had banished the rest of the children to their rooms upstairs. Since then she hadn't moved from her spot near the door where she now stood like a marble statue.

The only sounds were John's footsteps muted by the rug. Every once in a while, Father's voice rose. At those moments they all strained to hear what he was saying. It couldn't be good if Father was upset since he rarely lost his temper or spoke in anger.

"This is all my fault," John mumbled, as he had already a dozen times since the men had arrived.

Polly wanted to ask him what was his fault, but she already suspected the answer had to do with yesterday's run-in with Charlie's gang at the cave. They'd all been tense since last evening. Every passerby, every noise from outside, every knock on the door had made them jump. In some ways, finally having this confrontation was a relief.

At the *click* of Father's study door opening and the ensuing sharp footsteps in the hallway, John halted his pacing. His broad shoulders were tense and his expression grave.

The two customs officers made quick work of exiting the house, leaving Father behind with the constable.

"I'm sorry, George." The constable, Mr. Pickworth, was a long-time friend of Father's. Mr. Pickworth attended their church, and their families had grown up together. "The most I could do was prevent them from taking away your commission altogether."

Polly's pulse dove at the same time that Mother stiffened.

"You did the best you could, Sam," her father replied from near the front door. "It means a great deal to me that you defended my rights, especially since in doing so you put your own welfare in danger."

"You're a good man," Mr. Pickworth said. "One of the best I know. If I suffer for defending a man like you, then it will be worth it."

Father bade Mr. Pickworth good-bye and ushered him out. When the door closed and Father's weighted footsteps neared the drawing room, Polly couldn't keep from gripping Eliza's hand harder.

As Father entered the room, Mother reached trembling fingers for his. Father's hand shook as he took hold of hers. His forehead was grooved with deep lines, and his expression was somber.

Like the others, Polly stared at him, waiting for the news but not wanting to hear it.

"The good news," Father started, "is that I still have a job." He attempted a smile, but it was weak.

Polly held her breath and from Eliza's utter stillness, she knew her sister was doing the same.

"The bad news is that I've lost my position as a senior officer."

For a long moment the room was so silent they could hear the soft tap of raindrops against the window.

Finally, John spoke. "They can't do that."

"They did," Father replied.

"Because of Charlie Baldock?" John asked, his voice taut.

Father shrugged. "I suspect he paid one of the other senior officers quite a hefty sum to make sure my hands are tied."

John spun and stalked back to the window. Once there he
stopped and stared outside at the gray winter sky.

Guilt settled over Polly's heart like a coating of coal dust. If John
felt responsible, she was more so. "I'm sorry, Father—"

"Don't blame yourself, Polly." John turned, and Polly could see
his face was a mask of anguish. "This is all my fault."

"But I shouldn't have chased Miss Donovan's dog. Billy warned
me not to."

"Neither of you are at fault." Father squared his thin shoulders.
"I knew by taking a stand against the gangs that eventually I'd pay
the price."

Polly realized what he was leaving unsaid, that the price could
have been his death. Being demoted was certainly less costly than his
life. Even so, the loss of his prestigious position would bring shame
to their family as well as a reduction in her father's income. Would
Jack still be able to continue his education? And what of her own
schooling now? If her parents could no longer afford to pay for Jack
to attend school, then there would certainly be no chance for her.

For a brief moment she tasted the bitterness of disappointment.
But as quickly as it came, she swallowed it. She ought to be grateful
her father was safe. She ought to be grateful that this was the most
Charlie was doing to them for stumbling upon his hideout yesterday.
The punishment could have been so much worse. In fact, there was
still the very real possibility that he could attempt to recapture and
harm John. Or her.

She bowed her head as the shame of her selfishness pressed upon her. Tonight she would pray harder and longer. For forgiveness for wanting more. For safety for her family and John. But even as her prayers formulated, her soul echoed with emptiness. Would God really hear her? Why would he listen to her when she was riddled with faults? Would she ever be free of her sin and good enough to truly connect with God and feel his presence?

If only she could earn his favor. Maybe then he'd finally hear her prayers.

# TEN

*P*olly's fingers formed a new chord on the keyboard before her. "How does that sound?"

"Hmm . . ." John stood next to her bench and examined the notes with a solemnity that was almost comical. "Why don't you sing what we have so far?"

She couldn't contain her smile. "I think you're just looking for an excuse to hear me sing again."

"My lady, do you question my motives?" He put a hand over his heart as though she'd wounded him with her accusation. But his easy grin told her that she'd figured out his tactic.

"You have questioned my arrangements so often that I've decided either you think I'm a terrible composer or you're simply looking for an excuse to hear me sing."

His green eyes twinkled with the mirth she'd grown to love. "Or it could be that I take very seriously our task of developing music to go with these hymns."

Polly only shook her head and then worked her way through the page of music they'd already arranged. The music was meant to accompany the words of a hymn written down in a little book that once had belonged to John's mother. The verses were mostly taken from the Psalms, but his mother had composed them beautifully. And they begged for music to go with them.

From the worn pages and battered cover, she could tell John treasured the book, even if he didn't treasure the words of faith the same way she did. Although he didn't speak of his mother often, whenever he did it was with reverence and love. It was clear he adored her, and he'd told Polly that the hymnal was his last remaining link to her.

Over the past several weeks, the time spent composing with him had become one of Polly's favorite parts of the day. Usually they did so in the early afternoon, after their midday meal. And some days, especially during the past week, they had spent several hours at it. They'd written music for two of the hymns and had started a third. When she was deep in the development of the melody, she had the niggling suspicion that perhaps this was what God was calling her to do, to sit beside John and develop worshipful songs that would be an inspiration for others in their faith. And yet, how could it be if John didn't share her faith in God?

Her father had forbidden her to leave the premises of their home for fear that Charlie's gang might still attempt to harm her. As if the worry of reprisal and her father's loss of his position weren't enough, they'd had to release two of their servants, which left them with only one, not nearly enough help for a large household such as theirs. However, Mother had attempted to cheerfully embrace the new duties, explaining that the extra work would be good for all of them.

Thankfully, John's companionship had provided her with many hours of distraction. He willingly joined them in any task needing to be done. When the work was completed, he loved reading from the books in the morning room. She often found him there with a new book in hand, and he always discussed what he was reading with her. Not only that, but he resumed teaching her Latin. He also entertained her siblings and her in the evenings with his delightful rendition of one novel or another. And he introduced several new parlor games that they had fun playing.

She could hardly complain that she was a prisoner, not when John as her fellow prisoner provided such pleasant companionship. Nevertheless, spring would soon be upon them, and she was ready to resume normal life.

"When does your next voyage start, John?" her mother had asked only that morning as they ate toast and sipped tea to break their fast. "My recollection says you were due to set sail any day now."

He nearly choked on his tea and took overlong to respond. Although his tanned face didn't go red, Polly sensed a deepening color, especially when all her siblings stared at him and waited for his answer.

"I wanted to stay and protect Polly. I couldn't leave without making sure there was no longer any danger."

"Oh dear." Mother sat back in her chair. "I'm sorry that we've caused you to miss your voyage."

"Nay," he said quickly. " 'It wasn't your fault, to be sure."

"You should have let us know," Mother chided softly. "We would have encouraged you to go. You cannot neglect your other responsibilities for our sake."

"I've been carefully contemplating other options," he responded, "and I'm certain I can find another position at some point."

He took a bite of his toast and didn't notice Mother's narrowed eyes studying him with concern. But Polly saw the look, and it filled her with foreboding.

"As a matter of fact," John said after wiping the butter from his mouth, "I've considered going down to the dockyard and finding work there."

Mother had been made momentarily speechless by his declaration. Although the Royal Dockyard launched a new ship or two every year, some of the largest classes of ships, a man could not simply walk down to the dockyard and ask for a job. Most of the positions were filled by tradesmen and apprentices who specialized in their particular craft, including block makers, caulkers, blacksmiths, joiners, carpenters, and others.

Even getting a position in the ropery would have posed a challenge. Although the spinning of the hemp and rope making required many men, John hadn't been trained in any of the required skills. Perhaps there was a chance he could find work in the tarring house where the newly made rope was tarred to prevent rot. But Polly suspected, as Mother surely did, that the chances of John finding work beyond that of a common laborer weren't very likely. Would he really be happy with the backbreaking work and meager wages of unskilled positions that were reserved for paupers? At the same time, she couldn't bear the thought of him returning to seafaring life, not when war with France was looming so near.

Although her mother and father didn't often talk of the hostilities with France, of late they hadn't been able to shield her or her siblings from the growing threat of an invasion by the French under the guise of helping Bonnie Prince Charlie take the throne away from King George. She didn't understand what it all meant, except that since they lived so close to the coast and to France, her Father feared for their safety. And now she feared that if John returned to his sailing, he might get caught up in war.

But the truth was, John's only viable recourse was to continue in what he knew—sailing. Perhaps one day he'd earn enough to sustain a family through his voyages, like his father had.

Polly flushed at the thought and let her fingers linger on the keyboard. She wasn't thinking of a future with him, was she? Right now he wasn't ready, either financially or spiritually. But that didn't mean he never would be, did it?

He hummed a few more notes and then sang another line. He had a deep, well-tuned singing voice, and she had to admit she enjoyed listening to him.

In fact, there were so many things she liked about him—his wit, his laughter, their conversations, his helpfulness, his thoughtfulness, and his desire to see that she and her family were safe. She would miss him when he finally took his leave.

"Scoot over and make room for me." He lowered himself to the edge of the bench, giving her little choice but to move or have him sit on her lap.

Her attention shifted to the chair where Eliza had been only a moment ago embroidering an apron. The ivory linen was detailed with tiny colorful flowers, one tulip half-finished with the needle and thread hanging abandoned over the edge of the chair.

Where had Eliza gone? Even though Mother often referred to John as their brother and had enfolded him in their family as though he were her son, she had admonished them to have a chaperone whenever they were with him.

Polly had done her best to obey her mother's instructions. But now he was sitting directly next to her with his thigh pressed against hers. She had no more space to move on the short bench. Even though she ought to slide to the edge or even stand up, she couldn't make herself.

He leaned over the keyboard and placed his fingers on several notes as though completely oblivious to her nearness. He plunked out a few off-key notes. "How does that sound? Like a masterpiece, no doubt."

"If you keep it up, I think you shall likely put Mr. Handel out of work."

John grinned and played several more notes. "Aye, soon I'll be the one playing for the king and queen."

"I should like to see you in a long wig exactly like the one Mr. Handel wears." She glanced to his hair, tied back except for one sandy-brown piece that had come loose.

"I'm afraid I will have to disappoint you, my lady." He attempted a chord but clearly needed lessons. "I refuse to wear anything that resembles sausage links piled one on top of the other."

"Are you afraid that you might be tempted to snack on your hair in moments of hunger?"

He laughed softly. "Aye."

She couldn't resist studying his profile, the strong lines of his jaw, the slight layer of beard, and the smile lines near his mouth.

As though sensing her appraisal, he shifted his attention from his fingers on the keys to her face. Her mistake was not looking away quickly enough.

His beautiful sea-green eyes were wide and clear and light with the humor of the moment. And he didn't glance away either. She hadn't expected him to. He was bold and mischievous and sometimes even impious.

Heaven help her, she ought not encourage him in anything beyond simple friendship. And she'd done well during his visit to maintain boundaries. Thankfully he had too, in spite of his usual good-natured teasing. But there were rare moments when they were alone, like now, when all pretenses fell away.

The light faded from his eyes, turning them a darker green. The humor dissipated from his expression, replaced by a mixture of seriousness and determination that suddenly put her senses on keen alert.

He hardly shifted on the bench, but it was enough for him to lift his hand to her cheek. When his fingertips skimmed her cheekbone, she didn't move. She couldn't resist his gentle pressure. When his gaze alighted upon her mouth, the chaste part of her warned her to stand up, to flee temptation.

But another part of her longed for the thrill of knowing what it would feel like to kiss him. She could no longer deny that she'd been waiting for this moment since the day he'd held her in the stable. She'd wanted to feel his mouth against hers. She'd dreamed of what it would be like.

If he wanted to kiss her, she would let him.

As though she'd spoken the words aloud, he tilted his head closer. His fingers dropped to her jaw and grazed a line to her chin. She wanted to close her eyes and bask in the sweet sensation. But he'd captivated her, and she couldn't break eye contact any more than she could free herself from a swirling abyss.

He tilted a fraction closer so that now his breath lingered above her lips. When his nose touched hers lightly, the contact was so intimate and tender that she brushed the tip of her nose back against his, completely lost in the brief contact and the way their breath mingled.

If he'd had any doubt of her willingness before, the touch of her nose was all the invitation he needed. His lips grazed the corner of her mouth, feathery light. Even though the contact was infinitely soft, it elicited a gasp that came out of the depths of her naivety and new delight of such intimacy. But before she could express the completeness of her pleasure in that small kiss, his lips came against hers more forcefully.

The power of his mouth left her no room to utter a sound. She was too shocked by the strength of his kiss, the way his lips laid claim to hers, the way his mouth moved against hers. His lips demanded a response, stirring her passions, so that she closed her eyes and gave way to the driving need to experience him, to know him more deeply.

Oh God help her, but she'd never experienced anything so beautiful, so pleasurable. A moan begged for release, but his mouth covering hers gave her no escape. She wanted no escape. And when he lightened the pressure of his lips as though to pull away, she did the unthinkable. She refused to let him go. She initiated more. She crushed her lips against his.

He released a low groan, and his thick arms came about her, drawing her against his body even as his lips consumed hers again.

"Polly Catlett!" came a sharp cry from a distant land. Her mother's voice penetrated her desire. But it was John who broke off their passionate kiss. He scrambled away, fell off the bench, and landed on the floor with a painful-sounding thud.

For an instant Polly could only sit in dazed confusion as John jumped nimbly to his feet and stood to face what appeared to be a roomful of inquisitors.

Her mother stood at the forefront. Behind her stood Eliza and several of her siblings. And for some reason, Billy Baldock was there. Polly was too dazed to understand where he'd come from and why he was there.

"Polly Catlett," Mother said again. Her face was pale and her eyes wide with shock. She stood unmoving, her hands outstretched in a silent plea.

Billy, however, was not immovable. With the fierce guttural growl of an attacking boar, he charged toward John. His dark hair was unkempt, and his thick brows came together in a menacing scowl above eyes that flashed with deadly anger.

Before Polly could think to object, Billy knocked into John, sending the two of them backward. They slammed against the wall with such force that a small picture crashed to the floor, the gilded frame cracking into several pieces. One of Billy's fists flew into John's gut and the other into his face.

At the reverberating smack and ensuing grunt, Eliza screamed. The terror in her voice must have awakened Mother out of her stupor, for she cried out too. "Please, Billy. Please, John! Don't fight in front of the children."

Billy's fingers had found their way around John's neck, and he was cutting off John's air. A dot of blood pooled at the base of John's nose, but he'd clenched his fists at his sides in a clear effort not to strike back at Billy. Polly's chest tightened at the realization that John was letting Billy thrash him. She wanted to scream at him to defend himself, but she could only cup her hand over her mouth, her mortification paralyzing her.

"Billy," Mother pleaded.

Billy held John's neck in a deathly grip a moment longer before he finally shoved him hard and took a step away.

John sucked in a strangled wheezing breath.

Mother wavered and then quickly lowered herself into the nearest chair. Eliza rushed to Mother's side and took her hand in a comforting gesture.

"I'm sorry, Mother." Polly's voice came out much shakier than she wanted.

"Don't apologize for anything, Polly." John tentatively touched fingers to the bloody spot at his nose. "It's entirely my fault. I took advantage of the situation—"

"You're blasted right, you did," Billy interrupted, lifting a fist as though he would slam it into John's face again.

John didn't flinch. He didn't look at Billy but instead addressed Mother. "I beg your forgiveness, Mrs. Catlett. You entrusted me to keep Polly safe from smugglers, but it appears as though she's in more danger from my ardor."

"Oh John." Mother's face seemed to age with weariness and defeat.

"I beg your forgiveness as well, Polly," John said without looking at her. "I shouldn't have enticed you the way I did." She wanted him to turn and face her so that she could read the truth in his eyes and know that he didn't really mean his apology. She didn't want him to be sorry for kissing her. She didn't want him to have any regrets, although she knew they both should.

For a long moment the room was silent. Her younger siblings stood unmoving in the doorway, their expressions wide with all that they'd witnessed, filling Polly with renewed chagrin that she'd been such a poor role model to them.

Finally, her mother lifted a shaking hand to her chest. "I wish Mr. Catlett were home to advise me on what to do. But since he's not here, I must make the decision that I think is in everyone's best interest." She smiled at John sadly, a smile that sent worry pulsing through Polly. She wanted to stand up and protest what she knew was coming next, but what could she say? They were guilty.

"It's time for you to be on your way."

John nodded resignedly.

"A young man with too much idle time on his hands will only get into trouble eventually," she continued. "Whether you return to your sailing or something else entirely new, I believe that it's in your best interest to show yourself to be responsible, diligent, hardworking, and godly."

Like Billy. No one had to say the words, but she was sure everyone was thinking them. She glanced at Billy and had to give him credit for the fact that he wasn't gloating.

"Such qualities will hold you in good stead," Mother said, "and prepare you to take on greater responsibilities in the future."

"Aye, ma'am." John stiffened his shoulders. "You've been kind to me, kinder than I deserve. I thank you for your generous hospitality. Once again, I ask you to forgive me for taking advantage of the situation."

"I hold you no ill will, my child. I want you to know I will always have an affectionate place for you in my heart." Mother was offering him pardon, but not an invitation to stay with them or even to return in the future.

As though sensing the same, John let his head hang. Finally, he managed a grin and spoke with forced cheer. "Then I guess this is good-bye. I'll be on my way."

Billy stood back and crossed his arms, and Mother merely nodded.

John started toward the door, and the younger siblings scattered, their footsteps echoing in the hallway.

A strange sense of panic pooled in Polly's chest. She couldn't just let John walk out of her life without knowing when or if she'd see him again. And he certainly wouldn't leave without telling her good-bye, would he?

When he reached the door, the panic swelled and she rose from the bench. "John. Wait."

He stopped. He didn't turn right away but instead seemed to be fighting a personal battle to compose himself. When he finally shifted to look at her, the gut-wrenching agony in his eyes took her breath away.

She had a sudden overwhelming need to cross the room, fling her arms about him, and reassure him that everything would be all right. But would it be all right ever again?

"Good-bye, Polly." The words were soft and anguished as if he'd torn them from his soul.

Tears clouded her eyes, and she dropped her gaze before anyone could see them. Her sights landed upon the hymnal that had once belonged to his mother. She picked it up and closed it reverently. "Don't forget this." She held it out to him and couldn't contain the tremble in her hand.

He stared at it for a long moment and then finally met her gaze. "Keep it for me?"

Her throat ached. She knew how much the hymnal meant to him.

He didn't wait for her reply. Instead he spun and strode out of the room. After a few seconds the front door of the house closed with a resounding thud.

Polly collapsed to the pianoforte bench, overwhelmed with the need to weep. Instead, she sat silently and clutched the small hymnal to her heart. Or at least what remained of her heart.

## ELEVEN

*N*ewton wandered down the road that would take him into Chatham. Each step felt as though his shoes and stockings were drenched and weighted down with half the ocean. He didn't really care where he was going. He could get lost in the woodland for all he cared. Not even the brief thought that Charlie's men might be lying in wait for him bothered him. They could capture and beat him if they wanted.

One moment he'd been on the very brink of heaven itself, holding Polly and kissing her the way he'd wanted to since the day they met. Then the next moment she was ripped away from him and he'd become an outcast. If he'd ever harbored hope that the Catletts might consider letting him court Polly, that hope was dashed.

"You're a fool," he said kicking a loose stone in the road. "You're a stupid, stupid fool."

At the *clop* of horse hooves advancing behind him, he knew he should move to the side of the road to let the traveler pass by. But he stiffened his shoulders and stubbornly kept to the middle of the road. Whoever it was could go around him or try to force him aside. He'd relish a fight right about now.

"You're so pathetic you don't even have your own horse." John recognized Billy Baldock's contemptuous voice.

Newton's muscles tensed, but he forced his heavy feet to keep walking and didn't give the donkey the satisfaction of a response.

"Do you really think a sailor with nothing but the shirt on his back could ever be good enough for a woman like Polly Catlett?"

Aye, he had nothing, not even his father's horse this time. He had only the clothes he wore and the wages he'd earned from his months at sea. The leather pouch was tied beneath his pocket. But even that was only a small purse that wouldn't last long.

"I'll soon be in a position to offer her a lifestyle that she's accustomed to," Billy said louder. "And that's something you won't be able to do no matter how hard you try."

Newton's hands twitched. He'd like nothing better than to smash a fist into Billy's face. But he guessed that's exactly what Billy wanted. He was baiting Newton to attack him. He wanted the chance to finish what he started in the Catletts' drawing room. As much as Newton wanted a fight, he didn't want to kill Billy, and he was afraid that might happen if he lashed out right now in his current state of mind.

He walked a few more steps before finally shrugging his shoulders as nonchalantly as possible. "It doesn't really matter how much status or wealth either of us has. Polly's already chosen which one of us she wants. And it clearly isn't you, mate."

Billy's horse slowed and then stopped.

Newton spun to face Billy. At the raw disappointment and hurt on Billy's face, Newton inwardly smiled. He'd hit his mark and hit it hard. Even if all else failed, Newton could take some satisfaction in the fact that Polly had kissed him, had really kissed him back, not just to be polite and not just to experiment. Nay, he'd felt her passion. And he had no doubt Billy had seen it.

Just the mere thought of it fanned a low fire in his gut. It was the kind of kiss that could fill a man's dreams. It was the kind of kiss that a man could never forget, no matter how hard he tried. And he, for one, had no intention of ever trying.

"You've had months—nay years—to try to win her heart." Newton couldn't resist another low hit. "But obviously she doesn't want to be in your arms."

The hurt in Billy's expression darkened, and his brows came together over dangerously sharp eyes. "You coerced her into yours. That's the only way she would have fallen there. Soon enough she'll see you for what you really are. Ship scum."

Billy's declaration rang too close to the truth. Newton knew he wasn't good for much. Even though Mr. Catlett had taken the responsibility for his demotion, Newton still blamed himself. Now the Catletts, including Polly, would suffer as a result. He'd seen the disappointment in Polly's eyes. If her dream of going to school had been remote before, it was now impossible. And it was his fault.

If only he could find a way to turn it around for her. He considered asking his father for a loan. But if he returned to London, his father would discover he'd missed the ship officer's job and lecture him about how he'd thrown away another job opportunity. He'd remind him how hard it had been to find the position on a merchant ship now that hostilities with France were escalating and merchant vessels were leery of getting caught in the fray. His father would tell him how stupid he'd been, how he needed to grow up and become a man.

He could hear his father say, *"After all the work I went to lining up the position, how could you do this to me? What will my friends think of my son? That he's lazy? Irresponsible? Good for nothing?"*

His father wouldn't understand that he'd felt responsible to stay and help the Catletts since they'd had to let most of their servants go. He'd also decided that if he found work in Chatham perhaps he could give part of his income to the Catletts to make up for what Mr. Catlett had lost. More than that, he'd wanted to ensure that Polly was safe from any danger.

"You might have been able to charm Polly this time," Billy said, his voice laced with scorn, "but she'll grow up soon enough and see which of us is the real man."

"I think she can already tell."

Billy nudged his horse toward Newton, unhooking his foot from his stirrup as though he wanted to kick Newton in the stomach. Newton hardened his abdomen in readiness for the blow. But just as Billy drew up, several men stumbled out of a nearby tavern, laughing and cursing. Billy reined his horse with a rough jerk.

Newton used the distraction to start toward the tavern. The sign above the door had the picture of a sea god and the words Old Neptune painted in small letters. The tavern would be as good a place as any to spend the afternoon. He'd have time to nurse his wounds, think of what he would do next, and keep himself from thrashing Billy.

"Go away and stay away," Billy said after him. "We don't want you here."

"You can rest assured," Newton said over his shoulder, "I won't be leaving until I'm good and ready."

"Your days here are numbered. I'll make sure of it."

What was he planning to do, send his uncle's thugs after him?

Newton stopped in front of the tavern door and hesitated. Mayhap he was unwise to make an enemy of Billy Baldock. Sure, they'd never liked each other, not since the moment they'd met and both known they were vying for the affection of the same woman. But Billy had tolerated him because they were both trying to keep the Catletts safe.

Newton shrugged and opened the door. The waft of tobacco smoke and sweet rum made his mouth water. It had been about a month since he'd indulged himself. Truthfully, around Polly he hadn't missed the drinking, gambling, and other coarser activities of tavern life. But now, with the clink of mugs and coins and the rumbling of voices and laughter, his tongue felt heavy and dry.

He stepped inside the dimly lit interior and let the door close heavily behind him, shutting out Billy Baldock. The torture in his heart came back tenfold. For all his brave words and thoughts about not letting Polly go, about Polly having chosen him instead of Billy, all his insecurities charged at him, began to shout reminders about how he wasn't good enough, that he'd never amount to anything, that he was a failure, that a woman as kind and sweet as Polly would never be able to truly love a man like him.

He gripped his head to stop the noise. But the clamoring only grew louder, calling him names: fool, good-for-nothing, ship scum. He could think of only one way to stop the noise and names, the only way that had worked in the past. He would drown them out with drink. And mayhap he could drown the pain too, at least for a while.

Newton emptied his mug. The bitter liquid burned his throat. He slammed the mug down onto the table and fought back a dizzying wave. The air around him had grown stuffy. The voices and laughter from the men at his table had risen to almost unbearable levels. And his stomach gurgled with a sickening nausea.

He'd lost track of how much he'd had to drink. But it had been far over his limit of tolerance. By now, he wasn't sure if he remembered his name, much less why he'd come into the pub to begin with. Had he been there hours or days? He couldn't remember.

The door of the tavern suddenly opened with a bang that reverberated against the walls. Light from outside poured into the dank hovel. "Everyone leave!" someone yelled breathlessly. "A platoon is headed this way!"

Immediately chaos erupted around Newton. Men cursed. Benches and tables crashed to the floor. And people everywhere scrambled toward the exits.

Newton rose but swayed on his feet. He tried to grasp the table in front of him, but for some reason it had disappeared. He fumbled for something to hold but there was nothing. The room tipped and he found himself falling to his knees.

Why was everyone leaving? And where were they going in such a hurry?

"Don't go yet," he called, his voice slurred and heavy. "I know I can beat you in the next game if you give me another chance."

He patted his pocket to the spot where he kept his pouch. The leather bag was there, but it was much lighter than it should have been. In fact, if he didn't know any better, he'd almost come to the conclusion that it was empty. Surely he hadn't spent all of his earnings. Someone must have stolen from him.

"Who took my money?" he yelled, but again his voice was oddly thick. "I'll kill anyone who stole from me."

"You spent every last penny," said the tavern owner's wife as she rushed past with flushed cheeks, hurrying her two children to a set of steps that led to the living quarters above. "Now get on out of here before you get yourself impressed."

Impressed?

The one word was enough to clear his head for just a moment and fill him with alarm. He stood again and took a wobbly step forward. He had to get out of the tavern.

Harsh shouts and barked commands suddenly came from the door. Men wielding clubs barged inside. They shoved aside the women and went directly to the men who remained. The swaggering steps, loose pantaloons, and tarred cocked hats identified them as sailors. But it was the painted red crowns that sent panic slithering through every muscle.

These sailors were from the Royal Navy. A press gang. And they had only one job. To find men—willing or not—to serve on the king's ships.

Newton bolted forward, frantic to reach a door or a window. But his footsteps swerved, and he found himself tripping over an upside-down bench. He crashed to the floor. Before he could get up, a stout, pockmark-faced man stood above him.

"Where ye think you're running off to, lad?" The man reached out a ruddy hand and grabbed Newton by the back of his waistcoat.

"Just heading out to relieve myself," Newton replied, the fog in his brain clearing enough for him to know he had to escape. "You wouldn't want me wetting my pants, now would you?"

The man cracked a grin that revealed a browned top front tooth next to several gaps where he'd lost other teeth—likely to scurvy. "Ye can come with me nice and easy, lad," the man said. "Or we can do this the hard way. It's your choice."

"Nice and easy suits me." Newton pretended to submit. But as the man reached for the chain hanging at his belt, Newton attempted to make another dash for the back exit. His feet wouldn't work the way he needed them to. His body had lost its speed and agility. Before he could take two steps, something long and narrow crashed into his back. It came with such speed and fury that Newton cried out from the excruciating pain and sank to his knees.

He glanced behind him in time to see the stout sailor lifting his wooden club again. Newton crouched and covered his head with his arms just as the club came down a second time. A crack against his forearms had protected his head, but the bruising pain in his arms was unbearable. Instinctively he curled into a ball, tucking his head low and trying to protect himself from a concussion or worse.

The blows rained down on his back, battering his flesh and bones with such force that for a moment Newton thought he must have passed out. The next thing he knew, the stout sailor had chains around both of his wrists and was dragging him across the tavern floor slickened by blood and spilled ale.

When they reached the tavern doorway, the sailor jerked Newton to his feet mindless of the chains digging into his wrists. He propelled Newton toward several other men who were bleeding and battered and chained, standing with their heads down in clear dejection.

"We were told we'd find at least one sailor here among the lot of ye," Newton's captor said, giving him a shove toward the others.

*Were told?*

Through his pain and dizziness, Newton tried to make sense of the sailor's words. Had someone purposefully tipped off the press gang to his presence inside the tavern?

"But none of ye look sturdy enough for the sailing life," continued the sailor, "except for ye." He jabbed Newton with this club.

Newton didn't respond. Press gangs prized men with previous sailing experience over landlubbers. If he admitted he was a sailor, his chances of escape would dwindle to nil. He'd do best to say nothing and to act completely ignorant of sailing or the sea. Then at least he might have a chance of freeing himself. Although ignorance wouldn't mean much if the navy was desperate for men to fill the ships.

He took his place at the back of the short line and hung his head like the rest of the men. As the sailors of the press gang shoved them forward with their clubs, Newton stumbled. Although his mind was still numb from the effects of all his drinking, he knew he'd gotten himself into a terrible predicament.

He hadn't thought he could sink any lower or that things could get any worse. But they had. Much, much worse.

# TWELVE

ewton huddled in a corner of the twelve-foot-square gaol and folded his arms across his chest, attempting to find some warmth in the unheated stone building. The small barred window was open to the elements, allowing in not only the daylight but also a cold dampness typical of February. His fingers and toes ached from the cold, and his entire body shivered uncontrollably.

The two men who'd been thrown into the gaol in the wee hours of the morning moaned. They lay on the dirt floor in front of the door where they'd been dumped. Their faces were as bludgeoned and bloody as the other men. He guessed from the way one of his eyes was swollen shut that his face was just as bruised.

In spite of his conscience telling him to reach out a hand and at least help the new prisoners sit up, Newton couldn't make himself move. Like the four who'd been caught with him, he'd had no food or water since he'd been shoved into the holding room yesterday. And a gong hadn't stopped resounding in his head since he'd woken up at dawn.

His mind was finally clearing enough to know exactly what had happened. He'd gotten himself so inebriated that he'd lost his ability to think clearly. As a result, he'd been the perfect candidate for capture by a Royal Navy press gang.

Newton beat his palm against his forehead. Why had he been so careless? Why had he allowed himself to get so drunk? Especially in Chatham so close to the naval ships? He should have gone to visit his great-uncle in Maidstone as his father had encouraged him to do again this year. Of course, his father only wanted him to stay in his uncle's good graces and so set himself in a position to inherit something. But Newton had been too excited to see Polly to heed his father's instructions.

He should have left Chatham. Or at the very least he should have stopped imbibing earlier. Or he shouldn't have started in the first place. Then he would have had his wits about him when the sailors barged into the tavern. He was quick enough to elude any man. And certainly strong enough to fight back.

Now here he was stuck in a holding cell until the press gang had caught enough unsuspecting men to fulfill their captain's quota. Some of the men said that the HMS *Harwich* was riding at anchor just outside the port and that her lower deck was undermanned.

Even as they lay in the dark, foul-smelling gaol, the shouts and bawdy calls of sailors along with the waft of the damp sea air, told him the hovel was near the river, likely next to the Victualling Yard. Most of the Chatham ships were dependent upon Deptford, which had the largest Victualling Yard due to its close proximity to London wharves and markets. But Chatham still managed to retain a small yard with enough stores so that some of the naval ships due to set sail could be loaded up with provisions and preserved foodstuffs like hardtack, salted beef and pork, peas, oatmeal, butter, cheese, and beer.

"Fool," he murmured to himself.

"What did you call me?" the man next to him said in a gravelly voice, his body visibly stiffening.

"I'm calling myself a fool," Newton said, tempted to bang his head into the stone wall instead of his palm. "I should have known not to be anywhere near the waterfront."

Hadn't he recently spoken with Mr. Catlett of the imminence of the invasion from France? He'd known the king was preparing for battle and outfitting his ships. And he'd been a complete fool to take a chance at showing himself publicly anywhere in the area. Not when every captain of every naval vessel was in search of more men, especially men with sailing experience.

No matter how hated the practice of impressment was, and no matter how much people complained, recruitment of sailors by force had been lawful in England since the days of Queen Elizabeth. Once impressed upon a Royal Navy vessel, there was no way to leave. Except by desertion, which was an offense punishable by death.

Of course in recent years, Parliament had passed some legislation attempting to regulate the practice of impressment to make it more humane. Newton glanced at the man closest to the door lying in a pool of his own blood and vomit. He gave a snort of derision.

Humane? He wouldn't live to see the day when press gangs were humane. The navy wasn't concerned about treating any man with dignity. They simply needed more hands for their guns along with all the heavy lifting and hauling of supplies, powder, cartridges, and canons.

"If only Prince Charles, that pretender, would stay in France where he belongs," Newton muttered under his breath.

"It's the Scottish Jacobites stirring up the trouble," said the man next to him. "It's always the Highland Scots."

Newton rubbed his arms for warmth and blew the heat of his breath into his hands. And now the Scots and the French were ruining his life.

"We'll have to say extra prayers that young prince slinks back to his mummy with his tail between his legs," said another of the men. "Then the navy won't need us and will release us."

Newton nodded, needing to cling to any hope he could get.

But the man next to him cackled. "Even if there's no war with France, the navy won't let us go. No how, no way. They'll put us to work and keep us until we die or desert. Whichever comes first."

Newton stared at the door handle and wished he had some way to break it open. Then he'd run far away, which is what he should have done yesterday. But even as he thought of all that had transpired during his last moments with Polly and being forced to leave her home, heaviness settled over him, twisting his heart.

He hadn't intended for things to turn out with her the way they had. He'd wanted to prove himself worthy of her love. He'd wanted to win the favor of the Catletts. He'd wanted them to love him like a son.

Now he'd earned their displeasure. He could only imagine what Mr. Catlett would say to him if they reclined together in those worn chairs in his study, how disappointed he'd be. Mr. Catlett had warned him not to hurt Polly. And now he'd done the very thing he'd sworn he wouldn't do.

Why had he sat down on the blasted bench next to Polly? He'd noticed when Eliza left the drawing room, and he'd taken quick advantage of the opportunity to be alone with Polly. He wanted a chance to be near her for just a minute. After all the days of being around her but always at a safe distance, he wanted a moment of being close. He never meant to kiss her.

If only he'd been a stronger man. If only he had resisted the temptation.

He lowered his face into his hands. The truth was, he'd never been very good at resisting temptations. He always gave in to his desires too easily. And this time, look where it had gotten him.

"John Newton."

He thought for a moment he heard her sweet voice speaking his name. Perhaps the beating, his hangover, and his lack of food and water were making him hallucinate.

"Is John Newton still being held here?" That was no hallucination.

Newton sat up. The four other lucid men were staring at the window. Was it possible that Polly was here?

With an energy borne of desperation, he dragged himself off the floor and stood on shaky legs. Every inch of his body ached, and he could hardly make his feet work to hobble toward the window. He forced down a groan at the pain radiating up and down his back and shoulders where he'd taken the worst of the beating.

When he reached the window, he grasped the bars to keep himself from sinking to his knees. There on the other side, beginning to walk away, was Polly. Her head was down, and she was hurrying as though she didn't want anyone to see her near the gaol.

"Polly," he called, hoarse and desperate.

At the mention of her name, she spun. Her coat hung open, revealing a robin's-egg blue bodice and overskirt. Her hair was pinned loosely, and her flat-crowned straw hat was tilted as though she'd hastily donned it. She carried the basket she normally used for delivering her father's noon meal but had neglected to don her gloves.

"John!" she cried, her beautiful angelic features drawn with worry. When she ran back to the window, his heart gave a *thump* of relief that she was eager to see him, that she wasn't rejecting him just because her mother had.

She stopped abruptly a foot away, and her eyes widened at the sight of him.

He knew he looked like a monster with dried blood caked on his face, his eye swollen shut, and the bruises discoloring his skin.

"Oh John." She hid her trembling lips behind her hand, but she couldn't hide the tears in her eyes.

"I look worse than I feel," he lied. He'd never felt so awful, but he wouldn't distress her any more than she already was. "I'm just sorry I couldn't make myself more presentable," he said, trying to form a grin, but even that movement was too painful.

She dropped her hand from her mouth and seemed to silently chastise herself to be strong. She took a deep breath and then forced her lips into a tremulous smile. "We just got the news that you were pressed. Our servant heard it at market this morning."

"Aye, I was foolish enough to be in the wrong place at the wrong time." He hoped she couldn't smell the stink of rum on him and guess that he'd been drunk.

"Isn't there anything you can do to get out of it?" A thread of desperation wound through her voice and lined her face.

The desperation flowed into him, reminding him of the helplessness of his situation. "Could you send a message to my father?" he asked. "Mayhap he can free me." He wasn't sure what his father could do, but surely with his connections in the shipping industry, the captain could find a way to get him out of this predicament somehow.

"I'll send a note to him at once," Polly said, stepping closer to the barred window. She lifted the linen draped across the basket and pulled out a small jug. "I've brought you warm milk." She handed the jug to him, but it wouldn't fit between the bars.

He slanted the mouth of the jug in as far as it would go and bent his head to drink from it. He guzzled the milk, letting the creamy liquid soothe his burning throat and relieve the bitterness in his mouth. He took several long swigs until nothing more remained.

"Thank you," he said when he relinquished the jug back into her hands.

"I also brought you bread and cheese." She lifted the items out of the basket and passed them through the bars.

He was tempted to devour them both on the spot. But he held himself back. He'd already embarrassed himself enough with her and wanted to maintain some of his dignity. Besides, he wanted to share what he had with his fellow prisoners. He couldn't allow them to suffer while he filled his belly.

As if sensing his thoughts, she retrieved another loaf of bread from the basket. "For the others," she said, handing it to him.

His affection for her rose swiftly and made his throat ache with the pressure. He'd never met a woman like Polly Catlett. And he couldn't bear the thought of losing her. "No matter what happens, promise you'll never forget about me."

"You'll be set free," she said. "You have to be. Your father will find a way."

"Mayhap." Or mayhap once his father learned that he'd skipped out on the merchant-ship job, he'd be so livid that he'd decide to let him rot in prison.

Polly glanced over her shoulder as though to gauge who else might be nearby. Only Eliza stood a discreet distance away near a stone wall and stairway that likely led down to the wharves and the Customs House.

As much as he wanted Polly to stay and talk with him, she and Eliza weren't safe, not with scores of sailors roaming about the area. "You should go," he said reluctantly.

"Charlie Baldock and his gang left the area," she said. "That's why Billy came by yesterday. To let us know that we're safe."

Newton tried to make sense of what Polly was telling him through the lingering hangover haze. Charlie and his men had likely gone away when they learned that the press gangs were out in full force in the area. They'd gone farther inland for the time being to avoid any run-ins. At least Polly could walk about town again without worrying about Charlie.

Apparently Billy had known about the press gangs yesterday . . .

Newton's mind scrambled to make sense of the news and to remember all the things Billy had said to him during their heated encounter. Hadn't Billy told him his days were numbered in Chatham, that he was planning to send Charlie's thugs down on him? But if Billy had already known that the smuggler gang had left Chatham, then mayhap Billy had been plotting something else.

A sickening lump formed in the pit of Newton's stomach. Somewhere in the fog of his mind, he recalled hearing that someone had informed the press gang that a sailor was at the Old Neptune Tavern. Had that someone been Billy? After all, Billy had seen him enter, had known he was a sailor, and had obviously wanted him to leave Chatham.

"Billy said that with the chance of war with France, Charlie will have to lay low for a while," Polly continued. "And that I won't have anything to worry about."

The sickening lump only grew larger until the weight of it threatened to drag Newton down. The more he pondered all that had happened, the more sense it made that Billy had been the one to point the press gang in his direction. Of course Billy would have nothing to worry about since he was working for the Customs House and thus the king. He didn't have to fear impressment and so could easily have spoken with members of the press gang.

Newton had the sudden urge to blurt out his suspicions to Polly, to warn her to stay away from Billy, to at the very least ruin her good favor of the donkey. But uncertainty held him back. He couldn't be sure that Billy had indeed turned him in. And besides, while he was gone, Billy would watch over Polly. For all his faults, Billy would never let any harm come to her.

"Polly, listen," he said. "You're still not safe here, not even with Eliza. There are too many sailors in the area for you to be down here unchaperoned."

"Eliza and I are just fine—"

"Nay." There were too many sailors like him, who'd be getting drunk in the taverns. It was much too dangerous for two beautiful, innocent young women to be wandering around, even in daylight hours. "Don't come back to the gaol unless you have Billy or your father with you."

His voice must have been serious enough to give her pause, for her lips stalled around her rebuttal. He grabbed hold of the window bars, wishing he could rip them away and reach for her. But he was in no condition to hold or touch her, not when he was so filthy and foul.

"Go on now," he quietly urged her, though his heart longed for her to stay.

She surprised him by reaching up to the bars and wrapping her fingers around his. The warmth of her flesh enveloped his. The softness, the tenderness, the smoothness . . . For an instant he was back in the drawing room with her lips against his.

Her pretty blue eyes focused on his mouth for just an instant. It was enough for him to realize she was thinking about their kiss too. A flush rose in her cheeks. She broke her contact with his hands and folded her arms across her chest.

"I'll bring you anything you need." She stepped back. "What do you need the most?"

He was tempted to shout out that he needed her more than food or drink, more than freedom, more than life itself. But he could feel the eyes of his fellow prisoners upon his back. They were listening to every word he spoke and were likely anxious to have some of the provisions she'd brought.

"I'll be fine, Polly," he finally managed. "Don't worry about me."

She nodded once. "I'll have my father dispatch a message to Captain Newton at once."

He nodded in return. Then she turned and crossed briskly to Eliza. Without a backward glance, she linked arms with her sister and together they descended the stairs and were gone. He stared at the spot where she'd stood and tried to picture her again. He had the awful, gut-wrenching realization that he'd likely said good-bye to her for the last time.

## THIRTEEN

*T*hree more men were added to their prison. But one of them became deathly ill and was removed from their midst, leaving a total of nine. Newton considered whether he might be able to fake an illness for himself as a means of escape. But he had the feeling the navy wouldn't let him go that easily.

Thankfully, the victualling officer began to deliver food and water to them twice a day. Mr. Catlett also stopped by with provisions, including a coat. Newton wished Polly had come with her father but had the suspicion that Mr. Catlett had forbade her from going anywhere near the gaol. Newton missed her terribly and almost wished she would disobey her father and sneak down to the gaol anyway, even though he himself had told her not to come unchaperoned.

By the third day of captivity, he'd grown as morose as the other prisoners and lost hope that he'd find a way out until an officer opened the door and called his name. The officer bound him in chains before leading him out of the gaol and into the victualling building next door.

He was guided past a first-floor office that likely belonged to the agent victualler in charge of the storehouses, brewery, bakery, and any other facilities on the site and led him to a sparsely furnished room that had only two chairs on either side of a plain table. The whitewashed walls had a few rusty flecks, and Newton hoped they weren't bloodstains from some other sailor they'd battered.

Newton sat down without urging from the officer and was surprised when the young man exited and closed the door behind him. Newton sized up the room's only window. It was too high and narrow for him to use as an escape. And even if it had been bigger, Newton wasn't sure how he'd manage such a feat in his chains.

He suspected they'd brought him to the room to question him about his abilities. But he set his jaw tight, planning to not say a word about his past experiences as a sailor. They could torture him all they wanted, but he wouldn't admit to anything.

Footsteps clapped hollowly in the hallway and drew nearer, and then the door handle rattled. He ought to arise from his chair in respect for his authorities. But he couldn't make himself do it. When the door swung open, he stared insolently at his chained hands folded on top of the table. They were lined with grime and blood—his blood.

Someone stepped into the room, and the door closed again. Newton didn't move to acknowledge the new arrival. Finally, the newcomer released a long sigh, one that could fill a sail with the fullness of its disappointment. At the familiarity of it, Newton's head jerked up. He found himself looking into his father's sea-weathered face. The grooves at the corners of his eyes were especially deep, reflecting a sadness that made Newton shift on his chair.

Captain Newton was attired in a gray powdered wig that had side curls. He wore what appeared to be a new suit. At the very least, the breeches and coat were crisp and clean, with ruffles from his shirt-sleeve showing at the edge, advertising his growing wealth.

"Captain," Newton said, pushing away from the table and rising in deference to his father. "Thank you for coming." His father was an important man, well respected among both merchant and naval vessels. If anyone could save him from impressment, surely his father could.

"I was working in Deptford when I received the news. I came right away." His father's job was very similar to the naval victualler's, except that he worked outfitting merchant vessels. Newton had no doubt his father was incredibly busy right now in light of the imminent war with France. But he didn't seem unduly angry that he'd had to travel to Chatham.

Surely now that he was here, he would put things aright, just as he always did. Newton slid back down into his chair before his weak legs gave out. "I figured you could do something—"

"Why are you still here?" His father's tone turned decidedly clipped and frustrated.

Newton lifted his chained hands. "Does it look like I have a choice?"

His father crossed to the table in two long strides and slammed his palm against the plank so hard that it banged like a gunshot. Newton jumped and was half-surprised the officer didn't return to the room to see if he'd been shot.

"You know what I mean." His father's voice was a low growl. With his palms still on the table, he hunched over Newton and scowled down at him.

So much for his assumption that the captain wasn't unduly angry. He shouldn't have expected otherwise. That's the way things were between them. Never happy. Never easy. Never cordial for very long, if at all.

"You should have been on the *Astrea* last week." His father spoke the words through clenched teeth.

"I decided I wasn't ready to leave."

"When you returned from your recent voyage and asked me for help, I thought, John's finally growing up. John's finally being responsible." The captain's voice rose with each sentence. "So I asked for a favor from a friend, found you a good position. And what did you do?" He was practically shouting now. "You threw it away. Again!"

Newton wanted to defend himself, to share his plans to find work close to the Catletts so that he could help them financially as well as continue to make sure Polly was safe, but before he could speak, his father slapped his hands against the table, causing it to slam into Newton's chest. The force nearly knocked his chair backward.

"You threw it away just like you did the job in Jamaica!" His father yelled.

"I'm sorry—"

"And now look at you!" His father's appraisal was distressed. "Look at the trouble you're in as a result of your foolishness."

"Mayhap I should have gone last week," Newton admitted. At least then he would have had a certain job. And he could have saved his earnings to send back to the Catletts.

"Mayhap?" Again his father's voice rose. He backed toward the door as though he'd heard enough.

The movement sent a burst of panic through Newton. He couldn't let his father leave yet. Not without making some effort to get him out of the impressment. If he had to grovel at his father's feet to get the help, so be it. "I'm sorry, Father," he said again. "I know I let you down. It's just that whenever I'm with Polly I can't think straight."

"It isn't just this woman that's the problem," his father replied in a hollow voice. "You've always been irresponsible."

The defeat in his father's tone and posture pummeled Newton harder than his father's fists ever could. Apparently, he was an absolute failure in his father's eyes, in every way. There seemed to be nothing worthwhile and lovable about him anymore, if there ever had been.

An ache squeezed Newton's throat. "I'll try to do better, sir."

The captain nodded, although it was a dismayed half nod that said, *I'll believe it when I see it.*

"If you're able to help me now, I promise I won't let you down again." In his deepest heart, he meant it. He wished he could be the kind of man his father wanted. He wished for once he could make his father proud of him instead of always disappointing him.

"I've spent the morning talking with First Lieutenant Thomas Ruffin," his father said.

"Ruffin?"

"He's in charge of the platoon authorized to impress men for the HMS *Harwich.*"

Newton nodded in anticipation.

"He's agreed to recommend you to Captain Carteret."

"I don't understand."

"With your experience, I've convinced him to ask the captain to consider you for an appointment to the quarterdeck as a midshipman."

"I don't want an appointment. I want a release."

"It would be a prestigious award. You'd be a subofficer in training—"

"I could care less if I'm awarded first mate or even captain of the ship itself."

"You better!" His father's voice escalated again. "As midshipman, you'll be in line for promotion to the rank of lieutenant."

"The only thing I care about," Newton yelled back, "is staying as far away from that ship as possible."

"After all I've gone through to make these arrangements, you better not ruin it. Not again." The captain's eyes glittered with angry warning.

Newton could only stare at his father in complete frustration. This wasn't what he wanted. He had expected his father to help him out of this predicament. Not enmesh him into it further. Newton shoved the table, and it scraped across the floor. If his hands hadn't been chained, he would have pounded them into something. "Apparently you don't care that I'll be going off to war."

"Of course I care." His father's voice was low and agonized, and he glanced to the door as though anyone could be listening to their conversation. "Do you really think I want my son on a naval vessel, even one as big and new as the *Harwich*?"

Newton's angry response fell to the wayside.

"Don't you think I tried to get you transferred to a merchant ship? Don't you think I've pulled from every favor owed me to get you out of this press?"

"Then why didn't you?" Newton couldn't hold back his desperation.

"I've bribed, cajoled, and pleaded all morning," his father whispered hoarsely. "And this is the best I could do for you."

Newton slumped in his chair.

His father's broad shoulders sank, and he hung his head as though overcome by weariness and defeat.

Newton knew he should be grateful to his father for his efforts. His father had likely ridden through the night to arrive in Chatham first thing this morning. He'd groveled and pleaded on his behalf. He'd done the best he could to rectify a terrible situation. But his efforts had been for naught, and Newton couldn't conjure any thankfulness for the possible promotion.

"Rumors say the French army that was assembled at Dunkirk has now boarded ships," his father offered weakly. "The invasion could happen any day."

"Mayhap you can try to plead for my release directly with the captain—"

"Don't you understand, John?" his father shouted. "We're going to war with France. And the navy won't grant any favors. Not this time. Not to anyone."

Newton stared at the chains that bound his wrists. The heavy iron bands were cold and chafed his wrists. He could apparently no more free himself from the impressment than he could from the immovable metal that weighed upon his hands. He was stuck.

"What's done is done." His father's voice was low and resigned. "And now you must serve your king and country with honor."

Serve with honor? Devil be hanged. After the navy had beaten him senseless, bound him in chains, and then forced him into a position he didn't want, how could anyone expect him to serve with honor?

Nay, he would not give the navy his best effort. Nay, he would not give them any more than he had to, certainly not his life. He'd only do what he absolutely had to, and the first opportunity he had, he'd find a way to leave.

He stood abruptly, letting his chair tip over backward and clatter to the floor. He didn't look at his father as he brushed past him and opened the door. The officer standing guard in the hallway outside the room straightened in surprise.

Newton held out his chains. "Aye, then. You can take me back to the gaol."

The officer glanced toward his father with raised brows. Then with a shrug, the young officer took Newton's chains and began to lead him down the hallway toward the front door of the Victualling Office building. With every step Newton took, he could feel his father watching him, silently pleading with him to turn around, to understand that he'd done all he could, to recognize the effort he'd made.

Newton stared straight ahead, his gut churning with too much anger and resentment. If he had to go, he'd do it without any more complaints. He'd do it like a man. But he'd be sure his father—and everyone else—knew that he didn't like or approve of the injustice he'd been dealt.

Polly stood by the iron gate and peered down the road. The March day was warmer than any they'd had of late, which was just as well, since she'd been standing waiting for her father's appearance for the past hour. The late afternoon sunlight was beginning to fade and tinge the sky and clouds with faint pink. Although the winter wasn't quite over, the first green of spring was showing in the grass. In the distance she could hear the song of a marsh warbler having returned from the south.

The *yap-yap* of a dog drew her attention to the neighbor's yard. Miss Donovan had stepped outside with Prince. At a shout from inside the house, the young woman hurried after her dog and shushed him, her lean face wreathed in anxiety.

While Prince hadn't had any further runaway escapades, Polly had noticed that Miss Donovan hovered closer to the dog whenever he was outside. In fact, Prince never came out without Miss Donovan following it wherever it went.

Prince yapped again, and Miss Donovan bent and picked up the little dog, holding him like an infant and talking to him in a low affectionate tone that Polly couldn't help but hear. She placed a tender kiss on his curly white head.

At that moment Miss Donovan happened to glance up and catch Polly staring. Polly quickly returned her attention to the road and prayed she hadn't offended the woman with her staring.

For a long moment the neighbors' yard was silent, and Polly began to think Miss Donovan had gone inside. But then the woman spoke. "I didn't have the chance to express my gratitude to you for finding Prince." Eliza had been the one to take the dog to Miss Donovan since Polly had been too distraught.

"I'm happy that you have him back." Polly squirmed in embarrassment. Had Miss Donovan learned of the circumstances under which she'd found Prince and her father's resulting demotion? Was that why she was thanking her?

Miss Donovan ducked her head. "When you next see your young sailor, I'd be obliged if you'd thank him as well."

"Of course." Polly could feel herself flushing at Miss Donovan's insinuation that John was her sailor. Had she heard John was impressed too?

Miss Donovan made a move to turn and retreat but hesitated. "I'm sorry for your troubles and the impressment."

Polly nodded. Before she could think of a polite response, Miss Donovan was making her way back to the house. Apparently everyone in Chatham knew about her father's fall from favor and John's impressment.

It was several days since Polly heard that nine pressed men were rowed out in a tender to the HMS *Harwich* and that John was among them. Just yesterday, her father came home with word that Prince Charles was about to board the French ships that would bring him to England for an invasion when a fierce storm blew through the channel and stopped him. The storm had apparently grown so wild that it dispersed the French fleet anchored there. It seemed that many French ships had been damaged and that the invasion plans had been abandoned.

Surely today her father would know more about the situation. Surely he would bring her word that John would be set free. Without an attack, what need did the navy have of so many sailors? Maybe by this time tomorrow she'd see John again. He'd be waiting for her in the drawing room and sneak up behind her the way he did once before.

At the clomp of distant hooves and the sight of a horse and rider, Polly smiled and opened the gate. Finally, her father was coming. She began walking toward him and was rewarded with his tender smile and a wave of his hand.

"To what occasion do I deserve the honor of your sweet greeting this evening?" Father asked, reining his horse and sliding down. He drew her into a brief embrace. His tall body was lean, almost gangly, but he exuded a strength and solidness that always made her feel safe.

She pulled back and tucked her slender hand into his large one, just as she'd done when she was a little girl. "I was eager to see you," she started, overcome with embarrassment at the thought of broaching the subject of John with him. She walked for a moment in silence, swinging her hand in his as he led the horse with the other.

"And . . ." Father said. He was too perceptive. No doubt he could guess there was more eagerness to her this evening than his arrival home could warrant.

"I was hoping you'd have more information on what's become of the impressed sailors?" she said, focusing on the dirt road in front of her.

Her father didn't say anything for a moment, which only made her more embarrassed.

"Will they be released, now that we won't be going to war with France?"

Father walked in silence a few more steps before sighing. "I'm afraid we'll still see war with France before ere long."

"But if the French fleet was damaged?"

"They will find a way to fight anyway," he said quietly, almost bitterly.

The hope that she'd allowed to grow all day began to deflate, taking with it her energy and her enthusiasm. "Why must we wage war? Why must brother pick up arms against brother? Why cannot men resolve to live at peace with one another?"

She knew she was spouting the words Susanna had used with her on occasion when she'd protested violence. Susanna had likely developed such thoughts during her activities with the Quakers, who opposed not only slavery but also warfare. But England had been at odds with France as far back as Henry V, if not longer. It was wishful thinking to expect that an age-old rivalry would end during her lifetime.

Her father sighed wearily. "As long as men continue to harbor hate and greed in their hearts, unfortunately we will continue to have war."

As they reached the gate in the fence that surrounded the Catlett home, she slowed her steps and Father did too. She turned with her father down the side lane that led to the stable behind the house. "Even so, surely the navy won't have need for quite so many men."

Her father stopped and faced her. "Polly." His voice was gentle and knowing.

She reached for Pete, who'd come out to greet her, his long fluffy tail twitching in anticipation of a treat. He was no longer the wiry kitten John had rescued from the tree, but she still thought of him as such anyway. She scratched his head, attempting to ignore her father's probing eyes.

"The navy won't release John," he said. "You'll need to resign yourself to the fact that he's there to stay."

She rubbed Pete's back and received a head bump against her leg as a result. Why did father always have to be so honest? Why couldn't he give her platitudes? Or even a tiny thread of hope to cling to?

"I like John," her father continued, "but I'm afraid that he's lacking some qualities that I would want in a suitor for you."

Flames seemed to leap into her face at the bluntness of his words. She supposed her father was referring to the kiss she'd shared with John. She was every bit as much to blame for it as he was. Surely her parents couldn't fault him alone.

"Of course I don't approve of his forwardness with you," her father said, as though reading her mind. "But in spite of his indiscretion, I noticed a general lack of ambition and responsibility on his part."

"He just doesn't know what he wants to do yet." She felt as though she owed him some defense.

"That might be true. However, he should take measures to define the course of his life and have the means to provide before pursuing a woman."

She couldn't disagree with her father. Even if John didn't have much to offer her, he still needed to have something. Although he'd teased her enough about their relationship, they'd never spoken of him becoming a suitor. But after he'd kissed her, she couldn't remain naive to the fact that the bantering and friendship was no longer a safe boundary. More existed between them, whether she wanted to admit it or not.

As though sensing her distress, Pete rubbed his whole body against her. She scratched his neck, and the rumble of his purr reverberated against her fingers.

"What concerns me most," her father said, his voice growing more serious, "is that I don't know the condition of John's faith. Right now, he seems to be troubled and straying off course."

"He's shared his struggles," she replied. During their composing for his mother's hymns, he'd hinted at his doubts about God's love. She sensed that he didn't want to be irreverent to the memory of his mother, but at the same time, he'd treated the words more like pretty poetry than truth.

Father shifted the horse's reins and then squeezed her shoulder gently. "As hard as it is to watch John taken away in chains, I can't help but think that maybe this is God's way of protecting you from a potentially difficult situation."

She wanted to shake her head in denial. Surely John wasn't a threat she needed protecting from. But even as she tried to deny her father, her own conscience reminded her of her previous misgivings regarding him. Even if he could eventually provide for her, she couldn't consider becoming unequally yoked.

"I'm sorry, Polly. But I think it's best for you not to get your heart set on John." He waited quietly a moment, and as much as she wanted to ignore him, she couldn't disrespect or contradict him, no matter how much her heart protested his opinion of John.

She finally nodded.

After a moment's hesitation, her father led the horse toward the stable, his footsteps slower and heavier than before.

She absently scratched Pete's back as he arched into her fingers. Her heart ached with the knowledge that she not only wouldn't see John today or anytime soon, but also that if she truly wanted to obey her father, she would need to put John out of her mind altogether.

But how could she possibly put him out of her thoughts when he was woven there as surely as fine silken embroidery threads? How could she rip him out? And did she even want to?

# FOURTEEN

SEPTEMBER 1744

*A*ll loaded!" roared a nearby master gunner as his loader finished inserting the cartridge, a wool bag of black powder.

Newton ducked under a beam of the lower deck and peered out the nearest gunport. The French ship *Solide* was still in the line of battle and had been for nearly two hours. The foremast had split in half, the stern was afire from a direct hit, and the mizzen topgallant sail was hanging into the North Sea. Even though she was badly crippled, the French man-of-war kept fighting.

Devil take her. Would she ever give up?

Sweat mingling with soot dripped down his forehead and stung his eyes. His nostrils burned from the acridness of sulfur, and his head ached from the constant blasts from the HMS *Harwich*'s guns. Even though the two-decker was holding her own against the *Solide*, he'd heard reports that their rigging had suffered damage too.

"Prime!" the gunner yelled again, instructing the five men manning the cannon to ready it for another shot. One of the men rammed the bag of powder in place, and then the ventsman drove his priming wire down through the vent hole, puncturing the cartridge and exposing some powder.

Up and down the lower deck, each of the twelve cannon crews had been working nonstop. As midshipmen, Newton and another officer had been overseeing their efforts, coordinating their fire, and shouting orders. Another twelve cannons were firing from the middle deck above them. They brought their greatest weight of broadside guns to bear, but Newton wasn't sure it would be enough to dominate the gun ship of the French, which had sixty-four guns compared to their fifty.

"Get those matches lit," he called to one of the powder monkeys, a young lad no older than twelve. The whites of the boy's eyes were wide amid the black soot that covered his face. The long rope shook in his hands, but he managed to light it.

"Good," Newton called, as he watched the boy blow on it to keep it from going out.

Newton continued his way down the line of cannons. His neck and back ached from his stooped position. Only the powder monkeys and shortest sailors could stand at full height below deck. The ship was built to carry the maximum number of guns and men without sinking or being cumbersome in maneuvering. Comfort was the last thing on the designers' minds.

Even though the *Harwich* was close enough to the *Solide* to exchange the cannon fire, the tossing of the ship made aim difficult. Newton figured it was a miracle every time one of their cannon balls actually hit a target.

He wiped his shirt-sleeve across his eyes. For a September day, it was warm. But below deck, with the heat of the cannon fire, the choking smoke, and the cramped quarters, the conditions were nearly unbearable. Already two men had passed out.

If damage from the heat was the worst of their bodily injuries, he'd be grateful. He'd heard a man on the quarterdeck was hurt when a ball hit their main topsail and the rigging fell, but no one had been killed.

As much as he hated life aboard the naval vessel, they'd been lucky so far. They'd spent most of the spring and summer escorting convoys of merchant vessels. They'd traveled to Scotland, then to Ostend in Belgium, Gothenburg in Sweden, and Helsingør in Denmark. But apparently a run-in with the French had been inevitable.

Daily he cursed the French for persisting in war even though the early spring storm had prevented Prince Charles from his attempt at invasion and reclaiming the throne. Twelve French transport ships had sunk, including seven that went down with all hands. Many were calling it a "Protestant Wind" brought by God to keep the Catholic prince out of England. But of course Newton only scoffed at such superstition. The violent storms were typical of the conditions during the spring equinox in the English Channel and North Sea. Anyone stupid enough to attempt a crossing at that time of year deserved to be battered and lashed.

The French had abandoned plans for a second attempt at invasion, and the majority of the French force had marched to Flanders to fight British allies, the Dutch and the Hanoverians. Nevertheless, in April, the *Harwich*'s entire ship's company had gathered on upper decks to hear Captain Carteret read the declaration of war with France. Only the devil had any idea why England was continuing to fight this war. All Newton knew was that he was trapped. Indefinitely. And that thought fanned a slow hot flame in his gut, fueling his anger more than anything else.

"Aye now, mates, make every shot count!" he yelled at his men, his fury rising once again. "Let's bring the French she-dogs down once and for all." Maybe if they blasted every French ship out of the North Sea, they'd finally be set free to return to their normal lives.

The only light afforded to them was what came through the open gunports, which were filled with the cannons and blocked by the men manning them. The haze of smoke left from previous rounds darkened the deck even further.

"Ready!" Newton called, his throat dry and scratchy.

Farther down the deck fellow midshipman Job Lewis was calling orders to the men near him. Newton waved and tried to catch Lewis's attention so that they could launch their volleys at the same time.

Lewis waved back.

"Light the fuses!" Newton yelled.

The powder monkeys handed off the slow burning ropes that they'd already lit. The nimblest and most quick-footed of the men crouched and simultaneously touched the fuses on the cannons with the burning ropes.

Newton braced himself. The rocking force and the deafening roar came a moment later. He, along with the rest of the men, attempted to peer past the smoky openings as the coconut-sized balls flew across the water toward the *Solide*.

The first ball hit the broadside of the middle deck followed by a burst of light and explosion. It was dead on target, and Newton let out a whoop with the others at the fire that leapt into the air. From what he could tell, another of the balls had rammed into the fore-castle and caused a brief explosion.

A distant boom alerted them to the volley now headed their way. The gunners rapidly moved the cannons back out of harm's way before crouching a safe distance from the gunports along the side of the ship. Several of the men began the futile act of praying out loud.

An explosion sounded far above causing the ship to sway. New-ton guessed that a ball had hit one of their masts, adding to the wreckage among the sails and rigging. But better the rigging than the decks. After a moment of silence, he rose with the others, relieved that another round of the battle was over. Had it been enough to make the French ship finally give up?

Before he could straighten, a crash came from the aft gunport, followed by the splintering of wood and an explosive blast. Shouts and screams of agony mingled together.

Newton bumped his head against the overhead beam, but he was too concerned about the destruction at the last gunport to care about himself. He stumbled toward the destruction, trailing behind Lewis, who was praying fervently.

"You're just muttering nonsense to make yourself feel better." Newton called to Lewis whose fair hair and shirt were plastered to his body as surely as if he'd dunked himself in the water barrel. "Save your breath for something that really matters."

Lewis didn't respond, his attention focused on an unmoving form on the deck ahead. Several other men were down too, moaning and cradling injured body parts. Jagged pieces of wood littered the floor, and as Newton passed by one injured gunner, he could see a splinter protruding from the man's arm.

"Someone go after the surgeon," Newton called toward the foredeck. "We have injured men that need tending."

Without waiting to see if his order was obeyed, Newton knelt next to the unmoving form sprawled on the deck amidst the wreckage. The light coming in from the gap in the broadside illuminated the victim's face. It was the powder monkey he'd spoken to only minutes ago. Now the boy's face and eyes were devoid of fear or even pain. The boy didn't move, not even to blink an eye. And when Newton glanced down, he saw why. A sharp slab of wood penetrated the boy's chest at his heart. Blood already soaked his shirt and formed a pool beneath his body. He was dead. Likely killed instantly.

Lewis, who was kneeling on the other side, closed the boy's eyelids, unable to hide the tremor in his fingers or to conceal the anguish in his face.

Swift fierce anger swelled in Newton's chest, and he clenched his hands to keep from smacking something. "Where was God when this boy needed him?" Newton whispered harshly.

Lewis didn't respond. He simply sat back on his heels and looked at the boy with utter and complete despair. At the cries of the wounded around them, Newton could only shake his head and curse fate and God.

The *Solide* was too battered to escape. Seven of the French crew had been killed and twenty seriously injured, including the captain, who'd had his leg blown off. The *Harwich* captured the severely damaged ship and took the French crew as prisoners of war.

Newton had hoped that the *Harwich* was crippled enough that they would have to go in for repairs to one of the Royal Dockyards, preferably Chatham. But the ship's carpenter and his crew made the repairs, and all chances of a landing fell away, leaving Newton more dismayed than ever.

As one of ten midshipmen, his work was relatively easy. Mostly he exercised authority over the sailors on the lower deck. Because of his previous experience, he had the task of teaching some of the newer recruits how to climb the rigging, furl and unfurl the sails, haul the capstan, and all of the other duties that sailors needed to know.

His position also gave him more privileges than an able-bodied seaman. He'd been assigned to sleep and mess in the quarterdeck at the stern, which afforded him more space and better food than the three hundred other sailors who hung their hammocks and ate wherever they could find room in the dark, crowded lower and middle decks.

Every once in a while, guilt pricked him and reminded him that he'd shown no gratitude to his father for making the arrangements for his promotion on board the *Harwich*. His life could have been a whole lot more miserable. Even so most of the time he let his anger fester, anger that he'd been impressed, anger at Captain Carteret for sending out the press gang to begin with, anger that he couldn't control his own life and was always under the heavy hand of someone else.

Although he'd done what he could in battle for the sake of those over whom he had charge, he found himself slipping into a melancholy that not even the rowdiest game of cards and round of drinking could penetrate, at least not for long. As autumn passed into winter, he began to drink more, oversleep, and doze on his watch; one night he missed his watch altogether. His superiors rebuked him, but he couldn't find the will to care. He even thought that if he made himself detestable, mayhap they'd cast him from the ship.

"You're headed for trouble," Lewis warned him one December evening as the cold north wind blew off the sea through the caulking and boards.

Newton took a sip of the rum he'd located in Reverend Topham's cabin. The chaplain had more than enough rum and wouldn't notice the disappearance of a bottle or two now and then. The captain had already disciplined the devout man of the cloth once for his drunkenness and would probably need to again.

"Aye. But just one look at Polly and I'd be right again," Newton remarked. He pulled out the white lacy handkerchief she'd given him long ago and brought it to his nose. He dragged in a deep breath, trying to recapture the scent of her that had disappeared from the delicate linen.

Lewis and several other junior officers sat at the table. The sway of the oil lantern above them cast ghoulish shadows around the tiny room. Lewis was in the process of polishing the brass buttons on his coat as he did every evening. And the others were playing their usual game of cards with stakes.

"If you miss her so blasted much," said one of the midshipmen taking in his pathetic pining over her handkerchief, "then why don't you take a day's leave and go see her?"

"Because I don't know how to swim to shore." And because after the way things had ended, he had no idea if Mr. and Mrs. Catlett would welcome him back even if he should have the chance to visit. Newton tucked the handkerchief back into his pocket where he kept it at all times. His mates had ribbed him often enough about Polly, and he wasn't in the mood for any teasing tonight. "Smite my timbers, if I could swim, I'd have jumped ship long ago."

"I hear we're anchoring soon in the Downs," said Mitchell, the captain's clerk. "At Deal in Kent."

The bottle of rum froze midway between the table and Newton's mouth. "How far is Deal from Chatham?" His mind was too hazy to do the calculations for himself.

"It's a few hours' hard ride," one of the men said as he laid down a card. "If you hustle, you might be able to make it there and back in one day."

"It's more likely a half day's ride," Lewis cautioned. "And you can't forget to take into account the time it'll take for the tender to row him to shore and the time necessary to locate a horse. After all that, he wouldn't have much time left to spend with Polly before he'd have to turn right back around and leave. Even then he'd likely be riding back to Deal in the wee hours of the night."

Newton slammed the rum down to the table causing the amber liquid to splash out. "I don't care how much time I'd have with her. Even if I can only see her for a few minutes, it would be worth it."

"Several of the other senior officers are taking a leave for Christmas," Mitchell said, tossing a card onto the pile at the center of the table. "The captain won't give you as much time away as them. But he might give you a day."

Lewis shook his head at Newton warily. "You won't make it in a day—"

"You should know by now that John Newton can do whatever he sets his mind to doing." Newton pushed back from the table, his head reeling both with anticipation of seeing Polly and irritation at

Lewis. "I'm not a man who needs a mythical Being's help. I'm man enough to get by in my own strength."

Newton wouldn't begrudge a woman like Polly or Mrs. Catlett or even his mother her superstitions and the dependencies that came from relying on faith. But Newton couldn't resist sparring with Lewis, who took his faith much too seriously.

Lewis stared back for a long moment before finally shaking his head. "There's no talking any sense into you, Newton. You're a stubborn man."

"What? Now you're my father?" Newton tipped up the rum and took a long swig that blessedly burned his throat down to his stomach.

"I'm just saying—"

"Well, stop. I already have one father. I don't need another." Newton guzzled the last drops and let the warmth seep into his blood.

# FIFTEEN

DECEMBER 1744

*I*'ve had the settee reupholstered in an emerald green with a floral print," Susanna said as she followed Polly through the entry at the back of the house.

"It sounds lovely." Polly descended several steps into a hallway that led to the lower service rooms, including the kitchen, back kitchen, larder, and pantry. The steam emanating from the back kitchen told Polly that at midafternoon their servant was still washing laundry. The once-a-month task was an all-day affair, including collecting water from the rainwater butts and well, heating the water in a copper tank, and then scrubbing the linens on large corrugated boards inside tubs. The washing was followed by wringing water out of the larger and heavier items in a mangle. Then came the neck-aching task of hanging all of the damp items from the drying racks suspended from the ceilings.

Without the help of the servants who were dismissed when Father changed positions, Mother often assigned Polly to help with the task, but in recent months Mother had given Eliza the job. Mother wanted them both to learn all the work that was involved in running and managing a home. At least that's how Polly had consoled herself whenever she soaked her lye-reddened hands in lady's mantle at the end of a wash day. Such small tales held her guilt at bay.

"I'm having the tapestries made to match," Susanna continued, clomping down the steps and following Polly to the kitchen door. "Since Daniel loves the color gold, I've decided to have the tassels and ruffles made in a gold damask." Polly doubted that Susanna would ever have to help her servants do laundry. Daniel Eversfield was working for his father, a wealthy London banker, and apparently was able to give Susanna everything she wanted. After their wedding that summer, Susanna had moved into her very own home, a newly built four-storied terrace.

"I vow, I can't wait until Mother allows me to ride to London and see your home," Polly said, as she crossed to the large table at the center of the room and deposited the two heavy baskets she'd brought back from the market. Polly tried to douse another flicker of envy at the thought of Susanna's life. Since Susanna's arrival yesterday, it seemed she'd been fighting a losing battle. Even if she was still young, she couldn't keep from wishing she could have marriage and a home of her own too.

"Perhaps I will have to sneak back to London in one of your trunks." Polly tried to lighten the mood for both their sakes. "I'll stay until you tire of me, and then you can ship me back."

Susanna placed her basket next to Polly's and began to lift out their purchases: tallow candles, butter, cheese, milk, treacle, and barley flour.

"Just maybe I won't ship you back," Susanna said. A strange note in the young woman's voice caught at Polly.

Polly didn't say anything for a moment and instead studied her aunt's face. "Are you happy, Susanna?"

Susanna nodded and gave a short laugh. "Of course I'm happy. Daniel is spoiling me." Susanna reached for another package from her basket, this one a leg of mutton, and her fingers trembled.

Polly wanted to probe deeper, but she'd already given Susanna a chance to share. Maybe Susanna was still adjusting to her new life. Perhaps marriage brought more worries and responsibilities than Susanna had realized. Perhaps Susanna missed her secret activities; after all, she'd bemoaned the fact that as a married woman she would need to settle down. Polly couldn't help but think back to two years ago, to the winter day very much like this one when Susanna had tricked her into aiding an abolitionist rescue under the guise of wassailing. It was the day she met John for the first time, the day he came along to their rescue and saved them from certain trouble.

She hadn't seen him in months, since the day she'd walked away from the gaol. In fact, she didn't know if he was still alive. Her father had tried to shield her from news of the war, but she'd pried every piece of information she could out of Billy and had learned there had been several skirmishes with the French during the fall. Now that winter was settling in, most of the ships would find safe harbors where they could wait out the storms. The war would be put on hold until spring.

All she'd been able to do was pray John was safe. She'd prayed until she'd worn out the carpet next to her bed. And even though at times her prayers brought her comfort, she was often left strangely empty, as though somehow she still needed to try harder before God would hear her.

"There you are," Jack called from the kitchen door. He'd grown taller over the fall away at school, looking more and more like their father. She was relieved that Jack had been able to continue with his education in spite of Father's pay cut. What did it matter that her own dreams of school wouldn't materialize? Her father was alive, and Jack was still able to better himself. At least that's what she tried to tell herself every time she thought about all her friends who had left.

Jack's grin filled his thin face, and his eyes were bright with unusual mischief. He and Susanna had arrived together yesterday in time for Christmas festivities.

Susanna had explained her appearance without her new husband by telling them that Daniel was too busy to travel. Polly had been too excited at the time to question Susanna's excuse. But perhaps Daniel's absence accounted for Susanna's strange mood.

"You're bored already without me around to keep things lively?" Susanna smiled at Jack.

"Not quite," Jack replied mysteriously. "But I have been waiting for your return. Come up and join me for a game of whist."

"Card playing in the middle of the afternoon?" Polly asked. "Surely Mother has more work for us—"

"Mother said we've done enough for the day and now must enjoy ourselves."

That was all the invitation Susanna needed to put aside any thought of work. She tossed her coat and scarf onto the table for the servant to hang up and rushed after Jack. Polly couldn't begrudge either one a bit of merriment, but she finished unpacking the baskets and putting away the goods in the pantry and larder.

With Susanna's coat in hand, she peered in the back kitchen and noted that Eliza was no longer helping the servant with the laundering. Apparently Mother had dismissed her from work as well. Polly offered her assistance, but the servant waved her along.

Polly started up the steps that would lead to the main floor but stopped halfway up at the loud laughter and voices coming from the morning room.

"The poor sailor didn't know what had happened to him," came a voice filled with humor.

Polly sucked in a breath, and the world came to a crashing halt. Was it John?

"All he knew was that he was hanging head down from the main topsail yard, swinging in the wind like a flag." More laughter followed.

It *was* John. Polly's heartbeat pulsed forward at a dangerous speed trying to keep up with her feet as she raced up the stairs and down the hallway.

John was alive. He was here. She was suddenly frantic to see him, to know that he was safe and unharmed.

She skidded to a stop just outside the morning-room door and forced herself to take a deep breath, count to three, and then calmly make her appearance. Her gaze found him at once, at the table, flanked by Jack reclining in a chair on one side and Susanna on the other. Eliza and the younger children hovered near Mother, who was sitting in a chair by the hearth, mending in hand, but smiling at John's story.

All heads turned her direction, all except John, who continued to look at the cards he was holding in his hand. The sight of him made her heart career like an out-of-control coach on a bumpy road. His hair was tied back in a queue, which was longer than the last time she'd seen him. His features were browned from the sun and leaner, somehow stronger and more defined, as if he'd shed the last vestiges of his boyhood form and had finally become a full-grown man. The power of his presence was unmistakable, almost daunting. But it was also magnetic, not just for her but clearly for everyone else in the room.

She waited for him to look up, for his eyes to spark to life at the sight of her. She readied a smile, and when he glanced up, for the briefest second, his eyes filled with unmistakable thrill. But as he and Jack rose from their chairs, his enthusiasm disappeared and was replaced with nonchalance. "It's nice to see you again, Cousin."

*Nice?* For a moment she was taken aback by his greeting. But she supposed he couldn't very well admit much more than that with her mother sitting nearby. "I'm glad to see you too."

After she took a spot near the table, he and Jack sat back down and returned their attention to their cards. He launched into another one of his shipboard stories and soon had everyone laughing again.

Polly was tempted to walk over to him, shake him by the shoulders, and demand that he speak with her. In fact, she wanted to drag him away from the others and have him all to herself. But even as she watched the card game, she could feel her mother's eyes upon her, surveying her reaction to John warily.

Part of her was surprised her mother had allowed John to come into their home after the tense parting they'd had last time. Clearly Mother was too polite to refuse him hospitality. But Polly had the feeling that if John showed any romantic interest in her, Mother would insist that he be on his way before the day's end. She might send him away anyway. But the least Polly could do was attempt to maintain an appropriate distance. Then they could be together. Something—even simple friendship—was better than nothing.

As the afternoon turned into evening, Polly did her best to temper her eagerness, tried not to stare at him, and kept her distance knowing her mother was carefully monitoring her and John. She had no doubt her father would also expel John if he hinted at impropriety, and she didn't want to chance it. Still she couldn't keep her heart from racing faster every time he spoke or whenever she glanced at him.

Even though she longed for a moment alone with him, she contented herself with the brief friendly interactions he offered her. When her father saw John after coming home from work, his expression turned stern, almost grave, and she worried that he might ask John to leave. But as the evening wore on, her father seemed to relax, especially when he learned that John was on leave for only a few days.

It wasn't until the following morning, as they walked home from the service at St. Margaret's Church, that she finally had a moment of privacy with John. Her father and mother and little George had gone ahead in the gig. Eliza walked at the forefront of their party with her younger sisters. She and Susanna followed with Jack and John not far behind.

"Jack, come here a moment," Susanna said over her shoulder. "I need to speak with you about a matter of the utmost importance." She slowed her stride, and as she did so, she winked at Polly.

Jack hesitated. Polly had no doubt Father had instructed Jack not to leave John's side, not even for an instant. She suspected Mother had given Susanna the same command, that she was to chaperone Polly at all times and never allow her to be alone with John. But Susanna looped her arm through Jack's and dragged him forward, giving him little choice but to allow Polly a moment with John.

"Thank the stars for Susanna," John muttered, his lips quirking into a crooked grin. "I didn't know how I was going to live another moment without speaking with you."

At his declaration, Polly's stomach flipped. She focused her attention on her boots and kicked at the damp leaves that covered the road. Although the first day of winter was upon them and the sky was overcast, the temperature wasn't unbearable. In fact, the air wasn't even cold enough to nip her nose.

"We've spoken some already," she said.

"And I've been on my best behavior. I've been treating you like a sister, the way your father expects me to."

"You've done a fine job of it."

His voice dropped. "Aye, and it's nigh killed me."

She didn't want to admit the relief his words brought her. She'd been afraid his distance meant he didn't have the same affection for her anymore. Although her heart warred with her and told her it shouldn't matter, the thought had crossed her mind that perhaps he fancied another woman now.

"But I figured the only way your parents would let me visit is if I'm on my very best behavior." His footsteps lagged, and she had to slow hers to stay by his side.

"Heaven help me, Polly," his voice turned hoarse to almost a whisper. "I've gone crazy missing you."

Something in his tone made her body feel as though she were sitting too close to the coal fire. "I worried about you. I didn't know if you were dead or alive."

"Then you're happy to see me?"

"Can't you tell?"

"Say it, Polly."

She peeked ahead to make sure Susanna still had Jack's attention before she looked at John. The warm passion in his eyes was so different from the casual friendliness he'd shown her since he'd arrived. "I missed you," she whispered.

His shoulder brushed hers lightly. "Say it again."

"I missed you, John. And I wish you didn't have to leave."

His gaze caressed her face with such intimacy that her breath snagged in her chest. "Mayhap I won't go."

She smiled. "And risk getting in trouble for deserting?"

"It would be worth it." The low intimacy of his voice was making her insides curl. She could understand why her father was concerned about her relationship with John. There was something about him that was difficult to resist, an attraction, a deep pull that swept her along like an unstoppable current. "Although I honestly don't know how much longer I can go on with this charade."

"What charade?"

"Pretending to be your brother when you mean so much more to me than a sister."

Once again she couldn't look him in the eyes. His insinuation was so intimate that she had the feeling that if they'd been alone he would have kissed her. It had been months since their kiss in the drawing room, months of dreaming about the feel and taste of his lips.

Ahead on the path, Jack glanced at them, his eyes full of suspicion.

She ducked her head. "We have to be careful. I want my father to approve of you."

"Aye, good that. I want him to approve of me too."

"Then we agree to keep things as they've been so that he has no reason to think ill of you?"

"I suppose that means I can't ask you to sneak out of your room tonight and meet me in the stable?"

His scandalous request nearly made her stumble. "John," she softly chastised.

He chuckled. "I'm jesting."

She smiled in return, but the spark in his eyes told her that he wasn't entirely joking, and that thought made her insides burn again. "Please, John," she pleaded. "You must behave or Father will ask you to go."

She didn't have the heart to tell him all that her father had already said regarding his concerns over John's character.

"Don't worry," he said rather too cheerfully. "I may be a bad boy sometimes. But I know how to be good when I need to be."

Over the next few days, John kept his word. His behavior toward her was above reproach. On a couple of occasions that she'd noticed a slow smolder of desire in his eyes when he looked at her, he'd excused himself to take a walk. On both occasions when he'd returned a few hours later, he'd smelled of tobacco and rum. But he'd been considerably lighter in mood and able to renew his friendly stance with her.

"When does your leave end?" she heard her father ask John as the two sat in his study a week after his arrival. She hovered in the hallway outside the door. Eavesdropping was wrong and she needed to move away, but she was unable to force herself. Her mother and Susanna were in the drawing room talking and the younger children had already gone up to their rooms to ready themselves for bed. She should as well, but she was anxious to know John's plans, to know how much longer she had with him before another impossibly long separation.

John didn't answer, and the silence stretched uncomfortably.

"Am I to assume that you overextended your leave?" her father asked, and Polly was surprised by the sadness in his tone.

"I'm sure the captain won't mind," John finally replied. "He's probably off visiting family and friends himself."

"Exactly how long were you given?"

Polly's muscles tightened as she waited for John's reply. She suspected more was at stake here than just John's shipboard position.

"It's nothing to worry about—" John started.

"I've been honest with you," Father interrupted, "and I expect the same in turn."

Again John was silent, and in the interim Polly's heartbeat seemed to echo too loudly in the hallway.

"I had one day," John's voice was laced with defeat.

One day? And how long had he been there? At least seven? If not eight? Polly closed her eyes and leaned her forehead against the wall.

"John," her father said. The one word was filled with both sorrow and finality.

"They took me without asking." John's tone turned defiant. "They don't deserve my loyalty."

"If you end up swinging from the end of a rope, you know what will happen, don't you?" Her father's whisper was harsher than she'd ever heard. "She'll blame herself. Is that what you want for her?"

"Nay."

"Then go back and do your duty whether you want to or not."

"It's not my duty."

"It is until your captain says otherwise."

John didn't respond. And Polly could hardly breathe. She needed to leave now. But fear and sorrow had dropped upon her, and she couldn't move.

"I think it's best for you to return to your ship right away," her father said shakily. "Tonight."

"Of course." The scraping of chairs alerted her to the fact that the men were standing. She forced herself to start breathing again and glanced around for a place to hide, except that her feet still wouldn't work.

"I'd like to say good-bye to Polly if I may."

"No, John." Her father's voice again was filled with sorrow. "I'd like you to depart. And this time I don't want you to come back."

Polly pressed a hand over her mouth to keep from crying out her protest.

"Sir?" John asked as though he hadn't heard her father correctly.

"As much as I like you as a person, John, unfortunately you haven't proven to be the kind of man I want for Polly."

"Once I'm out of the navy, I'll be able to find another job—"

"It's not just your lack of means. It's your lack of character as well." Although the words were spoken gently, Polly guessed they must have slammed into John and knocked him speechless, for he didn't say anything in response.

"As hard as this is," her father continued, "it's better to put a stop to your feelings now, before one of you is truly hurt."

"I won't be able to stop what I feel for Polly. Ever. No matter how hard I try."

"Then do it for her. You know as well as I do, she needs someone who's trustworthy and reliable and able to take care of her the way she deserves."

Polly's chest ached and tears stung her eyes as the reality of what her father was suggesting began to penetrate.

"Give her the chance to forget about you," her father said urgently. "She's still young. Let her find someone else."

"Don't you think we should let her make that choice?" John asked.

No, she silently screamed. She didn't want either of them to force her to make a choice. She wanted to please them both and couldn't bear the thought of disappointing either of them.

"Or are you afraid of her choice?" John asked, and this time his tone turned condescending.

"John, please. If you care at all about her, then do the right thing."

Heavy footsteps plodded across the study. At the sound of them, Polly spun around and dashed to the stairway. But she wasn't quick enough. John thundered into the hallway, his features tight with anger.

He stopped abruptly at the sight of her. She had one foot on the first step, her hand on the banister, but she had no doubt that it was clear as summer sunshine that she'd been standing there listening and had heard every word they'd spoken.

She couldn't keep her lips from trembling. "Don't make me choose, John."

The fury in his slanted brow and the anger in his eyes raged for another moment, but then slowly began to lift.

Her father stepped behind John. At the sight of her, his eyes widened. "Polly, what are you doing here?" But from the sudden sag of his features, she knew she didn't need to respond. He could read the pain and confusion in her face.

"Polly," John said holding out his hands as if to attempt to explain himself. But then he dropped them. "I'm leaving tonight. I need to get back to my ship."

She nodded. She'd thought things were going so well. She hoped her parents would give John another chance. And she wanted John to change, even if just a little, so that he could be the kind of man her father would approve of, the kind of man she needed. But apparently he was the same man he'd always been.

John studied her for a long minute as though memorizing each part of her. "Good-bye, Polly." His voice cracked. Ducking his head, he crossed to the coat rack and retrieved his coat. He stuffed his arms in and then reached for the door handle.

Polly's chest ached. A sob rose up but her throat was too tight to let it pass. She wanted to call out to him to wait, not to go yet, that surely they could find a way to make things work between them if only they tried hard enough.

He opened the door a crack and then paused. His head was down, his shoulders slumped.

She silently called to him to look at her one more time.

He hesitated a moment longer, then he spun around. His sea-green eyes found hers. The desperation in them wrenched her heart. She didn't want to say good-bye any more than he did. Could he see that?

With a firm set to his lips, he lifted his shoulders and swiftly strode back across the hallway toward her. Each determined step made her pulse beat faster. And something in the hard line of his jaw made her stomach flip in anticipation.

When he reached where she stood, his arm snagged her and half lifted, half crushed her against his body. From her position on the bottom step, she was at eye-level with him. His mouth came down on hers decisively, without a moment of hesitation, as if her lips belonged to him and him alone.

His kiss was hard and demanding. She could do nothing less than respond, her mouth pliable and ready for him. After so many months of dreaming about it, the real kiss stirred her fiercely, scorching her with its heat.

In the distance she could hear her father yell, "No!"

In that moment, she didn't care. She mingled her lips with John's and lifted her arms to wrap them around his neck, to cling to him, to never let him go. But before she could do so, John was ripped violently away from her.

She gasped and stumbled back, bumping the next stair, just as her father swung a fist into John's face. A *thwack* was followed by a grunt.

John straightened quickly into a defensive stance. His shoulders stiffened, his hands balled at his sides, and his chin tipped up a notch, as though daring her father to hit him again.

Her father cradled his fist, likely having hurt himself more than John in the punch he'd delivered. Her father wasn't a violent man. She'd never seen him hit anyone before. But the fury in his eyes told her he'd hit John again if he had to.

"Leave," her father ordered hoarsely as he stepped in front of Polly. "And don't come back."

John glanced to the doorway of the drawing room where Mother and Susanna now stood watching with frightened expressions. A flicker of regret passed across John's features before he finally took a step backward.

His gaze connected with Polly's. The sorrow, the desire, the frustration in his eyes tore at her heart. "I love you."

The words crashed into her with such force the sob in her chest finally escaped.

"Someday, I will be the kind of man you deserve," he said. "I promise." And with that, he strode across the hallway, walked outside, and slammed the door closed behind him.

The walls reverberated and the hallway echoed with the thud. But it was nothing compared with the hollow bang that ricocheted throughout her body, jarring her bones so that her knees buckled and she slid into a heap on the step.

Her father reached for her, but she turned away from him. He'd only done what he thought was best for her, and deep in her heart she knew he was right about everything concerning John. But she couldn't face him right now.

She buried her face in her hands wanting to weep, but her soul was too anguished, her heart too raw to find tears. Her father and mother were whispering in loud, strident tones, and she knew she should apologize for deceiving them, for kissing John again, for encouraging his affection in any way. But for now she was too devastated to say anything.

A slender arm embraced her as Susanna sat down on the step next to her. Susanna pressed a kiss against her hair. When Polly lifted her face and saw the tears streaking down Susanna's cheeks, Polly's own tears finally came. She fell into Susanna's arms, the pain in her chest too much to bear. It was the pain of losing her heart to the man she loved.

Yes, even though she knew she shouldn't have, she'd irrevocably and irreparably allowed herself to fall in love with John Newton.

# Sixteen

Newton dipped the quill in the ink and touched it to the paper, trying to hold his hand steady. His scrawl was nearly illegible. The rough spring waters still rocked the ship, which had been badly damaged by a hurricane-like storm.

Many of the sailors who weren't injured from the storm were sick below decks. The constant wind and waves were hard for even the most seasoned of them to endure. They'd been lucky to come out of the storm alive. They'd been part of a naval fleet escorting a large convoy of Indiamen and Guineamen merchant ships. The ships had steered a westerly route until they reached the coast at Cornwall, on their way to Devon, where they'd run into the tempest head on.

Newton's only source of solace was writing letters to Polly. He'd penned a dozen over the past several months since he'd been apart from her. But he'd sent only two and had crumpled up the rest, pinings of his lovesick soul that would likely only scare her with his intensity. He hadn't sent the two worthy letters directly to her home for fear that her parents would burn them. Instead he'd addressed them to Susanna in London with the hope that eventually she could take them to Polly. If anyone would help him, she would.

The ship rocked sharply, causing his pen to jolt and the ink bottle to slide precariously close to the edge of the table. He grabbed it before it could crash to the floor, which was filthy with the stains of all that had already spilled.

He'd considered writing to his father as well. He'd recently learned that the captain was in Torbay, only thirty miles away, dealing with ship-repair contracts on several Royal African Company ships that had also been battered by the recent storm. Newton had heard rumors that the *Harwich* might be among the naval fleet that would escort the company's merchant and store ships. Mayhap, his father could work a transfer to one of the merchant vessels. At least then Newton would have a better chance at gaining his freedom at some point.

But even if his father worked out a deal, he doubted that Captain Carteret would do him any more favors. Ever since he'd broken his leave of absence in December, he'd been out of favor with the HMS *Harwich* captain and he hadn't recovered it. He knew he'd been extremely lucky the captain hadn't flogged him upon his late return to the ship. Mitchell, the captain's clerk, and some of his other fellow officers had thankfully come to his rescue, making excuses about how he was young and in love and had lost track of time.

A moan from Lewis's nearby hammock was followed by the heaves of retching.

"Do you need your Bible?" Newton called to the young man, who'd been ill for the past several days. "Mayhap if you pray harder God will heal you."

Once the caustic words were out, Newton detested himself for them. He was being a she-dog, but he couldn't seem to help himself when it came to Lewis. There was something about the man's simple, heartfelt devotion to God that put him on edge. Partly he supposed Lewis's faith reminded him of his mother and made him feel guilty that he was disappointing her by not living according to her values.

He bent his head over his letter again and tried to read his scrawled handwriting. Between the pitching of the ship and the wildly swinging lantern light, he could hardly focus.

"I will not mortify myself to think I shall return home to find you in another's possession before I have an opportunity of showing what I could do to deserve you." His chest still ached every time he thought of Mr. Catlett's words about not being the kind of man he desired for Polly. He wanted to prove to Mr. Catlett and to Polly that he could be the right man but feared she would find someone else before he had the chance to prove himself. After all, she was a beautiful woman, and if Billy didn't win her, then another man surely would.

"The first day I saw you I began to love you," his letter continued. "It has now been more than two years since, from which time till now I have been almost continually disappointed in whatever I have undertaken. It's true I hope to succeed. But I take love to witness; it is not wholly on my own account, for I shall not value riches but for the opportunity of laying them at your feet."

The truth was, he didn't care about wealth except for the fact that it could bring him closer to his goal of having Polly. Aye, Mr. Catlett had said that he lacked more than wealth. But Newton had concluded that the man wouldn't have pushed him away had he a large purse and a substantial income. Aye, Polly's father wouldn't have ordered him about like a dog and denied him Polly's affection if he'd had a better job and been a wealthier man. Sure, he had faults. He needed to improve himself in light of his drinking and gambling and cursing. But if he had Polly, he'd do better.

The cabin door swung open and Mitchell popped his head in. "I need a couple of officers to man a longboat going ashore for supplies."

"More supplies?" They'd been revictualling in Plymouth Sound for the past month in preparation for their next voyage, rumored to begin in April, just a few weeks away. Of course resupplying the ship had been made harder because Captain Carteret kept the ship a fair distance from the shore. Three sailors had deserted when the ship was at port undergoing repairs. And now, in order to prevent any further desertions, the captain kept the ship riding at anchor.

"Aye, we need more food," Mitchell said. "The admiralty has finally given us our orders, and we're headed to the East Indies."

"I thought we were going with a convoy to Lisbon."

"Nay. The plans have changed."

Newton shook his head feeling a sudden rise of panic. "We can't go to the East Indies. That's too far away. The journey there and back will take years." At least a five-year tour of duty.

"All the more reason to get the supplies we need."

Newton's head began to spin. "Why are we going? Why the change in plans?"

Mitchell swayed as the ship rocked back and forth under a fresh surge of stormy waves. The clerk's expression turned sharp. "Look. I don't know anything more than what I've been told. And today I've been ordered to put together a couple of crews to head to shore for more supplies. So are you in or not?"

Newton stared at the letter to Polly. Five years? He hadn't been able to make himself leave for the lucrative plantation position in Jamaica that would have been five years. He certainly didn't want to leave on a voyage to the East Indies with the navy. There would be no benefit to him in such a journey. Only heartache at being separated from Polly for that long.

Even though her father had told him he wasn't welcome anymore, he'd decided he wouldn't let that stop him from seeing Polly when he was between voyages. He'd planned to find a way somehow. But now . . . if he was gone for years instead of months, he'd certainly lose her.

The very thought made the panic in his gut swirl faster.

"After the favors I've done for you," Mitchell muttered, "I thought I could count on you to help out. But apparently not." The clerk slammed the door closed.

Newton slumped and let his head drop to the table. *Five years. Five years. Five years.* The words reverberated in his mind like a death knell. The East Indies was on the other side of the world, and anything could happen in the dangerous seas as they sailed around Africa and India. The ship could be attacked by the French. They could face pirates. They might be wrecked in a storm.

The Royal Navy may have forced him into service, but they couldn't force him to give up five more years of his life. It was too much to ask.

With a rage borne of desperation, he stood and slammed the table. The bump sent the ink bottle over the edge and crashing to the floor. The bottle didn't break, but the ink began to trickle out in a dark pool.

Newton stared at the bottle but didn't make a move to retrieve it. He had to see his father. His father could surely get him transferred. The hostilities with France were still ongoing, but not nearly as heated as they were last year. There had been no rumors of the French attempting another invasion. Of course, the Young Pretender Charles still wanted to reclaim the throne from King George. But if the French weren't willing to help him, what chance did the Bonnie Prince have?

Aye. Newton swiped up the ink bottle. His father would have a much better chance of getting him released this time. At least he hoped so.

Newton scratched out a quick note, folded it, and stuffed it in his pocket. Then he grabbed his coat, hat, and gloves and made his way to the larboard boom where a crew was assembling. A light freezing mist was falling, and the wind cut through his coat. He glanced with frustration at the distance from the ship to the far-off shore. The rowing would be long and difficult, especially with the ferocity of the white-capped waves.

He almost stepped back into the shadows of the mast, too weary and angry to help with the revictualling. He could send the letter to his father with one of the other midshipmen. But what if they forgot to post it? Or what if they read it and saw his request? He couldn't chance anyone discovering his intentions. It would only stir up more trouble with the captain than he already had.

"I'll go, mate," he told Mitchell, who was overseeing the boarding.

"That's a good man." Mitchell slapped him on the back. "The captain wanted me to tell the midshipmen that you have strict orders to make sure none of the sailors desert."

Newton surveyed the half-dozen men who would be under his

charge, huddled in their threadbare coats, with red and running noses and hats askew in the wind. He hadn't really gotten to know any of the sailors in his charge. As midshipman he'd kept separate from the others unless he had to exercise authority, like now.

"You heard the man," he called to his crew. "Don't even think of deserting under my watch. If I get a hint of anyone even thinking of running off, you'll be disciplined when we get back to the ship."

As they rowed to shore, the sailors were silent, some even sullen. But they had all the work they could handle fighting the wind and keeping the longboat from capsizing in the waves. When they finally reached the bustling docks with the busy port of Plymouth lining the waterfront, they were spent and chilled to the bone. The freezing mist had dampened their clothes through to their limbs.

The other midshipman in charge of the second longboat agreed to allow the men an hour's rest and warmth at the nearest pub before they began loading the waiting barrels into their boats.

"I need to post a letter," Newton told his fellow officer, "then I'll meet you at the pub."

The man nodded at him curtly before following the sailors as they sauntered toward the tavern, a new lightness to their steps and grins on their faces.

Newton spun and began walking toward the victualling office. He'd find someone there who knew his father personally and would be willing to make arrangements to send word of his predicament. As he neared the imposing brick building, his steps slowed with un-certainty. Even if he did locate an ally, what if the *Harwich* set sail before his father could help him?

Mayhap he should deliver the letter himself. He could find a horse, ride to Torbay, and be back to the ship by morning. If he rode nonstop, he'd make it. Even by foot he could do it if he kept a good pace.

He stood frozen in place for an endless moment. The bay and all the ships spread out before him. Dozens of ships and longboats were coming and going, some with sails all standing, others like the distant *Harwich* with sails furled. He was just one man among thousands. Surely he wouldn't be missed for one night. And if things went his way and his father got him transferred, then he wouldn't have to return at all.

He glanced at the road leading up through town. He guessed the path would cut across South Devon and eventually take him to the coastal town of Torbay. Even if it didn't, how hard would it be to find his way there?

With a deep breath, he ducked his head and started away from the pub, away from the *Harwich,* and hopefully away from his life in the navy.

## SEVENTEEN

*N*ewton stumbled over a rock in the road but caught himself. His head throbbed and his eyes ached from lack of sleep. He'd been awake for over twenty-four hours, and more than anything he wanted to find an old barn or large grove of thick woodland, any hiding place where he could lie down and sleep for a little while.

But for the past hour, he'd traversed the moorland landscape of South Devon, filled with newly plowed fields bordered with black-thorn and an occasional ash or poplar. He didn't see any safe place to hide. And even if he could locate a haven, the growing wariness in his gut told him he should keep going. In the distance a hamlet began to emerge with the outline of houses and the thin tendrils of smoke rising from early morning hearth fires.

The morning sun was hazy behind low clouds, and fog dusted the hills and poured into the valleys. The cool temperature of the long night still surrounded him, but he'd run on and off throughout the early morning hours to keep himself warm and to keep fatigue at bay.

Thankfully, the road had been deserted except for a lone shep-herd he'd met before daybreak. He didn't want to meet anyone and chance them wondering why he was traveling alone in the middle of nowhere at such an early hour. He couldn't risk locals thinking he'd deserted. For he hadn't.

Had he?

The thought had pounded louder with each hour that had passed. Yesterday he'd made an impulsive decision. He'd been rash. And mayhap too arrogant. Because after having time to think through his plan during the dark hours of the night, he'd realized that mayhap his father wouldn't want to help him get the transfer. After all, the last time he saw his father, Newton wasn't exactly congenial. And even if his father attempted to wield his influence for him, what if he failed again? Where would that leave Newton? Charged with desertion?

The rational part of his mind told him to return to the *Harwich* before it was too late. But he only had to remind himself of the fact that the *Harwich* would be gone for five years, and he kept walking. Besides now that he'd traveled hours away from Plymouth and his ship, what kind of explanation could he give the captain for his absence, especially after his unexcused leave at Christmas? His only course of action was to move forward and attempt to find his father.

As he drew nearer the village, he debated the possibility of skirting wide to avoid any questions or raised brows. But the rumble in his stomach and his growing thirst won out. Besides, he wanted to make sure he was still headed in the direction of Brixham and Torbay. He wasn't entirely sure where he was and didn't want to waste any more time than necessary.

He plodded forward and wished he wasn't attired in his filthy sailor garb. Like most seamen he didn't bother to wash his garments often. Shipboard life seldom provided the opportunity or means. That meant he not only looked like he'd jumped ship, but he smelled it too.

Ahead, the street flowed between a short row of connected buildings that lined both sides before tapering off again to farm fields and hedges. Across from a low, ancient stone building covered in moss and lichens stood several newer but weathered terraced structures. Newton directed his weary steps toward the one in the middle with the sign hanging above the door that said Moreleigh Inn. He had several coins in his purse that would be enough to buy a meal and drink. Surely a few minutes of rest wouldn't hurt him. He'd eat and then be on his way with renewed energy.

He hesitated at the door. The sound of voices on the other side gave him pause for only a second. He wouldn't stay, he told himself before pushing open the door. Only one drink and no gambling.

At the sight of him stepping into the tavern, the voices came to an abrupt halt. Newton nodded at the few patrons awake and eating, a table of four men in one corner and two others conversing near the barrels of ale.

"Top o' the morning to you," said one of the men at the barrels. He wore an apron around his rotund middle and gave Newton a welcoming smile that told him he was the proprietor.

"I'd be obliged for a drink and meal," Newton said, eyeing the table of four men who'd paused in their eating to watch him.

"Where you from?" asked the tavern owner as he filled a mug from the tap on one of the barrels.

"On my way to Torbay," Newton replied, avoiding the question. "And hoping I'm still on the right road."

The tavern owner happily made sure Newton knew about every route possible between Moreleigh and Torbay, even every cow path.

Newton was relieved when the four men in the corner took their leave and left him in peace.

One drink turned into two, and when the innkeeper offered him a third, Newton was proud of himself for pushing away from the table and declining even though his tongue was heavy with the need for it.

Once he was back on the road, the sun had risen higher and had burned away the fog. Although he was still tired, the ale had taken the edge off his worry. He ambled along whistling to himself, confident he'd made the right decision to leave Plymouth and look for his father. According to directions the proprietor had given him for the most direct route, Newton figured he had a half-day's walk left. Then he'd locate his father, get the transfer off the *Harwich,* and finally be able to set his own course for his life.

He crossed a footbridge leading across a swollen stream and relished the cool morning breeze as he climbed up a rise. When he reached the top, he stopped short at the sight of the four men from the tavern. Three were astride horses, and the fourth was driving a team and wagon. They blocked the path in front of him. From the way all four pairs of eyes were trained upon him, something told him they'd been waiting for him.

Thieves? Mayhap smugglers? He didn't know exactly, except that he'd fallen into a trap.

"Don't have much left to give you," he said as casually as he could, patting his nearly empty purse with one hand and inching his other to the small of his back where he kept his knife strapped.

"No worries," said the man positioned in front. "We don't need your pennies." His hair was greasy and pulled into a loose queue. His face had a long, thin scar running from his eye to his jaw.

"Good that." Newton's fingers closed around his hilt. "Then I suppose you mates will let me pass without any trouble?"

"You're a stranger to these parts. State your business, and then maybe we'll think about letting you pass."

Newton studied the leader more closely, noting the club at his belt. Was this another press gang? "I'm dispatching a letter." He said the first thing that came to his mind and reached in his pocket to retrieve the paper. He waved it as proof.

"Most couriers travel the coastal roads." The man's tone was laced with an accusation Newton didn't understand.

"I opted for the scenic route." Newton nodded at the newly budding leaves, his mind spinning. He couldn't risk capture by another press gang. He had to make it to his father. "Can you blame me?"

The man's eyes narrowed upon Newton. "I think you're a deserter."

A cannon ball seemed to barrel into his stomach and filled him with both dread and panic. He'd been discovered. This was no press gang. This was most likely a platoon that had been sent out by the navy to scout the area for deserters since recently there had been so many.

Newton tried to remain calm, but all he could think about was getting away. "Like I said, I'm delivering a letter. I only planned to be gone for a couple of days."

"I suppose you can show us the leave papers from your captain?" the leader demanded.

"He didn't have time to write them up."

"We have instructions to arrest any naval sailor who doesn't produce written leave-of-absence papers or orders from his captain.

Unless you can show us your papers, then we have to haul you to Plymouth."

He had to get away while he still could. He couldn't turn around and run the way he'd come. The men on their horses would easily overtake him. His only chance was to cut across country and hope for some luck in finding a hiding spot.

He hesitated only a moment longer before darting into the thick brush. He crashed through the sharp branches and brambles. Thorns clawed his body and twigs whipped his face. But he plunged forward and forced his way through the growth. His boots snagged roots. And fallen branches tripped him. Behind him came the shouts of the naval platoon and the crushing and breaking of brush.

A horse thrashed nearby, gaining ground. He could almost feel the hot snorting of the beast upon his neck. In the next moment, a club came down across one of his shoulders. The power and pain of the blast nearly sent him to his knees. He stumbled but then caught himself and kept moving. He couldn't stop. If he did, his life would be over. Literally. Many a recaptured deserter had been court-martialed and then hung from the yardarm of his ship. Newton had witnessed it several times during his life at sea.

The wooden club slammed into his back jolting him forward and throwing him off balance. He grabbed for the nearest tree to hold himself up. But the officer and horse trailing him were already on top of him. The weight forced him to his knees, and horse hoofs battered him. He cried out and tried to cover himself, but the club swung hard and fast toward his head, and the last thing he felt was searing agony before blackness enveloped him.

When Newton awoke, he found himself chained and in a gaol similar to the one in Chatham. While he couldn't see much of the town from the barred window, he surmised he was back in Plymouth. There were several other battered sailors in the hovel with him, and he guessed they were recaptured deserters. He insisted to the captain of the guard that he wasn't like the others, that he'd had every intention of returning to his ship after he delivered his letter. He cajoled, bribed, and demanded that he be given the chance to explain himself. But on the third day after he'd left the *Harwich*, he was led to a longboat. Lewis was the midshipman in charge of the crew, and at the sight of Newton bloodied, bruised, and in chains, he shook his head sadly.

"I don't need your pity," Newton said wishing he could pound his fist into Lewis's self-righteous face. Instead, he spat at the man's feet and lowered himself to a bench. With each dip of the oars leading him back to the *Harwich*, Newton's gut flamed with growing fear.

When he was hauled aboard the *Harwich*, no one spoke to him. He was dragged like a common criminal past the middle and lower decks to the hold, where he was finally manacled to the bulwarks. Except for the rats and cockroaches, he was alone in the dark.

Other than a sailor sent to deliver water and bread twice a day, he had no visitors. All he could think about was the fact that he'd ruined everything. He almost wished he could still believe in God. Then at least there would be someone to blame for his misfortune besides himself.

After what felt like an eternity, two men descended the ladder. The taller of the two carried a lantern, and as he approached Newton recognized him. Mitchell, the captain's clerk. He braced himself against the rough boards waiting for Mitchell to deliver a hard kick to his stomach. He deserved Mitchell's beating for betraying him.

The clerk stopped in front of him and held the lantern above him, almost blinding him and revealing his squalor. "You look like the devil got ahold of you. And you smell like a cess pit."

Newton squinted. "I'm sorry I let you down."

Mitchell shrugged. "You're the one suffering, not me."

"Aye."

Mitchell eyed him with clear disgust. "You're one lucky dog. Seems your father got word of your arrest, and he made contact with Admiral Medley. The admiral must really like your father."

Newton sat up straighter. His arms and shoulders ached from being in one position for so long. His backside was numb. And his toes and fingers were stiff with the cold. But for the first time in days, he allowed himself a tiny nugget of hope.

"Seems your father persuaded Admiral Medley to ask Captain Carteret for an exchange."

"I knew my father could do it," Newton said, letting triumph rise up and vindicate him. "I can't wait to get off this stinking piece of flotsam."

Mitchell laughed harshly. "Don't start celebrating too soon."

The clerk's tone sobered Newton.

"You're not getting transferred. You're not that lucky."

Newton swore softly under his breath, his hope and triumph dissipating.

"No, Captain Carteret wouldn't even consider a transfer. He's too livid for that. Besides, what kind of message would that send to any other sailors thinking of deserting? That you can break the rules and then get exactly what you want?"

Newton had angered the captain too many times already. He should have known the man wouldn't show him any leniency. "Then exactly how am I so lucky?"

Mitchell chortled again. "The captain's agreed not to court-martial and hang you."

"How kind of him." Bitterness made a winding path through Newton's veins.

Mitchell nodded to the sailor standing behind him. The man came forward and none-too-gently unlocked Newton's chains from the manacles embedded into the hull. The sailor cursed Newton with every foul breath he had to take. Newton knew he would have done the same if the roles had been reversed; nevertheless he wanted to slap the sailor, at the very least curse him back. He would later, he decided. Once he was topside, back into his position as midshipman, he'd make the sailor pay for his disdain.

When he was finally standing on his shaking, weak legs, he nearly collapsed again. Neither the sailor nor Mitchell made a move to help him. Newton's stomach cramped and nausea gurgled in his chest. He'd likely consumed contaminated water, and he had the feeling that he was in for a few days of being sick to his stomach.

Well, it would serve the captain right for relegating him to the hold and allowing him to sit in his own waste.

He held out his hands still bound by heavy chains. "You're not expecting me to get back to work wearing these, are you?"

Mitchell shook his head. "Of course not. An ordinary seaman can't climb the rigging or holystone the decks in chains."

Newton's mind raced with the implication of Mitchell's words. He was being demoted, degraded in rank.

"Have no fear." Mitchell shoved him toward the ladder. "We'll unshackle you after the captain's made an example of you. He wants to show the rest of the crew what happens to a dolt who attempts to shirk his duty to king and country."

So the captain was planning to flog him? While the news sent chills up Newton's back, he wasn't surprised. He tried to lift his foot to the first rung of the ladder, but he slipped and bumped his chin. His teeth sliced into his bottom lip, and the warmth of blood oozed onto his tongue. Of course the sailor showed him no mercy, battering and shoving him all the way up.

When he reached the main deck, the slow, solemn rhythm of two drums greeted him. The rest of the crew had already been assembled. They stood with hats off, in perfect silence to show respect for the law. Likely the captain had already read the article of war that Newton had contravened. Even though no one spoke, he sensed the scoffing glances at his condition. He guessed that not a man aboard the ship would be sad to see him flogged. He hadn't been particularly friendly or kind to anyone. Why would they show him any compassion now?

In spite of the bright sunshine, another chill rippled over his skin. Mitchell maneuvered him to the port gangway where the ladder had been removed, the brass eyebolts empty and waiting for him. The master-at-arms approached Newton, freed him of his chains, and then forced Newton to remove his coat and shirt so that he stood naked to the waist.

Newton guessed with the passage of time that March had turned into April. While the sea breeze was biting, it was decidedly warmer. Several seagulls glided in the cloudless blue sky above them, apparently having returned from their southern migration and ready to scavenge any scraps they could find, maybe even the flesh that would soon be torn from his back. Their laughing calls hung in the air, mocking him.

The master-at-arms forced Newton's arms upward and tied his wrists to the eyebolts of the gangway so that his arms were well above his head and angled into a wide V. Then he spread Newton's legs and tied his ankles to a grate on the deck. The ship's chaplain, Reverend Topham, stood nearby, his prayer book in hand. His eyes were bloodshot from a hangover.

*Hypocrite,* Newton wanted to lash out. *Don't stand there holier than thou and pass judgment on me when you fail to live up to your own standards.*

The boatswain broke through the crowd with the red baize bag. Everyone knew what it contained. The cat-o'-nine-tails. Newton focused his gaze on the porthole directly before him. Under normal circumstances, the hole was used as a means of leaving the ship. The irony of his position was not lost on him.

Behind him, he knew, the boatswain was pulling the cat out. Each of the nine tails was a rope of equal length as thick as a man's little finger. The thin whips eventually combined into a thicker cord near the handle. Altogether the whip was as long as a captain's boy. Newton had seen the devastation it could wreak on a man's bare back, and his mouth went dry at the realization that in just a few moments, he'd feel the torture across his own flesh.

The boatswain handed the cat to the chief boatswain's mate, who was positioned on Newton's left, his feet already spread wide to give him the most leverage as he swung the whip. The drumming tapered to silence.

"What the law allows, you shall have," came Captain Carteret's voice from above them on the quarterdeck. "But by the eternal God if any one of you disobeys that law, I'll cut out your backbone."

For a moment, Newton could hear the slap of the waves against the hull and the creak of mast and yards above them.

Then the captain spoke again, the words that all captains spoke at a flogging: "Boatswain's mate, do your duty, or by God, you shall take his place."

Newton swallowed hard and attempted to brace himself for the first blow. The whizzing of the nine tails through the air was followed by a *thwack* against his back. For a moment, the pain tore the breath from Newton's lungs so that he couldn't even utter a cry. The blow was so forceful that if he hadn't been tied in place, it would have knocked him to the deck.

He struggled to draw a gasp into his burning lungs. Just as he managed a small breath, the whip whistled through the air again, and the nine thin strands dug into his skin like the claws of a wild animal. This time he couldn't hold back a cry of agony. The scream was ripped from his lips just as the flesh was ripped from his back.

With each blow, thereafter, he determined not to utter a sound, to take the punishment without humiliating himself further. By the twelfth lash, his body felt as though it had been covered in tar and set afire. He couldn't utter a sound even if he tried. He couldn't move. Couldn't open his eyes. Couldn't lift his head.

For a long moment the cold sea breeze added torture to his back. He waited for another dozen lashes and was surprised when the boatswain began sawing the binding at his wrists. Apparently, the captain was giving him only a dozen lashes, which was the usual amount allowed without a court-martial, although the law didn't stop more from being issued when a captain thought they were warranted.

Newton supposed he should be grateful to his father for beseeching the admiral, even if he hadn't been able to arrange a transfer. The intervention had lessened his punishment significantly. Even so, he couldn't muster any thankfulness. The only emotion that swirled amid the pain was hatred.

He hated Captain Carteret for imprisoning him on the *Harwich*. He hated the rest of the men for allowing such an injustice, for standing back and doing nothing to stop it. He even hated his father for not being able to do more to get him released, for being so weak, so helpless, so ineffective.

The moment the ropes fell away from the eyebolts, he crumpled to the grate into splatters of his blood. The ship's surgeon was at his side, ready to transport him to the sick berth, where he would have salt water rubbed in his wounds to aid their healing before having bandages applied.

Newton wished he had the strength to push the surgeon away, to tell him to leave him. Even though his body would likely live, Newton wanted to die. If he'd had the strength at that moment, he would have risen, climbed through the porthole, and tossed himself into the sea.

# EIGHTEEN

APRIL 1745

*T*he letter in Polly's pocket burned against her leg. She shouldn't have it. Susanna shouldn't have given it to her. But her spirits had lifted the moment Susanna had secretively slipped it to her after her arrival a short while ago.

Although everything within her longed to find a private spot to tear it open and devour it, she let her fingers dance over the pianoforte keys, forming the melody of a song she hadn't played in many months.

"What a beautiful, cheerful song for this spring evening," Mother said with a smile from where she sat embroidering near the globe lantern that was already glowing brightly.

"It's lovely," Father added, his head leaned back against his wing chair, his eyes closed. In the oncoming shadows of the night, his face seemed more lined than usual, wearier, sadder.

"Sing us the words that go with it." Susanna glanced up from her spot on the settee next to Mother and Eliza. Her cheeks were pink, and her eyes sparkled with an all too familiar mischief. It was no secret that Susanna was involved in her clandestine activities again.

Marriage apparently hadn't cured her aunt's wildness after all. In fact, with each visit that spring, Polly had begun to suspect that Susanna relished getting away from London, that she wasn't as happy in her new marriage as she let on.

"The song is familiar," Susanna continued, the gleam in her eyes growing even more mischievous. "Isn't that one that you wrote with—"

"I composed it myself." Polly ducked her head before her family could see embarrassment coloring her cheeks. Even so, she felt her siblings' gazes turn upon her from where they reclined on the floor playing dominoes.

She wasn't being untruthful. She *had* composed it herself. But 'twas also true that it was the last song she had worked on with John that fateful day when he kissed her for the first time. The day when he'd been impressed.

She hadn't played the song since then. Hadn't wanted to. In fact, since the terrible parting with John at his Christmas leave, she hadn't wanted to play or sing much at all. Her heart felt flat and dreary like a discordant, off-key chord.

But somehow tonight with the promise of spring in the air and John's letter in her pocket, a lightness had returned and a sweet melody was running through her body.

"Sing to us," Eliza pleaded.

Polly smiled, remembering the way John had always been the first to beg her for a song. "If I sing, will you promise to empty the ash bins for me on the morrow?"

"Perhaps." Eliza smiled in return, knowing how little Polly enjoyed that particular task.

Polly's fingers moved over the familiar smooth ivory keys, but before she could begin the song, a loud knock on the front door brought her hands to a hovering standstill.

Every time there was a knock, she prayed it would be John coming to visit her again. Even if her father had told him to leave and not come back. Even if he'd told John that he wasn't the kind of man he wanted for her. Deep inside she hoped they would find a way to be together again. Surely they would.

She would plead with John to work harder at finding a job, to be more reliable, to be more serious about life. She could help him stop drinking and gaming and become a better man, a man of whom her father would finally approve. Couldn't she?

The banging on the front door turned into slamming followed by shouts. Her father rose swiftly from his chair, his features tightening with anxiety.

"George," Susanna said, rising from the settee. "The guest at the door is likely for me. Let me answer it."

"No, Susanna." Father stepped into the hallway without a backward glance. "Stay in the drawing room with everyone else. And don't come out."

Susanna pressed her lips together. Even if she remained composed, there was a slight tremor in her fingers as she took several papers from her pocket and stuffed them down behind the settee cushion.

The door banged open and was followed by an angry curse and "Where are those girls?"

"What girls?" Father replied.

"The two that are responsible for handing out all the pamphlets along the riverfront," said the gruff voice that sounded vaguely familiar—like the ox of a man who had beaten John outside the cave.

"My daughters and other female family members of my household are here resting for the evening with us. If you have any complaints, then you'll have to deal with me."

"That's fine," the visitor growled. "I'll be happy to make you pay. After all your past meddling, it could have been you behind it all anyhow."

Polly's pulse slowed with each word the man spoke.

Her father didn't respond, clearly willing to take the blame upon himself for whatever Susanna had done.

"You should know that Charlie Baldock doesn't like you," the man said. The hairs on the back of Polly's neck stood up at the menace in his tone. "He told me to tell you that he punished you once already, but that'll be nothin' compared to what he's gonna do if you and your family don't stay out of his business."

"You can tell him that I take my orders from God and the king," Father replied tersely. "Not from thugs who break the law so they can fill their pockets with ill-gotten gain."

With that, Father closed the door loudly enough to send a message that he was finished with the discussion. After a moment he reappeared in the drawing room. No one spoke. Polly guessed they were praying, just as she was, that Charlie's man would go away without threatening them anymore.

The mantel clock ticked away a minute before Father looked directly at Susanna. "You know I admire you for your desire to fight the ills of our society. But I cannot allow you to come here and put us all in danger—especially Polly."

Susanna nodded. "I'm sorry—"

"Charlie Baldock already suspects that Polly is against him. And now whatever you did today will only make matters worse for her."

"I didn't think handing out the pamphlets would put Polly in jeopardy." Susanna hung her head for only a moment before lifting her chin. "But if we're able to bring an end to the smuggling and trading of slaves, then isn't it worth the sacrifice? Look at what you've sacrificed for your convictions, George."

From their previous discussions about slavery, Polly knew her father wasn't convinced that the simple act of letting slaves go was the solution to what he believed was a much more complicated issue.

Mother lifted a weary hand to her forehead. "You have other matters that need your attention now, Susanna. Namely your husband and your home."

Susanna's lush brown eyes sparked with indignation. "My husband seems to be able to take care of himself quite well without me." Once the words were out, she blanched.

"Perhaps you're traveling here too often," Mother offered more gently. "Maybe if you were home more often . . ."

Susanna simply shook her head.

"You're newly married, and it takes time to adjust," Mother added. "Besides, I'm sure children will be coming along soon."

Polly squirmed in discomfort and was grateful when Father put an end to the awkward conversation. "Susanna, as much as we enjoy your visits, it's time for you to return to London and stay there." Susanna's eyes flamed with hurt. Before she could contradict Father, he spoke again. "And I'd like Polly to go with you. Perhaps she can live with her grandparents for a while." He glanced at Mother and she nodded. "Polly has always wanted to go to school in London, but since that's not possible, at least she can experience some of the cultured life—"

"I'll pay for her to go to school." Susanna stepped to Polly and drew her into a side embrace. Polly's pulse leaped at the prospect. She couldn't deny she'd experienced pangs of envy whenever Felicity Baldock and her other friends came home from school and boasted about what a lovely time they were having. They were full of such poise, elegance, and maturity.

Would she finally get to join them? She couldn't keep from squeezing Susanna with a new sense of excitement.

Her father shook his head. "No, we couldn't allow you—"

"Why not? I can easily afford it."

Her father's brows arched above troubled eyes. "Your husband may think differently."

"He gives me whatever I want. And if I choose to help Polly, he won't tell me no." Again Susanna's voice contained a bitter edge that Polly didn't understand. "Besides, it's partly my fault that she needs to leave Chatham. I owe you this, George."

Mother's expression radiated her approval. "Polly can stay with Susanna on her breaks and keep her company. Right, Susanna?"

"I'd be delighted to have Polly in London so close to me."

All eyes turned upon Father. Even the youngest of her siblings watched him expectantly. His astute gaze connected with Polly's, and it was as if he could see into her soul. "Perhaps London will help you think about other things."

Polly refrained from patting her pocket. Did he know about her letter? Even if he didn't, apparently he was quite aware that her feelings for John were still strong.

"Then it's settled," Mother said. "Polly will move to London. And you will leave as soon as arrangements can be made."

The rest of the family seemed to take that as their cue that they should return to their activities. Susanna hurried from the room, probably to begin packing. Polly moved to do likewise, the thrum of excitement radiating louder with each step she took.

As she crossed into the hallway, she could sense her father watching her. A moment later she heard his voice behind her. "Try to build some new memories, Polly."

She stopped halfway up the stairs and turned to face him. She couldn't pretend that she didn't understand what he meant. "I know I should, Father. But I can't keep from thinking he'll come back."

"Yes, I have no doubt he would have defied me and attempted to see you even though I've forbidden it."

*"Would have?"* The words sent dread skittering through her.

Her father's kind eyes pooled with the same sadness she'd seen there earlier. Even though he'd ordered John from their home, he would never wish John any ill will. "John deserted his ship but was recaptured."

"No." The word was a harsh whisper that contained all her confusion and horror.

"I'm sorry, Polly. I didn't want to tell you."

"Is he—" She couldn't make herself say the word *dead.* It was too awful, too final. But everyone knew what happened to deserters. "Did they—"

"They didn't hang him," her father said. "But he was flogged and demoted."

Polly shuddered and pressed her hands to her face to hide the sudden tears that sprang to her eyes. *Oh John,* her heart cried. Pain sliced through her as she pictured the cat-o'-nine-tails ravaging John's bare back. *God have mercy.*

"He'll live."

She nodded at her father's gentle words but couldn't speak past the tight ache in her throat. After his unexcused leave at Christmas, she wasn't entirely surprised by the news of John's desertion. No, she was more hurt than surprised. Why hadn't he stayed on his ship like he was supposed to? Why hadn't he tried harder to please his captain and get promoted? If he loved her as much as he said he did, then why hadn't he tried to find a way to make a life for them? Didn't he know a deserter would be hunted, shamed, and cast out? Didn't he know that as a deserter he'd lose all chances of winning her father's approval?

The prospects of having a future with John had been bleak before. But now any chance they may have had to be together completely disappeared.

Her father didn't speak the words he had every right to say: *I told you so.* Instead, she could feel his own deep sorrow at this turn of events.

She inhaled a shaky breath and blinked back her tears before dropping her hands and looking at her father. From where he stood at the bottom of the stairs, the sorrow in his eyes was almost her undoing again. "What will happen to him now?" she managed to whisper without breaking down and sobbing.

"The HMS *Harwich* is scheduled to act as a convoy to a fleet of Royal African Company ships that are headed to the East Indies."

Polly didn't know much about the East Indies except that merchant ships returned from the faraway eastern islands carrying expensive spices like pepper, cloves, nutmeg, cinnamon, and ginger. However, the main goods the merchants traded for were tea and coffee. The merchants could hardly keep up with the high demand for tea in the British Isles and provinces. Even the poor drank tea, buying used tea leaves from cooks of the rich who often used and reused the leaves themselves.

The voyage to the East Indies would involve months of travel down the coast of Africa and then more months of travel over to India and finally months more to the Far East. All told, John could be gone for years.

"It's time for you to go to London," her father said quietly, climbing the steps toward her. "And finally time to say good-bye to John."

She nodded even though the motion pained her. She didn't know how she'd ever be able to forget John Newton. He'd captured her heart in a way no one ever had and in a way she doubted anyone ever would again.

Her father stopped on the step beneath her. And when he opened his arms, she flung herself into his embrace. *Good-bye, John,* her heart whispered as her tears wet her father's shirt. *Good-bye. Forever.*

The sails above Newton flapped as the wind gathered in them. He couldn't straighten his back to look, but that sound was as familiar to him as his own breathing. His wounds were scabbing over and drying, yet any attempt to sit up pulled the skin taut and caused the welts to crack and bleed. The reopening stung like someone was slitting them open with a knife.

Holystoning the deck on his hands and knees was a demeaning chore, but at least his back was safe from too much stretching, especially if he didn't scrub too vigorously.

All around him were the noises of a ship that was finally underway. "Ship off the port stern," the boatswain called. There were shouts from sailors high up in the rigging and the swelling crash of the waves as the ship sliced through the water.

Footsteps slapped the deck, and before Newton could move out of the way, a boot crashed into his ribs and caught his back. The agony of the contact sent him sprawling. He bumped his chin against the piece of sandstone he'd been using to rub sand and water against the deck.

Coarse laughter came from above him along with another kick. "How's that feel, you stinking coward?"

Newton gritted his teeth and refrained from raining curses upon the passing sailors, the men once under his control when he'd been midshipman. Many of them relished ridiculing him every opportunity they could.

He couldn't fight them now, and if he attempted, they'd only beat him until he was a bloody mess again. But he would get revenge at some point. He clenched his hands and let the anger burn a slow flame in his gut. Once he regained his strength and movement, he'd make them wish they'd never touched him.

Slowly and painstakingly, he pushed himself back to his knees, retrieved his sandstone and began to brush it against the filthy deck. The wind blew hard, the coolness barreling into him, taunting and reminding him that the ship was well underway. The *Harwich* was finally leaving Plymouth and heading toward Madeira near the Canary Islands.

He was tempted to sit back on his heels and look over his shoulder at the fading coastline of England. It would be the last time he would see the shores of his homeland for at least five years. But he kept his head down and refused to give in to the urge. If he did, he'd only hate his life even more—if that were possible.

With every passing day, the thought of putting an end to his miserable existence grew more appealing. He didn't know what reason he had for living anymore, not when he was conscripted to this water-borne prison, not when he was in so much pain, not when he had absolutely no reason to keep going.

The only thought that had kept him sane over the past year of being in the navy was the prospect of seeing Polly, of being reunited with her, and of someday marrying her. But he couldn't expect her to wait five years for him to return. She'd surely be swept off her feet by another man and perhaps even married by the time he made it back to England. He'd considered writing to her and asking her to wait. But he loved her too much to ever ask her to make that kind of commitment. And yet, without her in his future, he didn't want to go on.

"This is all his fault," Newton murmured, his jaw clenching and his anger flaring. If only his father had tried harder to orchestrate his transfer. Instead, he'd likely stood back and crossed his arms and said to the admiral, "This is just the lesson my irresponsible son needs to make him grow into a man."

The truth was, he'd never been good enough for his father or for any sort of God. He'd always fallen short in pleasing them both. Being a Christian had been too difficult. So why bother trying—not that he'd tried all that hard in recent years to live an upstanding life. If God existed, he'd abandoned him just as his father had done. Now Newton would do the same to them.

He paused in his slow, halfhearted efforts at scrubbing and spat at the deck. He hated his father. He hated God. Most of all, he hated himself.

# PART THREE

A Year and a Half Later

# NINETEEN

*T*he carriage clattered to a stop in front of a towering home. Freshly painted white classical surround decorated the sash windows. The contrast of the white against the red brick was impressive. Then again, every home in the West End was meant to impress. The new homes had always made Polly gawk when she visited Susanna on breaks from boarding school during the past year and a half.

Even Daniel Eversfield's brand-new landau was striking. Polly ran her gloved fingers over the luxurious red-velvet cushioned seat and inhaled the strong scent of the leather carriage head that had been drawn to keep out the cold December drizzle.

The coachman swung open the door and helped her descend to the cobbled street that was clean and unpolluted for London. Even the air in the West End smelled cleaner and brisker than the stale sourness that pervaded most of the city. Of course, Mrs. Overing's Boarding School at Bethnal Green near Hackney wasn't quite as foul as some parts of London, but nothing could compare to the wealthy area where Susanna and Daniel lived.

Polly straightened her wide-brimmed hat and then proceeded up
the front walkway. A sharp iron fence that protected the house from
burglars also led to a lower entrance that the servants used. And fortunately, Susanna had several servants at her bidding.

Or maybe having extra servants wasn't fortunate for Susanna.
Polly's steps slowed as she remembered her last visit in the autumn,
when she witnessed Susanna slap one of the pretty young maids
across the cheek and then tell her to pack her box and leave the premises. Later when Polly prayed by her bed, she heard Daniel and Susanna arguing through the thin walls. Daniel said something about
not blaming the maid. And Susanna was crying.

Polly didn't understand everything, but with each passing visit,
she thought she was beginning to make sense of what was really
going on in the Eversfield home, and the very insinuation of impropriety was enough to make Polly squirm in discomfort.

Susanna had given her an open invitation to come whenever she
wanted. But Polly usually reserved her calls for school breaks and
holidays. Even then, she'd grown more reluctant to visit; the tension
in the home was something she couldn't quite get used to.

But besides the fact that her presence seemed to make Susanna
happier, Polly couldn't stay away from Susanna's six-month-old baby
girl, Mary. Even now the image of the sweet baby face melted Polly's
heart, and she didn't have to force a smile when she rapped against
the door.

The door swung open and before she could utter a greeting, Susanna was pulling her into her arms with the ardor of a long-lost friend.

"You're here at last!" Susanna said hugging Polly tightly, even
though their hoops collided and she knocked Polly's hat off in the
process.

Polly laughed. "I missed you too."

"Not more than I missed you." Susanna pulled back but didn't let go of Polly's arms as she examined her from her elegantly styled hair down to the tips of her shoes poking out beneath her petticoats. "You look lovelier and more grown up every time I see you."

At almost nineteen, Polly was the oldest girl at Mrs. Overing's. And her age was something her school mistress, Mrs. Arabella Manly, had been commenting on lately. "It's time for you to settle on a young man," the mistress said more than once in recent weeks. "If you don't find one now, you'll end up a spinster, and then all our work here will have been in vain."

The word *spinster* sent shudders through all the young ladies every time Mrs. Arabella Manly mentioned it. Polly couldn't keep from thinking about her neighbor back in Chatham, Miss Donovan, and her little white curly-haired dog, Prince.

Polly's insides curdled at the picture of herself carrying around Pete like a baby, cuddling him and kissing him, the cat sufficing as the closest thing to having a child. No, she wanted to find a loving man who could take care of her and give her a baby like Mary.

Polly peered over Susanna's shoulder to the glittering hallway with its high ceiling, chandelier, spiraling staircase, and gold gilt everywhere—in the mirror frame, the elaborate curves of the banister, and even the floral design of the wallpaper.

Susanna had outdone herself with the decorations throughout her spacious home. The rooms, like the outer facade of the home, were designed to show off her husband's wealth and growing status. While the luxurious interior did indeed mirror his position, it lacked warmth and was sterile and impersonal, much like Susanna's cold, almost impersonal marriage.

Polly listened for the babble or the cries that would direct her to Mary, but Susanna took her hand with a smile. "I can see that I'm no longer the main attraction for your visits."

"If you were short, bald, and had chubby cheeks, then maybe you'd regain your place."

Susanna gave a mock gasp. "I always knew you came to see Dopple."

Polly laughed at Susanna's jest about her aging butler, thinking that Mary and Mr. Dopple did indeed share many similarities. But as the smile faded from Susanna's face and her eyes turned dark and brooding, Polly's laughter stuck in her throat. She supposed speaking of illicit liaisons with servants only brought to the forefront Daniel's dalliances—if indeed that was his crime.

"Take me to Mary." Polly tried to infuse cheer into her voice, something she'd gotten quite accustomed to doing during her visits. "I'm sure she's been missing me terribly."

Susanna led Polly up the stairs to a cozy room across from the parlor where one of the servants was feeding Mary tiny spoonfuls of what appeared to be a creamy rice pudding. Polly insisted on finishing the feeding and then changing Mary's nappy. She'd just settled down into a chair near the hearth with Mary on her lap and had breathed a deep contented sigh, when a servant came to the door.

"I beg your pardon, Madam. I don't mean to disturb you." The young servant hung her head and cringed. Polly didn't recognize the girl from her last visit.

"If you're sorry," Susanna said, each word hard and brittle, "then please refrain from doing it in the first place." She sniffed and started to turn away from the girl.

The servant's cheeks turned a rosy shade at the slight, but she didn't move away. The girl wasn't overly pretty. In fact, she was petite with a long nose and small mouth. Perhaps Susanna had hoped that a plain servant wouldn't pose a temptation to Daniel. Had it worked?

"A visitor's come calling for Miss Polly Catlett," the servant spoke again timidly, as though at any moment she expected Susanna to lash out.

Polly sat up straighter in her comfortable wing chair. "A visitor for me?"

"Aye. He said his name was John Newton."

John? Polly's body forgot to function at the name no one spoke anymore. For a moment she could only sit in stunned silence. She'd tried so hard to obey her father and put John from her mind. The task had been excruciating at first, and she experienced too many painful nights when she wept silent sobs into her pillow. But over time she busied herself with all the new endeavors at school: reading classics and even some Shakespeare, memorizing poetry, performing in a play, learning to dance, and experimenting with all kinds of artistic pursuits, including needlework, japanning, paper cutting, and shell grottoes. She particularly relished their instruction in French. Best of all, she thrived with her music instruction, taking her composing to a new level.

Of course there had also been parties and outings with the new friends she'd made. They'd had plenty of suitors come calling. Several men had even paid her attention. Although none of the men had captured her affection, she'd eventually been able to spend time with them without comparing them to John.

Yes, she'd ruthlessly done all she could to eliminate the thoughts and feelings for John from her mind. After a year and a half, she'd almost come to believe she'd moved on, had put him in her past, had relegated him to a childhood crush.

But now, all the memories she'd tried so hard to wipe from her mind came rushing back in one instant, more vibrant than before, bringing back to life his quick grin, his bright green eyes, his swarthy handsome face, his thickly muscled arms and shoulders.

"By Jupiter, John Newton is here?" she heard Susanna asking. Susanna knew every last detail of what had happened with John as well as she did. Susanna knew the HMS *Harwich* had set sail out of Plymouth. She had even made further inquiries to learn that the ship had made a revictualling stop at Madeira, an important mid-Atlantic port, but had sailed out with the whole fleet of merchant ships and the rest of the naval escort.

"John should be in the East Indies by now," Susanna said. "There's no way he could possibly be back in England."

The servant girl hung her head, apparently unsure how to answer her mistress.

Susanna finally looked at Polly, her eyes reflecting both uncertainty and hope. "Shall I go see first?"

"No. I need to go." Polly stood, kissed Mary's downy head, and passed her back to her nursemaid. Then with shaking legs and a trembling heart, she made her way down to the drawing room. She paused outside the door and took a deep shaky breath. Next to her, Susanna patted her arm. Polly gave her a grateful smile. Steeling her shoulders, she tried to glide into the drawing room with as much poise and grace as she'd learned at Mrs. Overing's.

A tall man with broad shoulders stood peering out the wide front window, his back toward her. The strong stance, the rugged appeal, the set of the shoulders all belonged to John. And yet, he was thinner and not quite as muscular as she remembered.

Even so, she couldn't prevent her startled gasp at the ghost standing before her.

At her gasp, John turned. Only it wasn't him. Instead she found herself looking at a much older version, a man with the same build, the same tanned sailor skin, the same rough edges. His eyes were darker, and the lines at the corners and in his forehead were deeper. His features, while somewhat similar to John's, were decidedly more severe and angular, and his expression contained none of John's mirth or lightheartedness.

"Miss Catlett, I presume?" He stepped away from the window and faced her attired in a stylish frock coat and leather breeches. His black three-cornered cocked hat was under his arm, and his silver tye-wig with side curls gleamed in the lamplight. While perhaps not as fancy as Daniel Eversfield, he looked every bit a man of substance and means.

Polly nodded. "Yes. How do you do?"

"I'm Captain Newton, John's father." His tone was grave, and his eyes much too serious and sad.

Suddenly Polly's mouth went dry and any inkling of hope fled. She hadn't meant to harbor hope, had thought she'd extinguished every last trace. But her knees gave way, and if not for Susanna's quick catch, Polly would have dropped to the floor. There was no other reason for Captain Newton to visit and speak in so somber a tone unless he was delivering dire news. John was dead. That's what he'd come to tell her. John was dead and would never come to see her again.

"I'm sorry to call upon you unannounced." He surveyed the room, his sweeping gaze likely taking in the elegance of the new furniture, the thick tapestries, and the intricately woven carpet.

"What can we do for you, Captain Newton?" Susanna's face was pale, but her voice was unwavering.

Polly tried to remember the things John had said about his father during his visits to Chatham. But other than a few brief negative remarks, he'd rarely spoken of the man. He'd shared more freely about his mother and the love she'd had for him. Polly had surmised that he hadn't been as close to his father in the years following his mother's death.

She could understand why. From first appearance Captain Newton was an intimidating man. And when he turned his attention fully upon her and studied her, she had to resist the urge to press her hand to her head and the coiffure with ringlets hanging to the nape of her neck.

As though sensing her fear, he fumbled at the inner pocket of his coat and retrieved what appeared to be several letters, although from the outside they were torn and dirty, the ink smudged and almost illegible.

"Just this week I received letters from John," he started, but then his voice cracked.

"Letters from John?" she asked almost breathlessly. "Then you haven't come to tell me he's dead?"

Captain Newton's dark brows narrowed together, making his eyes look even sadder. "He was in a great deal of trouble when he wrote this letter to me months ago." He held up the most battered of the correspondence.

"What kind of trouble, Captain Newton?" Susanna asked, still clutching Polly and helping her stay steady on her feet.

Polly wasn't sure that she wanted to hear. But at the same time she couldn't make herself run away.

"It appears he wasn't on the *Harwich* very long," Captain Newton said.

As Captain Newton shared all that he'd learned, Susanna finally invited him to sit down and ordered tea from one of the servants. Polly could only perch on the edge of a chair as he shared the information he'd gleaned from John's letters as well as from the captains of passing ships.

Apparently after three weeks of sailing, the HMS *Harwich* had arrived at Funchal Roads, the chief port in Madeira, which was a Portuguese island colony to the west of Morocco. Since it was the only port of call before Africa, it was an important place to take on additional supplies and to make any necessary minor repairs. While the ship was anchored off the coast along with the rest of the convoy, two merchant seamen had been impressed from a nearby Guinea trading ship, the *Pegasus,* in exchange for two of the *Harwich*'s men.

Captain Newton explained that such an exchange was an accepted practice in the Royal Navy, that captains of merchant ships often gladly handed over unruly crew members for impressment. Apparently someone on board the HMS *Harwich,* perhaps the clerk or one of the midshipmen had taken pity on John and negotiated his discharge. Either that or Captain Carteret of the *Harwich* had grown tired of John's irresponsibility and so had given permission to the switch that not long before he'd denied.

Whatever the case, John ended up being discharged from the Royal Navy and placed on board the *Pegasus,* a slave ship that traded along the dangerous thousand-mile Guinea coast. As it turned out, the captain of the *Pegasus,* Captain Guy Penrose, was a friend of Captain Newton's.

"At first Captain Penrose was delighted to have John on board his ship," Captain Newton said. "I was informed that he reached out to John in kindness, believing that the son of an old friend would prove a loyal and hardworking sailor."

Polly knew what was coming and tensed.

"Unfortunately my son proved Captain Penrose wrong." Captain Newton's shoulders slumped with a discouragement that touched Polly. He loved his son. She could see it.

"I've been told by the *Pegasus* crew that John showed open disrespect to the captain, that he undermined the captain's authority with his insolence and disobedience. Not only that, he engaged in all manner of corrupt and vile behaviors—none of which is fit for a lady's ears."

"I'm sure John was angry after all that had happened to him," Susanna offered as she refilled Captain Newton's cup with more tea, which he took gratefully. "Being impressed against his will and then flogged would be enough to make any man bitter."

In an attempt to be polite, Polly picked up her tea and sipped the now tepid liquid. However, confusion and misery rampaged through her chest. She wanted to be sympathetic toward John like Susanna was, but John had been given a second chance by Divine Providence. He'd been released from the navy, which was exactly what he wanted. Why had he behaved so badly on the *Pegasus*? Surely he would have been relieved and grateful for the transfer.

"Unfortunately," Captain Newton continued, "Captain Penrose died suddenly in Sierra Leone, and the new captain, his first mate, despised John and was making plans to exchange him back to the Royal Navy as an impressed common sailor again. But apparently John made other arrangements before that could happen."

Captain Newton explained to them that while on board the *Pegasus* John met a man by the name of Amos Clow who'd become a successful businessman in Africa, owning and operating a large slave factory. John had signed up to become Clow's employee, and Clow had arranged for his release from the crew of the *Pegasus*.

Although Susanna hadn't been involved with her Quaker friends since Mary's birth, her shoulders now stiffened in protest at John's new line of work.

"From what I've been told," Susanna said indignantly, "the worst of the worst are the slave factory workers who separate families and strip, brand, fetter, and whip the poor helpless souls. Then they finally drag them aboard waiting ships where many of them die in deplorable conditions not fit for animals during their voyage to the slave markets."

Captain Newton stared into his teacup a moment before responding. "In all my years as a sea captain, I never got involved in the slave trade. I couldn't stomach the stench, the filth, or the ruthlessness." He didn't have to say that he was disappointed in John's choice. It was clear from every slumped bone in his back.

Susanna shook her head, her mouth pursed in disgust. "If he's hoping to make his fortune in such work, he'll only lose his soul in the process."

"And possibly his life," Captain Newton said softly.

Polly stiffened. This was the news he'd been leading to during the course of their conversation. Polly was certain of it. John had gotten himself into trouble again. Life-threatening trouble.

Captain Newton glanced up finally and looked at her with tenderness, as though he knew how much John had loved her and how much it would pain her to hear the truth.

She swallowed the growing ache in her throat and nodded at him. "What happened to John next, sir?"

"His letter doesn't tell me much," Captain Newton replied. "And no one I've talked to can give me additional information about John's situation after he left the *Pegasus*. But from what I can tell, he did something to anger his new employer, and as a result Clow put him in chains and locked him up."

"Then he's in the gaol again?" Polly asked.

Captain Newton began unfolding one of the letters. "He said he's enslaved by Clow, beaten and forced to work in the fields to exhaustion. He has to dig up roots and eat them raw in order to prevent starvation but has grown sick and weak."

"How long ago did he write the letter?" Susanna asked.

"Months." The captain's word echoed like the slamming of a coffin lid. For a moment no one spoke, the gravity of John's predicament too awful to grasp.

Captain Newton handed Polly two other folded pieces of paper. "He somehow managed to have my letter smuggled out of the Plantains along with these two for you."

Polly took the folded sheets of paper. They'd clearly been opened and read. But her heartbeat picked up pace. The paper had come directly from John. His hands had touched the sheets. His fingers had penned the words. His thoughts had been fixed upon her. "I've beseeched an old friend of mine in Liverpool, Joseph Manesty," Captain Newton said. "Manesty runs a shipping business and has alerted the captains of his African sailing vessels to make inquiries about John wherever they can. If they find him, they're to do whatever is necessary to bring him home."

*If he's still alive.*

The unspoken words hung over them.

"We shall pray that someone finds him," Susanna finally said, squeezing Polly's hand.

"One of Manesty's ships is leaving for Sierra Leone soon. I'm sending a letter with the captain." Captain Newton cleared his throat before continuing. "I wanted to inquire—at the very least I wanted to offer to have the captain deliver a letter from you, Polly. If you should choose to write. Although there's no obligation."

When he met Polly's gaze, his warm eyes were alight with hope.

Her first reaction was to tell him that she'd be delighted to pen a letter to John with the expectation that he was still alive and that the letter might encourage him to persevere.

But she'd come to finally accept that as much as she'd cared about John, a future with him was out of the question. Not only had her father and mother both cautioned her against it, the distance away from John and her own maturing had helped her realize that a union with John would have been fraught with frustration and disappointment.

She'd loved so many things about John. But the hard truth was that they didn't share the same values or faith, not when she tried so hard to earn God's favor and John didn't care about God at all. From the description of John's life in the last year, he'd only sunk deeper into sin. Thus any union would be uncommon.

Of course, after her time at Mrs. Overing's, she'd come to understand even more the need to find someone who could provide for her the lifestyle to which she was accustomed. Even though her father had never regained his officer position, she realized her family was still comfortable compared to the poverty she'd witnessed in London. But with someone like John who couldn't hold a job? What would her life be like then?

"I'm sorry, Captain Newton." She shook her head, the weight of her denial heavy. "It pains me to have to say so. But I will have to decline your invitation to write a letter. I cannot disobey my father or go against my conscience and offer John hope of a future."

The light in the captain's eyes faded, replaced with a grief that made her want to cry. She suspected the depth of his emotion wasn't directed at her but was instead the despondency of a parent with a wayward child who has caused much heartache. She had the feeling that not only was he grieving the loss of his son in a physical sense but even more he mourned the loss of hopes and dreams and plans for John's future.

"I understand completely," he said. "As much as I wish John were worthy of your love, I fully realize he's not."

Her fingers trembled so that the letters she was holding rattled.

"You are a good and kind woman," he said. "And I can see why John loves you. I'm only sorry that he's caused you so much heartache."

"I will continue to pray for him, that wherever he is God will spare him and return him to you, and more importantly return him to the One who holds all things in his hands."

Captain Newton rose and placed his hat on his head, adjusting it over his wig. As he took his leave, Polly felt as though her heart had been ripped out of her chest all over again. All the talk of John had brought him straight to the forefront of her hopes and desires.

But she'd closed the door on a life with John Newton. And now she had to keep it closed.

# TWENTY

*S*weat trickled down Newton's bare back. The African sun blazed with a heat that he still couldn't get used to, especially in February. On sweltering days like this, he missed England's cooler winter climate, although in a few months the rainy season would begin and bring some relief to the heat.

He dipped a hand into the Sherbro River and splashed his face with the warm salty water. Below the surface, the shiny silvery scales of a tarpon flashed in a glint of sunlight. The tarpon's large eyes seemed to peer up at him and accuse him, and its lower jaw protruded in a grim line as though in disapproval of his work.

The shallop swayed against the lapping tide that brought the ocean water upriver. The sailboat sat low, already filled with bundles of cloth, iron bars, brandy, and copper pots that he and his partner, Devon, would use to trade with local chiefs for their captives.

"I think we can squeeze in one more bundle of brandy," Devon said, shifting a pack under a bench to make room.

Newton shrugged, too hot to care. "I'll wait." He moved away from the tangled mangrove roots along the shore to the shade of a

tall patch of ferns. As he sat down in the swampy grass, several stri-
ated herons took flight. Even though he knew he needed to keep an
eye on the handful of chained slaves who would help man the shallop, he was ready for a nap. It was only midmorning, but the drinking and revelry from the previous night made him sluggish with a
hangover as it usually did.

Once he got moving, he'd gain the energy he needed. But it always took awhile. Thankfully his partner didn't mind. In fact, they
made a good pair, the two of them. Devon did all the organizing and
administrative work. And Newton took care of wooing the chiefs at
the villages deep in the countryside. He knew how to relate to them,
and they in turn liked him enough to invite him into their homes,
feed him, and even offer him his choice from among the concubines
at night, all of which Newton accepted.

The local chiefs loved trading for the British goods and weapons
that would help them gain superiority over rival tribes. In turn, the
chiefs provided Newton with captured enemies that he and Devon
would then bring back here, to their coastal base at Kittam.

Newton didn't care that they were cheating the chiefs. Each of the
slaves they purchased inland cost them about three pounds of traded
goods. But a single slave in good condition could be sold in the Carib-
bean for about twenty-five pounds.

At a nearby shout, Newton opened one eye and glanced toward
the barracoon where he and Devon kept the slaves awaiting transport to foreign markets. The shed was nothing more than a square
pen made of stone walls with a thatched roof. They'd recently had to
expand with a fenced area for overflow. Most of the slaves had ropes
tied around their necks or intertwined in their hair and then tied to

the roof beams overhead. Some of the more aggressive men had to be put in rough-hewn stocks fastened to their legs or hands.

The first time he'd seen a slave factory, back when he was still working for Clow, he was so nauseated by the sights and smells that he retched into a nearby ditch to the laughter of his companions.

"I see sails," came the shout again, this time clearer and from Devon, who was striding toward the white sandy beach that led to the ocean. "I'll get closer and let you know."

Newton nodded, his head groggy and his limbs as heavy as the iron fetters that had bound him not many months ago. He didn't like to think about those first months in Africa. He'd started out with such high hopes after the transfer from the *Harwich* to the *Pegasus* and then to his working arrangement with Clow on the Plantains. He'd been consumed with the possibilities of all the quick money he would be able to make as a land-based slave trader. Clow himself had become a very wealthy man through buying and selling slaves and had promised him the same.

He had visions of returning to England attired in a fancy new suit, walking into the Catlett home, and shoving a bag full of gold crowns in front of Mr. Catlett's face. He would say, "What do you think of me now, mate? Think I'm finally good enough for your daughter?" The man wouldn't be able to refuse him because John would have everything necessary to give Polly the kind of stylish and comfortable life she deserved.

During the first weeks with Clow, they'd made a couple of voyages upriver to Rio Nuna, and Clow had introduced him to the process of buying slaves from inland tribes. They would view slaves already captured by natives, pick out the strongest ones most likely to fetch a profit, and then pay the tribal leaders with the goods they'd brought with them.

At first Newton had struggled with the idea of buying people like one would buy tea or coffee. But over the weeks he eased his conscience by telling himself that the tribal leaders were to blame. They were the ones sending raiding parties into neighboring lands with the sole purpose of kidnapping people to sell to the Europeans. He'd heard tales of one African king in Dahomey who was making close to two hundred fifty thousand pounds a year selling other Africans into slavery. Newton figured if the Africans wanted to sell people, then he needn't feel guilty for his role in the slave trade.

Things had gone well working with Clow for a while. But then, during one of their upriver trips, a fellow trader had accused Newton of stealing rum out of the bundles of trade goods. Newton had been adamant in his innocence, but unfortunately, Clow had believed the other man. Newton could admit he was guilty of all kinds of other vices in his life, but he hadn't stolen this time. Not even one drop.

Nevertheless, Clow had chained him to the deck of the shallop for the remainder of the voyage. Of course it had been the rainy season, so he'd been constantly battered by downpours and had been wet and miserably cold. Clow had also denied him food, except for the smallest possible rations of rice. When they'd returned to the Plantains, Clow had treated him no better than he would a slave. And of course his mistress, Princess Pi, had relished joining in the persecution. She claimed to be a princess of her tribe, from an important family that had helped Clow get started in his business as an African trader. But she was nothing but a sadistic fiend.

Pi had taken great pleasure in thinking up new ways to torment him. One of the worst was keeping him on minimal water rations and allowing him almost no food. She summoned him into her presence while she was feasting and made him watch her. She'd toss him scraps, which fell to the floor, but she wouldn't allow him to pick up the dirty food and eat it. Instead she mocked and laughed at him. She forced her servants to throw stones and limes at him and heaped all kinds of verbal abuses upon him.

There had been plenty of nights during that time when he'd wanted to die. Sick with vomiting and diarrhea from the roots he attempted to eat, he'd lost all resolution to live. He could easily say that those months in captivity on the Plantains had been the lowest point in his life, even lower than when he'd been flogged and forced to leave England.

The only thing that kept him alive was his hope that his smuggled letters to his father would reach England and that his father would somehow manage to find a way to free him so that he could be reunited with Polly. He'd written a couple of letters to her too. But after months of not hearing anything in response, he'd given up hope that anyone was coming to rescue him. His father had failed him again.

Thankfully, a fellow slave trader, Smith, had persuaded Clow to release him. He wasn't sure why Smith wanted him—perhaps because he'd gained a reputation among tribal leaders for his ability to liven a party. As a result they liked and trusted him, and he could often manage to make deals that others couldn't.

Newton had been lucky—very lucky—that Clow agreed to Smith's exchange. He still didn't understand why the tyrant decided to let him go. He'd concluded that Clow and his wife had finally tired of belittling and humiliating him. The game had grown old, had no longer been fun. And Pi had likely found a new person to torment with her devious ways.

Whatever the case, he'd been freed from his long months of bondage and suffering and had been working for Smith in his Kittam slave factory for several months. Early on when working for Smith, he'd considered abandoning his new employer and boarding the first passing vessel that would take him back to England. But again the lure of easy money had kept him there. He could make more in a month in Africa doing this wretched work than he could in England in a year.

Nay, he was determined not to return until he'd amassed a fortune and could finally return to Mr. Catlett with his head held high. Surely he could do that within the next year or two. Already Smith had made him and Devon partners, which meant they had the right to own a percentage of the slaves they brought in and could then turn around and sell them to slave-ship captains for their own profit.

"Ahoy, Newton! There's a ship!" His partner was running back up the beach and stumbling in the ankle deep sand. "I'll start the bonfire."

"Do you want me to help?" Newton called without moving from his spot in the shade.

"Aye," Devon shouted. "Her sails are full and she's moving fast."

Newton struggled to his feet and tried not to stagger even though he was dizzy. He waved at the Africans still waiting in the shallop and motioned them ashore. Their chains clanked as they crawled out of the boat, and their ebony skin glistened with sweat after having sat in the tropical sun for the past hour waiting to leave.

"We'll set sail later," he explained, although none of them spoke English. With the barrel of his pistol he prodded them back to the barracoon, to the outer fenced area, and made quick work of binding them. The stench emanating from the nearby slave hut was putrid since most of the slaves sat in their excrement. Every few days, he and Devon would force a couple of the women to clean out the hut as best they could. They had to keep the slaves strong and alive until they could sell them to a passing ship. But the fact remained that it was highly impractical to loosen the slaves bonds every time they needed to relieve themselves. After all, he and Devon weren't being paid to be nursemaids. They were being paid to sell valuable stock.

Newton dragged his heavy feet through the hot sand until he reached the wide-open, level spot on the beach that they used for lighting large fires. When men on passing ships saw their smoke, the captain would know they had slaves to sell. If the ship was a slave trader and had room for more cargo, then the captain would send a longboat ashore to make purchases.

"We're nearing capacity," Devon said, as he tossed another log onto the flames, sending sparks shooting into the air along with the black smoke that they needed. "We'd do best to delay our trip inland for a day. If we sell most of the slaves we already have waiting, then we'll be able to make room for the new slaves we bring back."

"Aye. Good that." Newton threw on a dried tangle of mangrove roots. The heat of the blaze hit him full in the face, forcing him to step back. Even so, the hair on his arms pricked, singed from the close contact.

He unhooked his shirt from his gun holster and used the linen to fan the flames and smoke higher until it was rising in billowing clouds.

In the distant northwest, he caught sight of the sails and rigging that Devon had already spotted.

They took turns adding wood for the next hour until finally the ship drew close enough that they could see several of the crew on the poop deck.

"Is she dropping her anchor?" Devon asked. His face was black with the smoke and streaked with sweat. The young man was serious almost all the time and reminded Newton of his fellow midshipman on the *Harwich,* Job Lewis. Whereas Lewis had been enamored with the Bible and God, Devon had begun dabbling in some of the local witchcraft, necromancies, and divinations. Newton had seen plenty of black magic and voodoo practices during his visits inland among the tribes. He'd witnessed dances and ceremonies that were fascinating, and he could understand why Devon was infatuated with some of the amulets and charms. He'd participated as well.

There were times he could almost believe Devon was under some kind of demonic spell—if that kind of thing was truly possible. Yet if he admitted that the strange things he'd seen were real and not just a figment of his drugged imagination, then he'd have to admit that a supernatural world really did exist and with it the possibility of God. After the past couple of years of denying the existence of God and living his life as he pleased, he didn't want to think too deeply about all that he had witnessed in recent séances.

"I'll paddle out and meet the captain," Devon said, already dragging the canoe toward the water. "That way hopefully we can sell the slaves today and be on our way upstream tomorrow."

"They'll send in some men eventually," Newton said, his exhaustion hitting him again. He could admit he was lazy. Why make the effort to row out to the ship when the crew would come to shore before the day's end?

"I don't mind going out to meet them." Devon flipped the canoe over and shoved it into the relatively calm water that was lapping with a gentle rhythm against the shore. "I'll be back shortly."

Newton dropped the log he'd been holding back onto the pile. His attention shifted to a hammock tied between two palm trees. The spot was covered with blessed shade. He didn't wait for Devon to reach the ship before he crossed to the hammock, climbed inside, and closed his eyes.

The first vision to float before him was Polly's beautiful face, the fairness of her skin, the elegance of her cheeks, and the sparkle in her blue eyes. After all the time away from her, he could still feel the softness of her lips against his and the silkiness of her blond hair in his calloused fingers. He could still hear her angelic voice. He could still see her sweet smile. No one would ever compare to her. She was pure. Undefiled. And the picture of all that was good in this world.

He dug in his pocket and let his fingers trace the embroidered initials on her handkerchief. The linen that had once been so white and perfect was now dirty and frayed. And yet he still clung to it, still kept it with him everywhere he went.

He pushed aside the thought of all the women he'd been with during his time in Africa. None of them meant anything. None of them mattered. If he was honest with himself, he knew he was using them to sate his lusts and nothing more. He was, after all, a man with physical needs. He had no religious rules holding him back. He could live however he pleased.

Yet he squirmed at the guilt that flamed in his gut. What would

Polly think if she discovered his unfaithfulness? Even if he wasn't married to her, even if they didn't have a binding commitment to each other, he couldn't keep from feeling as though he'd betrayed her faith and trust in him.

He shouted a string of oaths and draped his arm across his eyes. The hammock swung back and forth. For a moment, he tried to conjure a feeling of peace and happiness. But instead he felt only discontent.

As time had worn on and as he continually gave in to the passions of his flesh without regard to anyone else, he'd experienced pleasure. He couldn't deny that. But it never lasted. Like now.

His eyelids grew heavy, and he dozed until shouting on the beach awoke him. He pried his eyes open to the sight of Devon pulling the canoe back onshore. A glance at the palm tree shadows and the position of the sun high overhead told him that he'd rested for a couple of hours. Even so, he still felt lethargic.

He forced his feet out from the hammock and pushed himself up with a groan. Not far behind Devon, halfway between the ship and the shore, was a longboat.

"Looks like we're in luck," Newton called to his partner. "How many slaves do they have room to take on board?" He was always relieved to get rid of the slaves awaiting transport. Looking at them day after day, watching them waste away, listening to their pitiful cries and pleas always began to wear on him.

There were times early on when he was tempted in the middle of the night to sneak into the barracoon, loosen the ropes, and leave the gate unlocked so that the slaves would have the chance to escape, especially some of the women with infants. Those times always made him think of Susanna and her abolitionist friends. Mayhap they were made of stronger conscience than he was to be able to put their own lives at stake to free people they didn't know.

He'd had to restrain himself on more than one occasion by drinking himself into a stupor. He always got himself dead drunk before Devon branded the new slaves so that he could avoid the screams of agony and the charred scent of burned flesh.

"Hopefully they can clean us out," Newton called again to Devon.

"No such luck!" he shouted across the span of beach. "The *Greyhound* isn't a slave ship."

The relief Newton had experienced only a moment ago was replaced by a choking heaviness. If the ship wasn't trading for slaves, she was likely trading for other African goods, like gold, ivory, beeswax, and camwood, of which they had none. All they had were slaves, and he wanted to get the slaves out of here, get paid, and then assuage his guilt. But it looked like they were to be stuck with the suffering mass of humanity awhile longer.

"Why are they coming to shore?" he called angrily. "I hope they don't expect us to ply them with our rum if they have nothing to give us in return."

"Nay, nothing like that." For the first time Newton noticed the hint of excitement in Devon's voice.

Newton stared at the longboat, which was almost upon the beach now. He searched the forms and faces of the sailors at the oars, but none impressed him with familiarity. "What do they want?" he growled.

Devon came closer. His long hair was greasy from unwash. His face was in a constant state of red, either from exertion or sunburn. And his sour stench preceded him by a league. Newton guessed he himself wasn't much better. "Believe it or not," Devon said with a rare smile, "they want you."

"Me?" He scoffed. "Who the devil would want me?"

"Your father."

All the dark noises in the recesses of Newton's mind ceased to clamor. The breeze blowing off the Atlantic seemed to die, leaving him standing in a hot void of nothingness.

"Captain Swanwick of the *Greyhound* has been charged by his master, Joseph Manesty, and your father to find and rescue you from your imprisonment."

Newton's attention shifted to the tall man at the bow who was sitting stiff and erect. Eying his blue coat and waistcoat, Newton had no doubt he was the captain. Newton suspected that attired as he was, the man was dripping with sweat. Nevertheless, like any good English ship captain, he'd come visiting in style.

Apparently Newton's father had received his letter. His heart gave a leap like that of flying fish. But then just as quickly sank. After hearing of his plight, his father had clearly been moved enough to ask for help finding him. But as usual, the help was too little too late.

Nevertheless, he approached the captain and the crew eagerly, hoping for letters and news from home. They exchanged pleasant-ries, and Newton invited the captain and his mate inside the low stone home that belonged to his boss but that he and Devon lived in while in Kittam. Servants prepared them a large meal, and when the men had their fill and were reclining on the open front veranda that faced the ocean, Captain Swanwick finally broached the reason for his visit.

He'd removed his hat, coat, and cravat, and between puffs on his pipe, he explained how he'd come to be in Kittam. He'd been given orders by Joseph Manesty to make inquiries along the Guinea coast during his trading ventures. He called at the Bay of Sierra Leone and at Benanoes Islands and asked about Newton in both places. Although he talked to several people who remembered Newton, no one was able to give him clear information about his current location. In fact, one trader had said he'd last seen Newton many miles inland. With that news, Captain Swanwick had given up hope of finding Newton and decided to finish his trading mission without any further delays.

"After losing time already, I was planning to pass by your smoke signal," the captain said. "We had a fair wind behind us, and I wanted to make use of it to further our progress."

"Aye. Understandable. You had no need to stop here since you have no interest in buying slaves." Newton sat on a stool near the captain, his back against the cool stone wall, his gaze on the sun beginning to set on the calm waters that met the horizon. "I'm lucky you decided to drop anchor. And you're lucky I was still here. Devon and I were minutes from departing for an inland trading journey."

"It wasn't luck at all," the captain countered. "It was clearly the hand of Providence that orchestrated our meeting. I still can't explain the feeling that came over me that made me decide to drop anchor even against my better judgment, except that it was Providence miraculously intervening to bring us together."

Their meeting was purely coincidental. But Newton held his mockery in check. Captain Swanwick was obviously a devout man and wouldn't take kindly to any sacrilege.

Captain Swanwick handed him a letter, and Newton tried to reach for it calmly instead of snatching the sheet and tearing it open as he was wont to do. He hoped it was a letter from Polly, but was only slightly disappointed to see his father's neat penmanship on the outside addressing the letter to him.

"Your father will be happy to know you're alive," Captain Swanwick said, as Newton unsealed the letter and perused it. The note was brief and to the point, indicating his father's willingness to pay any fees that were necessary to free him from his bondage and return him to England.

"I've got orders to bring you home with us to England," Captain Swanwick continued as he released a ring of tobacco smoke. "Your father promised to pay your passage in full if you should be found, and of course pay a handsome reward to the one who brings you home."

Newton folded the sheet, his emotions suddenly swirling in a vortex of confusion. "My father is a generous man." While the captain had done well for himself in recent years, surely such costs would require him to sacrifice of himself and his family. Why would his father do such a thing for him? Especially after the contempt Newton had shown him. It made no sense.

"I'll write a letter this very night to your father," the captain said. "He'll be relieved to get the news we found you."

Newton didn't know quite how to answer. Was it feasible he hadn't given his father enough credit for loving him? Mayhap his father's love ran deeper than he'd ever known was possible. Newton's throat tightened at the thought.

"We'll need to set sail again on the morrow at daybreak," Captain Swanwick said. "Think you can be packed and ready by then?"

The words jarred Newton's attention from the horizon to the ship anchored offshore. Had the invitation reached him when he was sick and starving at the Plantains, he would have received it as life from the dead. But now . . . He was free. He was his own man. He was finally setting his own course for his life without anyone controlling him. And he needed more time to earn his fortune, especially considering the fact that he hadn't saved much yet but had been spending it all too freely on his imbibing and gambling.

"Of course I still have some trading to finish up before I'm ready to set sail for home," the captain continued. "I'll be making stops at ports along the coast down to Cape Lopez before I catch the trade winds across the Atlantic."

Newton nodded. Following the trade winds covered a greater distance and took ships to Brazil, then north to Newfoundland before pushing them back to England. Newton knew that Captain Swanwick was probably looking at another year before he'd be back in England.

Only one year and he could be reunited with Polly. He'd get to see her beautiful face. He'd get to talk with her and spend time with her and mayhap even hold her in his arms. The prospect was too tempting to resist.

He sat forward, his body tense with the need to go. Part of him was ready to run to the longboat and get on the ship before anything else happened to prevent him from going back home. The impulsive man he'd once been would have jumped at the chance to return to Polly regardless of the cost or consequences.

But another part of him—the cynical man he'd become—held him back. As eager as he was to see Polly, he doubted whether she'd be happy to see him. No doubt she'd heard about his desertion and flogging. He'd been disgraced, and what woman would want him with such a blemish on his reputation? He'd always known he wasn't good enough for her, but now he was even worse.

Nay, the only way he could win her was by returning with a fortune. He had to stick with his plan to remain in Kittam, start saving his money more carefully, and then go home after he'd amassed enough to win Mr. Catlett's favor.

"I can't go yet, sir," Newton said.

"How many days do you need to wrap up your business?" the captain asked. "I really don't have much time to wait since all my querying after your whereabouts has put me behind."

"I can't go at all."

Captain Swanwick took his pipe from his mouth and stared at Newton with surprised eyes. "I don't understand. Don't you want to be rescued?"

"My situation has changed since I penned that letter to my father. I'm no longer in such dire straits."

"But you must be ready to go." The captain's features grew taut. "This pagan place is not appropriate for any decent, God-fearing man to live."

He was tempted to tell the captain that he was safe since he wasn't decent or God-fearing. But he knew what the captain was alluding to—the fact that inland slave traders had a less than stellar reputation. They'd gained a reputation as exploitative, self-serving, and cruel. Many of them had taken on the lifestyle and habits of the natives. Not only that, but the work was inherently dangerous and the death rate high. He would be putting his life in continued peril if he stayed.

"As much as I'd like to return with you, sir, I cannot leave yet."

"May I ask why?" The captain returned his pipe to his mouth and took several quick puffs.

Newton stared at the dot of flaming red nearing the horizon, partially covered by pink and purple clouds that stretched across the sky. "I can't go home empty-handed."

The captain was quiet for a moment and then sat up so rapidly that it startled several flycatchers that had perched on a low post at the front of the house. "You have no need to worry about going home empty-handed. Not when you have a large inheritance waiting for you."

It was Newton's turn to be startled. "Inheritance?"

The captain's stoic expression became animated. "Yes, as a matter of fact, the inheritance is worth about four hundred pounds a year."

Newton slid forward on the stool and nearly fell to the veranda's stone floor. Then he caught himself and shook his head. "Nay. 'Tis impossible." The amount was too large to be true.

" 'Tis entirely possible," Captain Swanwick insisted. "A distant relative has passed on during your absence and left you his estate."

"Why are you just telling me this now?"

"I thought I'd have plenty of time to relay that information during the voyage."

Newton's heart began to pound at the thought of four hundred pounds a year. With that amount Mr. Catlett certainly wouldn't be able to refuse him. Newton would be able to offer Polly a life far above anything she'd ever dreamed of. He would be able to give her anything she wanted—an enormous house, a country estate, the latest fashions, numerous servants, a new pianoforte, and luxury in every form.

He shook his head again. "Nay, this can't be true."

"I was instructed to pay a ransom for your release. Up to half the cargo of the *Greyhound* if need be. How do you think your father could afford that if not for the inheritance?"

His father would never be able to afford to repay half the cargo without some other means. Mayhap that was how his father could also afford to pay the reward for finding him. Even so, Newton couldn't believe that such fortune would come his way. Nothing good like that ever happened to him.

"And of course, your father has also paid for your first-class travel home. You won't have to work. In fact, you shall lodge in my cabin and dine at my very own table."

Newton could only sit in stunned silence, the thudding of his heart echoing loudly in tempo to the waves lapping the shore. What if his great-uncle in Maidstone had died? He was a wealthy man, and since he had no children, he could have left his estate to Newton. That's what his father had always hoped would happen and had been one of the reasons he'd sent Newton to Maidstone on occasion.

But four hundred pounds a year as an inheritance? Surely his uncle hadn't been a man of quite that means.

Mayhap the captain was misinformed on the exact amount. Mayhap he'd inherited two hundred pounds a year. Even that would be more than enough to go home with pride, to hold his head high, and to be able to finally propose to Polly without anyone having cause to object.

"So what say you, young man?" Captain Swanwick asked. "Will you be ready to leave on the morrow?"

Newton searched the captain's face. The captain seemed a man of integrity, much like his father. He certainly wouldn't have cause to lie.

Across the yard, a flash of movement caught Newton's attention. Devon was dragging a young African woman away from the area of the slave hut and toward the house. Even though the shadows of the evening had lengthened, it was still light enough to see that the woman was naked and dripping wet.

Newton glanced away in sudden embarrassment, hoping the captain hadn't seen the woman. He knew Devon was only doing what they always did when they had special visitors. He'd washed the slave girl up and would give her to their company to use as they saw fit during the night. The first mate and the sailors who'd come ashore could take their turns with her. After the deprivation of shipboard life, the sailors would be indebted to him and Devon for such an offer.

But the captain was clearly a righteous man. Surely he wouldn't approve, and he wouldn't take kindly to him leading his officer and sailors astray. Newton certainly didn't want the captain to tell tales of his hedonistic lifestyle once they returned to England.

Newton stood, his mind made up. "I'm ready to go tonight, sir. Right now as a matter of fact."

# TWENTY-ONE

SEPTEMBER 1747

*P*olly hugged her mother tightly.

"It's so good to have you home, my love," her mother murmured against her ear.

Polly pulled back with a smile. "I'm glad to be home."

"You look so fancy and grown up," cried Eliza, who ran to her and threw her arms around her.

"I haven't changed all that much since I saw you in the spring," Polly replied with a laugh. The autumn sunshine was warm and bathed her childhood home in a soft glow as if to welcome her back.

"I hope you're home for good," Eliza said, linking arms and strolling with her up the walkway to the door.

After finishing at Mrs. Overing's in the spring, Polly had spent the summer traveling with school friends, first to Bath, then to visit Jack at Oxford, and then finally to one of her friend's country estates in Elsfield. While the summer had been delightful, full of parties and introductions to more men than she could keep count, she was relieved to have the quiet of home again.

"I'm not going anywhere soon," Polly spoke playfully with her sister. "Unless of course you refuse to listen to all my new songs and praise them highly."

Eliza giggled. "I will be your greatest fan and demand that you play them over and over."

"Then I think I shall have to stay forever." Polly leaned into her sister for a half hug.

Her mother linked her other arm, and they strolled together. "You needn't do anything but just enjoy being home," Mother said, her eyes sparkling with a gladness that made Polly realize how much she'd missed everyone. Seeing them on school breaks had never been long enough.

But even as her mother's gracious words flowed over Polly, she wasn't naive enough to believe them. She had work to do—the work of finding a husband. No one would say those words to her. But at twenty years of age, she knew it well enough. It was her primary job now. She was polished and perfected, the prime marriageable candidate. Now she needed to choose before the eligible men were snatched up.

The front door opened and her father stepped out. He was as tall and thin as he'd always been. Except for more gray hairs mingled with the brown, he was virtually unchanged. His warm eyes met hers, and his smile radiated true joy at seeing her.

She broke away from her sister and Mother and ran to him. With a laugh of delight, she found herself wrapped into his arms. "Welcome home, Polly." He kissed the top of her head before releasing her. "I can't tell you how much we've all been looking forward to this day."

He searched her face for a moment as though silently assessing how she really fared. He'd always been able to see deeper inside her, past her facades, past her smiles, to the truth. She knew he was at-tempting to gauge how she was feeling about John Newton, whether she still cared for him or if she'd been able to forget about him and move on.

She gave him a genuine smile hoping he could see that she was finally free. Yes, she'd struggled in the few weeks after Captain New-ton's visit to Susanna's London residence last December. Yes, his visit had awakened emotions she hadn't wanted to feel again. Yes, she'd ached with a need for John she couldn't deny.

But that was all gone again. She'd had even more time in the ensuing months to cut her ties with him. After all, Captain Newton's visit had confirmed that John was all but dead anyway. There was little hope that he'd survived his captivity in Africa. Even if he had, that didn't matter to her. She made clear to Captain Newton that she didn't want to have anything more to do with John. Either way, John was dead to her. Just as he should be. Just as her father had hoped for.

Her father brushed her cheek before returning her smile. "You grow more lovely every time I see you."

Before she could respond, her younger siblings surrounded her, clamoring for hugs and talking all at once. As her trunks and boxes were unloaded, she updated her family on news of Jack at the univer-sity and shared some of the experiences she had during the summer.

They'd only just finished eating dinner when a knock sounded on the front door. Eliza smiled dreamily when the servant announced that Billy Baldock had come calling.

Her father was the first to approach Billy, who was standing in the front hallway.

"Good evening, sir," Billy said with a slight bow. He was wearing a crisp navy-blue customs officer's uniform, a long frock coat with gleaming silver buttons down the front over a long waistcoat. He'd already removed his hat to reveal his wig.

His attention shifted to her standing in the dining-room doorway, and in one sweeping glance he took in her stylish garments, the elegantly embroidered and beaded stomacher decorating the burgundy-colored bodice and matching skirt. The dark red contrasted with her pale skin and fair hair. It was one of her least fancy garments, one she often wore for traveling. But nevertheless, it was a flattering outfit, and she couldn't prevent the small measure of satisfaction at Billy's reaction.

His eyes widened and his Adam's apple rose and then fell before he finally tore his attention away from her and back to her father. "I heard Miss Catlett had returned from her travels, and I hoped I might be allowed to invite her and one of her sisters for a brief stroll since it's such a fine autumn evening."

Her father studied Billy for a moment. "She's spent a long day traveling and is weary from the ride."

Billy bowed his head in acquiescence. "I understand completely, sir. May I have the privilege to come calling on Miss Catlett tomorrow evening?"

Father glanced at her with a raised brow. She couldn't help noticing the concern in his eyes and wondered at it.

She gave Billy what she hoped was a reassuring smile. "It would be lovely to visit with you, Billy."

Billy broke into a grin, highlighting his dashing good looks. Surely he had caught the eye of some local girl? Next to Polly, Eliza gave a soft sigh and gazed at Billy with undisguised admiration. Polly had to force back a chuckle. At the very least, he'd captured Eliza's attention.

Billy put his hat back on and gave her a nod. "I'll look forward to tomorrow evening and hearing about your time away at school."

"I'll walk you out to the front gate," Polly offered.

His eyes lit up, but he looked at Father for permission. Father nodded and took a step back. He appeared as though he might say something more to caution her, but then he smiled and waved her forward.

As she stepped outside in the fading evening light, she glanced overhead and saw the first star of the coming night. The air was cooler than when she'd arrived, but still pleasant enough.

"It's good to see you again," Billy whispered, with a glance over his shoulder at the open door behind them where several of her siblings stood watching.

"I'm glad to see you too."

"Do you mean it?" He slowed his steps to almost a crawl.

"I wouldn't say it if I didn't." She smiled up at him.

His expression turned suddenly serious. "I've been waiting for the day of your return, Polly. I've nearly worried myself sick that you may have met quite a number of men while you've been away."

"I did."

"And . . ." His feet came to almost a standstill. "Did any of them capture your heart?"

She didn't want to admit that only one man had ever captured her heart and that man had been John Newton. But that was in her past, a past she wanted to forget. Instead, she focused on the present, on the important task of picking a husband from among the good men available to her. "I've given permission to a couple of gentlemen to call on me now that I'm home."

"You have?" Billy's voice rose with dismay.

"Surely you wouldn't have me become an old spinster?" she tried to tease, but remembered that Billy was a much more serious man than John.

"You won't become a spinster," Billy said, as gravely as she expected.

She glanced to the window next door where the figure of a woman half-hidden in the draperies of a second-floor room watched them. It was Miss Donovan, and she was holding her dog. At the sight of Polly peering her way, she fell away from the window.

"I'd like permission to come calling on you too." His words tripped over themselves awkwardly, but that didn't stop him. "And not just as a friend."

They'd reached the front iron gate, and he stopped and faced her. She had the feeling that if her younger sisters hadn't been giggling in the doorway, Billy might have even reached for her hand. She searched his eyes, seeing in them a sincerity and kindness that reminded her of Father. She supposed she would inevitably compare every man to her father. She couldn't help it. She wanted a man with the same character, the same solid integrity, the same abiding faith, and the same love of family.

"I've been promoted to a riding officer," he said earnestly. "And I've been saving everything I make. By spring, I should have enough to buy a house."

"I'm glad to hear you've done well for yourself—"

"For us," he interrupted. "For you."

His face was darkly handsome, and she tried to conjure an attraction to him, something, anything. She willed her stomach to flip, for warmth to pulse through her veins, for her fingers to crave the touch of his skin.

He paused as if waiting for her reaction, but then he rushed forward again as though he needed to prove his worthiness even more. "I'm doing well, Polly. I'll be able to give you everything you need or want. I promise."

Her stomach finally gave a small flip—more like a tiny ripple. But it was something, maybe the sign that she ought to consider Billy as a suitor. He was prepared to take care of her.

"Will you give me a chance?"

This time when his gaze caressed her face, her heart pattered forward with an unexpected *thump*.

What reason did she have to refuse him? She knew Billy better than any of the men she'd met in London. He would make some woman a good husband. She just wasn't sure that woman was her. But it wouldn't hurt to spend time over the winter and spring discovering if they truly were compatible enough for marriage.

"Very well," she said, feeling suddenly shy with him. "You may come calling on me. And not just as a friend."

His grin warmed her heart. After he took his leave, she ambled back down the path to the open door. For a moment she thought she was alone and hugged her arms to her chest, trying to make sense of what she'd just promised Billy.

"Billy's a nice young man," came her father's voice as he stepped into the doorway.

A flush of heat moved into Polly's cheeks, and she wondered if they were as red as they felt. "He's always been a good friend."

"I can see that he's no longer satisfied with friendship."

"He's asked to call on me."

Her father leaned against the doorjamb. "I figured he might."

A note in his voice stopped her. "You don't approve?"

"I like Billy," Father replied slowly. "But you know already that I don't approve of dishonest gain."

"He said he's become a riding officer."

"Yes, he's done well for himself in that regard. But I'm sad to say that he's fallen prey to his uncle's bribing. It's partly how he was granted the position in the first place. Charlie wanted a riding officer who was on his side."

"He's likely doing no more or less than anyone else," she said, wanting to defend Billy.

"That's true. But just because everyone is cheating and stealing doesn't make the sin right in God's eyes."

Now she understood the concern she'd seen in her father's eyes when Billy had come calling. He didn't like the fact that Billy was accepting bribes from smugglers like so many of the other officers.

But should that really stop her from considering him as a suitor? Besides, maybe her father was being too particular about her suitors. He hadn't liked John, hadn't considered his character to be strong enough, hadn't believed he was worthy enough for her. That was understandable. After all, John was lacking in many areas.

But how could he disapprove of Billy? Billy was everything he should want in a son-in-law. Obviously he wasn't flawless. But there were no perfect men. If she waited for someone perfect, she'd most definitely end up as a spinster like Miss Donovan next door.

"You have high standards for my suitors," she said cautiously, not wishing to be disrespectful of her father but also knowing she was old enough to make up her own mind now.

"I only have God's standards in mind for you, Polly" he replied in a tender voice, as though he sensed all her thoughts. "And if you lower those standards, you may find yourself content in the short term but unhappy long term."

"But if I'm too choosy, I may end up with no one."

"If you're not choosy enough, you could end up with the wrong person."

Her mind flashed to Susanna, to her miserable marriage. Susanna had started with such high hopes, had thought Daniel was someone who could love her. But perhaps Susanna had put too much stock in the lifestyle Daniel could give her and not enough in the things that mattered most, like his character.

"If we hold true to God's Word and walk according to his way—no matter how tempting it is to take the easy path—he'll bring us to green pastures eventually."

She wanted to believe her father, wanted to trust that he was right. After all, he was the kind of man she aspired to marry. Billy was close enough. Wasn't he?

Her father smiled warmly and beckoned her inside. "There's no rush. You can take your time discovering if Billy is truly the man God has for you."

She returned his smile and walked into his embrace.

"In the meantime," he said, draping an arm around her, "I shall enjoy seeing you every day while I still can."

# TWENTY-TWO

MARCH 1748

ewton sat at the table in Captain Swanwick's cabin and stared at the open pages of *Euclide's Elements* in front of him. He'd sat often at this table over the past year of traveling on the *Greyhound*. The round port window afforded little light, especially in the dismally rainy spring evening. The lantern hanging above him cast swinging flickers. But even with the poor conditions, he'd done nothing but read since the *Greyhound* sailed away from Newfoundland eight days ago.

They'd caught a strong westerly wind, which was blowing them rapidly back across the Atlantic. With each passing day, his mood had considerably sobered. He wasn't exactly sure why, except that perhaps the realization he was heading for home had finally hit him. In a month's time, he very well could be standing in Chatham proposing marriage to Polly.

His sights shifted to the other book lying on the table, the book he hadn't wanted to read but had been drawn to again and again over the past week.

With a sigh he shut the well-worn copy of Isaac Barrow's

textbook of mathematics. The geometrical designs, diagrams, and calculations had set his wits a-woolgathering many days during the months on board the ship. He realized he had a natural turn for mathematics and enjoyed the study. Perhaps if he'd continued with schooling, he may have even become a mathematician.

But during the past few days, *Euclide* hadn't held his attention. Instead, he kept opening the only other book—besides the Bible—in the captain's cabin, which was a copy of *The Imitation of Christ* by Thomas à Kempis. The four volumes had originally been written in Latin, but fortunately the edition was rendered in English, having been compiled by George Stanhope. Stanhope had added a commentary with many explanations of passages.

Newton had only picked up the book to pass the time. He was bored and had nothing better to do. He'd begun reading it with the same indifference he would a novel.

But once he started, he wasn't able to stop. And no matter how hard he partied with the ship's crew late into the night, no matter how much he tried to use rum to drown out the thoughts the book was awakening, he invariably came back to it. Every day.

As if his fingers had a will of their own, he cracked open the book again. The pages fell open to a familiar spot, and the words jumped out at him: "True peace of heart, then, is found in resisting passions, not in satisfying them."

The ship crested a wave and came crashing down, sending the books sliding toward the edge of the table. Newton grabbed *The Imitation* to keep it from crashing to the floor.

He pulled it back in front of him and read the next sentence. "There is no peace in the carnal man, in the man given to vain attractions, but there is peace in the fervent and spiritual man."

He could attest to the fact peace wasn't found in satisfying the desires of the flesh. He'd certainly tried in Africa. And subsequently during his time on the *Greyhound,* he'd done all he could to live the way he wanted, to find fulfillment in easy living. After all, Captain Swanwick had promised him that he wouldn't have to work while aboard the ship, that he could lodge in his cabin, sup at his table, and be his guest for the duration of the voyage.

He'd taken full advantage of those privileges, so much so that he'd alienated himself from the captain. He should have known a religious man like Captain Swanwick wouldn't tolerate profanity and blaspheming. And he should have known that he wouldn't be able to hide his true self from the captain for long, especially when they were living in such close proximity.

As it was, he'd finally given up trying to hold himself in check and had given himself the freedom to live the way he pleased, just as he'd been doing in Kittam. He drank heavily with the crew, gambled, and delighted in all kinds of mischief while the *Greyhound* finished trading in Africa. Finally, in January after revictualling at the port of call in Annabona, they'd set sail across the Atlantic. Once they were within sight of Brazil, they'd steered a northward course up the eastern coast of the American colonies before dropping anchor in Newfoundland on the Grand Banks. They'd spent a leisurely half a day fishing for cod. But since they already had plenty of provisions for the final leg of the trip home, they didn't linger.

It seemed that the entire crew was preoccupied with thoughts of home and ready to move on. Although Newton had been able to round up a few of the men to drink and play cards with him that week, most had seemed to grow weary of his antics, especially the captain. Captain Swanwick likely rued the day that he'd stopped for the smoke signal in Kittam. Only yesterday the captain had rebuked him again for his foul language and told him that he wasn't fit for any decent Englishwoman, that he indeed felt sorry for the young woman he planned to marry.

The captain's disgust shouldn't have bothered him. But for some reason it had, probably because there was a measure of truth to his words. They echoed Mr. Catlett's parting words all too closely. And reminded him that while he may no longer lack means, he still lacked the character Polly needed.

Perhaps this innate desire to become better for Polly was now driving him. He didn't know except that his attention turned again to the pages of *The Imitation of Christ* spread open before him. "Yet if he satisfies his desires, remorse of conscience overwhelms him because he followed his passions and they did not lead to the peace he sought."

The words, as before, clanged in his mind. They glared out at him with a truth he couldn't deny no matter how hard he tried. He had followed his passions, and they hadn't led to the peace he desired. In fact, over time he'd only grown more discontent, restless, and anxious, which in turn only led him to drink all the heavier.

A crack of lightning flashed in front of the window. The pattering of footfalls overhead told him the sailors were likely reefing the topsails to reduce the area exposed to the wind. He couldn't deny he was glad to be out of the cold rain in the captain's cabin. Nevertheless, fresh discontent ate at his stomach as surely as acid.

Newton reread another passage. "'He who follows Me, walks not in darkness,' says the Lord. By these words of Christ we are advised to imitate His life and habits, if we wish to be truly enlightened and free from all blindness of heart. Let our chief effort, therefore, be to study the life of Jesus Christ."

He tried to bring to the forefront all his skepticism and the scoffing that had kept him in good stead over the past few years. What did he care for the things of God? He didn't even believe in God. He'd thought he was truly enlightened, free from the bondage of ancient tradition and the antiquated rules of the Bible.

But what if he walked in darkness? What if he was blind? What if the words of the fifteenth-century monk were true? If so, he was doomed.

Newton slammed the book shut and stood. Frustration twisted his insides, making him want to fling the book across the room against the hull. Instead he took a deep breath and forced himself to respond calmly. If the book wasn't true, then why was he letting it bother him so much? If *The Imitation of Christ* and the Bible were merely full of superstitions and myths, then he should be able to set them down and walk away without any further anger.

He shoved the book back into a nook next to the Bible, extinguished the lantern, and then climbed into his hammock. He wouldn't open either one again. He'd put the matter of peace, truth, and God's existence from his mind once and for all. He wouldn't let a mere book have power over him. It was meaningless. It was irrelevant. And it was useless.

He closed his eyes and let the sway of the ship soothe him. He must think of something else, anything to get his attention off the morbid thoughts that had been plaguing him lately. Usually thoughts of Polly could help him forget about anything. But as soon as he began to try to picture her beautiful face, a fresh wave of despair crashed over him.

The fact was, he wasn't good enough for Polly. He was just as vile, contemptible, and despicable as Captain Swanwick accused him of being. As Mr. Catlett knew.

Polly deserved a much better man than he.

He fell into a restless sleep, a sleep that wouldn't last. He knew eventually he would have to get up and drink himself into a stupor to truly drown his troubles. Nevertheless, he was surprised when a spray of icy water hit his face.

He sat up in the blackness of the cabin, a curse ready to level at the man responsible for the jest. But the pitching of the ship tipped him out of the hammock and to the floor where he landed with a splash. The coldness of the water seeped into his trousers and took his breath away. He jumped to his feet only to have the sudden dive of the ship throw him against the narrowed stern. His head slammed against a low beam, and for a moment he hovered on the brink of consciousness.

The howling wind and crashing of waves all but drowned out the panicked shouts of the crew. A flash of lightning lit up the cabin for a second, illuminating the water that was rushing in from a crack in the planks. It was difficult to tell how much water the ship was taking on due to the swaying, but he guessed the water was already up to his ankle if not his midcalf.

With a shake of his head, he tried to focus. He shrugged into an oiled coat and jerked open the cabin door only to find chaos. The shouts of orders and cries of frightened sailors were whipped away by the wind.

As he climbed up the slick ladder and out the hatch, hard rain pelted against his face. Once topside, his heartbeat slammed to a halt. The boatswain managed to hang on to a lantern that illuminated the windward side where several planks had been torn away, leaving a gap that was allowing the onslaught of high waves to crash right onto the deck. The ship's carpenter and several sailors were attempting to make repairs. Two men were manning the bilge pump. Others were bailing water with buckets.

At the rate they were taking on water, they would sink before the hour was out.

"I need a knife!" called the carpenter.

Newton reached for the small of his back where he normally wore his, but he'd neglected to strap it back on before ascending. "I'll go below and get mine!" he shouted.

Before he could reach the ladder, one of the other sailors had already jumped onto the top rung to run the errand. At that instant, a giant wave rose over the forecastle and came crashing down on them. Newton wrapped one of his arms around a spoke in the capstan. The wave shoved against him with clawing force. The water sucked at his hand, trying to pry it loose. It knocked against his feet, lifting him from the deck.

To Newton's horror, the wave swept the sailor off his perch on the top ladder rung. In one fell swoop, it picked him up and flung him over the side of the ship.

"Man overboard!" Newton cried, but his call was cut off by another wave that splashed against the deck, causing him to splutter and cough. Another crack and cry of dismay told him they'd likely lost another plank.

Without waiting for assistance, he strapped a rope around his waist, tied it to the capstan, and then crawled to the port side where the sailor had fallen into the sea. Rain slashed Newton's face. The spray of waves all but blinded him. But he squinted over the side attempting to locate the floundering sailor. Nothing but blackness and foaming waves greeted him.

"Hey mate!" He gathered the excess rope and tossed it overboard. "Grab on!" But his words were lost. Even though he shouted again and again, a burning ache formed in his chest. The man was gone. There was no hope for him. None in the least.

Yet Newton couldn't stop staring. It should have been him on the top rung. If not for a split second, it would have been him. Then he would have been the one swept overboard and drowning in the ocean.

"Stop standing there doing nothing!" Captain Swanwick shouted near his ear. "We're taking on more water than is going out. I need you to join the others in bailing."

Although he wasn't a crew member, he knew that all hands were needed to survive. Newton nodded but as another wave thrashed the vessel, he had the feeling that ere long they would all join the man overboard in an icy death. The ship was sinking, and no matter their efforts, they were at the mercy of the storm and the sea.

Each minute of the night seemed like an hour. For every bucket they bailed, double the seawater poured inside. The foot pumps couldn't keep up with the bilge. All the sheep, cattle, and poultry they'd brought on board at Annabona were swept overboard.

No one expected to survive more than a quarter of an hour, so when dawn broke and the storm began to subside, several of the sailors fell onto the deck weeping. The waves were still rough and the wind biting. The clouds above them were dark and stormy and spitting rain. But at least the worst seemed to be over. They were shivering and exhausted. But they were alive.

Newton approached Captain Swanwick on the main deck where he was still bailing with some of the men, while others were bailing from below.

"I'll take a few men and attempt to plug up holes, sir. We'll use bedding, blankets, and any clothes the men can spare."

The captain nodded, his face ashen, his lips blue.

"If we take planks from the inner walls, we can use those to patch up some of the bigger gaps in the hull." Newton wiped the water out of his eyes, a useless gesture as the rain continued to slash them. He tried to still the chattering of his teeth, another futile move.

"That's a good plan," the captain said wearily. "I can think of none better."

Newton met the captain's grave eyes. They were carrying bees-wax and camwood, both of which were unusually light and floated in the waterlogged hold, buoying the ship. If they'd had a heavier cargo, they would have sunk by now. Even so, Newton was an experienced enough sailor to realize they weren't out of danger yet. The *Greyhound* was badly damaged, and there was still the great likelihood that she could sink in the stormy waves.

"Do what you can, Newton," the captain said gratefully, "and God bless you for it."

"If this will not do, the Lord have mercy on us." As soon as the words were out, Newton froze in astonishment. Where had those words come from? He hadn't spoken the Lord's name in anything but a curse in years. Nor had he desired God or his mercy in just as long.

Throughout the morning as he helped to make the repairs and plug the holes, he couldn't stop thinking about his passing reference to God's mercy. He could only conclude that somewhere in the depths of his being, he'd never truly stopped believing that God existed. He supposed that all those like him who tried to deny the existence of God wouldn't face such a battle to eradicate the concept of God, wouldn't be so angry and threatened, and wouldn't be so antagonistic if God weren't alive and truly a threat. Deep down he supposed he'd always known that but had made excuses so that he could live whatever way he pleased.

He'd even rejected God in his anger, anger toward his mother for leaving him, anger toward his father for not being there for him in the way he'd needed.

But mayhap his anger toward his parents had been misplaced. Or at the very least the anger of a child who didn't understand the bigger picture of loving and losing. Now that he'd experienced love and loss for himself, he could finally begin to understand what his father had gone through after the death of his mother. Whatever the case, he felt as though he'd awakened to the reality of God's existence.

Once the repairs were completed, Newton organized shifts so that the sailors could begin to sleep a few hours at a time. He helped man the pump all morning and was frustrated when the wind began to pick up. As the waves crashed over their heads again, Newton tied himself to the pump and instructed the others on deck to hold themselves fast with ropes too so that they wouldn't be washed overboard.

He worked for hours expecting that every time the vessel descended into the sea she would rise no more. Fear radiated from every exhausted face near him, every face red and raw from the cold. The men uttered prayers, cried out, and pleaded with God. And for once, he didn't mock them—not even in his thoughts.

He'd tangled with death many times in his life, especially in the past two years during his time in the navy and while living in Africa, but never with such fear. He supposed he'd blocked out all thoughts of eternity, and that had made the task of facing death easier. If he didn't believe in God or an afterlife, then he could assume that once he was dead that was it. He was done. His body would decompose. And that would be the end of all things.

But if God existed and heaven was real, then he was in grave trouble. After the life he'd lived, what mercy would there be for him?

"You've given everyone else a break," the captain shouted at him, as he staggered toward the pump. "Now it's your turn."

The rain had finally ceased, but the clouds above them were still dangerously gray. The wind blew fiercely against every board and beam on the ship, which creaked and moaned in the throes of death.

Newton shook his head and pressed the pump handle. Beneath his gloves his skin was wrinkled and chafed from the water and cold. The muscles in his arms and shoulders were numb from the hours of nonstop work. He could no longer hold his head up from weariness. But he could do nothing less than put forth his best effort. It was the least he could do.

He was Jonah. He'd run from God, and in some ways he couldn't keep from thinking that the storm was his fault, that God was pouring down his wrath upon them all because of him. Mayhap if he suggested to the captain to throw him overboard, the storm would stop.

"You need to rest!" the captain said again, above the roar of the wind and waves. "Let someone with more strength do the job now."

"Then put me to work somewhere else," Newton called back.

The captain glanced to the stern and then to the helm.

"I'll relieve the helmsman," Newton offered, taking in the hunched shoulders and waterlogged condition of the man at the wheel. "My father taught me to steer a ship, and I've done it enough times I could keep her on course even with my eyes closed."

The captain hesitated only a moment before nodding. The gratefulness in the captain's tired eyes only served to stir Newton's regrets, especially the regret that he hadn't done more to help the captain during the rest of the voyage. Instead he'd only been dead weight, taking the rest of the crew down with his lewd behavior. Newton took the helm and waged war with the wheel, attempting to keep the ship from being tossed every which way by the waves. Because of the hole in the upper bow, he had to keep the damaged area leeward and protect it from taking on any more water than necessary.

As the day moved into another stormy night, he didn't care when no one came to relieve him. Even though his body was battered and weary, his mind was keenly awake.

His thoughts kept turning to the question of God. He wanted to pray for God's mercy like the other sailors. A desperate part of him longed to cry out for God to save him. But how could he? He'd ridiculed, mocked, and blasphemed God so much that he was completely unworthy of God's salvation during this hour of need. In fact, he deserved nothing more than to be smashed and choked by a crashing wave, swept overboard, and drowned in the deepest sea.

But the truth was, he wasn't ready to die. Not so close to home. Not so close to being reunited with Polly. He hadn't survived so many escapades only to die now, had he?

His mind replayed all the times his life had been spared from death. Even in the past year of sailing aboard the *Greyhound,* he'd had two near-death encounters. The first he'd been drinking with some of the crew when they'd been moored in the mouth of the River Gabon before leaving Africa. He'd convinced his shipmates to mix rum and gin in an enormous seashell. With such a potent mix and in such large quantities, he was inebriated after several rounds. Amidst the hooting and cheering of his mates, he jumped up and performed one of the wild African dances he'd learned during his trips upriver trading for slaves. During the frenzy, a gust of wind caught his hat and blew it over the side of the ship and into the river. He'd been irrational and had climbed up onto the rail intending to get his hat back. As he was about to jump into a longboat that he thought was tethered to the side of the *Greyhound,* one of the other sailors grabbed his shirt from behind and kept him from plunging down.

Later he learned that the longboat had been at least twenty feet downstream. If he'd jumped he would have sunk where the strong current would have pulled him under. In his drunken condition and with his inability to swim, he surely would have drowned.

The other time he was saved from death was when the *Greyhound* had anchored at Cape Lopez and he traversed inland on a wild buffalo shooting expedition. He was excited to fell a buffalo on his first shot. When he went with his companions to locate the carcass, they got lost in a dense wood that was renowned for its predatory animals. By the time darkness had settled, he'd almost given up hope of surviving. They didn't have light or food, and they had used up their ammunition.

They wandered around in the suffocating blackness until the clouds parted, allowing the moon and stars to come out and light their way so he could lead the men back to the ship.

Both times he'd considered himself lucky. But what if Divine

Providence had been watching over him? What if God had spared him?

Polly's words from one of their first meetings came back to him: *"It sounds to me like God has intervened in your life in each of the occasions, miraculously saving you from death. Perhaps he deemed that your time on earth isn't finished, that he has more in store for you yet in this life."*

Her confidence and belief in him had always encouraged him. No one had ever accepted him or loved him as unreservedly as Polly had, although she didn't know the worst of what he had done. But God did, and certainly God didn't love him as unconditionally. How could he, after how foul and wretched he'd been? After the horrible life he'd lived, especially during his time in Africa? He was the worst of sinners. There never was nor could there ever be a sinner as depraved as himself. His sins were too great to be forgiven.

*"The LORD is merciful and gracious, slow to anger, and abounding in mercy."* The long-buried words of Psalm 103 reverberated in his mind, a passage his mother had made him memorize as a boy, a passage he hadn't thought about in years. *"He has not dealt with us according to our sins, nor punished us according to our iniquities. For as the heavens are high above the earth, so great is His mercy toward those who fear Him."*

During the long hours at the helm, other Scriptures he'd once memorized began to come back to him as well. Yet no matter how many verses filled his mind about God's love and mercy, he couldn't shake the feeling of unworthiness. God surely wouldn't save him. Not again.

After navigating the ship for endless hours, he wasn't sure if the course was growing easier and the waters less turbulent or if he was beginning to suffer delirium from cold and hunger. When the captain finally sent a sailor with orders to relieve him, Newton rubbed a wet sleeve across his eyes only to realize he wasn't imagining things. The sea was growing calmer. The storm was dissipating.

"It would appear that the pumping and bailing efforts have availed," the sailor said, his thin body shaking in the cold breeze. "We're not going to sink."

At the news, Newton released his grip on the wheel and crumpled to his knees. A cry of relief crowded his throat. He buried his face in his hands with the overwhelming need to weep.

Had God once again rescued him from the clutches of death?

The very thought was too much to comprehend.

"Thank you, God." Once the words were out, Newton realized it was the first prayer he'd uttered in years.

## TWENTY-THREE

APRIL 1748

ewton's stomach rumbled with an ache that burned deep. His limbs were numb and stiff with the constant dampness and cold that came from spring in the North Atlantic. But he didn't move from his spot at the table in the captain's cabin, where he'd been reading most of the night since his watch had ended.

What if the Scriptures that he'd long opposed were true? What if they were not only historically accurate, but what if the message of the gospel was real and applicable?

Over the past three weeks since the storm had battered the *Greyhound,* he'd done little else but pour over the captain's copy of the Bible. As he read, the messages he'd heard as a boy from both his mother and the pastor of the Dissenters' chapel in Wapping kept surfacing. Mayhap his mother was even now in heaven smiling down on him, happy to know that all her teaching, all the seeds she planted those long ago years, were still there. They were dormant. But they'd never left him.

His stomach growled angrily, enough that Captain Swanwick

across from him glanced up. "Are you sure you won't take your ration today?"

"You need it more than I do, Captain." Newton pressed a fist into his gut. "I'm dispensable. You're not."

After the storm subsided and they'd taken stock of their supplies, they realized that they faced starvation. Not only had all their live-stock been lost during the storm, but the seawater and the violent swaying of the ship had battered and ruined most of their other food stores in the hold. They'd salvaged a few sacks of grain and some pig feed along with the cod that they caught during the fishing expedi-tion in Newfoundland.

Under normal circumstances, such stores would have fed the crew for a week. By careful rationing they'd made them last three. Even so, they were slowly starving to death. And now that the cap-tain had distributed the last remnants of the cod at daybreak, they would have nothing.

At least they had plenty of water, even if the food was gone. Five full casks of water remained in the hold, so they didn't have to ration that.

The captain sat back in his chair, abandoning his pen and his logbook and studying Newton until he began to squirm. "You've changed, son."

"Aye, sir." Newton couldn't deny it. "Guess that's what a storm will do to a person."

It wasn't just the storm, although that had been the catalyst that forced him to think more about God than he had in a long time. Nay, it went deeper than that. It was the deliverance from death time and time again. As though God truly had a grip on him and wasn't letting go.

But the question always came back to haunt him. Why him, the worst of sinners? Surely God should be busy rescuing other people, righteous men and women who hadn't ridiculed and profaned him over and over.

He wasn't worthy of God's mercy or love.

His cold, stiff fingers moved back to the fifteenth chapter of Luke and the story of the prodigal son. He'd already read the passage numerous times. He could certainly place himself in the role of the wayward son who'd rejected everything he'd known and who'd lived his life as he pleased. He'd blamed his father for so many of his problems when his father had only wanted to help him. Nay, his father hadn't done everything right. Nevertheless, Newton could see now that the captain had truly only wanted what was best for him.

All along, with each mistake, his father had always been there for him. He'd come to his rescue time after time. Even after Newton had shunned and hated his father, the man hadn't given up on him. He'd even sent a ship to free him from captivity in Africa.

Even so, how would his father feel about him when he returned? Would he welcome him home with open arms like the father in the parable? The truth was, he didn't deserve his father opening his arms and receiving him back. He didn't deserve his father's kindness any more than he deserved God's. As much as he longed for forgiveness, he wouldn't ask. He couldn't.

At a commotion on the deck above, Captain Swanwick pushed back from the table and stood. He retrieved his pistol from a drawer and then nodded at Newton. "Best to stay below in case the men get any more ideas."

Newton had heard the whispers, had seen the angry glances his way. In their hunger, the men were growing desperate. They'd even begun to talk of cannibalism.

According to the captain's compass and calculations, they were on course for Ireland. In fact, they should have reached the coast by now. But because of the gaping hole in the bow and because most of the sails had been damaged or blown away, the *Greyhound* had limped forward like a wounded and dying horse.

Even though they'd plugged the smaller holes and leaks in the hull, they still were taking on water and had to man the pumps and bail around the clock to keep the flooding below decks under control. Not only that but they were all damp and freezing since they'd used up most of their extra clothes and blankets to make repairs. The temperatures and wind had only added to their misery.

And now the hunger was reaching a crisis point.

The shouts topside grew louder. The thuds against the planks above him indicated a fight.

He stood and glanced at the ceiling. The captain had told him to stay below. But if the crew was mutinying, the captain would need his help.

Newton sprang forward, out of the cabin, and up the ladder. He was topside in seconds. The boatswain was holding back one sailor, pinning his arms behind his back. And the captain had his pistol pointed at another.

As Newton straightened, every pair of eyes on deck shifted toward him. The morning was crisp. The sky was cloudless. And the sun was beginning to rise. Maybe today it would finally lend them some warmth.

In the far distance mountainous points seemed to form on the horizon. But no one paid them any attention. They'd already been fooled once during the past three weeks. They'd thought they sighted land, had passed around the last of the brandy to celebrate, and then realized they were only seeing a mirage. As the sun had risen higher, the land had grown redder. Even though they'd wanted to deny what the red meant, any good seafarer knew it was the sign of an illusion created by the sun and clouds. As the morning progressed, the island and mountains vanished. And so did their excitement.

Now all that remained was bitterness, and that bitterness hit him with full force.

"He's the cause of all our problems," said the sailor being held back by the boatswain. Through brown-stained teeth the sailor spat at Newton on the deck.

"We decided we need to kill and eat him first," said another of the sailors whose lean face and skeletal frame beneath his shredded garments attested to the severity of their hunger.

"We're not killing or eating anyone," the captain spoke sternly. "Least of all Newton. If not for his quick work at making repairs, this ship would be at the bottom of the ocean and all of you with it. Not to mention that he steered this ship for hours during some of the worst of the storm. Keeping her afloat was no easy feat, something only a skilled seaman could do."

Newton glanced at the hardened faces staring at him, the very men he'd led astray with his lewdness and profanity during most of the voyage. Where had all his antics led him now? The sailors he'd caroused with certainly didn't like him any better. In fact, in the face of their worst challenge yet, they valued his life so little that they were willing to sacrifice him to save themselves.

"We've got to do something, Captain," said the ship's carpenter, "or we'll all die."

The captain straightened his shoulders as though to bring dignity back to the situation. His bones poked through his thin shirt showing him to be just as decimated as the rest of them. "If we must die, then we'll die with honor."

Newton knew the logical and safe thing for him to do in this situation was retreat to the captain's cabin, where he should have stayed in the first place. Four weeks ago, maybe even three, he wouldn't have ventured out. He'd been just like the sailors—thinking only about himself.

But during all his soul searching since the storm, something calm had come over his soul, a peace that had been growing with each passing day, something he couldn't explain. Mayhap it was the peace he'd been looking for all along.

Now in the face of mutiny and the threat of murder, that calmness held him in place. Even the wind didn't blow through his scant garments as it had in recent days. If they wanted to sacrifice him, he wouldn't fight it.

"If you feasted on each other's flesh," the captain continued, "you might save your lives now, but you'd forever be haunted by your deed."

This time only a few grumbles met the captain's rebuke, and several of the sailors dropped their gazes to the deck.

Only the wind and waves made their unending conversation, except that Newton noticed a softening, a gentling from the harsh noise of past days. He glanced upward to find that the mainsail was shifting. The wind was changing direction. Already he could feel the ship lightening in the waves, which would make it easier to keep the broken bow out of the water.

One by one the other men began to notice the shift. Before any of them could move, a cry came from the lookout above them. "Land, ho!"

The crew moved cautiously to the rails. Newton didn't join them. He was an outcast among them, but he knew with certainty that he'd done the right thing this time in standing his ground instead of running and cowering below. He hadn't taken the easy way out as he was prone to do. He'd faced difficulty with honor. And it felt right.

Maybe right living was hard. Maybe at times it was even excruciating. But the reward of knowing he'd lived with integrity made the sacrifice all that much more fulfilling.

With every eye trained upon the distant horizon, not a man dared to breathe. They'd been disappointed once before. As the sun moved in its course, would the mirage vanish like it had last time?

They waited and watched the sun slowly make its way upward in the sky. The streaks of pink and orange reflected against the tattered sails and lit up the sky. As Newton watched, another verse he'd memorized at the knees of his mother pushed to the front of his mind. *"Where can I go from Your Spirit? Or where can I flee from Your presence? . . . If I take the wings of the morning, and dwell in the uttermost parts of the sea, even there Your hand shall lead me, and Your right hand shall hold me."*

He'd tried to run away from God. He'd tried to sail as far away from God as he could possibly get. But God had a hold on his life and always had. God had never let go, had never given up, and had never lost hope, even during Newton's darkest moments of rejection.

A swell of gratitude rose in Newton's chest. "I'm unworthy of such grace," he whispered. "So unworthy."

The murmuring at the rail began to turn into shouts of excitement. Newton peered into the distance along with everyone else. This time there was no mist of red, no disappearing horizon, no mirage. The outline of an island was clearly visible and growing larger. "Ireland!" someone cried.

The gratefulness in Newton's heart almost hurt. God had saved him from certain death once again.

They passed the island of Tory off Donegal and less than a day later rounded Dunree Head and sailed into the calm inlet of Lough Swilly on the north coast of Ireland. There, on April 8, the battered and barely sailable *Greyhound* dropped anchor.

Newton attempted to wait patiently for his turn to go ashore in the longboat. When his time came, he sat in front of the captain and pulled at the oars with the little strength he could muster in his exhausted body.

"The wind's changing," Captain Swanwick said, glancing to the northwest where the inlet led to the Atlantic. "Another storm's headed our way."

Newton followed the captain's gaze to the dark clouds piled on top of one another that were blowing in from the north. They were ominous, even frightening.

"If we'd stayed another hour at sea," the captain said in a low voice only Newton could hear, "we likely would have been pushed far out into the Atlantic again."

Newton shuddered at the prospect. If the *Greyhound* had been forced to weather another storm, she wouldn't have been able to survive the blows.

"I didn't say anything to the rest of the crew," the captain continued. "But of those five remaining casks of water that we had in the hold, yesterday I discovered they were all empty."

The oars in Newton's hands became suddenly too heavy and his stomach hollow. "Devil be hanged. You're certain?"

Captain Swanwick's eyes were old and tired. "Aye. They must have cracked open during the storm. We had but a few drops left."

They'd nearly emptied the cask they'd drunk from that morning. If they'd had no further fresh drinking water, then they most certainly would have died from thirst within days if not hours, even if they'd been able to weather the storm that was currently brewing.

Starvation. Dying of thirst. Another brutal storm. All had been lurking much too close.

Newton plunged the oars deeper into the water for the last few strokes that brought them to the rocky beach of Lough Swilly. With a choking gasp of relief and eagerness, he jumped out of the boat and helped drag it the rest of the short distance to the shore. He didn't care that his boots and trousers were soaked. He didn't care that he was impatient. The other sailors in the longboat did the same thing in their frantic need to be on firm ground.

When his feet hit dry land, he fell down, pressed his face to the cold, slippery stones, and breathed in the wet scent of the rocks and soil. "Oh God. Oh God. Oh God," he whispered, unable to contain the deep sobs that rose in his chest.

He pressed his face into the earth. He could no longer deny that there was a God in heaven. He couldn't deny it any more than he could deny the solid ground beneath his body. The blessed solid ground, ground he'd never thought he'd step on again.

"Oh God," he breathed again, knowing deep in his heart that

God had heard and answered his calls for mercy, had in fact answered them when he'd least deserved it.

He lifted his face, and the growing breeze from the stormy north blew across his cheeks, across the tears that wet his flesh. Bright green pasturelands stretched out in the craggy hills before him. Flocks of sheep grazed contentedly, seeming unaware of the dark clouds moving swiftly into the inlet.

His heart opened wide with the need to acknowledge not only the existence of God but also the existence of a merciful and loving God. He'd been an undeserving wretch, but God had saved him—not only from the clutches of dangers, toils, and snares, but from the very brink of hell itself.

"I don't deserve your amazing grace," he said as another tight sob rose in his chest at the thought of all his many sins. He wanted to weep over them. The remorse for all he'd done overwhelmed him, and he pressed his hands against his face.

But that was the beauty of the gospel. God could choose to pardon his sins. In fact, God had done that pardoning through the death of Jesus Christ. He offered forgiveness to everyone, even to the vilest sinners.

Suddenly Newton knew God would embrace him and forgive him just the same way the father in the prodigal son story had embraced his son.

Tears wet Newton's hands, and he bent to the ground again, broken, humbled, and overwhelmed that God could love him.

He felt almost as if he were seeing life for the very first time, as if he'd been blind and now could see the truth. He'd been lost but now was found.

# TWENTY-FOUR

MAY 1748

*P*olly pressed her face in the bluebell bouquet Billy had picked for her and breathed in the heady scent. He strolled next to her, their steps unhurried in the warm afternoon sunshine.

Behind them, Billy's younger sister and Eliza followed at a discreet distance as chaperones. Polly didn't mind the constant companionship of the others, especially in light of Billy's growing ardor and attention over the past weeks. Somehow the presence of one or more of their siblings kept the time together safe, kept the boundaries firmly intact, and kept Polly from having to make a decision about Billy.

But her time was running short. Although Billy was always patient with her, she knew that he was ready to marry her.

As they reached the back gate of the house, Billy stopped and touched her arm. His expression pleaded with her to allow him a moment to speak with her alone.

Eliza stopped and quirked a brow.

"Go ahead, girls," Polly said even though her stomach quavered at the prospect of being alone with Billy. She was fairly certain what he wanted to say—or ask.

She'd been stalling him and avoiding this moment. And she couldn't do it any longer. She had no reason to say no to Billy Baldock—except the word of caution from her father when she'd come home last autumn. Every once in a while, remembrance of his concern returned to admonish her. But of late, especially after Felicity's wedding, she'd been able to shut it out.

Felicity had married a young man like Billy who was gaining possessions and moving up in his social standing. Such a life was everything a girl like her, of the middling class, could aspire to: status and wealth, comfort, the approval of her friends. Billy could offer her all that and possibly more. What need did she have of a higher purpose, a greater calling to do more, especially with the hymns and her music? Perhaps that was simply the wish of a young girl and nothing more. She could certainly find contentment in her charity work with Mother at the almshouse, couldn't she?

Besides, she'd come to the conclusion that perhaps it didn't matter so much that Billy was helping his uncle from time to time. Billy claimed that it wasn't often and assured her that it was all just part of his job. Riding officers couldn't possibly stop every smuggler. No one expected that of him.

Billy cleared his throat and glanced down at his feet. The tall grass brushed his legs, and a small wood white butterfly flitted near her skirt. The sunshine was warm on her back and her large hat, reminding her that summer would soon be upon them. And summer was the deadline she'd given Billy for making the decision. She couldn't put him off any longer.

"Polly . . ." Billy said, folding his hands together. Then he unclasped them and lowered himself to one knee in front of her.

Her heart began to patter faster at the implication.

"Polly." He reached for her free hand and took it between his clammy ones. The nerves in his jaw twitched. "You would make me the happiest man in the world if you would do me the honor of becoming my wife."

She smiled at him, hoping to ease his discomfort.

He released a small breath and smiled in return. "I love you," he continued with more confidence. "And I've dreamed about marrying you for as long as I can remember."

As much as she wanted to say the words, to reassure him of her own love in return, she couldn't bring herself to make such a declaration. Not yet. Yes, she cared about him. But was it love?

Her heart betrayed her with the memory of the last time she'd seen John Newton nearly three and a half years ago, of the kiss he'd given her, of the power of her longing and passion in that moment and others with him. She'd never experienced anything close to that with Billy.

But love wasn't just a feeling. It was a decision. And all she had to do was decide to love Billy. Didn't she? That certainly wouldn't be hard to do since he was such a good man.

Billy lifted her hand to his lips and pressed a kiss to her fingertips. Although her hands were gloved, the heat of his lips and breath seeped through the silk and made her flush. It was the first time Billy had made any overt physical contact with her, and she wasn't quite sure how to react.

His eyes suddenly blazed with longing, a desire that was only natural and normal for a young man his age. He was ready to be married, to settle down, to start a family. He had the means. He'd worked all year, and as he'd promised, he'd saved enough to buy her a home. In fact, he already had his eye on a lovely cottage close to the

River Medway. He'd taken her past it only a week ago and asked for her opinion on it.

She must not keep him waiting any longer. She wasn't being fair to him. "I think you know my answer, Billy," she said quietly.

His smile widened and moved up into his eyes.

"But I should like to have my father's approval first."

The brightness of his expression wavered. But he rose and gallantly offered her the crook of his arm. "Then let's go ask your father together," he said. "Perhaps we can set the wedding date today, and I shall have the banns posted on the morrow?"

She took his arm and allowed him to lead the way through the back door. They followed voices to the front drawing room. Billy squeezed her arm as they stepped into the room.

The voices tapered to silence. At first Polly was confused as she took in her mother and father seated on a settee across from Captain Newton. Her heart gave a rapid painful pang against her chest at the sight of his broad shoulders and muscular build, so similar to John's.

Captain Newton rose to his feet, as did her father.

"Polly, come in, my darling," said her mother with a smile, which only served to confuse Polly further. Her mother had always spoken somewhat negatively of Captain Newton, her cousin's husband. Polly had sometimes gotten the impression that her mother disapproved of the captain for not being there when his wife had died. But now she had apparently been chatting with him as though they were long-lost friends.

"This is Captain Newton," Father said nodding at the man amiably, which surprised Polly too, considering how much he'd disapproved of John. "We were just speaking of you."

At the mention of Captain Newton, Billy's arm stiffened beneath her fingers.

Polly took a deep breath. Whatever the news, she was long done with entertaining thoughts about John Newton. "Captain Newton and I had the pleasure of meeting in London at Susanna's some time ago."

"I'm pleased to see you again, Miss Catlett," Captain Newton said, and she was surprised to realize that his eyes truly were brimming with pleasure. The sad ghosts that had haunted him when she'd visited with him in London seemed to have vanished.

Polly curtsied. "What brings you to Chatham, Captain Newton?"

The captain looked first at the bouquet of bluebells she still held and then at her hand tucked firmly into Billy's arm. "I was hoping that I might speak with you and your parents privately about the nature of my visit."

Billy's body turned into an iron pike. "Polly and I were hoping to speak to you alone, Mr. Catlett."

Her father also glanced at the bouquet and then briefly searched Polly's face. His knowing expression told her he'd guessed exactly what Billy hoped to speak with him about. "Since we have this rare occasion of visiting with Captain Newton, I'd be grateful if we could put off the matter for another day."

Billy looked as though he wanted to say more, but after a moment he nodded briefly and then released Polly. "Then may I have the pleasure of calling on you tomorrow evening?" His words were directed at her, but he tossed Captain Newton a challenging glance.

The captain assessed him coolly in response.

Polly was relieved when Billy left. She sat in a chair near her parents and willed her heart to stop its frantic racing. She tried to tell herself that she didn't care what had become of John. But she couldn't fool herself. She was suddenly desperate to know that he was alive and safe. Even if he could never be hers, at least she would know he was well.

"Miss Catlett, you look even lovelier than the last time I saw you," Captain Newton said with a gentleness that contradicted a man of his size and power.

"Thank you, sir." She wanted to squirm under the three sets of eyes that were trained upon her but remained poised as she'd been taught at school.

"I got a letter from John yesterday."

Her gaze snapped up to his. "And . . . ?" She hated that her voice was breathless.

"And . . . he's alive and safe in Ireland."

Something wild and fierce gripped her chest, and she couldn't prevent the tears from springing to her eyes. He was alive. Thank the Lord. He was alive and safe. She tried to speak, to ask more, but her lips only trembled, and she had to cover them with her hands and blink back rapid tears.

"I thought he was dead," the captain whispered hoarsely, his eyes brimming with tears too. "I'd heard that the *Greyhound* rescued him. But for the past eighteen months I haven't had one word. No one knew what had become of the *Greyhound*. We assumed that it had sunk and all its crew with it."

Captain Newton paused and pulled out several sheets of paper. He opened them to reveal John's handwriting. The captain cleared his throat before continuing. "From what John wrote, and from what I've since heard about the *Greyhound,* they're mighty lucky to have made it as far as they did."

For several long minutes he relayed John's rendition of the storm, the starvation conditions, and finally how the ship had made it to Ireland with one miracle after another, too many to simply be a coincidence. Polly's body was taut on the edge of her seat by the time the captain finished.

"The Lord intervened so far to save me," Captain Newton read the letter now. "I cried out to him who alone could relieve me. I was sorry for my misspent life and committed myself to an immediate reformation. The powerful hand of God had at last found me out."

A thrill of wonder swept through Polly, and she reveled in the sweet words, utterly amazed that they'd been penned by John, who'd had such a hard heart toward God for as long as she'd known him. She was grateful that he'd finally made peace with God.

While awaiting repairs on the *Greyhound,* he was staying in Londonderry. He said he was going to church twice a day for morning and evening prayers, was taking Communion, had stopped cursing, and was studying religious books. "I rose very early and with greatest solemnity engaged myself to be the Lord's forever." The captain read for a moment longer, and Polly wondered if perhaps John had finally made peace with his father too. Perhaps that was why Captain Newton had a new light in his eyes.

"We're truly pleased for you, Captain," Mother said.

Father nodded his agreement. "It's just too bad you won't get to see him before you leave."

Captain Newton smiled faintly then. "Aye, I wish that I might.

But at least I have his letter to take with me to reassure me that this wayward son of mine is now walking the right path."

"Take with you?" Polly asked.

"I've been offered a position as governor in Hudson Bay at York Fort, a northern outpost. I'd hoped I might be able to see John before I leave, but the damage on the *Greyhound* was so extensive that the repairs have delayed his departure. He won't be able to make it back by the time I leave in two days."

John was coming back? The realization overcame Polly with such force she couldn't think. When? How? What would she do? She sat back in her chair flustered.

As though sensing her discomfort, Captain Newton looked at her with sudden expectation. "He still loves you."

Her pulse sped so that she could feel the blood racing through her veins.

"He doesn't know that I'm here in Chatham. He didn't ask that I come. But I knew it was the last gift I could give him before I leave England."

"Gift, sir?" she managed.

"The gift of reconciliation." With that he looked at her father and mother. "I'm sorry for any hurt I may have caused you at Elizabeth's death." Mother started to speak, but Captain Newton continued, his voice cracking. "I loved her more than anything. And not a day goes by that I don't regret not being here for her. If only I'd been a better husband, she might have lived."

"No, that's not true," Mother said quietly, her voice just as anguished. "There's nothing you could have done, nothing any of us could do."

"I don't want John to go through what I did," Captain Newton said, sitting up straighter and visibly attempting to bring his emotions under control. "I don't want him to miss out on life with the woman he loves."

They were all silent for a moment, save the twittering of a nest of birds outside the window that drowned out all Polly's thoughts except one—John still loved her. John still loved her. John still loved her.

"At our last visit, you made clear to me that you couldn't offer John a hope of the future," Captain Newton said, meeting her gaze head on. "I know I have no right to ask you to reconsider your position on the matter. But I wanted you to know that John's a changed man." He shifted to look directly into her father's serious eyes. "And I wanted to gain your permission for John to marry Polly, if Polly should be in agreement."

Polly almost gasped out loud at the bold request. Surely Captain Newton couldn't expect that after all this time she'd save herself for John. And surely Captain Newton couldn't expect her father to put aside his reservations so easily after one letter from John declaring himself to be a changed man.

Her father hesitated, as if thinking the same thing.

"I sent a letter to my friend Joseph Manesty in Liverpool requesting a job for John on one of his vessels. And I had word from Manesty before I rode out this morning that he's planning to offer John a position as captain of the *Brownlow*."

Her father's brows rose. "That's a big promotion."

"Aye. With big pay. But Captain Swanwick of the *Greyhound* wrote to Manesty and personally recommended John. He attested to John's change of character. And he said that if not for John's expert seamanship, skill, and courage, they may not have survived."

Father exchanged a look with Mother. She smiled at him, as if to give her approval.

Polly's heart flipped with a tiny current of hope, a hope she hadn't known was still there. When her father looked at her with wide, calm eyes, she didn't dare breathe.

"If John is truly a changed man and is walking with God," he said, "then I have no objection to him pursuing Polly."

The current of hope turned into a hum of wonder. After all her father's reservations about John, after throwing him out of the house, after banning him from seeing her again, could her father really approve of John now?

As if reading her unspoken thoughts, her father continued, "If he's given himself over to God, then I know his heart is in the right place."

"I have no doubt John will still struggle," Captain Newton rushed to say.

"No one is perfect," her father added.

"He'll still have a lot of growing to do."

"Don't we all?"

The men nodded at each other, and Polly sat back, all the tension easing from her body. In all her dreams, she'd never imagined this conversation taking place, much less with her father. But watching him, she could see that he was genuinely pleased and so was Captain Newton.

"So what do you think?" Mother was smiling at her in a way that made Polly want to blush. When both men looked at her with questioning eyes, she was sure her cheeks did turn pink.

She longed to nod yes, yes, yes. That she would consider John, that she'd never stopped considering him, that he'd always been woven into her heart even though she'd tried so hard to pluck him out. But she couldn't just invite him back into her life and into her heart at the spur of the moment, could she? Surely they needed to meet again and determine if they still felt the same way about each other. After all, they'd both grown up in the years they'd been apart. What if John saw her and no longer felt the same way? Or what if she wasn't attracted to him anymore?

And what about Billy? Her stomach clenched at the memory of his proposal and declaration of love. She'd all but said yes to him. How could she say no now?

The lines at the corners of Captain Newton's eyes began to form a frown.

"It's been so long since John and I have spoken," she explained, not wishing to disappoint him but knowing she couldn't rush into a commitment. "What if things have changed?"

Her mother nodded. "That's perfectly understandable. You both had a childhood infatuation. And that may no longer be the case."

Captain Newton shook his head solemnly. "I don't think this was ever an infatuation for John. From the first time he met Polly, he was in love with her. And it never wavered. Everything he's ever done was so that he could be with her, including leaving Africa. If not for his love for Polly, he wouldn't have had any incentive to return home."

The captain's words flowed over Polly like the warmth of a gentle summer rain shower. Even so, she glanced at the bluebells on the side table where she'd laid them. Their fragrance was still sweet and strong.

She cared for Billy too. He was a good man who loved her and who would always be there for her. He'd been a steady presence in her life all along, and marriage to him would offer stability and predictability. Such qualities were appealing—and had always been lacking in John. "We shall welcome John into our home," her father said as he searched her face. "And then we shall let the Lord will whatever he desires."

# TWENTY-FIVE

MAY 1748

*I*t was a lie," Captain Swanwick admitted. "I'm sorry, Newton. But at the time, it was the only thing I could think of to make you leave Kittam."

They stood together in the Liverpool shipping office of Joseph Manesty. The dank front room smelled of whale oil and tobacco. It was cramped, with the crates and barrels shoved into every corner a testament to the thriving shipping business that Manesty owned. "I knew it wasn't four hundred pounds," John responded as disbelief and despair churned in his gut. "But maybe I've inherited two hundred from my great-uncle? Maybe even one hundred?"

"There's nothing." Swanwick lowered his head, the shame radiating from his stricken expression. "For all I know your uncle is still very much alive and well."

Newton could only stare at the captain who had become his friend over the past month. After waiting for repairs in Londonderry, being well fed and well dressed and welcomed by the people there, the *Greyhound* crew had shed their sunken eyes and haggard appearance and had begun to fill out again. Now back on English soil in Liverpool, they were finally at the end of their journey together. "I beg you to tell me that I have at least a small amount."

Swanwick didn't respond. And this time, Newton hung his head. Pain, regret, and confusion hit him with such force he had to close his eyes to keep himself from crying out with frustration.

When they landed an hour ago, he had every intention of finding a horse and riding as fast and hard to Chatham as he could. The journey was at least two hundred fifty miles, and he didn't want to delay another minute, another second. He'd been away from Polly for nearly four years. And the need to see her had grown steadily more intense with each passing day.

Only prayers throughout the long night had kept him from doing something stupid like stealing one of the longboats and rowing himself to shore. When they finally arrived on the docks after daybreak, a messenger from Manesty was waiting for them. Manesty requested that Newton and Swanwick meet him at his office.

In his haste to leave town, Newton had almost tossed aside the request. Every minute of delay made his muscles tighten until he thought he might explode from the pressure. But he forced himself to accompany Swanwick to the office with the anticipation of leaving the second his meeting with Manesty was completed.

But now . . .

"Then that means I have absolutely nothing," Newton said, "not even a farthing to my name."

"I'm sorry," Swanwick said again.

Newton shook his head. "It's not your fault." He should have known.

"But I did put in a good word with Manesty for you," Swanwick said.

"Manesty would never hire me." Not after he'd been irresponsible with the first job offer Manesty had given him on the Jamaican sugar plantation. Manesty wouldn't consider him, not even if he was the last man available.

Newton's mind spun. He couldn't go to visit Polly now, not without anything to offer her. Mr. Catlett would see him coming down the front path and tell him not to walk into Polly's life again. Already Newton would have a battle regaining Mr. Catlett's good favor. Without a fortune, the task would be impossible.

He would stay away from her until he had something he could offer her, even if it tore his heart out to do so.

But as he contemplated all the ways he could earn money quickly so that he could win her, he shook his head. "I need to give her up, Swanwick." His throat ached just saying the words, but once they were out, he knew them to be true. "I can't keep holding on to her."

"You don't need to go to that extreme," Swanwick started.

"It wouldn't be fair of me to visit her now. Even if she still wanted me, it could take years before I'd have means enough to be worthy of her. She deserves to get married and have a family before she's too old for all of that." Besides, it was possible she already had a serious suitor, was in love with another man. After all, she'd never written back to him, even after he asked her to.

"Even if you aren't a rich man," Swanwick said, "not many women can boast of a man loving them the way you do her."

Joseph Manesty's deep booming voice jarred Newton. For such a loud voice, a tiny wisp of a man stepped out of the adjoining room and strode briskly toward them. Thin and bald, Manesty wiped a sheen of perspiration from his shining head.

Newton had met Manesty on several occasions as a boy but

hadn't seen him since before the failed job opportunity when he neglected to show up for the ship that was set to sail for Jamaica. He braced himself for well-deserved censure.

"Newton, my boy," the man called almost jovially. "The *Brownlow* will be outfitted and ready to set sail this summer."

"Aye, good that, sir," Newton said tentatively. Could it be the man was giving him a second chance after all?

"When can you be ready?" Manesty cocked his head and pinned him with a serious stare. "Will three weeks suit you?"

Was the man offering him a position as a sailor on one of his ships? "What are your expectations, sir?"

"I'd like you to outfit her and find a crew. Then I expect you to command my ship with as much expertise and skill as I heard you did the *Greyhound*."

"Command?" Newton could barely get the word out.

"Of course command. What do you think I expect of my captains?"

Newton scrambled to make sense of Manesty. Was the man offering him a position of captain on the *Brownlow*?

"Your father and Swanwick both testify that you're ready for the position," Manesty continued. "And after your time in Africa and familiarity with the coast, I think you're just the man I need."

Swanwick nodded. "Aye. Newton is one of the most skilled sailors I've met. He'll make you a very fine captain, sir. Not only that, but he's not the same man I met a year ago. He's completely changed his life for the better."

Newton nodded at Swanwick, grateful for the words of praise, although he wasn't sure that he deserved them. The front door of the office opened and several more men ducked inside. Their rolling gaits identified them as seafarers, likely sailors coming to sign on for a voyage on one of Manesty's many ships.

"So we're all set?" Manesty asked, starting to move toward the newcomers. "Swanwick, you'll take the *Greyhound* out again once she's ready?"

Swanwick nodded hesitantly, and Newton could see the fear in the back of the man's eyes. After barely surviving on the floating wreck of a ship, he wouldn't be too eager to take her out again, even if she was repaired. The many months in Africa's equatorial waters had rotted the *Greyhound*'s timbers. Besides that, Manesty was known for his frugality and for reducing the cost of his ships, often sacrificing safety and durability for profit. But he also offered incentives and bonuses to his captains who could bring back the most cargo.

Manesty didn't give Captain Swanwick a chance to protest. He was already skirting several barrels halfway across the room.

"And Newton, I'll see you back here in three weeks," Manesty boomed. Manesty was giving him a second chance the same way God had. A growing sense of unworthiness came stealing back. He didn't deserve Manesty's confidence any more than he deserved God's love. Would he be worthy of the man's trust? He prayed he would but knew deep inside he still had a long way to go in becoming a new man.

Polly paused by the front gate. "Good afternoon, Miss Donovan."

The woman was scratching Prince's curly head, and at Polly's greeting she straightened. Other than a few more creases in her forehead, Miss Donovan's appearance hadn't changed much while Polly had been away to school. Unfortunately, neither had her spinster status. She was still dependent on her brother.

"Miss Catlett." Miss Donovan managed a smile, her lips thin, the lines in her pale cheeks crinkling like flaxen linen that was stiff from disuse. "Visiting the almshouse again, I see?"

"Yes," Polly replied. Her mother had finally allowed her to accompany her to the almshouse in the months since she'd returned home. She'd hoped the charity work would fill the gap inside. She'd hoped that by focusing on those less fortunate, she could forget about her own maladies, not that she had many. She had so much for which to be grateful. Even though her father had never regained his position and still struggled to provide for their family, they had more than the unfortunate souls residing at the almshouse. She had to remember that every time discontentment surfaced.

Polly swung the empty basket draped over her arm and glanced ahead at her mother, who was already entering the house. "We decided to do so early today, to avoid the rainstorms."

Miss Donovan tipped the brim of her hat back and peered up at the darkening sky. The wind was beginning to blow with more force, swaying the branches with their new leaves. "Oh, what do you know. It is looking like rain."

Droplets had already dampened Polly's cloak on the long walk home from the almshouse, but she refrained from remarking about the obvious since she suspected Miss Donovan purposefully came outside when she knew Polly would be returning home. Polly couldn't begrudge the woman a few moments of visiting, even if the conversations generally went about the same every time they met.

Their meetings were always short. Miss Donovan wasn't particularly talkative, and Polly didn't want to risk being impolite by prying with questions of her own. So they always ran out of things to talk about after a minute.

"You are such a saint to take provisions to the poor," came Miss Donovan's usual praise.

"I'm only seeking to please God," Polly countered with her usual response. She only wished that going to the almshouse brought her a measure of satisfaction. But as with her prayers, her charity work felt empty. No matter how many prayers she offered, how content she tried to be with her life, or how often she visited the poor, she couldn't keep from sensing that somehow she'd failed to live up to God's expectations for her.

And now after Captain Newton's visit yesterday, she was even more restless. Of course, she'd concluded that she wouldn't entertain any thoughts about John Newton. Even if he had really changed and could provide for her, she'd already told Billy that she'd marry him. It wasn't official yet. At her father's request to wait, Billy hadn't posted the banns.

"I saw that your sailor is back." Miss Donovan shifted her attention to Prince and began scratching him rapidly up and down his back as though he hadn't had any attention in weeks.

"My sailor?" Polly was confused for only a moment before realizing that Miss Donovan must have noticed Captain Newton coming and going from their home yesterday. She likely had confused him with John, which wouldn't have been hard to do, especially from a distance. "No, that was Captain Newton coming to give us news about his son."

Miss Donovan scratched her dog for another long moment before speaking again hesitantly. "It was good news, I hope?"

"Yes, John—Mr. Newton is alive and well in Ireland."

"Wonderful." Her pale cheeks took on a pink hue.

"It is wonderful." Even if she wouldn't allow feelings for him to fan back to life, Polly couldn't deny the deep relief that still swept through her every time she thought about John being alive.

Another long silence stretched between them. When a fat raindrop splattered against her cheek, Polly gave Miss Donovan a parting smile and turned to go. "Good day to you."

"My fiancé was a ship captain." Miss Donovan's words tumbled over themselves and barreled into Polly.

She pivoted and faced Miss Donovan again. This time the flush on the woman's cheeks had turned as bright as the magnolias that lined the fence. Polly didn't know why she should be surprised by the news that her spinster neighbor had once been engaged and perhaps in love. She supposed she'd assumed spinsters were somehow deficient in matters of love.

She hadn't considered that Miss Donovan may have once been exactly like her. What had happened, then, to prevent her from marrying her fiancé?

"He and all his crew went down with his ship during a terrible storm," she said, as though sensing Polly's question.

Like the storm that had almost killed John? From the way Captain Newton had described the squall and the conditions afterward, John should have perished. It was a miracle the *Greyhound* had made it to Ireland. John had certainly had his fair share of lifesaving miracles over the years. Surely by now he'd used up his allotment.

Miss Donovan hefted Prince into her arms and buried her face against his neck.

"I'm so sorry for your loss," Polly said in a vain attempt to ease the awkwardness of the moment. What more could she say? She supposed that Miss Donovan had waited for her captain to return from voyages, much the same way she had for John. She'd likely placed all her hopes for the future on him. But then one time, he'd never returned. And by then she'd been too old to start courting other men. Or perhaps she'd been too grief stricken. Either way, Miss Donovan was now reduced to a life of dependence with only a dog to love and be loved by.

As though sensing Polly's pity, Miss Donovan hugged Prince tighter and spun away. "Good day to you, Miss Catlett."

Newton held the letter from his father in his hands, too frightened to open it. He'd been sitting at the writing table in his Liverpool dormer room for the past half hour unable to work up the nerve to read it.

He'd written a couple of letters to the captain when he was in Ireland. In them both he told his father he was deeply sorry for his disrespect and disobedience over the years. He felt burdened to make reparations almost as soon as he landed on the shore. He didn't ask for forgiveness. That was too much to ask. But at the very least, he needed to tell his father he was sorry for all the years of grief and disappointment he'd caused him.

Newton realized now that he had to forgive his father for his harshness at times. Although his father had faults, deep down he was a good man. Even when Newton harbored petty and immature grudges, his father had come to his aid. The captain was always willing to help him, even when he was a clot in return. In fact, his father had done it again by recommending him to Manesty for the captain's position.

Why had his father come to his aid once more? Especially after the disdainful way Newton treated him the last time they were together? Newton's throat tightened. Certainly the captain couldn't still love him, could he? Not after how horrible he'd been.

Newton pushed back from the rickety writing table and stood. The cloudy window of the dormer room overlooked the bustling Liverpool harbor and docks with the ships coming and going. The street outside was just as busy with shopkeepers setting out their wares and the many merchants and sailors preparing for their next voyage.

Liverpool was one of the busiest trading ports and also flourished from its shipbuilding, rope making, and iron working. Sugar refining was also a booming industry as ships delivered sugar grown in the West Indies.

The instruments hanging in a ship chandler shop across the street glared at Newton as they did every time he peered out. Handcuffs, leg shackles, and thumbscrews. Also a surgical instrument with a screw device used to pry open the mouth of any shipboard slave who tried to commit suicide by refusing to eat.

He glanced quickly away and pushed down his discomfort and guilt. Liverpool was also the world's largest slave-trade port, sending dozens of ships to Africa every year.

Although part of him longed to be elsewhere, Newton had accepted the spot Captain Swanwick graciously offered him in the dormer room that he was renting in the King's Arms tavern.

Newton dropped his gaze back to the letter from his father and released a shaky breath. This would probably be an easier letter to

read than the one he hoped to get any day from Susanna. He'd
written to Susanna over a week ago, not long after arriving in
Liverpool.

The words he'd written still tore at his heart every time he remembered them:

"I have long loved my cousin Polly. I love her still, as well as ever,
and it is that love that makes me now endeavor to relinquish my
pretenses. The chief business of this letter is therefore to assure you
that I am determined from this moment to divert my thoughts from
Polly as much as possible. And though I do not expect ever wholly to
conquer my passion, I will endeavor to keep it within my own breast
and never trouble either her or you anymore with it."

After he posted the letter, he questioned a thousand times
whether he'd done the right thing. Mayhap he shouldn't have sent it.
Mayhap he should have gone one more time to see Polly. Mayhap he
could have talked to her and discovered how she felt.

He dug in his pocket and pulled out the handkerchief she'd given
him so long ago. It was threadbare in spots. The lace along the edges
was frayed down to nothing. Her monogrammed initials were all but
gone. But it was still a part of her. He'd never be able to give her up
completely. No matter how hard he tried.

Nay. He shook his head and started to open his father's letter. He
couldn't keep second-guessing himself. Although the decision tortured him, he'd done the honorable thing for once in his life. He'd
released Polly to pursue a life without him. And he wouldn't go back
on it now.

The paper shook in Newton's fingers as he unfolded it. The date
at the top told him his father had written it on the day before he'd set
sail for Hudson Bay. When Newton first heard that his father was

leaving England and that he'd miss seeing him by only a few days, he wasn't sure whether to be relieved or disappointed. Though he'd written the letters of apology, he wanted to make his amends face to face too. As hard as that would have been, especially not knowing how his father would receive him, Newton longed to humble himself before the man as he should have years ago.

But now he would have to settle for his father's response in a letter. Anxiously, Newton began reading his father's words. The tone was formal and related mostly to business matters. His father explained his new position in Hudson Bay and expounded upon Manesty's offer to be captain of the *Brownlow*. Newton was relieved the tone was cordial but was disappointed that his father made no mention of repairing their relationship. He knew he didn't deserve it even though he longed for it. He should be grateful his father had written back to him at all. Even so, he couldn't keep from wishing for more.

Newton dropped back into the stiff chair, the heaviness of despair settling upon him. As his attention turned to the postscript, Newton's pulse came to a sudden halt.

"Addendum: After writing this letter, I rode to Chatham and visited with the Catletts to discuss a possible marriage match between you and the object of your affection. They received me warmly and are willing to give you their blessing in such matters. We all agreed to leave the final decision to you and Polly. They shall be expecting your visit soon."

For an endless moment, Newton could only stare dumbfounded at the paragraph. He blinked to see if the words were a mirage, if they would disappear much the same way land did on the horizon. But after several blinks they were still there. He drew his thumb across them and reread them a dozen times before finally releasing a shaky breath.

He didn't fight to hold back the tears that stung his eyes. His father had forgiven him even though he hadn't asked for it. Nay, his father hadn't said the words. Nay, he hadn't written them.

Rather he'd proven his forgiveness by doing the one thing that would mean the most to Newton. He'd given Polly back to him. He'd made a way with Mr. Catlett where there had been none. He'd gained approval when Newton hadn't been able to. He'd done it all for Newton when there had been nothing for him to gain in return.

Newton dropped his face into his hands and wept for the man who'd never given up on him. The man who'd loved him through all the difficulties and disappointments and failures. The man who'd never stopped loving him.

"Thank you." His voice cracked. "I love you too, Father."

# TWENTY-SIX

JUNE 1748

*P*olly pressed a kiss against Mary's forehead, then straightened and gazed down at the sleeping child's peaceful face for a long moment, the feathery lashes resting on her rosy cheeks. Polly's heart ached with both love and loss.

She fought back the tears that came whenever she thought about the letter from John that Susanna gave her when she arrived yesterday. The awful letter in which John informed her that he was giving her up, that he wasn't worthy of her, and that he wouldn't visit her again.

The letter had broken her heart. She knew it shouldn't have mattered. She knew she shouldn't have cared. She thought she had convinced herself to go ahead with marriage plans with Billy. She didn't want to marry a ship captain and have to live with fear every voyage that she'd lose him.

Even so, she had to admit to herself that she'd still been harboring the hope of seeing John again.

There was something about the idea of being with him that excited her in a way that being with Billy never had. And now that he'd devoted his life to following God, she couldn't keep from thinking of how well they had worked together on his mother's hymns. What if God had a purpose and a ministry for them together?

So she'd been waiting. And she'd even been watching the road.

Until Susanna arrived yesterday and delivered John's good-bye letter. Susanna still used every excuse she could to get away from her London home. It was no secret anymore that Daniel regularly committed adultery with the female servants, whether they were willing or not. Apparently he had always felt it was his right to dally with the servants, even as a young man still living under his father's roof. Though he'd agreed to Susanna's pleas for him to stop, she told Polly that she caught Daniel fondling one of the chambermaids earlier in the week.

The idea of getting into a marriage like Susanna's frightened Polly. If only Susanna had known about Daniel's problem with lust when they were courting. She'd known he was a flirt but admitted to Polly that she thought he would change once they were married, that he'd settle down, that he'd have no need for anyone else.

But it had become all too clear that marriage wasn't the cure for a man's sins. The issues didn't magically disappear after marriage. In fact, if anything, the problems only came more into the light.

Of course Susanna had brushed aside John's good-bye letter as nonsense, had insisted that John wouldn't be able to resist coming to see her, that he'd never follow through on his resolution. But Polly had the feeling that this time John was determined to prove himself a changed man. He wasn't planning to come to her again.

He'd set her free.

Polly pressed her hand over her mouth to keep a sob from escaping and waking Mary. She backed slowly out of the room that had been given over to Susanna and Mary for the duration of their visit.

Susanna met her in the hallway. "It's about time—"

"Shh." Polly cut her off with a finger to her lips and a warning glare. "She's finally napping."

"You've been in there for an eternity," Susanna said as she followed her down the stairway. The hallway was dark with the shadows of the late afternoon.

"I like holding her."

"You like spoiling her."

Polly smiled. "She's easy to spoil."

"Well, you're needed in the stable," Susanna said, steering her toward the back door. "Apparently one of the new kittens is lost."

Polly tensed. "Oh no." Pete had found himself a mate, and they'd had another batch of kittens as they did every spring. She didn't wait for any further instructions from Susanna but hurried outside and across the backyard. "And of course, Billy rode by," Susanna said breathlessly in her effort to keep up. "He asked if he could come calling later this evening."

Polly sighed. Billy had been much too patient with her over the past two weeks. They'd had the meeting with her father, and he'd asked for permission to marry her. Father had acquiesced, but Polly had sensed his reservations, the same reservations he'd had all along.

She'd told Billy she needed more time to think about it. But after John's letter, she would tell Billy tonight that she would marry him and let him post the banns as he'd been waiting to do.

"You check inside," Susanna said, stopping several feet from the open doorway. "And I'll search around the perimeter."

Polly nodded and waved Susanna away before ducking into the cool shadows. The soft neigh of her father's horse greeted her, along with the earthy scent of the fresh hay strewn on the dirt floor.

"Here kitty, kitty." She started toward the far side of the stable to an old wool blanket where the mother had been nursing and sleeping with the kittens.

At a *thump* against one of the stalls, she swung her attention around.

"Looking for these?" Out of the shadows stepped the broad-shouldered man she'd never thought to see again.

She gasped and covered her mouth to conceal the breadth of her surprise.

He held one kitten in his palm, and three others were crawling up his arms and on his shoulders. His face was leaner than she remembered, and he seemed taller. But otherwise he looked the same. His skin was browned and his hair windswept with sun-bleached streaks. The scruff on his cheeks told her he hadn't taken the time to shave. But he was attired in clean garments, likely the best he owned even if they were slightly frayed.

She took him in, hardly daring to believe he was standing in front of her, living and breathing and altogether too attractive.

His sea-green eyes were taking her in too, growing wider with each inch of her body that he perused so that she couldn't keep from flushing under his scrutiny. "You're all grown up," he whispered, wrenching his gaze upward to her face.

"It's been a long time," she whispered back, drinking him in with wonder.

"Aye. Too long."

She studied his face and wanted to reach out and touch him to make sure he was real.

One of the kittens chose that moment to begin crawling up the front of his shirt. He grimaced from the tiny claws that were likely digging into his skin.

At his pain, she rushed forward and reached for the orange tabby. "Now, Pasqual," she chided, "that's no way to treat our company."

"Pasqual?" One of John's brows lifted.

Polly rubbed the kitten behind his ear. "This is Pasqual. Then there's Posie, Petunia, and Pembrose." She pointed at each one.

"Don't tell me the father is Pete." Newton grinned, and it took her breath away.

"Yes, Pete's the father and the mother is Priscilla."

"It sounds like you have an admiration of the letter *p*."

"How could I not?" she teased back. "There are so many good things that start with the letter *p*. Pockets, parcels, pastries, and pies."

"Don't forget the best thing of all." He bent down and allowed the kittens to jump off him. The mother cat came from out of the shadows to gather them to her side.

"Peace?"

"Aye, peace is a good one. But I know something even better."

"Paradise."

He chuckled softly. "Aye. Something even better."

"There's nothing better than paradise." She'd forgotten how much fun she had bantering with John and loved how easily they could fall back into such camaraderie.

John took another step forward so that he was only an arm's length away from her.

"What could possibly compare with paradise?" she asked again, her attention dropping to his broad chest and the strength exuding from his torso.

"Being with a woman named Polly." The words came out light, but when she glanced up to his face, his expression was so intense that she sucked in a sharp breath.

Her thoughts flitted to the past, to the other time when they'd been in this exact spot together. Apparently Susanna had orchestrated another meeting alone. Polly was grateful for the privacy.

"Polly." He uttered her name with such reverence that her heart began to thud in anticipation. Of what she did not know. All she knew was that she'd been waiting for this moment far too long.

"I can't believe I'm finally looking at you," he whispered and reached out to touch the ringlet dangling next to her ear. "I feel like I'm dreaming."

His touch was as light as the whiskers of the kittens. She held her breath and waited for him to move his fingers from the curl to her cheek and to graze her skin. She wanted it. Needed to feel his touch on her face. She could see in his eyes that he desired her, and when his attention shifted to her lips, her stomach burned low and deep.

She'd relived his parting kiss a thousand times. Even now, she could feel the hard pressure of his lips, the passion in his mouth, the taste of him, the warmth of his breath.

Something flared in his eyes, and he began to lean closer as though he had every intention of kissing her again. But then just as suddenly he shut his eyes and dropped his hand. His nostrils flared, and he took a step back before opening his eyes.

Although he still regarded her with desire, the muscles in his jaw clenched and the corners of his eyes wrinkled, showing a new maturity. "I missed you." His voice was hoarse. "Not a day has gone by in which I neglected to think of you at least a dozen times over."

She wished she could say the same thing to him. But the truth was, she'd spent nearly every waking moment trying to forget about him. It had taken months before she could finally make it through a day without her heart ripping open at the thought of him. Just the remembrance of her struggles and the intense heartache gave her pause.

Was it really such a good idea to see John again, especially in light of the letter he'd sent to Susanna? Maybe he'd been right to cut off their relationship rather than put them through this torture of wanting each other but being unable to be together. She took a step back. "Susanna brought me your letter."

He exhaled a sigh and his shoulders drooped. "I was hoping it hadn't reached you yet. But I suppose that's why Susanna rode out to Chatham."

Polly nodded.

John kicked at a loose piece of hay. "I wrote the letter before I received the news from my father that he'd come to visit your parents and that your father is willing to give us his blessing."

"So you had no desire to see me before that?"

"Nay," he said rapidly. "I was desperate to see you. The minute my feet touched ground in Liverpool I was planning to ride here to see you. But . . ." The afternoon sunlight slanted in through a crack in the siding illuminating the anguish in his expression. "I discovered that the fortune that I thought I could offer you was all a lie."

She wanted to tell him that a fortune didn't matter. That she didn't care what he had to offer. But she knew that wouldn't be the truth. It did matter. She did care. After the years at Mrs. Overing's Boarding School, after the time mingling with wealthy young ladies, after a lifestyle of ease and pleasure, she couldn't imagine throwing all that away.

"I have nothing, Polly," he said, splaying his hands out to his sides as though to show her all he had was himself. "I can't offer you the kind of life you deserve. I can't even come close."

She'd always known that if she chose John she'd lose her status and end up poor. At one time, when she was younger and more naive, she might have been able to overlook such prospects. But now after seeing Susanna's marriage, after seeing that marriage wasn't the cure to all of life's problems, she could only imagine how her life would be once the newness of married life wore away. Would she be disappointed?

"Your father said you've been given the captain position of a ship," she said. "Surely that will be a good start to a new career."

One of the kittens scampered across John's shoes and started to climb his trouser leg. In one easy but gentle swoop, John scooped the kitten into his palm and began petting it. "On the ride here I decided that I'm not going to take the captain position."

"What? Why?"

"I'm honored to have been offered the job. But for my first voyage, I think God wants me to be in a humbler position where I can practice obeying a captain and acquiring further insight and experience before venturing to lead others."

Polly stared at John in amazement. The young man she'd once known would have boasted of his position. At the very least he wouldn't have deliberated over the prestigious offer or claimed the need to gain obedience and insight before taking on such a role.

"When I go back to Liverpool, I'm planning to tell my boss that I'd like to be the mate, the second in command, as long as he's able to find a replacement." John's words were spoken with a finality that echoed through her. Regardless of how such a move would affect his financial situation, he was doing it. No matter how it might affect his ability to provide for her, he was humbling himself.

Even if eventually he became a captain and could provide modestly for her, he'd be gone for long months at a time. She'd see him only for a few weeks a year. How would she endure the long separations inherent in being married to a seafarer? Her thoughts returned to Miss Donovan's revelation about her fiancé. Every time she told John good-bye, would she be wondering if it would be her last? She couldn't bear the thought of allowing herself to love him, only to lose him. With John, she could very well end up a spinster. Like Miss Donovan. And that was the last thing she wanted.

"Since I have so little, I know I have no right to ask you to consider a future with me," he said in a tremulous voice. "But my father's letter gave me hope. I thought that if your father had given his blessing in spite of everything I've done in the past, I hoped—and prayed—that you might be willing to give me another chance."

His eyes were wide and expectant upon her face. The green was calm with a peace she'd never noticed there before.

She couldn't give John a decision at this moment. She needed more time to think about everything. She swallowed her unease and tried to smile. "I think we need some time—"

"I don't need another minute to know that I love you, that I always have, and I'll never stop until I take my dying breath." The passion in his voice matched the sudden flare of passion in his eyes.

Heat rolled like lapping waves through her stomach. She wanted to do nothing more than fling herself into his arms and give herself to him. But shouldn't they spend more time together first? After all that had happened to Susanna with her marriage, she couldn't rush into a decision as big as this. "I need more time, John. Please."

Disappointment flashed across his face. But he ducked his head to hide it and didn't say anything.

"At least we have some time this week that we can spend together," she said, trying to ease the strain between them. "When must you return to Liverpool?"

"I might be able to stay a few days," he started, but then stopped and glanced almost painfully at the open doorway. Outside, Polly caught a glimpse of Susanna's petticoat and wondered if Susanna had listened to their bittersweet reunion. "Nay," he said, his voice spread thin and tight, "as much as I'd like to stay for a week or even a few days, I have to leave on the morrow if I'm to make it back by my deadline. Manesty gave me three weeks to report back to the office, and I've already squandered two."

Polly stared at him in wonder. Deadlines had never stopped John in the past. He'd always stayed as long as he wanted. Was he truly a changed man as his father had declared? She regarded him again, as if for the first time, taking in the serious bent of his brow, the gentleness of his expression, and the sincerity of his stance.

"I'm thrilled to know you've made peace with God," she said. And for a brief moment, she was jealous of him and wished that she too might find peace for her restless heart.

He nodded. "I'm far from perfect. I'm much like Saint Paul, who persecuted believers. He was blind but then had his eyes opened to the truth. I'm now on the path toward righteous living and will be striving down that path to the end of my days."

She smiled at him, genuinely pleased to know that he'd come through his storms a stronger and better man.

He smiled in return, and she was relieved when the light danced back to life in his eyes. "Mayhap I can join you tonight . . ."

His suggestion shocked her, and her lips stalled, unable to find a suitable response.

He quirked a brow.

"What do you mean?" she finally squeaked.

"I'll join you in prayer. What did you think I meant?"

She could feel herself flushing, and he laughed, clearly enjoying her insinuation. "You're still in the habit of nightly prayer, aren't you?"

"Of course I am."

"Then we shall meet and pray together."

The idea was entirely appealing. But was it appropriate? "I don't know . . ."

"On the other hand, if you'd rather meet for other reasons"—his tone was nonchalant—"then I suggest we have a hasty wedding."

"John," she said, in shock once again.

His laughter rumbled between them, and she couldn't keep from giving him a playful push. He feigned a stumble backward, allowing himself to fall into a mound of hay.

She reached out a hand to help John back up, but when he caught it, he tugged her down, leaving her little choice but to fall into the hay next to him. He tossed a handful of straw, and she threw a handful back at him. Soon they were both laughing and covered in bits of straw.

She was glad to know that though John may have changed in some ways, he was still the fun-loving, mirthful man he'd always been. Sitting shoulder to shoulder, his hand was next to hers in the hay, and suddenly his fingers brushed hers. His touch was soft and tentative at first. When she didn't move away, he slowly, almost gingerly, laced his fingers through hers. The slide of his skin against hers was so exquisite that she had to close her eyes at the pleasure.

His head brushed hers, and she could hear the heavy drag of his breath close to her ear. All she needed to do was turn ever so slightly and her lips would meet his. She almost trembled with her need to kiss him. But she instead reveled in the feel of his warm palm, his fingers fitting together with hers, and his calloused skin.

"I love you," he whispered again in a thick voice that did strange things to her body. His words contained a finality that told her he wasn't expecting her to respond, that he simply wanted her to know of his undying adoration.

Her own declaration of ardor welled up from deep within, but before she could find the words, several giggles at the stable door alerted them to the fact that they were no longer alone. Susanna had apparently held off everyone else for as long as possible.

The rest of the evening passed in a whirlwind of seeing John and being near him, but never having another moment alone. She was all the more grateful to Susanna for somehow orchestrating a few stolen moments with John.

When Billy came by after dinner, he was understandably angry to see John. Neither man spoke to the other, and the tension between them was palpable. Billy's expression lightened only after Newton made the announcement that he was heading back to Liverpool the next morning. Her father nodded his approval and invited John to visit again during the summer if he had the chance before setting sail. Later her father beckoned John to his office to talk. She lingered outside the closed door for only a few moments to assure herself that this time the conversation was more pleasant than John's last visit.

When she finally made her way up the stairs to her bedroom, she couldn't keep from smiling at the remembrance of her conversation with John about joining her tonight. The thought of praying together with him was as delightful as the thought of spending the night wrapped in his arms.

"You love him," Susanna whispered, stepping out of her bedroom into the dark hallway. "I can see it in your smile." Polly started to shake her head, but Susanna cut her off with a grip that was so tight Polly winced. "Daniel never loved me the way John does you. And Billy doesn't love you that way either."

Even though Polly couldn't see Susanna's features clearly, anguish radiated from her tense hold and in her voice.

"Don't let him go."

Polly didn't have to ask to know that Susanna was referring to John. "But he can't provide for me." Once the words were out, Polly realized how selfish she sounded, and she hung her head.

"Wealth and prestige won't make you happy," Susanna said harshly. "Look at me."

"Billy's a kind and loving man too."

"Maybe. But are you willing to settle for a man you don't love, simply to have the kind of lifestyle you think will make you happy?"

"No man is perfect," she retorted. "John has his faults the same as Billy."

"The difference is that John wants to change. Billy sees no need for it." Susanna's quick answer silenced Polly. After a long moment of silence, Susanna finally sighed and released her. "I just don't want you to make the same mistake I did, Polly."

"I know."

"Then think about what I said."

Polly nodded. "I'm scared of making the wrong decision." Could she give up everything to be with John? Or should she give up John's love in order to have everything?

# TWENTY-SEVEN

JUNE 1748

*D*olly played the last note on the pianoforte before looking up at John, who'd come into the drawing room while she was immersed in the song. She'd already indulged him by singing last night when the whole family was gathered. His eyes had been bright as he watched and listened. She tried not to pay attention to his de-light, but she adored knowing that she still had the ability to please him with her singing.

"Did you compose the music?" he asked, nodding to his mother's songbook that was open above the keyboard.

"Do you like it?"

"I love it."

"Then yes," she responded with a smile, "I'll take credit for writ-ing it."

"Thanks for taking such good care of the book while I was gone."

As much as she'd wanted to bury the book at the bottom of her chest of drawers in her efforts to forget about John, she hadn't been able to. Every once in a while on a trip home, she'd pulled it out and fingered the worn pages. And then after Captain Newton's visit last month, she'd been unable to resist keeping it out and had even written music for another of the songs.

"I should give it back to you now," she said.

"Nay. It has a good home with you. I want you to have it." He grinned somewhat nostalgically, the sadness suddenly putting her on edge. "Besides, maybe I'll write my own hymnal. I'm working on a new song, one about God's grace. I have a couple of verses completed."

"I should like to hear the song," she responded, trying to dampen her eagerness. "Perhaps I can compose the music."

"It will have to wait for another day," he said, clutching his hat in his hands. "If you'll allow me another day?"

Her heartbeat tapered to silence. He was getting ready to leave. He really was doing the responsible thing this time. He'd dallied for the past couple of hours since their morning toast and tea, and she'd begun to wonder if perhaps his old habits were harder to break than he expected.

She wanted to promise him another day. She wanted to promise him all her days. But even after her sleepless night, she didn't think she could make that promise, not after having visions of sinking ships and sad spinsters.

"How long will you be gone this time?" she asked.

He looked at his hat, at the black brim that his fingers were busy twisting. "It'll be awhile. Eight months. Maybe a year."

Her throat tightened so that she could hardly swallow. "That's so long," she whispered, not daring to meet his eyes lest he see the torture in her own. How could she wait a whole year to see him again? How could she spend the rest of her life this way, being with him for a few hours, a few days, a few weeks only to have him leave her for months at a time? And how could she live with the constant worry that he may never come back?

"I know I have no right to ask." His voice had dropped to a hoarse whisper too. "But will you wait for me?"

Everything inside her longed to tell him yes. But she couldn't make herself say the word. She hung her head.

After a long moment she felt him move behind her. He bent, pressed a kiss against her head, and then spun and left the room without another word. She heard him in the hallway say good-bye to Mother and Eliza, and then finally the door closed behind him.

She sat unmoving on the bench. Her chest ached and her throat burned with the need to sob. She loved him. She probably always had. But love was too painful. It was filled with too many heartaches and disappointments and good-byes. She wanted to run up to her bedroom, close the door behind her, and stay there forever. Why bother with relationships at all?

The faint yipping of the neighbor's dog floated in through the open front window. What about Miss Donovan? The picture of the spinster neighbor on the day she'd lost her dog came back to Polly, the downtrodden, defeated, and disheveled appearance. Miss Donovan certainly was miserable.

But the thought of ending up in an unhappy marriage like Susanna's was frightening too. There were no guarantees that marriage would bring fulfillment. Whether she chose Billy or John, she could very well still end up miserable.

Cool fingers brushed her neck accompanied by the scent of rose water. "I can't presume to know all that you're going through right now, my darling," her mother said quietly. "But I have a suspicion that John's lack of means is at the forefront of your mind."

Polly nodded and squeezed back the tears.

"I know there have been times when you've been discontented with what your father could provide for you."

"I'm sorry, Mother——"

"The truth is, if we're focused on material possessions, no matter how much we have, it will never be enough." Mother's fingers skimmed Polly's hair and brushed back loose strands. "Many people spend their whole lives trying to gain more status and wealth, but in the end they're shallow and empty."

"But John has nothing."

"He has everything now," her mother responded. "He has the wealth of God's grace in his life. And that counts for so much more than anything here on this earth. That's the lesson your father has learned, and I'm proud of him for living according to his principles, even if that means we have to go without the luxuries many of our friends have."

Polly nodded. She deeply admired her father, and she'd always wanted to find a man like him. Was John now that man?

"I'm not saying your father is perfect. No one can expect a perfect marriage. Both partners are sinful human beings, and we bring those sins with us to marriage. However, when two people are committed to growing in holiness, there is hope for any problems that arise."

Polly's head bent again under the weight of her own sins. She'd tried so hard over the years to throw off the weight through her regular prayers. She'd tried charity. She'd tried to live a good life. But none of it had taken away the feeling that somehow she was always falling short. "I don't know if there's any hope for me. I've tried to connect to God, but he always seems out of reach."

Her mother's gentle combing came to a standstill.

Once her confession was out, Polly wished she could retract her blasphemy. "I'm sorry, Mother. I shouldn't have spoken—"

"Polly, look at me." Her mother's fingers came under her chin and gently prodded her head up.

When she met her mother's gaze, she expected censure for her doubts. But instead she saw tenderness. "My darling, none of us can earn God's favor with our own efforts. Whether we're a sinner who's strayed far from God, like John. Or a saint who attempts to please God, like you. None of us can stand before God on our own merit. We all need his grace."

*His grace.* What did that mean?

"Perhaps you've been trying to earn God's love," Mother said in answer to her unspoken question. "But we can't ever be good enough on our own. Instead, God offers to love us in spite of our failures and imperfections."

Was that what had happened to John? Had he somehow come to accept God's love in spite of his shortcomings? Perhaps there was still hope for her to learn to connect with God like that too.

"So do you think I should tell John that he may visit me again?" Polly asked.

"Your father and I agree the decision is yours." Mother took a step back. The warm June sunlight streaming in the front window illuminated her fading blond hair. "Whatever you do, my darling, don't let fear enslave you."

As Mother left the room, Polly was tempted to call her back and beg her to tell her what to do. But except for Miss Donovan's barking dog next door, silence enveloped her.

Was she letting fear enslave her? The fear of marrying wrong or not marrying at all?

Maybe she'd have an easier, more comfortable life with Billy. But should she let her fear of poverty or an uncertain future hold her back? If God could change John's life and free him from his past insecurities, could he not do that her for as well?

She slid off the bench to her knees and bowed her head. She didn't know all the answers, but she could pray and start by asking God to free her from her fears. And she could run after John and tell him that even if she didn't know what the future would hold, she did want to see him again. She truly wanted to see him. In fact, she couldn't imagine life without him in it.

Sudden desperation pushed her to her feet. She needed to run after him and speak to him before he left town. Her heart pulsed with a new urgency, and she darted across the room and into the hallway.

Her mother was already standing next to the door as though she'd been waiting for Polly. "His coach is leaving from the Gull Inn," Mother said, opening the door and shoving a hat into Polly's hands. "If you hurry, you'll catch him."

Polly rushed outside and ran. Behind her she heard her mother call for Susanna to accompany her. But Polly didn't wait. She sped as fast as her heavy skirts and hoops would allow her. The Gull Inn was on the road that led to London, and the quickest route was to cut across the fields on the old sheep path that she and Susanna had always used. She didn't let the overgrowth slow her down. Instead she pushed forward frantically, stumbling over roots and clawing at bramble that clutched her gown in her effort to reach John before he was gone.

If she didn't stop him, he would leave thinking that she never wanted to see him again. She couldn't allow that, not when it was the furthest thing from the truth. With each frantic step she took, she knew she wasn't ready to let John go.

"Oh God," she prayed, her breath coming in gasps. She fought her way through the last of the branches and nearly fell into the clearing onto the road. Her hair had fallen loose during her run and filled her vision.

She scraped the loose strands back. In the distance she caught sight of a man striding swiftly away. His rolling gait, the strength of his stature, the tousled hair all belonged to John. His broad shoulders were slumped, not just from the weight of his bag slung there.

A chord of despair clamored through her chest. She'd discouraged him. She'd pushed him away. What if he didn't want her now? She wouldn't blame him.

Her breath came in uneven gulps, and she wasn't sure she could speak past the burning in her lungs. Did she dare stop him? What if letting him go was for the best after all?

She gulped for air and pushed aside the hesitations that threatened to make her a coward. If, after all that had happened, he could summon the courage to come to her, then she could do likewise. She could go to him now and show him that she didn't have to cling to the easy and secure way of living. She could step out and be brave, just as he had.

"John!" Her voice was weak from her exertion. When he didn't pause, she stopped in place and called again, louder. "John Newton!"

He glanced over his shoulder, and when he saw her, he halted. Slowly he pivoted, his shoulders still slumped and dejection evident in every limb.

She waited a moment for him to run back to her, to grow excited at seeing her, or to even say something in response to her presence. But he stood unmoving and silent.

A lump of uncertainty wedged in her throat. But she forced her feet to move forward toward him, hoping she stepped toward a future with him, a future quite possibly filled with many more good-byes.

When she was finally a dozen paces away, she stopped. The wind caught her loose hair and tossed it into further disarray. But she clutched at her skirt, unable to move her hands for fear he'd see them tremble.

"John?" she said, her voice dropping to a whisper.

He didn't respond except to lower his bag away from his shoulder.

What should she say? How could she explain all her confusion? The heartache she'd experienced while he'd been gone? The fresh pain that shredded her insides at the thought of him walking away from her again?

No matter how much anguish his leaving now would cause, the alternative was worse. Tears stung her eyes. "I lost you once. I thought you were dead to me. I prepared myself to live without you, even though it nearly killed me to do so."

Other than a slight flicker in his eyes, he didn't seem to react.

The despair rising in her chest threatened to choke her. But she forced out the words she knew she must finally say. "Even though I loathe the thought of being parted from you every time you leave on a voyage, even worse is knowing that if I let you walk away, I'm losing you again. This time forever."

She wished he'd say something—anything. But he watched her with an unreadable expression.

"The truth is," she said, admitting to herself what she'd known all along, "it's always been you. And that will never change."

He studied her face, his features taut.

Her hands shook again, and she buried them deeper into the folds of her skirt. "John," she finally whispered in the silence that hung thickly between them. "Say something."

He let his bag drop with a thud and then crossed the distance between them with determined steps. When his sights fixed upon her lips with a steel set of his jaw, her stomach tumbled with strange anticipation.

Upon reaching her, he lifted his hands to both sides of her face and bent in swiftly, taking her lips with a force that seemed to sweep her into the air so that both her heart and stomach felt weightless. He moved against her with the longing and passion of a man brought back from the brink of hell. A man who'd tasted death and now thirsted for life, for her, for them.

She knew without a doubt that this was where she wanted to be. Always.

Breathless, he broke away for a fraction but kept his lips against hers. "Tell me."

"Tell you what?" Although she already knew.

"You know." His low gravelly whisper made her tremble again, but this time not in fear. Although they would likely face many struggles in the days and months to come, a sense of God's pleasure washed over her. She was where God wanted her. In his grace, ready to be used by him. With John by her side.

She wrapped her arms around him, feeling the solidness, the surety, and the simplicity of who he was. "I love you," she whispered against his lips.

This time his kiss was sweeter, more tender, but still with a thread of desperation that matched hers.

"You're my saving grace, the only reason I came home." It was his turn to whisper against her lips. His hands slid from her cheeks to tangle in her loose hair. "The only reason I'll ever have for coming home."

"I beg of you to always come home to me."

"Always?"

She nodded.

He leaned back slightly so that his grave eyes met hers. "I'm still a poor man with only heavenly treasure. And I'm still a sinner living only by God's grace. I have nothing to give you but my love and my Lord."

The sweet truth of his words brought tears to her eyes. "That's all I need."

He brushed his rough, unshaven cheek against hers until his mouth found her ear. "Be mine and only mine as long as we both shall live?"

"I already am yours," she whispered.

"Then that's a yes?"

"Yes."

He pressed a kiss to her ear. "I pledge you my love, my devotion, and my undying affection through every storm as long as life endures."

# EPILOGUE

*N*ewton peered into the beautiful blue eyes of his angel bride. Her bright floral-patterned gown with silvery quilted petticoat fitted her body to perfection, showing off every exquisite curve and line. Light filtered through the stained-glass windows behind the altar and formed a halo among the ribbons woven into her fair hair.

He hadn't been able to stop staring at her since she'd arrived at St. Margaret's.

The curate, Reverend Jonathan Soan, was holding open *The Book of Common Prayer*. He turned to Newton and nodded that now was his turn to recite his vows. But Newton's throat clogged with a thousand different emotions that stole away his voice and his breath—wonder, amazement, joy, and overwhelming love. This day that he'd been dreaming about for seven years was finally here. Aye, he'd met Polly over seven years ago and had loved her from the moment he first laid eyes upon her.

As if sensing his difficulty in speaking, Polly squeezed his hand gently and smiled up at him, her own eyes filled with a love that he'd spent years hoping for and dreaming about, a love he didn't deserve, but a love that he cherished more than anything. There were still days when he woke up and could hardly believe that she truly did love him.

During the time he was mate on the *Brownlow,* he wrote to her almost every day. Of course, he had to wait to send the letters until he found a ship heading back to England. So the letters piled up in a drawer in his cabin for up to six weeks at a time. As the months passed, he grew more and more agitated to return to England, praying that he'd find her waiting for him as she'd promised.

All told, the voyage had lasted from August of 1748 to December 1749. He'd been gone for over a year. In the end, he'd been in agony. If not for all his reading and studying while aboard the ship, he would have gone mad with his longing to be reunited with Polly.

During the many days at sea, he renewed his studies of Latin with *Odes of Horace.* More importantly, he'd devoted himself to the study of Scripture as well as William Law's *A Serious Call to a Devout and Holy Life.* He committed portions of the book to memory, including a passage that resonated deeply with him because of all that he'd experienced so far in his life.

"If anyone would tell you the shortest, surest way to all happiness, he must tell you to make it a rule to yourself to thank and praise God for everything that happens to you. For it is certain that whatever seeming calamity befalls you, if you thank and praise God for it, you turn it into a blessing."

He had to quote Law's words to himself many times in the days after he reached Liverpool and learned that his father had died unexpectedly in a swimming accident in Hudson Bay. Upon receiving the news, he wept bitterly over the loss. And every day since then, he lived with the regret that he'd never had the opportunity to apologize to his father face to face.

Mayhap his father hadn't said that he loved him, but he'd shown him in countless ways over the years in the sacrifices he'd made, the willing help he'd given when Newton hadn't deserved it. His father had continued to fight for him and love him even when he'd been his ugliest and nastiest. He respected his father more with every passing day.

And he respected his mother more too. He might have had her in his life for only a short while, but she'd left a lasting impact. He realized that now too. And he wished that she could be present to see him marrying the godly daughter of one of her best friends.

Aye, even on this glorious day next to the woman of his dreams, both sadness and regret mingled through the joy.

Whispers came from the nave among the parishioners who had come to witness his marriage. Polly's eyes hadn't wavered from his, but they filled with worry. Did she think he was having second thoughts? Surely she should know better.

He grinned, hoping to alleviate her concern. The day was God ordained. Providence himself had saved him from the clutches of death so many times that it was no small miracle he was present and standing beside Polly.

He cleared his throat again. "I, John, take thee, Polly, to be my wedded wife, to have and to hold from this day forward, for better, for worse, for richer, for poorer, in sickness and in health, to love and to cherish, till death us do part, according to God's holy ordinance and, thereto, I plight thee my troth."

As Polly stated her vows in a clear, sincere voice, he thought back to their reunion only six weeks ago, the first time they'd seen each other since that day she'd run after him and promised to marry him. Never had the desire to stay and be with her been more tempting. Even though he'd nearly killed himself tearing away from her and continuing down the road without her, he'd wanted to prove to himself and Manesty that he was a man of his word, a man of integrity just as his father had been. Just as Mr. Catlett was.

Reverend Soan gave him another nod.

Newton dug into his pocket, and his fingers closed around the smooth metal band that he found among his father's possessions when he stopped by his boyhood home in Wapping. Thomasina and his half siblings had greeted him kindly, sharing in the sorrow of their loss together. He'd vowed to watch over them as best he could. He knew his father would have wanted him to.

The ring had belonged to his mother. And Newton wanted to believe his father would have been happy to know he was now giving it to Polly, to know that he loved Polly with the same deep and abiding love that his father had once given his mother.

Reverend Soan held out the open prayer book, and Newton placed the ring onto it as was the custom. The curate lifted the ring, said a blessing over it, and then handed it back to Newton. Newton reached for Polly's left hand and her fourth finger, reveling at the smoothness of her skin.

He held the ring above her finger and at the same time spoke words of commitment from his heart. "With this ring I thee wed, with my body I thee worship, and with all my worldly goods I thee endow: In the Name of the Father, and of the Son, and of the Holy Ghost. Amen."

His worldly goods were few. But Polly had reassured him again over the past six weeks that what mattered most was their relationship, not where they lived or what they owned. Manesty had offered him another voyage, this time as captain of the *Duke of Argyle*. He'd make more money this time. But even so, he still wouldn't have enough to provide her a home or possessions. They'd agreed that Polly would continue to live in Chatham with her parents at least for this next voyage. Then she wouldn't have to be alone while he was gone.

He knew he wouldn't sail ships forever. If God had saved him, the worst of sinners, then he must have something important for him to do. He would use him for some purpose. Newton wasn't certain what that would be. But he could do nothing less than give himself completely over to the One who had saved both his body and soul more times than he could count.

Polly's tender gaze told him that she would be by his side through it all. Whatever God sent their way, she would be the anchor in his life, always believing in him, always drawing him back home.

He slid the ring down her finger and had the overwhelming urge to lean down and kiss her until they were both breathless. From the heat that flared in her eyes, he could see that he'd sparked the same desire in her.

Reverend Soan took a step back and then waved to the prayer cushion.

Newton took Polly's arm and together they knelt. He intertwined his fingers with hers, and his heart leapt with gladness to think that they would start their marriage the way he hoped they could keep it going—through prayer.

"Let us pray," the reverend said solemnly.

Newton bowed his head.

"O eternal God, creator and preserver of all mankind, giver of all spiritual grace, the author of everlasting life, send thy blessing upon these thy servants, this man and this woman."

Giver of all spiritual *grace*.

The words resonated deeply in Newton and brought forth the words of the song that had been forming since the storm at sea when he'd finally begun his journey back to God.

> Amazing grace! How sweet the sound
> That saved a wretch like me!
> I once was lost, but now am found;
> Was blind, but now I see.

> 'Twas grace that taught my heart to fear,
> And grace my fears relieved;
> How precious did that grace appear
> The hour I first believed.

> Through many dangers, toils and snares,
> I have already come;
> Tis grace hath brought me safe thus far,
> And grace will lead me home.

> The Lord has promised good to me,
> His Word my hope secures;
> He will my Shield and Portion be,
> As long as life endures.

# AUTHOR'S NOTE

*A*fter his voyage as mate on the *Brownlow,* John Newton became a ship captain like his father and went on to make three more voyages between 1750 and 1754 before a strange illness finally put an end to his seafaring career. During his illness he remained unemployed for ten months, a time fraught with anxiety, especially because Polly became ill too. However, as was the case many times in Newton's life, God miraculously intervened. He opened a way for Newton to become appointed as Liverpool's surveyor of the tides.

He and Polly moved to Liverpool, where Newton remained in his position for many years. During that time Newton felt certain that God was calling him into full-time ministry. He studied Greek and Latin during his spare time and applied to become ordained by the Church of England. For seven years he faced rejection in his quest to become a pastor. But in all that time, he never gave up. In 1764 he gave up his surveyor of the tides position and was appointed as curate of the Church of St. Peter and St. Paul in Olney, a town sixty miles north of London.

During his years as a pastor at Olney, he became friends with a man by the name of William Cowper. The two collaborated in writing hymns and eventually put together a hymnal called *Olney Hymns.* One of the songs that became a part of that hymnal was "Amazing Grace."

Newton wrote the song in 1773 in preparation for a New Year's Day sermon. Unlike other pastors of the time who used only the King James Bible and *The Book of Common Prayer* for their church services, Newton strove to make his services something that his congregation (made up primarily of laborers and tradesmen) could understand. He often wrote hymns that tied in with his sermons in order to make the message more meaningful for uneducated people.

Perhaps Newton didn't pen "Amazing Grace" until he became the pastor of Olney, but I would like to believe that the words had been forming long before that during the many toils and tribulations that he experienced early in his life. Whatever the case, "Amazing Grace" has gone on to become the most beloved hymn in the world, as well as the most recorded and most sung. It has been sung for over 240 years across all continents and all cultures by billions of people.

But how many people know the amazing story behind the writer of "Amazing Grace"? And even more importantly, how many know just how instrumental Polly Catlett was in bringing him to his amazing grace moment? God used her in an incredible way to lure John out of his life of degradation and slave trading in Africa. If not for her, John likely wouldn't have left Africa or his wayward life there. If not for her, he wouldn't have been aboard the *Greyhound* when it encountered the storm that changed his life. If not for her, the prodigal son might never have returned to England to make peace with both his earthly and heavenly fathers.

The truth is Polly Catlett played a critical role in the development of "Amazing Grace." Her story deserves to be told and lauded every bit as much as Newton's. It's my prayer that this book finally gives her the recognition that she's due.

Although they were never able to have any children of their own, they went on to adopt two children of deceased family members. In addition to infertility, they faced other challenges. But through it all, they continued to pray together. John's love for her remained as strong as always. Later in a letter to Polly, he said, "My love has been growing from the day of marriage, and still it is in a growing state. It was once as an acorn, but it has now a deep root and spreading branches like an old oak. It would not have proved so if the Lord had not watered it with his blessing."

Two of the many resources I used in my research and highly recommend are *Out of the Depths: The Autobiography of John Newton* and a well-researched and thorough biography, *John Newton: From Disgrace to Amazing Grace* by Jonathan Aitken. As with most of my novels that are based on the lives of real people, readers want to know what's true and what I made up. Well, most of what I've included in the pages of this book really did happen. Newton and Polly really did meet at a young age. Newton really did claim to have fallen in love with her at first sight. He overspent his time at the Catletts on numerous occasions and lost his jobs in the process. Because of his lack of character, the Catletts forbade further contact with Polly. He was impressed into the Royal Navy but later deserted; he was whipped and demoted. He was transferred from the *Harwich* to a merchant vessel and from there spent time dealing in the slave trade in Africa.

Captain Swanwick of the *Greyhound* did lie to Newton about a supposed inheritance in order to entice him to leave Africa. The ship did experience a terrible storm at sea. I tried to portray everything about that voyage and storm as accurately as possible, including the starvation conditions and the miraculous intervention that landed them in Ireland only hours away from being swept out to sea in another storm without any drinking water left.

After learning that the inheritance didn't exist, Newton did write to Susanna Eversfield, ending his relationship with Polly. A few days later, he learned that his father had beseeched the Catletts on his behalf and that now the Catletts had given their blessing on the union. Polly was hesitant about renewing her relationship with Newton. He had to propose to her three times before she finally accepted.

Most of the minor characters mentioned in the novel are true, including all the family members, shipmates, and captains. The settings and timelines are mostly accurate too.

I did have to adjust Polly's and Newton's ages slightly. When she first met John, Polly was only thirteen. Since most modern readers wouldn't be able to relate to a passionate romance between a thirteen-year-old and a sixteen-year-old, I made them slightly older.

I also added in the subplot of dealing with the smugglers. We do know that at this particular time in Kent, England, smuggling was a huge problem. Dangerous smuggling gangs existed in abundance, particularly in and around the River Medway and the coast near Chatham. The practice of customs officers taking bribes from smugglers was commonplace. While many people were threatened and even killed by smugglers, I invented the threat to Polly and John for the sake of the story. Billy Baldock is also a completely fictional character, although he is representative of a riding officer of the time and of someone in the middling class striving to improve himself and move up in status.

Finally, I purposefully neglected to mention that the *Brownlow,* the ship that Manesty wanted Newton to command, was a slave-trading ship. It's nearly impossible for modern readers (including myself) to reconcile that a truly repentant Christian who'd experienced a saving grace moment as powerful as Newton's could turn around and agree to be the assistant to the captain of a slave trader.

Essentially a slave-trading ship would sail along the coast of Africa and buy slaves from the slave factories (like the one in Kittam that John and his partner managed). They would trade for months before finally having enough slaves crammed into the hold. Then they would make the voyage from Africa to the West Indies or American colonies where the slaves were in high demand. They would sell the slaves in an auction-like format before returning to England to be outfitted for another slave-trading voyage.

The journeys aboard those slave ships for the Africans who had to endure them are too horrible to imagine. Reading accounts of such voyages is enough to make even the strongest stomach churn. In our modern times, we see the bondage of other human beings as intolerable. We see racism as inexcusable. We see the mistreatment and cruelty of another life as unacceptable.

That's why it's so difficult for us to imagine how Newton, as a repentant prodigal son who'd experienced God's unconditional love and amazing grace, could go back into such an awful occupation as that of a slave trader, not just once but a total of four times.

As unjustified as it might seem to us, very few people in the mid-

1700s questioned the practice of the slave trade. It was a perfectly acceptable occupation, even for Christians. While it may have made people squeamish and while their consciences may have convicted them, the abolitionist movement didn't take off until much later in Newton's life, when he was an old man. Newton eventually came to a place of great remorse and repentance for his role in the slave trade. He published a book, *Thoughts upon the African Slave Trade*, in which he said: "I hope it will always be a subject of humiliating reflection to me that I was once an active instrument in the business at which my heart now shudders."

His book became widely read and highly influential in the growing abolitionist movement. And later his testimony in Parliament against the slave trade helped sway public opinion in support of the abolitionist movement. His book stood out not only because of his reputation as a beloved pastor but also because of the authenticity, his eye-witness reports and his firsthand experiences in the slave trade.

As appalling as Newton's slave-trading voyages were after he became a Christian, I'd like to think that God was still directing Newton's life then just as he had been all along. He allowed Newton to experience such depravity so that later he could use him as a pivotal instrument in bringing about the abolition of the slave trade in England.

I also take comfort in knowing that even after Newton experienced God's saving grace, he still wasn't a perfect man. He made mistakes (some very big ones!). His life reminds me that transformation into holiness is a lifelong process. Experiencing God's grace is only the beginning of the journey. God doesn't expect us to be perfect. And he can in fact use our imperfections to make an impact, sometimes even world-changing impacts.

I pray that Newton and Polly's story will encourage you on many levels. But most of all, I hope it reminds you that there is a God who loves you. Unconditionally. No matter where you've been. Or what you've done. He will always love you and welcome you home.

# READERS GUIDE

1. If not for Polly Catlett, the world might not have the classic hymn "Amazing Grace." John Newton freely admits in his autobiography that "hardly anything less than this intense and compelling passion [for Polly] would have been sufficient to awaken me from the dull melancholy habit I had formed [while slave trading in Africa]." Had you ever heard of Polly Catlett before reading this novel? Did you realize how instrumental she was in bringing John out of his life of sin?

2. John also says in his autobiography that "almost at the first sight of this girl, I felt an affection for her that never abated or lost its influence a single moment in my heart. In degree, it equaled all that the writers of romance have imagined; in duration it was unalterable." Do you believe *love at first sight* is possible? What are some of the pros or cons to falling in love quickly?

3. John overstayed his visits with the Catletts on multiple occasions and overestimated his abilities to find and retain work without much effort. How did you feel about John repeating his mistakes? Why do we often do the same thing? We've all heard the sayings, "History has a way of repeating itself" or "Children grow up to make the same mistakes as their parents." How can we stop the cycle?

4. At times Polly wondered why her father had to be different
   from so many of the other customs officers who turned a blind
   eye to the smuggling going on around them. If so many people
   thought smuggling was okay, then why was her father taking a
   stand against it? We face the same controversy in our modern
   culture. How can we take a stand for what's right, even if we're
   in the minority?

5. What did you think of the practice of impressing men to
   become sailors on the king's ships? Do you think John was
   justified in being angry that he'd been forced to serve in the
   navy? How could he have handled his situation better?

6. When he realized during a voyage to the East Indies that he
   would be bound to the navy for a term of five years, John said,
   "I think nothing I either felt or feared distressed me so much as
   being thus forcibly torn away from the object of my affection
   under a great improbability of seeing her again." When the
   English shore disappeared from sight he said, "I was tempted to
   throw myself into the sea." It was at this point that John utterly
   abandoned God for a life of atheism. What drives people to
   abandon belief in God? Discuss how people of faith and those
   who don't believe can have positive dialogue about their
   choices.

7. John's relationship with his father was always strained. Yet his
   father never stopped loving him or trying to help him. Describe
   some of the ways Captain Newton tried to help John. How did
   John treat him in return? Have you experienced or known of a

"prodigal" son or daughter who seemed ungrateful and contemptuous toward his or her family?

8. In hindsight, John could see how God intervened on multiple
occasions to save his life. Can you compare any personal
experiences in your life to the catalyst for John's change?

9. It became clear to John that God had saved him for a purpose,
but John didn't understand what that purpose was for many
years. In fact, it's safe to say that John died not knowing what a
legacy of faith he left through "Amazing Grace." God asks us
to trust him even when we don't understand our situations.
When we're in difficult situations, why is it often so difficult to
trust God's higher purposes?

10. Before John's mother died, she prayed for him daily, interceded
on his behalf, and begged God for his soul. She was faithful to
plant seeds early in his childhood with Scripture memory and
biblical truths. While those prayers and seeds took many years
to come to fruition, her example offers hope to all parents.
When a child seems lost, we need to resist Satan's lie that our
prayers and seeds won't make a difference. Why is it so easy to
give up when we don't see results right away? How can we
persevere in prayer and planting seeds?